SILVER ON THE ROAD

THE DEVIL'S WEST, BOOK ONE

SILVER
ON THE
ROAD

LAURA ANNE GILMAN

SAGA PRESS

LONDON SYDNEY **NEW YORK** TORONTO NEW DELHI

SAGA PRESS
AN IMPRINT OF SIMON & SCHUSTER, INC.
1230 AVENUE OF THE AMERICAS, NEW YORK, NEW YORK 10020

Saga Press is a trademark of Simon & Schuster, Inc.
For information about special discounts for bulk purchases, please contact Simon & Schuster Special Sales at 1-866-506-1949 or business@simonandschuster.com.
The Simon & Schuster Speakers Bureau can bring authors to your live event. For more information or to book an event, contact the Simon & Schuster Speakers Bureau at 1-866-248-3049 or visit our website at www.simonspeakers.com.
The text for this book is set in ITC Galliard Std.
Manufactured in the United States of America
First Edition
2 4 6 8 10 9 7 5 3 1
CIP data is available from the Library of Congress.
ISBN 978-1-4814-2968-9 (hardcover)
ISBN 978-1-4814-2970-2 (eBook)

FOR

JOE MONTI

AND

BARRY GOLDBLATT,

WHO BELIEVED IN THIS PROJECT

WHEN OTHERS DIDN'T.

Northern Wilds

Unclaimed Lands

Junction

Flood

The Mother's Knife

De Plata

SPANISH PROTECTORATE

THE DEVIL'S
WEST

0   200   400

Miles

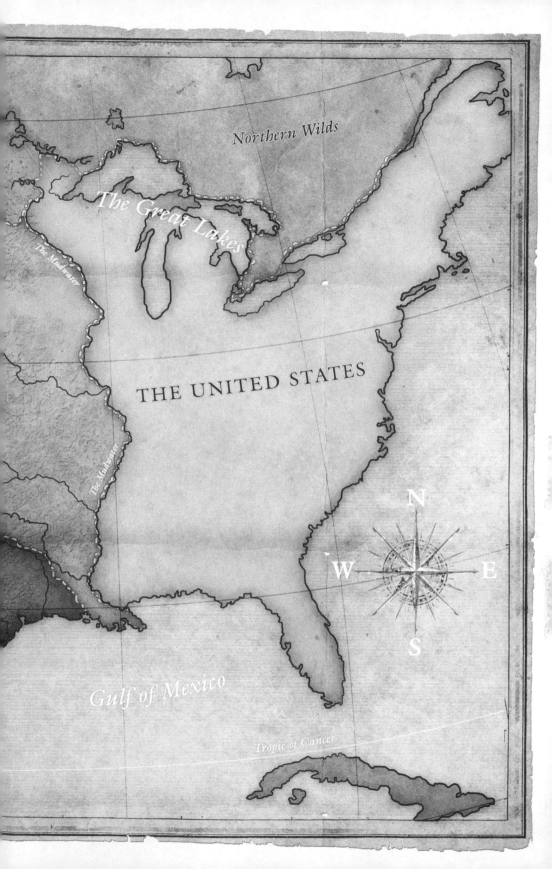

Northern Wilds

The Great Lakes

The Mudwater

THE UNITED STATES

The Mudwater

N

W   E

S

Gulf of Mexico

Tropic of Cancer

PART ONE

FLOOD

Izzy leaned against the railing and watched the sun rise over the far end of town. Flood wasn't much to look at, she'd admit. Sun-greyed planks and local stone: there wasn't much point in prettifying with paint when the wind and sun would only beat you back down to plain again.

The way the story'd been told her when she was younger, a gospel sharp had ridden into town before there was much of a town at all, just the saloon and a couple-three homesteads, looked around, and pronounced that they'd be the first washed away, come the Flood. The name'd stuck. But the sharp had been wrong about the import-ant thing: Flood had dug its roots in deep and stuck, too. In addition to the saloon, there were a dozen storefronts now, and a bank, and thirty families living within town limits. "Thirty pieces of silver," the boss called them, and would shake his head and laugh, and say they'd gotten that story all wrong, too.

The boss had a sense of humor, Izzy thought. Not a man could say he didn't.

The sun was stretching higher over the rooftops now, and the town was beginning to stir; she could hear Missus Wallace calling to her chickens, and then the blacksmith's hammer rang out, a pause followed by a series of steady blows. Hiram was always the first to work each morning, and his forge never cooled entirely, the scent of brimstone and hot metal always in the air. Izzy breathed in, letting the familiar stink settle in her chest. Her bare toes curled and relaxed against the dry wood of the verandah, the morning sun touching her upturned face.

Winters were bad, dry and cold, and in summer, the sun got hot and the ground got hotter and mostly folk stayed under shade if they could. Just now, though, Flood was nearly perfect.

At that thought, a shiver ran through her, and she wrapped her shawl more tightly around her shoulders against an imagined chill. *Today*, she thought. *I have to decide today.*

As though her thought had called him, a voice came from the doorway. "Izzy. What are you doing awake so early?"

She didn't turn around but smiled, a gentle curve of her lips the way she'd seen the older women do, that she'd practiced late at night, looking in the mirror over her washstand until she got it right. "It's my birthday."

"All the more reason to sleep in." The boss's voice was deep and smooth, and always gentle, even when he was angry. In all her years, Izzy realized, she'd never heard him yell. Angry, yes; his temper was legendary. But he never yelled. He never had to; nobody ever dared cross him. Flood was his town, not the buildings or the land, but the people who lived here. They were all of them his, one way or the other.

"I'm sixteen today," she said, as though testing the words.

"Yes. You are."

He had been the one to draft her indenture papers fourteen years before; he knew what that meant.

She turned, keeping the smile on her lips with an effort. He was standing in the doorway of the saloon, the morning light silvering his dark hair, two tin mugs in his hands. The mugs were battered and dented, and tendrils of steam swirled over the tops as though an unseen finger stirred them. She could smell it from where she stood: chicory and coffee, and a chunk of sugarcane boiled with it.

She stepped forward and took one of the mugs, the thick dark brew sloshing slightly against the rim. "Thanks." He was the boss; he shouldn't be bringing her coffee.

"Not every day a girl turns a woman," he said, as though knowing what she'd been thinking. "And today's twice special. No doubt you've been thinking on it for a while."

She sipped the bittersweet brew, wincing as it burned the inside of her mouth, and nodded. For months now, tangled thoughts that each time she thought them neatly sorted would tangle again while she slept. He knew. He always knew, even when he didn't say. That was the boss through and through, though; you had to come to him.

His smile turned faintly mocking. "Well, if you're determined to be awake, put yourself to use. Marie tells me Catie's got the headache, so Ree could use help in the kitchen."

It might be her birthday, but there was always work to be done, and idle hands were the devil's tools. She nodded again.

"And Izzy?" he said before going back inside.

She looked up.

"Happy birthday, dearling."

She smiled then for real, cupped her mug in her hands, and turned back in time to see the sun come full above the horizon, turning the sky from dark to pale blue.

Sixteen. Fourteen years since she'd first come to Flood. This was the only home she'd ever known: the two-story building of the saloon and the wide, rutted street in front of her, and the *flickerthwack* of cards laid on faded green felt, the clink of glasses, the scrape of boot-heels on wooden planks, and the stink of sweat and hope and desperation on human skin.

Flood was home, the only one she could imagine.

3

But she was sixteen now. A woman grown in the eyes of the law, and her indenture ended.

Everything changed. If she wanted it to.

Ree was already arms-deep in work when Izzy slipped through the kitchen doorway. The morning air might be cool, but the kitchen was steamy-warm already, the smell of bread baking mixing with the tang of fresh meat, and the sharp, warm spice that tasted like licorice. Her mouth watered, anticipating. "Good morning, Ree. Boss said you could use some help?"

"Knead dough," the cook said shortly, not looking up from the haunch he was cutting up. Ree was stern and mostly silent, but he was that way with everyone, even the boss. He might've known it was her birthday or might not, and most probably didn't care.

She made a face—breadmaking wasn't her favorite chore—but tied a kerchief over her brow to keep the sweat from her face and reached for an apron hung on a hook to cover her clothing. She'd worn her best dress today, a brown gingham that had been made for her, not handed down and mended. She'd tried to add a new bit of ribbon to her bodice when she dressed, but her hands had been shaking so badly, she finally left off.

Izzy prided herself on steady hands and ordered thinking. Lapses in both irked her. The boss had put his finger on it and tangled all her thoughts again. He did that: she'd be going along with her day, and he'd say something out of nowhere, and she'd start *thinking* again.

Mostly, she liked that. Working through a problem, looking at all the details. But this wasn't something she could think on forever. Today was her birthday. Today, she had to choose.

Izzy pulled the dough out from under its cloth cover and turned it into a bowl, digging her fingers into the spongy mass. Soon enough, her arms ached with the effort of turning it into something useful, but the quiet warmth of the kitchen and the repeating actions of her hands and arms let her thoughts go where they would.

Unfortunately, they seemed to go around and around, without cease. Her whole life, there were things other folk decided. Where she slept, what chores she did, and what lessons she was put to, even after she left school last year. Marie, who ran the saloon for the boss, had no use for what she called chickenskull girls. They could all read and figure as well as pour drinks and shuffle cards, know how to charm a stranger and listen to confidences. And most of the girls seemed content with that, night in and night out, the same routine safe and soothing as running water. Izzy, though, she kept *thinking*.

"Now leave alone."

Izzy started, then realized that Ree was talking about the dough. She'd been kneading longer than she realized, and her hands were beginning to cramp. She shook her arms out, wiping them with the warm cloth he offered, and rolled her sleeves back down. Sweat had formed under the kerchief, and she lifted her braid to wipe the back of her neck as well.

Ree had already gone back to work, and she looked across the kitchen at him, frowning. He was a big man; sallow-skinned, round-shouldered, and bald. His arms were covered with lines of dark ink, and he never covered them, not even when the wind turned bitter cold and the horses grew their coats out thick. He was a good cook, good with the horses the boss kept, good with his hands when something needed fixing. He could have done anything, anywhere, pretty much.

"Why did you come here? To Flood, I mean." To the saloon, she meant. To work for the boss, out of all his choices.

She'd never asked before. Never dared to. You didn't poke into someone's privacy unless they offered first.

Ree didn't say anything for the longest time, and Izzy thought maybe he wouldn't, until he did. "Nothing where I started for me. Nothing out there for me. People scattered, land shuffled like cards to whoever won. So, I went west, came here."

She chewed on that a little while she turned the dough into its bowl, covered it, and set it on the shelf at the far end of the kitchen, where it could rest. Everyone who came to Flood wanted something: an answer, a Bargain, a way to get out of a mess you'd made. That was why you *came* to Flood. But most of them took what they got and moved on. If you stayed, Izzy thought, it was because the devil had need of you.

If you stayed, it was because you'd made a Bargain. But if you never asked what someone came for, you never asked what they paid.

"Was it worth it?" The question slipped out anyway, like she was still a little girl who didn't know better.

Ree chopped a handful of carrots, shoving them off the board into the stewpot, every motion focused on what he was doing. If she had been rude, he didn't seem to care. "For me, yes." He reached for another bunch of carrots and the knife cut into them, a quicker, lighter thunk than the blacksmith's hammer, but with the same steady rhythm. "This I know: when you deal with the devil, first know what you want, and what you can pay."

Izzy opened her mouth to ask another question, but no sound came out. How did you know? she wondered. How could you know what you were able to pay, and what did you offer when you had nothing of value except what he already owned?

Flood was the boss's town. He owned everything—and everyone in it. Including her.

For one more day.

Her hands clean and dried, Izzy wandered to the single window, waiting for Ree to give her another chore. She rubbed a finger against the pane. The glass was flawed, thick and wavy, but it let in light from the alley that ran between the saloon's backside and the Judge's office. A clowder of cats prowled there; Ree tossed scraps out for them every evening, but she'd seen the remains of rats and birds there, too. Like everything else in Flood, the cats served a purpose.

One more day, she thought, letting her fingers rest on the sill. "What's out there?"

Ree knew she didn't mean the alley. "Beyond Flood? Open space. Plains, mountains, deserts. Indígena, los nativos do país. Some homesteads, some towns. Go too much west, Espanhóis. Go east, cross the Mudwater into the States, there are cities. Lots more people."

"How many more?"

Ree looked at her, his eyes dark and unblinking, until Izzy started to feel nervous. She had known him all her life, it seemed, but just then, he was nearly a stranger, thinking of things she'd never seen.

"More people than you have ever met. More people than in all of the Territory, north to south. Too many people."

She had no basis for "too many people"; the words were only words. "Have you seen a city?"

He shuddered. "No. No desire to."

She ran her fingers along the frame of the window and looked through it as though she might see something new. Nueva España didn't like folk crossing the border; she knew that much. They considered the Territory unclean, dangerous, and everyone who lived there lost souls, to be saved or burned. But the stories about the States said people there didn't care, so long as you could earn your way. If she wanted to, she could go to the States. Head across the River to Fort Cahokia, or all the way east to one of the cities, Boston or even New York.

And do what, once there? No one knew her, there. No one would even notice her. She thought about being somewhere nobody knew her name, tried to imagine living somewhere like that, and found the one thing that scared her.

The kitchen only got warmer as the morning went on, and Izzy sighed with relief when Catie, Ree's usual helper, came in to take over.

"Sorry, sorry," she said to Ree. "Megrim this morning wouldn't let go." Then she saw Izzy. "Lord, child, don't try to carry all that at once. Give that to me, here." Catie was slender, red-cheeked, and blunt-spoken, and rumor had it she'd been born across the River, in the States, though she never spoke of it, or anything before coming to Flood two years before.

"Sit, eat something," Catie said. "You're still a growing girl, and if I know Sundays by now, odds are you won't have a chance to sit again until supper."

Izzy willingly sat at the long worktable and tucked into the corn dodgers and cold pork Catie handed her, then wiped the grease carefully off her fingers before rinsing her plate and cup. She waited a moment, but the two of them seemed to be knowing exactly where to be and what to do, with no more need of her. Izzy returned her apron to its hook and left them to their work.

It was still early by the saloon's usual hours, and the main room was quieter than she was used to. Izzy knew that she should take advantage of the time, get to her usual chores before the day got busy. The saloon officially opened midmorning, but sometimes someone wandered in earlier off the road, and Iktan never turned anyone away, serving up coffee and whiskey to the men—and some women—who came in.

Instead, she sat on the wide wooden stairs leading to the second level where the living quarters were, tucked her skirts up under her legs, and watched the others.

Iktan was nowhere to be seen, although his apron and rag lay across the gleaming wooden bar that filled much of the left-hand wall. Young Sarah was helping Feeny set up the tables, the girl as usual more trouble than help. Alice, at ten the youngest and newest saloon girl, was sweeping the floor, while her brother, Aaron, wound the mechanism of the striking clock. They'd come to Flood over the winter, half-starved and terrified, dropped off by a stern-faced man with a road marshal's badge. Their parents had been outlaws, and nobody else would take them, certain the twins would be trouble, too.

The boss had promised to beat it out of them, if so.

The boss had beaten her once. She had been their age and spoken rudely to a customer who'd insulted her. The boss had taken her side in public, but that morning, after the saloon closed, she had been summoned to his office. Marie had assigned her chores to keep her standing up the next day, for mercy.

The boss had a temper, yes, and a strong hand, but never undeserved. Every now and again, a gospel sharp would come to Flood. He'd set up outside the saloon—never coming in, despite the boss's own invitation—and would preach for hours in his coat and collar, sunrise to sundown, about how the devil was evil, the devil was wrong, the devil was a risk to their immortal souls and ruining these lands, beside; that without him, the high plains would be fertile, the rivers lush even in summer, and no one would ever die of hunger or thirst or native attack.

Izzy had never been sick, never gone hungry, never been threatened by real danger—at most, a customer might tug at her braid or pat her backside until one of the women distracted him, took his attention back where it belonged. She was safe here.

She thought about that, and again about what she knew of the States, still in turmoil after their rebellion, and Spain's holdings south and far west of them, where everyone bowed to the Church.

People didn't bow in the Territory. Preachermen and gospel sharps here would call to you, cajole and harangue you, but nobody had to listen to them who didn't have a mind to. You just went somewhere else until they were gone.

But no matter how much she thought on her options, of Nueva España or the States, or the wild lands far to the north, they slipped through her thoughts like trying to catch minnows, too slick to hold. She couldn't imagine herself there . . . but she couldn't imagine this, either, doing the same thing tomorrow she'd done every night before.

But she would be an adult, come sundown. She would be free.

Izzy had said the word "free" so many times in her head, she didn't know what it meant anymore. Ree's words came back to her: "First know what you want." How could she know what she wanted when she'd never wanted for anything her whole life?

With the front doors open to the street, the sounds of the town filtered in: voices raised in greeting, the occasional clop of hooves or rattle of wagons, a horse's neigh or dog's bark. She heard the laundryman's voice: fresh linens were being delivered. Inside the saloon, though, it was hushed, the occasional scrape of a chair or clink of a glass, Alice's broom on the floor, and the sound of cards in the boss's hands.

He'd come in while she was thinking, sitting down at his favorite table while everyone worked around him. His hair gleamed dark red now in the dusty light, slicked back and curled down to the turn of his collar, a neat goatee turning silver trimmed close against his bronzed jaw. Only his eyes never changed, golden brown and deep as the moon.

He knew she was watching him.

"What should I do?" she asked, not raising her voice a bit.

"Your cards, your call," he said, slicing open a new deck and spreading it out underneath his hand. "All I can do is wait and see how they're played."

An entirely unsatisfactory answer. Izzy rested her chin on her hands, her elbows on her knees, and watched him deal out the cards to invisible players. Supple hands, strong wrists, his shirtsleeves pulled back to show the sinews moving under his skin. The working girls said he was a particular lover; only a few ever felt his touch, despite what the preachermen said. He liked women; he liked men. But he liked them willing. That was more than she could say about some of the men who'd come into the saloon. You knew them, the way they looked, the way they moved. You learned to tell, and evade, and not give them the chance to make trouble.

If they did, the boss gave them what they came for, twice over, and they never came back again.

"Tell me about my parents," she said.

"They were young. And stupid." He said it without condemnation; stupidity was a natural state. "In over their heads and looking for a way out."

"But there wasn't one." She knew the story by heart but liked hearing him tell it, anyway.

"No. There wasn't. They'd planted themselves in Oiwunta territory without asking permission, built themselves a house and had themselves a child, and never once thought there might be a price to pay."

Everything had a price. Every resident of Flood knew that. Everyone who survived a year in the Territory knew that. "And then the Oiwunta came."

"They came back from the summer hunting grounds and found a cabin in their lands, where the creek turned and watered the soil, and the deer had roamed freely." He set aside the deck of cards and slit open another pack, fanning the pasteboards easily, frowning as he did so.

The backs of the boards were dark blue, pipped with silver. The last pack had been pipped in gold. They got a new shipment in from the East every month, and the old ones were burned so nobody could say the cards were worn or marked.

"That was offense given, thrice over. The Oiwunta would have been within their rights to kill everyone, burn the cabin down, and steal all that was within." He paused, fingers splayed over the cards. "Although it's easier to steal, then burn. They're a tricky folk to predict, though." He smiled, closed-mouthed, as though that pleased him.

The natives didn't come to Flood, mostly; the boss said they had their own ways of getting into trouble, didn't need him for it.

"But they didn't," she said, bringing the story back to her parents.

"They didn't. They'd been watching, the Oiwunta had, watching what happened elsewhere when settler folk moved in, and they were smart—smarter than your parents, not that it took much doing. The strangers could stay, but they had to pay. Just once, but something that would tie them to the land, tie them to the welfare of the tribe. Their child."

"Me."

"You." The boss shrugged, shuffled the cards, and laid down a new hand on the felt, all his attention on the pasteboard. "They could have had other children; if they wanted to make a go of it out there, they'd have to have other children, take in orphans, or hire help from somewhere else. But they were stupid, like I said. They refused. And the Oiwunta burned 'em out. Stole everything they had but left 'em alive."

"And then they came here," Marie added as she passed by, unable to resist adding her piece. Marie had been here then. Marie, Izzy thought, had always been here, much like the devil himself. She had the smooth skin and straight back of a young woman, but she had always been here, for as long as Izzy could recall.

"To the saloon?" she asked.

"To Flood," the boss said. "And, eventually, here."

Everyone who came to Flood came to the saloon, eventually. To see, to deal, to press their luck, or to pay homage. The newspapers back East called everything this side of the Mudwater the Devil's West, but Flood especially was the devil's town. He came and he went, but you could always find him there if you came calling. And people did, even if they didn't always know they was looking for him.

"Nothing but the clothes on their backs and a single horse—and you, little mite, all wide-eyed and closed mouth, barely walking. Didn't say a word, even when your daddy handed you over." The boss chuckled, looking up at her then. "Thought I was getting a quiet one. Proof even I can be wrong."

She remembered that, maybe. Her father was a hard-handed blur in her memory, and her mother only a soft voice and tears, but she remembered being handed over, the boss's face peering down into hers, and him promising that she'd never be sick, never be hungry, never be lonely, so long as she worked for him.

The boss kept his promises.

"What happened to them after that?"

"They took the money from your indenture and they left town."

"Where did they go?" She had never asked that question before, either, in all the times he'd told the story.

"Back south across the Knife? Or headed north, maybe. No idea."

They weren't his; he didn't worry about them.

Izzy thought about that for a minute, then got up from the steps and headed for the storeroom. If the laundryman had been here, there were linens to fold and put away. Her birthday didn't mean there weren't still chores to be done.

"You thinking of following them?" Sarah was nine and not a saloon girl; her mother was one of the faro dealers, so she helped out and generally got petted and spoiled by everyone. She perched on the edge of the worktable now, watching while Izzy worked.

"Of course not," Izzy said, sorting the linens into piles, a familiar, mindless routine. "Why would I?"

"They're your parents." Sarah's eyes went wide when Izzy shrugged. She liked hearing the stories, liked imagining the house she'd been born in, on the banks of a creek with fierce natives lined up outside on their painted ponies, strong and true. But the people who had birthed her had less relevance than the farmers and gamblers who came through Flood, and left even less of a mark on her life.

"You gonna stay?" Sarah's voice was hopeful.

"I don't know."

Until now, it had been a story, like the story of how she came to Flood, only she could change this story, play out all the endings she could imagine. But at the end of the day, she would be sixteen for real. The term her parents had sold her into would end, and in the eyes of the law, she would be a legal adult. She could choose to sign an employment contract, name her own terms . . . or she could leave.

The possibilities taunted her, ticking down the hours until she had to give the boss an answer. Stay, and her future was decided. She would never be ill, or lonely, never be without food or shelter. It seemed foolish to consider any other choice, and yet, and yet. Izzy pressed her hands into the pile of linen and closed her eyes. And yet, the thought of remaining as she was filled her with upset, like a bird trapped inside a too-small cage. She was ungrateful; she was a fool for wanting more.

Especially since she could not say what that more might be.

"Izzy?"

"Take these to the storeroom," she said, pushing the folded linens into Sarah's arms. "I've other things to do."

By midafternoon, the upstairs rooms were filled with noise and voices as the women woke up, and the arrival of the Lees' new baby too early meant that Rosa was called out for her healing skills, meaning Izzy added hairdresser and bodice-lacer to her usual chores. No matter how busy her hands, though, Izzy's thoughts kept wandering, picking one possibility up to consider it, then setting it aside for another, the need to make a decision weighting her shoulders. Nueva España. The States. Heading north to the Wilds to make her living as a trapper. Settling down in one of the Territory towns, maybe become a store-keeper or marry a farmer. Stay in Flood. Leave Flood forever. Each time she thought she'd come to a decision, then a new thought would wind its way in and tangle the threads again, only now her chest got tight every time she thought of something new, the need to make a decision pressing against her and making it hard to breathe.

"You have wrinkles in your forehead, Izzy." A tall brunette paused as she walked past the window seat where Izzy had taken refuge for a moment, and reached out to rub at Izzy's forehead. "Men don't like girls with worry-lines."

"Men don't look that high up," Izzy retorted, batting at the help-ing hand. She was trying to fix her hair; a braid was fine for daytime, but she was due on shift soon, and the thick black mass needed to be pinned up neatly.

"Oh, here, let me do that. How someone so nimble with her hands can so muddle a coil, I'll never understand." Peggy settled in behind her, making swift work of rolling the braid up into a neat knot. "There you are."

Izzy didn't bother to reach up with a hand to check it; Peggy wouldn't say it was ready if it wasn't.

She tilted her head to look up at the older woman. Peggy had come to Flood seven years before, after her husband died. She had to be nearly forty, but despite her sorrow, her face was unlined now and she still laughed easily. Even the hardest customers relaxed when she rested her hand on their shoulder. "Have you ever been East, to the States?" Izzy asked, trying to keep her face equally calm.

"Not me, no." Peggy didn't sound surprised by the question, but then, Peggy rarely was surprised by anything. "My brother was born there, but we came out when he was only five."

Her brother was a road marshal, one of those who settled disputes and kept the daily peace. A hard job, the boss always said, but some folk were born to it, and Tom was one of those. He'd ridden through town last year and visited with them for a while. He didn't laugh the way his sister did, and kept the six-pointed star pinned inside his vest, but he'd smiled at her and given the young 'uns store-bought candy.

"And west, out to the Spanish lands?"

"Now, why on earth would I want to do that?" Peggy's hands rested briefly on Izzy's shoulders, her fingers warm and hard through the cotton of her shawl and dress. "Izzy, dearling, whatever is in that head of yours, with all these questions?"

Izzy looked down at her hands, rubbing fingertips together and feeling the soft calluses there. People came to Flood for a reason. But she hadn't come here; she'd been brought. What reason did she have to stay? "Just thinking, is all."

"Well, you think too much and you'll be late for your shift. Go on; shoo, now."

Izzy ducked back into her room to catch up a shawl to drape over her shoulders against the evening chill, and came back out just as the clock called four chimes. She went to the stairs and looked down; it was a quiet start to the night, with only half of the six gaming tables in use, but that would change soon enough. Catie was right; Sundays were always busy. She looked back up at the balcony, where Peggy was leaning against the railing. The woman smiled and winked, then went back into her room to finish her own preparations.

Peggy was content here. So was Rosa. So was mostly everyone. Why couldn't she be the same?

Izzy was the only girl working that afternoon; Lisabeth had a bad head cold, and Alice was too young to work with customers yet. Sarah's mother was working the far left table, dark brown hair piled elegantly on her head, a periwinkle-blue gown half-covered by her lace shawl, her pale, slender fingers distributing cards. Jack's table was the other side of the room from hers, only two men at it just then, talking among themselves while they waited for a third. Jack had shed his jacket, his shirtsleeves gleaming white like the store-bought finery they were, emphasizing the odd coppery redness of his hair.

This was her home. She knew every pulse, every shift, the way she knew her own heartbeat.

Suddenly aware that she'd been moon-gazing, Izzy picked up a tray from behind the bar and began circulating around the tables, collecting empty glasses and filled ashtrays. As she worked, she looked over the crowd, habit and curiosity sorting them out. There were a few locals passing time and gossiping, a handful of strangers with the look of professional gamblers come to test their luck against the devil, and two men who sat shoulder-slumped at the bar, drinking too slow to forget but too fast to be calm. Only one woman among them all, watching the tables, wearing widow black trimmed with purple. That meant she was nearly out of mourning, or was out but decided black made her look exotic. Her dust-veil was tucked back, showing wisps of pitch-black hair and a pale, square face that had never seen the noon sun, not without a parasol, anyway.

Men came to Flood for a hundred different reasons, the boss always said. Women only came for one reason: revenge. Izzy thought that he would deal with this woman last, after the easier tasks were done.

Izzy waited patiently for Iktan to finish filling the new orders, then carried them to the main table, where the boss held sway, his hands sorting and delivering cards with nonchalance, as though gold and souls were not on the table.

Three men were playing him, two sweating, one too cool. He was the one with the worst hand, she thought in passing.

She delivered her drinks, then paused by the boss in case he had direction for her.

"What do you think, birthday girl? What do you see?" The boss's voice was scented with the cigars he carried but never smoked, and the lighter taste of the gold-colored whiskey he drank a sip at a time.

Izzy knew what he was asking. They played this game often. "The woman." She was the most interesting, of all the people here tonight. "She's glad he's dead. There's something else she wants."

"A lover? Scorned, or unresponsive?"

"Another woman." Izzy didn't know how she knew that; something about the way the woman's head turned, the way she listened or simply how she wore her hat. "She hates another woman."

"Ah." He had already known, of course. But she felt a flush of satisfaction hearing his voice confirm her suspicion. People were so easy to read, sometimes. She finished delivering their drinks and turned to go.

"And that gentleman, last seat at Jack's table?"

And sometimes, they weren't so easy to read. Izzy studied the stranger from under her lashes, careful not to draw his attention. Despite that, he turned and looked directly at her. His smile was sly and sweet, and promised things she knew that she'd like. Izzy composed herself, looking her fill, until she had his measure.

"A charmer, that one. He's winning and doesn't care." Most men cared very much. Whatever they brought to the table, they clung to—until they gambled it away in a moment of passion or hunger, and then the devil had them.

"Yes." The boss agreed with her assessment. "Why is that?"

It was a question, and an order.

When she'd been younger, Izzy could get away with walking up to someone and asking a question. Even if someone had been offended, they'd laughed rather than take it out on a child. Now she had to be more careful. She ghosted to the man's elbow, her tray balanced on her palm, a saucy pitch she'd stolen from Peggy in her voice. "You like a freshening?"

"That's all right, darlin'." He had a soft voice, faded around the *R*s and *D*s, and he didn't look up from his cards when she paused at his elbow.

"I can get you something else, if you like?"

He looked up then, and his gaze took her in, crown to toe. Close up, she noted that he'd dark blue eyes under thick brown lashes, and his crooked, sly smile was all the more powerful when he wasn't trying for sweet. Izzy felt herself blush; there was no way not to, under such a look, but she made herself stand and take it.

She could tell that he wasn't one of those men who came here for the women and not the cards, but he looked his fill anyway and didn't seem to mind what he saw. "Your boss send you over to distract me?"

"If he wanted to do that, he'd send Molly or Sue."

"Get me drunk, then, drinking his surprisingly fine whiskey?"

There was good whiskey and rotgut behind the bar; Iktan decided what you got, no matter what you paid. She let his wink go and tilted her head at him, curious. "Why would the boss do that?"

"Why, indeed? Because I've got a tidy pile of his house's money under my palm?"

Izzy almost laughed. "He doesn't mind that. The boss admires a man who takes chances and plays them well."

"And to entice us in, he offers the only honest faro game in all the Devil's West." His smile was cheeky, his dimples showing, and there was laughter in his eyes, too, the way they crinkled around the edges and made him look older than he probably was.

"The devil's table is an honest one," Izzy said, not quite scolding him.

The crinkles around his eyes eased a little; he wasn't laughing now. "So I've heard."

She had his measure now: likely a professional gambling man, or maybe a law's advocate, someone who held things close. A sharp man, either way. The charm was on the surface; she couldn't tell yet what was underneath.

"You're one of his girls. Young for it, aren't you?"

"Sixteen." She put her hand on one hip, shifting her weight the way she'd seen Molly do when she sassed a man.

"Still young for this world, barely a woman grown," he said. "But good bones, bright eyes, smart mind, and a mouth that doesn't say half of what that smart mind's thinking. You'll be a handsome woman soon enough."

"Handsome?" Her pride was stung. "Not pretty?"

"Handsome's better than beauty," he said, leaning back in his chair, the cards under his fingers not forgotten but put aside, for now. "Lasts longer. Does better. A handsome horse, a handsome woman, they'll never give you grief. Pretty is heartbreak waiting to happen."

"That's a man's take on it. Beauty is power."

He laughed and moved on his cards, proving he was watching what happened at his table, too. "Power is power. A good hand of cards, a bank filled with gold, a loaded gun, a pair of fine eyes and a bewitching smile . . . The trick isn't what you've been given but how you use it."

He studied his cards, then studied her again with the same look. "A young girl with wits and looks could do well beyond Flood."

Izzy cocked her head, looking at him differently now, studying the new turn he'd taken. "Is that an invite, mister . . ."

"Kasun. Gabriel Kasun. You're a bit young yet for me to be offering any invites to, missy, sixteen or no. But if you happened to be out front when I ride out, I would not be unwelcoming of the company. I've mentored before; not against doin' it again for the right rider."

She stared at him, her hand still on her hip, all sass forgotten. An offer like that to come along on this of all days, only a fool'd ignore it. A mentor, someone who knew the Territory, could teach her what she needed to know, how to get by on more than her wits. . . .

"You mean that?"

He was paying full attention to his cards, not her. "I don't offer what I don't mean, girl."

"Iz-sobel. My name is Isobel." Her full name felt odd-shaped in her mouth, but she didn't want to use her nickname, not with this man. Not when he talked to her like that.

"Isobel, then."

The weight of the tray in her hand reminded her she had other drinks to deliver. He might have watched her as she walked off: Izzy didn't look back to find out. She made her rounds as though nothing had changed, watching the way cards were held, the shift and lean of bodies, keeping a tally of whose glass was nearly empty and who had waved off a refill already. She couldn't afford to think on it, not while she was working, not when she was meant to be *looking* and *seeing,* not thinking.

Eventually, she made her way back to the main table and stood behind the boss while he finished a game, waiting while the players took their winnings or left their losings. In the brief space before new players came, she gave her report. "House is clean. Nobody cheating too obvious; nobody looking to cause trouble."

"And the young man over there?"

"He's a sharp, passing through. Likely wanted to see how the devil's house laid down the cards."

"And he is satisfied?"

"Said you run the only honest game in the West."

"Hah." The boss seemed pleased. "And so I do."

"He said I was handsome."

The boss skimmed her with his gaze and smiled. "And so you are."

"And he thinks I could do well, outside of Flood."

The boss put his cards down and swung around in his chair. Izzy quailed inside but stood her ground. He wasn't angry, just paying attention, hearing what she was—and wasn't—saying.

"You could. But not because you're handsome."

"Because you trained me well."

"Exactly." He turned back to the table, new players taking their seats, and she was dismissed.

The rest of the evening kept them all busy, although true to her read, there wasn't any trouble worth mentioning, not even an overenthusiastic drunk. She took advantage of a moment's breather when she could, leaning a little to take the weight off her feet while she waited for Iktan to fill her orders.

"You all right, Izzy?" he asked, even as he poured out the whiskey and rye.

"I'm fine."

Iktan didn't look convinced, but he didn't push, just slid the drinks onto her tray and let her be. He had to be nearly a hundred, his bronzed skin wrinkled like a dried apple, but there wasn't a man in town who'd want to take him in a fight; the boss said he hadn't been born so much as forged out of iron and stone, and there were some who claimed that wasn't a joke.

But when she looked down at the tray, a stick of sugar candy was tucked between the glassware, tied with a scrap of pink ribbon. Birthdays weren't generally fussed over, but that Iktan had remembered this one, specifically, made Izzy's eyes itch. She blinked back the tears, and slipped the candy into her pocket for later.

Time slipped by, drinks to be served, reports to pass along to the boss. The gaming tables were all full and the noise level had risen considerably when Peggy, Molly, and William finally came down, dressed in their working best, to join the others already on the floor.

"Eat something," Will said as he passed her then, his stern tone at odds with his boyish face and the welcoming smile he cast at a customer. "You look like half a shadow."

Part of her rebelled at being scolded like a child, but that thought triggered the realization that their arrival meant it was past eight o'clock. Her breath caught; how could she have missed that?

Izzy looked around the room, catching a nod from the boss. Released, she ignored the supper waiting for her and fled up the stairs to her room, closing the door carefully behind her.

She had lived in this room for nearly four years, since she earned a space of her own rather than a cot in the room the younger girls shared. It was small, but there was a window that looked out over the front porch, directly into the top floor of the mercantile across the street, a narrow bed that squeaked when she turned at night, a chestnut dresser and a washbasin that had come all the way from the East, its bowl painted with green vines and tiny yellow flowers, and a wood-framed mirror set against the wall. She lit the oil lamp by her bed and stood in front of the mirror now. The last tracings of sunlight were gone, the oil lamp casting more shadows than light.

Sundown had come. She was free.

Izzy took a deep breath, watching the dim shape in the mirror do the same. She looked the same as she ever had: dark hair and eyes, the ruddy tones of her skin washed pale by shadows. Her teeth were good, and Molly had said once that her eyes were her best feature, round and wide-set. But she was nothing remarkable.

Yet the stranger had seen something in her. Handsome. Strong.

"A young girl with wits and looks could do well beyond Flood."

Izzy made a face at her reflection. The cardsharp man—no, Gabriel his name had been, Gabriel Kasun—had thought she was unhappy here, that she wanted something more. She wasn't . . . and she did. All the thinking she'd been doing, all the sorting and watching, and the threads of her thoughts had finally come clean and smooth, without her even noticing.

You trained me well.

The boss had taken her in, barely walking, and indentured her, the work of her hands and back at his command. Clothed her, fed her, trained her, to be . . . what? What did she want?

"Your cards, your call. All I can do is wait and see how they're played."

One thing she knew like her own breath: it was the devil's game, life in the Territory, but he ran it honest. Mister Kasun had the right of that. The boss would wait to see what she chose; for the first time in her life, the decision was solely her own. She could do whatever she wanted.

Mister Kasun would ride out tomorrow morning. She could be there. And maybe, in the greater Territory or beyond, she would find what suited her.

Or she could stay. And be what?

Not a saloon girl, nor a shopgirl. She had considered both, off and again, and rejected them. She didn't like the kitchen; she wasn't much for the stables, nor being a shopkeep girl. She wanted *more*.

Riding with a mentor gave her options she hadn't considered, hadn't even *thought* to consider. Riders—"road vagrants," Marie called them, not always kindly—had freedom, could go wherever they wished, do whatever they wanted, pick up whatever skill they thought handy . . . but they were loners, too. They could go anywhere, but they didn't have anywhere to come *back* to, not really.

Izzy couldn't imagine being alone. But crossing the River into the States, with all those people, their noise and bustle . . . she couldn't imagine that, either. And Nueva España feared those who came over the Knife, the taint of the Territory; without something to offer, some skill or wealth, they would not welcome her. North held some appeal, but she lacked the skills to become a trapper or trader; Izzy knew she'd come to grief during their cold, hard winters if she went north. And it was a lonely thing there, too, she'd been told.

All these choices, but the truth was, this was her home.

The knowing of what she wanted rose up the way waters did from streams underground, so quietly you didn't notice until you slipped on the slicked-down stone. All those choices, like the spread of cards facedown on the table, but she'd spent her entire life learning the devil's game . . . and she was good at it. Good at seeing underneath the bluff to what people held, what they wanted.

She looked at the girl in the mirror, and the girl smiled back at her, quiet and sly.

Bargaining with the devil was tricky, but he didn't cheat. He never had to. Ree had been right: the devil took nothing you weren't willing to give. Her parents had taken money and handed her over to the devil they knew rather than the copper-skinned one they didn't. They'd abandoned her, maybe with tears and maybe not, and it didn't matter, because she hadn't been their daughter, the only child of Alfonso Távora and Felipa Lacoyo; from that moment on, she'd been Izzy, indentured to the Devil's House.

And she wasn't that Izzy any longer. Sixteen and free.

Without thinking, Izzy rose, opened the door, went to stand by the railing, looking down.

The night was in full swing. Molly was sitting in someone's lap; William was deep in discussion with the woman in black and a freedman, the three of them leaning against the bar while the others circulated, refilling drinks and flirting, making everyone feel at home, whether they were there to gamble, gossip, or just drink their troubles away. Most of the tables were still full, and the dealers were flipping cards smooth as butter.

Marie passed behind the boss's table, her hand touching his shoulder as she went. To Izzy's eye, he took no notice any more than he looked up to see her standing there, but she knew he knew where they all were, every moment of every day. They were his, for as long as their contracts ran, and the devil never lost anything he cared to hold.

And he knew the things you don't even tell yourself. He just waited until you figured it out.

Panic gripped Izzy when she woke to the sound of the blacksmith's hammer already ringing out. The light coming through the window told her she had slept well past dawn, and she sat upright, her heart racing, before remembering that she had no duties to perform that morning.

Free.

She slipped from bed and washed up quickly at the basin, then brushed out and rebraided her hair, feeling the weight of it swinging between her shoulder blades. That done, she paused, staring blankly at the wooden brush still in her hand. With the end of her indenture, she had no responsibilities today, no chores that needed doing, no obligations or . . . anything. The lack felt like an itch under her skin, uncomfortable and awkward.

"And what do you do when there's nothing to be done, Izzy?" she asked her reflection in the mirror. The words she'd heard nearly every day of her life came back to her, shaped by her own mouth but sounding suspiciously like Marie: "Find something that does need to be done."

She didn't have far to look, although the thought of it unnerved her enough that she thought for a moment to crawl back into her bed, pull the covers over, and pretend.

She placed the hairbrush on her dresser, smoothed the fabric of her skirt, and left the room.

All the bedroom doors were closed, and no one else seemed to be about, although there was the usual muted clatter coming from the kitchen when she came down the stairs. The tables were covered with their usual sheets to keep dust and dirt off the felt, the chairs tipped forward or stacked against the far wall. Somehow, she had thought that everything would change today. Instead, it felt exactly the same.

A door opened and shut above her, the wood creaking the way it always did, and someone shuffled into another room. When the saloon was open, everyone wore hard-soled shoes that tap-tapped merrily on the wood. After hours, though, the women wore sheepskin slippers, upswept hair came down over shoulders, and tired faces smiled only when they wanted to, the saloon a refuge rather than a place of business. Izzy felt guilty for wearing her shoes this early, as though she were making too much noise, but the thought of facing this in slippers . . . Izzy blanched. No, for this, she would be dressed and ready.

The boss was in his office, coffee by his elbow, the steam rising lazily into the air while he entered figures into the ledger book.

"You're up early again, dearling." He didn't look up when she paused in the doorway. The boss's office wasn't exactly forbidden; she'd been in there often enough, usually when being scolded. But she waited anyway, and finally he sighed, closed the ledger book, and looked up at her.

The boss hadn't aged in all the time she'd known him, but he looked . . . tired this morning. There were no windows in his office, but she thought sunlight might pick out a few more silver strands in his dark blond hair. He was clean-shaven today, his shirt open at the neck, vest undone and no cravat around his neck, so she could see his Adam's apple move when he spoke.

"I didn't sleep well," she admitted.

"Not well or not at all?" He pointed at the chair opposite his desk, and she sat in it obediently. Unlike yesterday, she wasn't wearing her best, just a simple brown wool dress that she thought made her look older, more serious. She crossed her feet at the ankle to keep from tapping her toes nervously on the floor. What had seemed so obvious, so plain, before she fell asleep last night now fluttered like a butterfly, too flighty to consider.

"Not well—barely at all," she admitted. Her fingers twisted together in her lap, and she sighed, giving up on any pretense of maturity, solemnity, or dignity. "My indenture ended last night."

"So it did." He was giving her his full attention now, his eyes still arrowhead-sharp, the brown tinged with gold, his skin sun-weathered and creased. She'd always liked this look best on him. "A grown woman with her life spread out in front of her."

His tone was teasing, but his expression was serious. She nodded, and suddenly the words, rather than being locked up in her throat, flowed easily.

"I've been thinking. Like you said yesterday. I've considered my options, and I want to stay. I want to work for you. Not the saloon, not . . . I don't want to work the back rooms or the bar. I want to work for *you*."

It had sounded better, clearer, when she'd rehearsed it in her head, lying in her bed last night. Izzy felt her skin flush, and she looked down at her fingers again, embarrassed.

He wasn't going to make this any easier, reverting to the formal posture and voice he used when someone came calling for a Bargain. "What is it that you want, Isobel Lacoyo Távora?"

The sound of her family name, her birth name, brought a flash of memory, voices and warmth, but she pushed it away. The past was past. Her future was what mattered now.

"Respect." There was no thought of lying to him or shading the desire. There was no point: if she were to bargain with the devil, she needed to be honest. This was what she wanted, what she had been bought and trained for. "Power, maybe." You could not have the first without the second; she knew that. "To be part of what you do. To help . . ." Her mouth was so dry, but she managed to get the words out. "To be part of all this."

"And you think to find that here, in this House? To be my faithful right hand in all doings?" He smiled, and it was both sweet and cold. "You want Marie's job?"

"I . . . Maybe? Someday, yes." Izzy licked her lips nervously. This wasn't going the way she'd thought it would. In her imagining, the boss had laughed and told her he'd been waiting for her to say that, and Marie welcomed her, saying her help would be priceless, and . . .

In daylight, she saw how foolish that had been. The devil was honest, but he gave nothing away, and Marie had no reason to share, no need of help.

"Or something else," she said. "Some way I can help . . ."

"Help what?" He was still watching her, still with that smile. It should have made her angry or uneasy, but instead, her nerves steadied. She was a free woman come to make a Bargain. She knew that look, knew *him*, as much as any soul might. Izzy waited, and watched him in return, the way she had watched the woman in black the last night, the way she'd watched so many other people come and go over the years. She had lived her entire life in the devil's house, and she had no fear of him. He had taught her that, as well.

"Help you do what you've been training me to do all these years," she said finally. "To see what people are, what they want. What they need. And how to give it to them."

She was right; she knew she was. She *had* to be right.

He leaned back, his left index finger tapping thoughtfully at his lips, his gaze unblinking as ever as they regarded her, looking bone-deep in that way he had.

"Marie runs this house," he said. "She is my steady right hand and will continue to be so for many more years."

Izzy refused to let her shoulders slump, but inwardly, all of her hopes and courage crumbled. If he had no need of her, then what?

The boss sighed, then brought both of his hands up in front of him and held them up, turning them back and forth as though to show he held nothing in his palm, nothing up his sleeve. He had strong hands, long-fingered and supple, and his right hand was unadorned, while his left bore a silver-and-black signet ring on his index finger. She had never seen that ring before—but a similar one, with a clear stone, encircled Maria's right thumb.

"We each have two hands, of equal strength and dexterity. Each with things it does well, better than the other. All this time, you've seen the day-to-day business, the gathering-in and the granting, the bargaining and the dealing, the work of my right hand." His voice changed again, slipping to a soft growl she had never heard before. "Did you never think beyond that, Isobel? Did you never wonder what the other hand held?"

"I . . . No." She never had.

"Most don't. I prefer it that way." He let his hands fall, resting them palm-down on the desk, graceful even in stillness. The growl was gone, but his voice remained sharp. "The States see us as some empty wilderness to be claimed and tamed, while Spain and their holdings call us evil, a cluster of heathens and sinners in need of cleansing—by sword and fire, if they had their way. Both sides press on us, coveting us. Those who leave their homes and come here, who cross into our borders in search of something, even if they never make their way to Flood, they see more clearly what the Territory means, but even so, they see only the one side . . . until they need the other. Then they grab onto it, with desperate strength.

"The right hand gathers and gives, visible to all. But the left hand, Isobel, the *manu sinistra*? It moves in shadows, unseen, unheard . . . until I deem it time for it to be seen and heard. And when it moves, its work cannot be undone. It is the strength of the Territory, the quick knife in the darkness, the cold eye and the final word."

She looked up, away from his hands, and was caught by a gaze the burnt gold of the morning sun.

"I have been lacking a left hand for too long. Are you strong enough for that, Isobel née Lacoyo Távora? Is the iron in your spine, the fire in your blood, ready for my forging?"

Née? Marie was née too when she introduced herself. Marie née Aubertin. Izzy didn't let herself hesitate, didn't let herself feel fear. "Yes."

"And what do you have to offer in return?"

She had nothing. Everything she owned, everything she carried, belonged to him. "Myself," she said. "All I have is myself."

"I accept your terms," he said abruptly. "Marie will write up your new papers."

Then his eyes faded to the more soothing, familiar brownish-gold, and the smile in them was familiar, and fond. "They won't be ready for several hours. You have this day of freedom, dearling. Go, enjoy it."

Marie, doing her predawn rounds, had seen Izzy go downstairs dressed as though for battle, her hair braided and coiled, and her boots laced. She had leaned over the railing and watched as the girl paused, then found her courage, and went to the boss's office, not bothering to knock. Despite her worries, Marie smiled. It wasn't guts the girl lacked, for certain.

She went back into her room and finished her morning preparations, keeping an eye on the sunlight rising through her window. When she thought enough time had gone by, she draped a shawl around her shoulders and went to check on how things were progressing.

The office door was still closed. Normally by then, she would be meeting with the boss, discussing the day over her first cup of coffee, but that could wait a bit yet. There would be another pot of coffee in the kitchen, and Ree wouldn't dare smack her fingers if she snitched a piece of the fry bread she could smell cooking. But even as she thought that, the door opened and Izzy walked out.

Marie studied the girl's face. She didn't look angry, or happy for that matter. She looked as though a horse had kicked her, and she wasn't yet sure if it hurt. Her heart ached for the girl, but she held her tongue as Alice came out of the kitchen, an apron two sizes too large for her wrapped around her middle. Clearly, Ree had her in search of something, because Izzy directed the child to look behind the bar before the older girl pushed open the front door and disappeared outside.

Marie waited a hand's count to make sure that the girl wasn't coming back before descending the stairs herself, nodding to Alice in passing, and entering the office without knocking. The boss was writing, his fountain pen making faint noises as it scratched its way across the paper. He didn't look up, but he didn't tell her to go away, either.

She gathered her skirt in one hand, sorting it out of the way, and perched herself on the edge of the desk. "Are you sure about this?"

He didn't bother asking how she knew; he'd trained her to know what went on within the walls of the saloon, given her the ears to hear, and had only himself to blame when she used those skills on him. "The only question was if she was certain. And she was."

Marie frowned at him, unable to argue and yet unsatisfied with the response. "I know she's not a child any more, not legally, but she's still so young."

"Old enough. And she came to me, quite clear in what she desired." He looked up from the ledger and studied his Right Hand. "You doubt her capabilities?"

"She is quick-witted and steady-minded," Marie said, taking the question seriously. "And her heart is neither tender nor cold. She listens as well as any girl her age and has a healthy dose of doubt for what she hears. She was born to the Territory, feels it in her blood and bones. No, I don't doubt her capabilities or her desire." How could she, when she too had quietly fed and encouraged it all these years?

"And yet you question my decision?"

Marie leaned past him, picking up the paperwork, buying herself time. She looked at the cream-colored paper, reading the words inked there with an odd expression, part resignation, part hope, and then handed the sheet back. "I suppose I'm too fond of the girl," she said. "I may have hoped that she'd find a nice farmer, or maybe the blacksmith's boy, and settle down somewhere nearby."

The boss laughed. "Our Izzy? Woman, get out of my office; stop wasting my time. And if that boy is still around, the northern cardsharp from last night? Find him for me."

She knew better than to ask what he had in mind. Whatever it was, they'd all learn soon enough.

‡ ‡ ‡

When the young boy knocked on the door of his hired room about midmorning, Gabriel was already packed and ready to ride out.

"Sir? The boss would like to see you. Right now, if'n it's convenient."

"The boss?" Even as he asked, Gabriel knew. The master of the saloon. The master of this town. The Master of the Territory, some said.

Gabriel hadn't moved to the main table the night before, although that had been his intention when he arrived. Every man jack thought, in his heart of hearts, that he could face the devil across the green felt and come out the winner, or at least hold his own long enough for bragging rights. Gabriel had played out his hands and waited for the tables to shift, for his turn to come along, but somewhere midway through the evening, he'd discovered that it was enough to be there, to see the way the man worked, to feel the power that shimmered around him, steady as the wind and old as the stone.

Gabriel had questions; there wasn't a man alive as didn't. But he'd realized the last night that he could find the answers on his own or he'd never know, and that would have to do. The devil, it turned out, had nothing he would bargain for.

So, to be summoned now, when he was preparing to leave? That was . . . disturbing.

"Give me a minute," he told the boy, and got his hat and coat from the rack, leaving his bags on the bed.

The boardinghouse was only a few steps down from the saloon, and in that time, Gabriel considered and rejected half a dozen reasons why he might have been summoned. The only one that held water was his conversation with the girl the night before; what had been her name? Isobel, that was it. A cheeky smile and a serious eye, and he'd made the offer without thinking, but surely that wouldn't be enough to bring him to such notice? If the girl was thinking of riding out, there was no reason she shouldn't, unless she'd made a Bargain preventing it. He couldn't have given offense just for offering, if he hadn't known. Could he?

His blood chilled, but he kept his hat at a jaunty angle, the brim shading his eyes from the sun but also keeping them from view. The weight of the knife in his boot was no comfort, for once. Weapons of steel and bone couldn't defend him here. Still, he'd noted that the devil kept an honest house, and he had no reason to doubt that yet.

Gabriel had never been in a saloon or gambling house before opening hours. To his surprise, it was busy even in the daylight, as innocuous as a storefront, with a handful of youngsters underfoot sweeping the floor and washing glassware, carrying linens and laundry to and from, and generally keeping busy. An older woman, dressed in her night-wrapper, was seated at the bar, swinging her legs gently, a hint of bare flesh showing as she moved. She winked at him, and Gabriel felt himself blush like a schoolboy, but he touched the brim of his hat in acknowledgment and was rewarded with a laugh.

The boy didn't pause but led him across the main floor to a door in the back and knocked once on the frame.

"Send him in, Aaron," a voice called.

The door opened, and Gabriel walked into the devil's lair.

The man behind the desk had blond hair and a square, clean-shaven chin that did not match Gabriel's memory of the man he had seen at the tables the night before, but by the time he took the indicated seat, removed his hat, and looked up again, that first impression changed again, angular features softening, chin and lip now covered with morning stubble, although the eyes, keen and golden brown, remained the same.

Riding the Territory, Gabriel had encountered odder in his time; he let the shift go without comment.

"You are, no doubt, wondering why your presence has been requested."

"No doubt."

The devil leaned back in his chair and tilted his head, studying Gabriel. "You spoke with Izzy last night while at the card table."

"I did." Gabriel knew when he was being studied—and judged. He waited, his hat in his lap, boots on the floor, conscious again of the knife in its sheath, and how utterly useless it would be if the judgment went against him.

"She's a comely girl, serving drinks; most would flirt, perhaps tease her, or try for something more. But you spoke to her seriously; you took her seriously, despite her youth and gender. And then you left. Before your turn at my table came around. You did not feel the need to play against me."

"No."

Gabriel had been born to the Territory, but he had trained back East to face judges and juries with men's liberty on the line. He wasn't afraid of silence, nor the moment before the storm. And if his stomach muscles tensed or his shoulders drew back, his lead hand kept still against his thigh, neither of them remarked on it.

Those eyes brightened to pure gold, the skin tone darkening from native bronze to near black, the cheekbones sharpening. Gabriel waited, his gaze steady, his hands resting on his knees, his hat on his lap.

"You're an advocate, not a cardsharp."

"A man mightn't pursue two distinct interests in his time?" He hadn't meant for it to sound so much like a question.

"I have an offer to make you," the devil said, as casual as he might deal out a new hand, all friends around the table, no cards up his sleeve. "Or perhaps I am accepting your offer. Either way, I think it may be of interest, and of worth, for you to accept."

He had made no offer to the devil, only Isobel, but Gabriel was not fool enough to argue the point. A cautious man thought out his plan, and his price, before he went to the devil. If the devil came to you . . .

Gabriel raised a hand to indicate that he was listening, but he would not speak again, not until he'd heard the offer out.

‡ ‡ ‡

Izzy felt lost. She stood on the wooden steps of the saloon, the door closing firmly behind her, and was filled with an unfamiliar, unwanted sensation of having nowhere to go, nothing to do. She had no place in the daily routine anymore, her old chores would have already been reassigned, and despite her meeting with the boss, she had no idea of what her new status, her new role might be.

The uncertainty made her uncomfortable. The boss had told her to enjoy herself. . . . But her mind went blank at the thought. She didn't want to go back inside, waiting in her room like a scolded child anticipating her punishment, as though she had done something wrong.

She took a deep breath, letting the dry air fill her lungs. The sky was blue overhead, the breeze a cool counterpoint to the sun rising bright and warm. A walk along the river would take her away from questions she could not answer, and perhaps clear her head a little.

Resolved, she stepped along the planked sidewalk, walking toward the edge of town. Flood, for all its importance, was not large, and there were few people out and about this early, save an older man heading toward her, down the middle of the street. A small wagon trundled behind him, piled high with burlap bags, the wooden wheels making a *rattleclack* noise as they turned. "Good morning, Miz Izzy," he said, tipping the brim of his hat to her.

"Morning, Mister Dash." He and his son, Samuel, grew enough on their farmstead a few miles out of town to support themselves, and contracted to sell what remained. Molly said that outside the Territory, a black man couldn't enter into a contract, nor a native, nor a woman of any race, in most places. The boss didn't seem to care so much about that, so long as they stuck to their terms and didn't cause troubles.

She had no contract, no agreement, no terms sealed and signed. The thought made Izzy's skin itch. Not that there weren't folk who did just fine without them, she supposed, here and elsewhere. It just felt strange. Uncertain.

The planked sidewalk ended just before the smithy, and Izzy stepped down onto the road, puffs of dirt rising around her ankles. It hadn't rained in nearly a week; that wasn't good. The smithy's door was open, but there was no steady *clank-clank-clank* of the hammer, just the slow breath of the fire, waiting.

Past the smithy, there was only the icehouse, a low-slung building built into the rise, and then the grasslands that led down to the river's edge. The low ridge of hills to the west was only a faint purple smudge in the far distance. The river itself was as high as it'd ever be, and old Duarte's boys would be bringing his cattle through soon enough, heading for summer pasture. The saloon was always busy then, with Duarte's oldest son paying a visit to the boss, the hired hands spilling their cash on the tables, although few of them sat at the boss's table.

She had never been allowed to work the cattle drive; the boss thought the hired men were too unpredictable and prone to abusing their drink, so the younger girls never worked those days. She'd spent the last year's drive in the kitchen, sneaking peeks when there was a lull, before Ree slapped the flat of a wooden spoon on her backside, herding her back to chores.

"He'll have to let me work out front this year, won't he?" Marie did, but the boss had said that the left hand was different from the right, hadn't he? She tried to remember exactly what he had said, but the words were blurred in her memory now. Something about having the last word?

Despite herself, Izzy laughed. Nobody ever got the last word with the boss. Even if he let you speak last, he always had the final say.

Birds chirped overhead, and a pair of rabbits disappeared into the tall grass as she approached the river, but otherwise she might have been the only living thing for miles, the town quiet and invisible behind her. Suddenly, Izzy wasn't so sure that this walk had been a good idea. She paused, then licked her lips and forced herself to continue. She was perfectly safe here, so long as she didn't try to cross the river, and she had no intention of doing anything so foolish.

Izzy paused when she reached the edge of the river, listening to the water flowing over rocks, a pleasant, steady gurgling sound. She felt too restless still to sit quietly, so she kept walking along the riverbank, letting the morning sun gentle her skin and the sound of the water ease her worries, until she came to a section of the bank that was too steep, the footing too uncertain. She dug the toe of her boot into the dirt and considered working her way around it, then shook her head and turned around. She had gone far enough; there was no need to tempt fate.

Despite that soothing of the creek and sun, the unease that weighed on Izzy's shoulders remained. How long could papers take to write up? Should she go back now, or would the boss think she was hovering, that she didn't have the patience to do the job? Might he change his mind? The worries chased each other until she determined that going back would be no worse than staying here and fretting herself into a state.

The path seemed longer going in than walking out, and she paused when she reached the border of town, feeling the ground rumble faintly through the soles of her boots, part warning, part welcome.

"It's me, Izzy," she said quietly. It wasn't necessary: the town knew her, had known her since she was knee-high. But this was the first time she'd crossed the border without *belonging*. Better to be cautious.

There was no indication anything changed, her feet still feeling an odd tingling, but she stepped forward anyway. Nothing struck her down, or set off an alarm, or whatever the boundary was supposed to do if someone came with ill intent. It never had done anything, not in all the years she'd lived there, but then, no one had ever come with mean intent, either. Not that they made it into town, at least.

Aaron ran down the street to meet her, the afternoon sun lighting him from behind and making him look like a dusty angel.

"You're to come, Izzy," he said, jigging with enthusiasm, as though finding her had been the best part of his day. "Boss wants you. Now!"

The boss was in his office, along with Judge Lenn. They both stubbed out their cigars when she walked in, and the judge stood, taking her hand and bowing over it like they'd never met before. His short-trimmed mustache tickled the back of her hand. "Miz Isobel. May I wish you belated but heartfelt felicitations on your birthday?"

Izzy fell into the moment, dipping a curtsey like she had seen Marie do when she was being formal, and smiled up at the older man. "I thank you, sir."

He squeezed her fingers gently and then released her, his face falling into the more familiar serious lines. "The old man here asked me to witness your signatures. You do understand what you're doing? This is more than an indenture. This isn't only a contract; it's a Bargain. There's no leaving his service once you sign, save death, and I'm not so certain even that can break this."

"I understand," Izzy said, because the judge seemed to be waiting for a response.

"And this is of your own free will, with no coercion."

Izzy nodded. "Yes, sir." She wasn't quite sure what that last word meant, but she'd made the decision, nobody else.

The judge looked at the papers again, then nodded once. "All right, then. I can't say as I think this is a wise choice—no offense, sir," he said in an aside, and *none taken*, the boss responded, smiling, "but it's your choice and none of us are as wise as we think we are at your age."

The judge was the only one who talked like that, and the only one who not only sassed the boss but went toe to toe with him on a regular basis. But he spoke for the Law in Flood, and the boss said Law was useful to have on your side, so he looked over every contract and witnessed its signing.

Izzy reached for the pen, but the boss held out a hand, stopping her. "Read them first, Isobel. Never sign a thing you have not read first."

"Yessir." She picked up the paper and looked over the terms, resisting the urge to skim them quickly.

"To bear faithful service," she read silently, forming the words only with her lips. "To obey in word and in deed the trust given." In return, she was promised five full coin a month, plus all supplies and training needed for her to carry out those responsibilities.

Izzy came to the end of the page, then leaned forward and picked up the pen. It was heavier than she'd expected, the barrel cool and smooth under her fingers. The prick against her fingertip was a sharp pinch, the nib cold as it drank its fill, and then she was signing her name on the creamy paper next to the *X*, all her penmanship lessons coming back to her, leaving a smooth line of text when she was done.

The boss took the pen next, pricked his own finger, and scratched his name on the next line. The blood glistened, then sank into the paper, turning darker as it dried. *"Maleh mishpat,"* he said quietly. "Isobel, thou art bound to me."

It was done. Izzy had expected . . . more, somehow. She had expected to feel different.

"Congratulations, my dear," the judge said, and she took the hand he offered, smiling up at him when he shook it this time, the way he might another man. "You will give credit to your Bargain, I am certain." There was something in his eyes, a flicker of something deep and troubled, and then it was gone, even as he turned to offer his hand to the boss as well.

Izzy, left alone, looked down at her hands, and . . .

She did feel different. The uncertainty she'd been hauling was gone, and . . . She tilted her head, listening to something running under the two men's voices. She could tell every movement within the saloon, the hum of voices, the move of bodies, the *flickerthwack* of cards and clink of glassware, the swallow of throats and the beating of hearts. It pressed against her, squeezing everything out of her until she began to panic, fingers splayed as though to push back against empty air.

"Isobel."

The boss stood in front of her, his hair tousled as though he'd just run a hand through it, disturbing its earlier stylings, and the sense of pressure faded.

"Yes, boss?" She relaxed her fingers and waited; now he would tell her what her duties would be, what she had to learn, what responsibilities she would have.

"Come with me."

Gabriel had spent much of the day with the devil's right-hand woman, a terrifyingly efficient woman named Marie who would have put the dean of the College of William and Mary to shame. If your plans were suddenly rucked off course, he could think of no better soul to straighten it again.

"Ah, about that," he had said when she handed him the route they were to take. "I do have . . ."

"Obligations, yes. We have taken those into consideration as well."

Of course they had.

She had deposited him at the bar an hour before, but the glass in front of him was the same pour he'd started with, never mind that it smelled much the same quality he'd been drinking the night before. There were days you wanted to numb your thinking, and others you wanted it keen, and there was no doubting which sort of days he'd be having going forward. Behind him he could hear the hum of conversation, the sound of cards being dealt and drinks served, and his spine itched with the need to turn around, keep an eye on all corners of the room, note who was where and doing what, as though he were caught in a crossroads.

He should have been on the road already. He'd had a schedule, an agenda. . . .

"Mister Kasun."

He hadn't heard the man come up alongside him. Of course he hadn't. Gabriel gave his drink one last, final swirl, then turned to face the man who'd tossed his entire life into chaos.

"Sir." If the man had a surname, he'd never heard it used. "Boss," most called him in public. Or "sir." The girl was with him, dressed more soberly in a plain brown dress, her hair pulled back in a single braid. She had a plain enough face, he'd noted before, but the bones were strong, her mouth full and well drawn, and her eyes dark-lashed and expressive. Right now, they showed nothing but a faint curiosity and a flicker of apprehension.

"Isobel, you've met Mister Kasun."

"Briefly, yes." She offered him her hand, and he took it. She had a firm grip, with soft calluses at the fingertips and along the heel. No stranger to regular work, then. Good.

"I've decided to take him up on his offer to mentor you. You'll leave tomorrow morning."

Gabriel would've rather run backward onto a saguaro than say a damned thing just then. Those expressive eyes were expressing something more than apprehension, the sort that a single bit of tinder could spark into something ugly for man and beast.

"You . . . what?" Her voice was soft. She didn't shriek or yell or bring any attention to herself, and yet there wasn't a doubt in his mind that she was somewhere past shocked and well into hopping mad. Suddenly, that rye in his glass seemed like an excellent idea.

"Izzy." Just that one word was enough to close her down. Gabriel cast his gaze back down into his now-empty glass, damned himself for a coward, and looked back at the pair.

"You will ride circuit for me, be my ears and eyes beyond Flood," the devil said. "Mister Kasun will teach you what you need to know. You seemed open to his suggestion the night before; has something changed?"

Gabriel would've rather run *forward* into a saguaro, with his *face*, than say a damned thing at that moment.

The girl—Isobel—looked as though she were more foolhardy than he, then she closed her mouth, swallowed, and shook her head. "No, boss."

A brief, too-white smile, deeply unnerving, flashed across his face and was gone. "I'll leave you two to get acquainted, then. Get a good night's sleep, Isobel. You'll be leaving first thing in the morning."

And then the bastard left him with Isobel, who still looked as though someone had drowned her kitten rather than given her the chance of a lifetime.

Izzy heard the boss's words, but it was fuzzy, like there were a dozen people yelling at her all at once, until she couldn't hear anything at all. And then he was gone, and she'd agreed to leave. Agreed to go away.

"Buy you a drink?"

"What?" She looked blankly at the man, as though she'd never seen him before, then the words settled into something comprehensible. "Yes. All right. Tea, please, Iktan?" The boss never forbade them anything stronger, but Marie frowned on the girls drinking while they were working, saying men could make themselves foolish, but a woman never should. She slid onto the chair next to the stranger—not a stranger, Gabriel his name was, Gabriel Kasun—and accepted the glass the bartender slid toward her. The dark, astringent liquid was familiar on her tongue, pushing away the noise, the odd sensations, and leaving her firmly seated and utterly flummoxed.

And, she admitted, tasting it on the edge of her tongue, like a pepper in her tea, angry. Incredibly, unutterably angry.

"So." Mister Kasun looked uncomfortable, but she couldn't find it in herself to feel sorry for him. "This was a surprise to you."

"Yes." All of it, a surprise. Being tossed out of her home, told to go away . . . when she chose to stay, she'd thought that she would be *staying*. "I mean, I . . ." She took a deep breath, sipped her tea, then started again. "The boss has his reasons. And I do appreciate your willingness to mentor me."

Nobody did anything without a reason, and nobody did anything without exchange. And the way the boss had spoken to him . . . No, whatever Bargain had been made, it was between him and the boss; Izzy wasn't fool enough to ask. But that didn't mean she wasn't deadly curious.

"Your boss took care of the details—including, apparently, where we're to go." His voice was lacking the humor she'd heard in it before, his gaze somehow harder. "You know how to pack for the road?"

"No. I . . . No."

"Light, and dense," he told her. "If it's purely sentimental and won't fit in your pocket, leave it here. If it serves no purpose, leave it here. No fripperies, nothing breakable. Boots, not shoes. Durable. No fancy dresses."

Izzy thought of the remade dress Molly had just given her, pale pink with lace at the trim, and nodded.

"Bring only the extras that're important. A book. A memento you can't be without. The things that'll get you through a long cold night, or a day where all you see is mud and rain."

"You're talking from experience?" The question slipped out despite her sulk.

He laughed. She liked this laugh; it wasn't mean or even really amused. More thoughtful, remembering. "You get out on the trail, a gullywasher comes through and you're up to your hocks in water. If you can't find shelter, you're either sleeping in the mud or you climb a rock or a tree and shiver until it all blows through. And then the next morning, everything you own is sodden and mud-covered, including you and the horse."

"It sounds delightful." She was borrowing Molly's tone again, sass and vinegar.

"It's a hard thing, taking the road," he said. "But if you're meant for it, then yes. It can be."

Izzy didn't know if she was meant for it. She hadn't chosen it; this wasn't what she'd wanted, not what she'd expected. But it was what the boss wanted her to do. So she'd do it.

The first morning of her new Bargain, Izzy woke all at once, not the panic of the day before, but her body braced as though expecting something to happen. The morning light was clouded, the shadows darker than ghosts, and she lay still a moment longer, breathing in the air, feeling the linens cool under her skin. Distantly, she heard the floor clock downstairs chime, too muffled to count the hour, and she slid out of bed, each movement uncertain, as though she had a fever, or was moving in a dream. There were no sounds outside, as though the entire Territory slept, even the morning birds. It must be before even dawn.

Mister Kasun—Gabriel, he had told her to call him Gabriel—had said they would leave with the sunrise.

She lit the lamp and bathed quickly at the washbasin, then dressed in one of the three new outfits that had been laid out on her bed when she returned to her room the night before: a plain brown skirt falling to her ankles and buttoned halfway up the back to allow her to ride astride, the bodice a looser fit that she was accustomed to, with plain cuffs and no embroidery or ribbons anywhere. The stockings were a thicker knit than she was used to and dyed brown to match her dress. Over all that, a jacket made of a rough waxed cloth that was overlarge in the shoulders, as though it had been sewn for a larger body, or one wearing multiple layers underneath. The boots, too, were new: oxblood leather rising to her calf, with a slight heel, and laced on the outside rather than in front.

Dressed, she felt awkward, uncertain, her body unfamiliar in unfamiliar garb.

The sky outside her window was beginning to brighten. She brushed out her hair and then braided it again, a single plait hanging against her back. Her face in the mirror didn't seem quite hers anymore. She made a face, mouth drawn down, eyes wide, like a frog, to see if that helped. It didn't.

Her bags were waiting by the door, the rest of her clothing already packed, but as she went to place her necessities into the saddlebag that had also appeared on her bed, she noted something on the dresser that hadn't been there the night before: a plain hammered-silver band and a small leather journal with a pencil tied to it by a leather thong.

Izzy picked the ring up and slid it onto the littlest finger of her left hand. It fit perfectly, the cool silver warming against her skin, and felt right, as though she'd been wearing it since forever.

Silver was for cleansing and protection. Inside Flood, there was no need, but on the road . . . She wasn't sure if such a thin slip could do anything, but wearing it made her feel better.

She picked up the notebook next, feeling the smoothness of the cover, the careful stitching of the binding, the double-looped swirl-within-a-circle of the devil's sigil burnt into the front. There was no note, no clue as to who had left it there. Izzy frowned at it and then slid it into her saddlebag before leaving the room, closing the door behind her one final time.

Marie was the only one awake in time to see her go. The Right Hand was leaning against the bar, a mug of coffee in her hands, watching as she came down the stairs. Izzy reached the main floor and let her bags drop to the ground, bending down to check the tie of her pack again, even though she knew that it was secure. The canvas was scratchy against her fingers, the leather smooth, and she was afraid that she packed too much, that he was going to make her empty it out and leave more behind.

Just as she began to think that she should go upstairs and pack again, the Right Hand stepped forward. The swish of silk under her skirts only emphasized Izzy's awareness of the strange feel of her unmentionables, the fabric rubbing oddly against her skin, and the hard sole and stiff leather of her boots laced too loosely against her calves. Everything felt wrong, awkward, immodest somehow despite her skin being decently covered.

"Isobel."

Izzy's hands stilled and her shoulders stiffened, years of obedience forcing her to look up at the older woman. Did she know that Izzy had wished for her position? But Marie didn't look angry or even upset. "It's all right," she said, one hand touching her shoulder, urging Izzy to stand. "It's all right to be scared." And she didn't allow time or space for Izzy to deny it. "You're leaving the only home you've ever known, and if you weren't scared, you'd be a fool, and we don't raise fools here, do we?"

"No, ma'am." She wasn't scared. She was *angry*. But she wasn't fool enough to tell Marie that. She looked around the main room, pained to see it still empty. She hadn't gone out of her way to tell anyone she was leaving, but everyone had known by the time she went to bed, no doubt. Gossip spread anywhere there was breath. She'd thought maybe someone would have come down to wish her well. . . .

"This is the way of the world," Marie said, as though knowing what she was thinking. "Some come, some stay, some go . . . and come back. You'll come back to us, Isobel. You belong to the Devil's House now."

Hadn't she before as well? But no, the judge had said so: a Bargain was different from just a contract or indenture.

"It's a hard road you'll be traveling," Marie went on, stepping back and giving Izzy a long, assessing look. "Not one I would have chose for you, but that's all and done now. Just you remember this: we don't serve our own whims, not here nor out there. We play the devil's tune, and he calls it as he will."

"Yes, ma'am."

Marie shook her head, as though aware that Izzy didn't understand, not really. "When you hear it, you will understand. Now go; the sun's almost up, and you should be on your way. A journey's best started before dawn."

Izzy moved almost without thought, following Marie's gentle order. Her bootheels sounded impossibly loud against the wooden planking, the swing of the door shut behind her sharp as a thunder-crack. Something snapped inside her with that noise, and she straightened her back, refusing to let it cow her. She'd wanted something more, wanted to *be* more. If this was how it came, then that was how she would go.

Two horses waited, tied to the rail, along with a rough-coated, long-eared mule already loaded with packs, neck extended so flat teeth could snatch at a sparse patch of grass, probably not so much because it was hungry as because the grass was there. Izzy was wise to mules: she stepped to the side, out of reach, just in case it thought she might be more fun to bite.

Gabriel Kasun came around from behind the taller of the two horses, a deep-chested bay with black points and a head like a rock, nothing graceful and all power behind it. The cardsharp was gone, his fine-cut coat replaced by a heavy canvas duster, a striped shirt with the placket done up underneath, his eyes half hidden by the wide brim of his hat. Her gaze dropped, and then she remembered Marie's words and raised her head again, meeting his stare squarely.

"There you are," he said. She thought there was approval in that smooth rumble, and her forehead creased, not understanding, before he turned away and put a hand on the second horse's neck, pulling loose her reins with a simple tug. "Your boss said you had some skill at riding. This is Uvnee."

The mare turned its head toward her, as though aware they were being introduced. "Hello, Uvnee." Izzy let her pack slide to the ground again, the saddlebag slung over her shoulder, and stepped forward, moving to the left side and holding her hand out palm up and flat, to let the mare sniff at her. "I'm sorry; I don't have an apple for you this morning." She should have thought of it, should have planned better. A horse that associated her with treats was a horse less likely to fuss when asked to do something.

The mare lipped her palm, the blunt teeth brushing against the skin without nipping. Izzy took that as a good sign and reached up to rub between the ears, bits of dust and dander clinging to her fingers. The mare's coat was reddish brown, the color of river clay, and when she snorted, her breath was warm against Izzy's face.

"That what you're bringing?" Gabriel asked, indicating her pack with a rough jerk of his chin.

"I . . . Yes." Her pack, and a saddlebag.

"Hunh," he said, and she braced herself, one hand still on Uvnee's head, the other pressed uncertainly against her stomach, forcing it to settle. "That'll do." And then he looked at her and smiled, teeth showing and the corners of his eyes squinting, a real smile, not something forced or mean. "I'll load this, then, and we'll be on our way."

She had passed the first test. Izzy felt the tightness in her stomach ease just a bit.

The pack went onto the mule, who accepted the additional burden without complaint, chewing the grass with seeming content. Izzy tried to determine what the other packs were, but they were tucked in so neatly, it was difficult to tell one from another, tied down with leather straps that, she hoped, the mule wouldn't be able to chew through.

"All right, then," Mister Kasun—Gabriel—said, giving the mule a firm slap against one hindquarter and tying its lead to his horse's saddle. "Let's go."

He didn't offer to help her fix her saddlebag's straps, nor offer her a boost into the stirrup, just swung into his own saddle and gathered the reins, waiting until she was ready. Izzy frowned at the saddle, then unbuttoned the lower half of her skirt, letting the fabric flare slightly as she fitted her foot to the stirrup, grabbed the pommel horn, and swung onto the horse's back with less grace than she might've wished for but enough for the job. And it wasn't as though anyone were watching. She was familiar with riding astride; the boss didn't hold with sidesaddle, said it was a good way to get a broken neck for some excuse at modesty, but Uvnee was broader than the old gelding she was accustomed to. Fortunately, the saddle was well made, and it took her only a minute to find her balance and adjust the skirt decently around her.

"We'll stop in a bit and adjust your gear once you're used to her," Gabriel said. "Got any farewells you need to say?"

Isobel looked over her shoulder at the saloon, the shuttered windows, and then turned to look up at the sky, the faint streak of dawn starting to cross the horizon, the fresh hint of brimstone and hot iron coming from the blacksmith's. She shook her head, letting the leather of the reins slide between her fingers until she was comfortable, feeling Uvnee shift underneath her, anxious to be moving.

"No," she said softly. "No, I'm done."

Every deal has two sides, the devil had said. *I've told you what I want. Name your price.*

Gabriel tightened his fingers on the reins, remembering. He hadn't gone into the saloon to make a deal, neither contract nor Bargain. He'd had his chance the night before and passed on it, declined to face the devil across the felt.

I didn't make the offer to you. Your accepting it on her behalf don't change that.

The devil had seemed amused by Gabriel's sass: his smile was thin, but it reached his eyes, a comfortable amusement that had nothing cruel about it. Gabriel'd heard the stories when he was back East, over the River, the warnings of brimstone and betrayal, but he'd never been able to believe them. What he'd been raised on was more truth: the devil ran an honest house. But for him to be asking the price rather than telling it . . . that ran contrary to everything anyone knew, and it made a man suspicious.

To be offered his price for a thing he'd been willing to do for free . . . It made a man more than suspicious.

Steady snorted, as though the gelding knew what he was thinking. He kneed the horse forward as though to tell it to shut up and focus on the trail, but it was a wide-open road, cleared of rocks and smooth of holes, exactly the way you'd expect the road to perdition to look.

The girl rode behind and to his left, Uvnee falling into place like she'd been riding with Steady her entire life instead of coming fresh out of the stable. Still, he'd picked the mare out of the ones offered, and he had a decent sense of horseflesh.

I'm sure we can come to an equitable agreement. . . .

Gabriel tugged his hat down farther over his eyes, the morning sun up high enough now to be annoying but not high enough to start warming the air. His gaze flickered to the girl, noting the way she held her reins, the way she shifted, trying to find the most comfortable position, adjusting to the mare's movements. She'd need a hat, he decided. Probably used to spending all day indoors, out of the sun, and had no idea how bad it could get come midday. When they stopped, he'd rig something, but the first town they hit, she needed a decent hat.

Studying her now, he looked past the strong bones and smooth skin that had first drawn his attention, trying to see what about the girl was worth so much to the devil. Her gaze was on the road, but he got the feeling from the tension in her jaw that she wasn't seeing it. Girl was terrified and trying hard not to let it show.

Good. Being scared right then meant she was smart. Being scared could keep her alive until she learned better. And not showing fear would keep her alive after.

And him ignoring the fact that she was terrified right then was all the comfort he could give her.

Marie stood in the middle of the room, her arms wrapped around her as though she were cold, her ears straining for sound of hoofbeats moving away. The signet ring on her thumb had rarely felt so heavy, not since she first slid it on. "Winds go with you, Isobel," she said, "and bring you back home again."

There was a crash from the kitchen and the sound of someone's door opening overhead, soft voices beginning to float down the hall-way, and she exhaled finally, a long, shuddering breath. The day had begun. What was done was done and out of her hands. She turned and picked up the tray she had placed there before Isobel came down, lifting it with both hands and carrying it to the narrow door behind the bar. The stoneware of the cups rattled slightly, but the carafe, ten-drils of steam still rising from it, did not spill.

She paused outside the closed door behind the bar. "Boss?"

"Here." She knew he was there, but it was manners to ask first. His office was open to the staff, and anyone with a need could enter, but this room was his own space. Private.

The walls here were light brown wood paneling, not textured the way the walls in his public office were but smooth-hewn and polished by time and use. There were no windows, no desk, and one wall entire was covered by a map, careful black lines and lettering on a fine-grain calfskin larger than any calf ever grew.

The boss stood in front of the map, barely a handspan away, intent on something. His jacket lay across the back of the chair, his shirtsleeves rolled to the elbows, hands resting on his hips. She could not see his face, but she knew that pose.

"Figured you might want some coffee." Marie placed the tray down on the narrow sideboard opposite the map. "With a dash or two of Iktan's finest." She poured the coffee into the cup and handed it to him, then fixed one for herself, sipping gratefully. Only then did she turn and study the map, looking at it from a safe distance.

The lines moved as she watched. Small shifts, quivers, trembles. Changes. A patch of red shaded to pink; a shadow of blue melted to yellow. She did not understand the map, did not understand how things shifted and shoved each other, but she imagined it was similar to managing the house, one personality driving the next, storms blowing themselves out or building to something larger.

They called it the Devil's West, but they didn't know the truth of it.

"They're gone," she said.

"I know." There was a note of rebuke in his voice: why was she wasting his time telling him the obvious?

She took her coffee and left him there watching the Territory shift and turn.

PART TWO
THE ROAD

THEY TOOK THE WESTERN ROAD out of town, away from the river and the half-circle of farms. Izzy, focused on learning the mare's movements, adjusting to the unfamiliar saddle, was achingly aware that every pace the horses took led away from everything she knew, every step that was familiar.

She would come back. Marie had said so. But when?

The thought made her heart stutter, her chest contracting in fear. She turned in the saddle, looking back the way they'd come, as though to assure herself the familiar buildings still stood, would be standing when she returned.

"Best if you don't look back," Gabriel said. "If anything's riding to catch you, you'll hear it soon enough."

She took him at his word—he was her mentor, his responsibility to teach her, so it would be foolish not to listen—and looked down the road in front of them instead. Not that the road was much to see, she thought, half disappointed. It was the same firm brown dirt that ran through town, wide enough for two wagons to pass without one of them going in the ditch, pocked with hoofmarks and wheel ruts.

There wasn't anyone else about, just a long ribbon unrolling in front of them, occasionally disappearing up over and down a hillock as they rode. The land around Flood was flat, rolling away from the river-banks; the soil there was good for farming, soft and rich, but past that, it was grassland. Sere and low in the winter, dull enough to drive you to tears if you looked at it too long, but now with spring well along, the grassheads were speckled with tiny bursts of color where flowers reached toward the sun, yellow and blue against the endless shades of green. Not all pretty, she reminded herself; some of those grasses were sharp enough to pierce your skin if you weren't careful. But the road was cleared—the marshals made sure of that each spring, clearing brush and filling the worst of the ruts in. So long as they stayed on the road, they would be fine.

Her mentor did not speak, and she could not think of a way to break his silence. After the constant hum and mumble of the saloon, the quiet was like a weight, pressing her down into the saddle. Accustomed to keeping busy, her hands were restless on the reins, her thinking jumbled until she finally lost herself, the steady, even plod of the mare's walk, the quiet snuffles of the mule behind her, even the swish of tails and occasional rattle of leather and metal, rubbing away the unease and uncertainty.

But as the morning passed and they didn't pause, she'd been on horseback longer than she'd ever ridden before, and even the mare's steady pace made her ache. Izzy pressed her heels down into the stir-rups, lifting her backside up slightly, trying to stretch her legs without jostling the reins or unsettling the horse beneath her.

"Coming up on a crossroads." Gabriel's voice floated back to her, and she straightened in the saddle, rolling her neck to loosen her spine the way the dealers did at the end of a long night, and tried to seem more alert than she felt. She must have passed through a crossroads at least once, when she was a baby, before she came to Flood, but she'd no memory of it. Gabriel had slowed his horse enough that the mare caught up, coming alongside the gelding. "Tell me about them," he said.

The sudden conversation threw her as much as the question. "What?"

He spoke louder, as though she hadn't heard him. "Tell me about crossroads."

"Oh." Every child learned that. "A crossroads is where two roads pass over each other, a straight line meeting a straight line. The more traveled the road, the more powerful the crossing." She didn't know why, only that it was so.

"And?"

"And . . . crossroads are dangerous," she continued. "You wish in one, and it might come true, but more'n likely it will get turned around and come back on you all wrong. And magicians . . ." Her voice trailed off. They'd all been told about magicians, warned about them, but not more than that. *"If you ever see a magician, run. Do not pause, do not speak, by all that you value, do not catch their attention, just run."*

"Magicians use crossroads for their rituals. They pull all the power out and into themselves. A crossroads that's been used up is twice as dangerous as one that's been left alone, because it will try to refill itself." She bit her lip, thinking that again she knew what but not the why. Had never thought of it, any more than she'd wondered the why of the sun rising or the rain falling.

"And how do you know if a crossroads' been drained?"

This she knew—and she knew *why.* "A coin. A silver coin tossed ahead. If it tarnishes, the crossroads isn't safe to pass through unprotected." Silver for cleansing. Silver for protection.

"Good. And do you have a silver coin?"

Izzy was embarrassed that in all the supplies she'd handled the night before, picking over each piece before placing it into her pack, she had never thought to gather the few spare coins in her dish. "No."

"Fortunately, I do."

He fell quiet again, but her numbness had been broken, her body aching and her thoughts disordered. She wished for something to fold, even something to darn, but her hands were occupied by leather that needed to be held quiet and low, and whatever testing her mentor had seen fit to do, he was clearly done, now.

And then, after another turn cutting through the tall grass, there was the crossroads visible in front of them: an unmarked intersection in the middle of the plain. It looked peaceful, still, and Izzy had a difficult time seeing it as dangerous. And yet, anything could lurk within, unseen until it was too late.

"Watch what I do," Gabriel said then, and kneed his horse into a gentle trot, leaving her behind. She kneed her own mare into a faster walk, careful to stay well behind him, the mule still bringing up the rear, more cautious than its cousins or their riders.

Just outside the crossroads itself, he halted and looked up to check the position of the sun, not quite yet overhead, then reached into his waistcoat pocket and pulled out something pressed between his fingers. It glittered, catching the sunlight, before he flicked it into the spot where the two roads crossed. It landed in the dust, the silver still shining.

They waited a hundred breaths, the horses shifting and snorting at each other, uneasy but trusting.

"Clear," Gabriel said finally, and swung down from the saddle to reclaim his coin. Izzy held her breath, helpless to prevent herself, until he'd picked up the coin and slipped it into his pocket, then walked back out again unharmed.

"Needn't be a coin, although they're best, but you should always have a bit of silver," he said to her as he reached up to reclaim his gelding's reins.

"Oh. I do!" she said, holding up her hand, the ring visible on her little finger, feeling foolish for not having remembered it before.

He glanced at it, then nodded, swinging back into the saddle. "Good. Not perfect, but at least you can find it easily. And make sure you always, always keep it polished. Tarnished silver does nobody any good."

‡ ‡ ‡

The crossroads safely behind them, the sun passing overhead and down into the sky ahead of them, Izzy decided that her earlier aches had been nothing. Now she *hurt*. Her face felt too tight, her neck and shoulders ached, her feet were oddly swollen inside her boots, and her hips and legs didn't bear thinking of, the shift of the mare and the creak of the saddle chafing and stretching her muscles in ways that she blushed to think about.

"You all right?" Gabriel's gaze when he turned to look at her was sharp, his eyes bright under the brim of his hat, and Izzy was sure she'd flushed.

"Yes. I'm fine." It might be foolish pride, but she couldn't admit to even the slightest discomfort, not on their first day. She took a small sip of water from the canteen hanging at her knee, letting the liquid sit in her mouth the way Iktan said was smart when he'd told them stories of riding the dust roads. She'd never understood before, but now, with her entire body begging for moisture, the way the water filled her entire mouth instead of simply sliding down her throat, she couldn't argue. Even warm and stale, the water was the most glorious thing she'd ever tasted.

Gabriel sighed, reining his horse in until they were walking side by side, the mule holding a few paces behind. Uvnee's head turned slightly to look at the bay, then swung back to watch the road in front of them. Izzy did the same, stealing a sideways glance at Gabriel before looking away. He looked as comfortable on Steady's back as he had sitting at the card table back in the saloon, his body alert but relaxed at the same time, like he was part of the saddle, part of the horse.

"Don't," he said. "You push yourself too hard, tomorrow will be worse. The road cuts by a creek in a bit; we'll stop there, stretch our legs. We're not rushing anywhere; there's no need for you to damage yourself from sheer muleheadedness. We already have one of those on this trip."

She wanted to deny that she was being stubborn, but bit the retort back. She might sass the man in the saloon, but not her mentor. Not until she'd earned that right, anyway, the way she'd earned the right to sass back to the boss. And he wasn't wrong: a chance to stretch her legs would be welcome.

Gabriel had spent much of the morning cursing himself for having offered to mentor in the first place, for putting himself in a position to be manipulated, used. And for not having the courage to tell the devil where he could put his offer.

The devil ran a fair game: if he'd said no, there would have been no repercussions. But the devil also knew what bargains to offer; that was why he was so dangerous, that even sober, sane men lost their wits around him.

And Gabriel had offered before he knew what he was stepping into. More fool him.

He had never ridden with a woman before, not a new rider, anyway. The female riders he'd met were older, harder. Trained. They knew their limits, knew better than to let pride get in the way of survival. He needed to temper what he knew, what he'd planned. Miss Isobel might have come out of the devil's own lair, but she was in some ways as innocent, as helpless as an Eastern lamb.

He grinned, imagining her reaction to that. She'd be in a prickle, her fine eyes alight with indignation, her hands fisted on her hips in a way that on a larger woman might be fearsome. She might be young, but he'd no doubt she was fierce. Still, he'd need to teach her how to throw a punch before they started tangling with others; a little thing like that needed to be able to protect herself with more than the side of her tongue. Although he'd noted a blade strapped to her saddle; he wondered if she knew how to use it.

He should have asked before. He'd assumed the devil would not send her out unprepared, but that was not an assumption he should have made.

"Is that the creek?" she asked, and he lifted his head to see the road drop slightly, disappearing out of sight before picking up again in the distance.

"Good eye," he said; the slight hollow of the creek wasn't obvious from here. "We'll stop on this side; it should be dryer."

"Dryer" was a relative term: the creek was high with early spring runoff, and even the wider bank on this side was slick and slippery, with a few scrub willows stretching branches and roots toward the water. He turned Steady off the path before the slope and slid out of the saddle.

He turned to see Isobel attempt to echo his movement, but her body was stiff from so many hours in the saddle, and the moment her feet touched the ground her entire body buckled, only the mare's solid presence keeping her from going to her knees in agony.

"Here now, let go." Gabriel was at her side in an instant, his hands steadying her until she was able to stand again. "You should have said something if you were that sore." He tried to keep his tone even, but he was annoyed: at her, at himself, at the devil and all his machinations that put them here.

"I'm all right," she said, wobbling at the knees, but upright.

"Of course you are." He led her away from the mare, watching how she moved, noting how her body shook under the stress. "Don't sit down, not just yet. You need to stretch. Walk if you can, but don't sit down."

The horses had lowered their heads and were already nibbling at the grass. The mare might be new, but she was settling in well, and he trusted her to stick with Steady even if something were to spook them. The mule, faithful as ever, wouldn't spook if someone blew the Gjallahorn in one floppy ear. All three of them scented the air, nostrils blowing, but none seemed inclined to test the slippery bank to find the water themselves.

"Yeah, all right," he said to them. "You'll get yours; just wait a moment."

"Tell me it gets easier?" Isobel had taken a few more steps, wobbly but determined, and then stopped, grimacing as she pressed her hands into the small of her back.

"It does. But getting back on, that's going to hurt like blazes for a bit. Walk some more; it'll help." He took his hat off and ran fingers through his hair, scratching where the sweat left his scalp itchy, and watched her move. Her shoulders slowly straightened, and she shook out hands that were clearly cramped from holding the reins too tightly.

"Where are we?"

"Still inside your boss's hand," he said, turning away to give her some privacy for any stretching she might need to do, bending to adjust Steady's belly strap. "Another few hours' ride, we'll be in Patch Junction. We'll stop there for the night."

"I know Patch," she said, sounding surprised. "Know of it, anyways. One of our girls, she went to live there."

"You want to stop in and say hello?"

She seemed to be considering that. "No. I . . . It's been a while. I wouldn't know what to say to her."

"You might find different, seeing her again."

"Maybe. I—"

The sound of hoofbeats made them both stop and look up. His hand reached for the knife in his boot, letting three fingers rest on the leather sheath without unsnapping it. Isobel merely stood there, waiting. She made no move to reach for a weapon of any sort, and he sighed. He knew Flood was safe a place as existed, but did they teach their girls nothing?

There was splashing from the creek, and the sound of voices. Four horses, he determined, going at a trot but not in any great hurry. And he could hear the moment they noticed the horses, when they slowed, coming up out of the water.

"Isobel. Behind the horses." She didn't hesitate, didn't question, but ducked down, using the mule's packs to hide behind. He could hear her breathing, heard her trying to calm it.

And then the riders were in sight, and he stood, turning so as to draw the riders' attention. Four of them—too many for a knife alone to handle. He placed a hand on Steady's flank, then slid it forward to where the flintlock, a short-muzzled carbine, was strapped to his saddle, sliding it free and loading it with a practiced hand. He missed his longrifle, but its accuracy was set against the fact that it took twice as long to load, and danger came up fast and close more often than it hung back at a distance.

A single shot wouldn't do much against four, either way, but it might make them hesitate if they meant mischief. And he could take one of them out before they came any closer, leaving only three to deal with.

"Gentlemen," he said in greeting as they drew to a halt. Good horseflesh, deep-chested but not flashy, their riders a somber bunch likewise, dusters and battered gear, and not a star or sigil among them. That could be good or ill.

"Two horses and a mule, but only one rider," the lead man said, easing in his saddle. "Armed, yet. You afeared of us?"

"Cautious of strangers," he said, keeping the musket's barrel tilted toward the ground for now.

"Well I'm Jed, that's Dickon, Jared, and Rainy." Each of the men nodded as they were introduced, the last one clearly native, although he was dressed in the same canvas and cloth as the others, his hair cut short like theirs. "And now we're not strangers, are we?"

He didn't like the situation, but they weren't being hostile. He needed to keep it that way. And it was clear they knew there was a second rider. "I'm Gabe. Iz, c'mon out."

He watched as their attention shifted to the girl. There was interest there but no aggression, no lust obvious on their faces. Gabriel kept the carbine in clear sight just in case. "This is Isobel. She's green on the road."

An innocent. Under his protection. The warning was clear, as was his steady hand on his weapon.

"Ma'am," Jed said, tipping his hat. "Welcome to the road."

"Thank you." She was using her saloon voice again, softer and wispier. He'd have to break her of that; this was no place or time to be soft.

"Don't suppose y'all have seen anything on the road as shouldn't have been there?" Jed was asking him now, looking away from Isobel. His message was clear: they were on business and had no interest in the girl. Or they were trying to lull him.

"Can't say as we have, no. What's gone missing?" Four men chasing down something, and not a sigil-badge among them, so they weren't marshals. Could be a posse, although they were supposed to identify themselves too. But they had a look in their eye he knew too well: trouble.

"Someone rousted a fetch a few nights ago. Got a bit ugly."

"A fetch?" Isobel sounded far too excited, considering where she'd lived. Although he supposed a fetch wouldn't go anywhere near Flood, not unless it wanted to be knocked all the way back to its body.

"Nasty thing," Dickon, Gabriel thought, said, a clear Eastern clip to his voice. Not born here, then, and come late in life. Rare, that— and odds were he'd left trouble behind him, too. "But nothing you should fuss your pretty eyes about."

"My eyes, pretty as they may be, have seen worse things without a fuss," Isobel said, and the sudden cool in her voice could've put ice on the brook. Maybe he wouldn't have to teach her so much after all, Gabriel thought, although he could have wished she'd found a different time to become fierce.

The boys were eyeing her with a little too much interest now, so he shifted ostentatiously, pulling their attention back to him the way he would if trying to redirect a jury. "Anything specific we should be looking for?" Fetches—the incorporeal form of a living body—could be a significant problem or just be a general nuisance, but he liked to know which was what. Mostly, though, he just wanted these men gone and on their way, elsewhere.

"Nah, this one's a mischief-maker, most likely, but we want to find it before it decides to grow a purpose. And so we can pick up the bounty, of course." Jed's smile was a death's head rictus, drawn too far back over his jaw, and his gaze flicked over to Isobel, quickly enough that a soul not watching for it might have missed it. Posse, then, but not a sworn-in one, he'd venture. Not bound by Law.

"Of course," Gabriel said. Bounty on a fetch wouldn't be much unless they had cause to worry about it. More than likely they enjoyed the chase, the excuse to cause trouble and not catch trouble in return. "Good hunting to you. We'd like to avoid even mischief, this trip," he went on. "Road ahead's clear?"

"Clear as the noon sky. Just stick to the road and you should be fine. You heading over to Whiskey Springs?"

"Yes, we are."

"Then we'll likely see you there when this is done." Jed tipped his hat to Isobel, with another quick flicker of his eyes, and chivied his men on their way.

Gabriel waited until they picked up a trot again before he exhaled, then set his attention to unloading the flintlock—a tricky task but better than discharging the shot and risking more attention. He was sweating, he realized, far more than the day's warmth would excuse.

"We're not going to Whiskey Springs," Isobel said, frowning.

"I didn't say we were going there; I said we were heading there. We are. Mostly." Finished with the weapon, he secured it again, then turned to her and knelt on the ground, picking up a stick and laying it on the grass. "This is the road. We're here"—he placed his left-hand thumb on one side. "Patch Junction is here"—his hand spanned over the stick, stretching out to mark a spot at the other end. "Whiskey Springs is here"—his right hand reached over and tapped a spot just a little off from the first town's marker, southwest as the map was laid out. "Same direction."

The girl studied the makeshift map, her face still scrunched in a frown that made her seem even younger. "They were a posse?"

Why didn't you trust them? she was really asking, clear as day.

"No sigils to say they were sworn in proper, so they might've been a bounty mob. But the only difference between the two is how official they are. The sort of men sign on for that, they're not the sort you want to travel with."

She considered that, and nodded. "But you didn't want to lie to them. Not outright."

"If you can avoid lying, you should," Gabriel said. "That's the third rule."

"What are the first two rules?" she asked, reasonably enough.

"Things to be learned later. Now collect the horses; sore or not, I don't want to linger, in case those four decide to circle back."

Her body still ached, but Izzy pulled herself into the saddle and followed Gabriel back onto the trail and down to the water. Although the creek wasn't overly deep, the current was swift and the water chilled enough that the scattered drops that landed on her skin made her shiver. She couldn't imagine how the mare felt, slogging through water halfway up her legs. But Uvnee followed right after Steady, her nose practically in his tail, while the mule was already on the other side and waiting, like a patient dog.

She wasn't a child; she knew what Gabriel had been worrying at. The way that man had looked at her wasn't anything new: men looked, even when they weren't supposed to. But this had been the first time it'd happened where the boss wasn't, and she knew—and Gabriel knew—that one against four wasn't enough to stop 'em if they'd a mind for violence.

Knowing that the world outside was dangerous and having it shoved up in your face were different things entire. Izzy was almost glad for the soreness in her body and the wet stink of horseflesh and leather, giving her something to think about other than might-haves and what-ifs.

Halfway across the creek, something twitched inside her, not a pain so much as a gentle twist against her ribs. Izzy dropped the reins and pressed the palm of her left hand flat against her stomach, like she'd felt it gurgle from hunger, even though it hadn't felt like that at all. And then it was gone, and Uvnee was slogging up the other bank as though nothing had happened, Izzy leaning forward like she'd been taught, pressing her legs into the mare's side in encouragement.

The road picked up again on the other side, but half as wide as it had been, the dirt far more rutted and pitted with wear. She twisted in her saddle, feeling muscles protest again, and looked back at the other side.

"Something changed." She knew that, but she didn't know what, or why, or how she could tell.

"Been a while since you crossed running water," Gabriel said, and it was like he was laughing at her, but polite-like so she couldn't take offense. He was her mentor: she wasn't allowed to take offense, anyways.

She shook her head in agreement. Folks in Flood stayed on their side of the water, mostly, unless they had cause to do otherwise. "What?"

"Running water's like the opposite of a crossroads," he said. "If it's deep and fast enough, anyway. Not much magic can pass over, not without being watered down itself. You remember that, if anything's ever chasing you." He sighed. "They didn't tell you much of anything, did they?"

Izzy felt the insult sharply. "I know how to tell if someone's cutting their cards or watering a drink," she said. "I can tell you if someone's flush, or if they're going to run a tab they can't pay. I can tell you what pain a body's suffering inside. And I know when someone's lying to me."

"Do you, now?" He didn't sound impressed at all.

"Yes. But that won't be much use here, will it? If nobody lies on the road."

The sass came unbidden and she drew a sharp breath, but it made him laugh that warm, not-really-amused laugh she'd heard from him before, not angry. "Never said nobody lies, Isobel. I said if you can avoid lying, you should. You ken the difference?"

Yes, she started to say, exasperated, but the word caught at her teeth. That was like one of the boss's tests, his question. Wasn't about answering but thinking on.

He didn't seem to expect her to answer, only turned his horse to face the road and set off again, that same slow and even walk. They rode on while the sun shifted into afternoon, and if he hummed a bit under his breath and looked sideways at her a time or three, he left her and her thoughts be.

Eventually, though, she let both the question and the worry fade, sinking back into the sensations surrounding her: the creak of leather and the roll of the mare's body beneath her, the smell of sun-warmed flesh and dry dust, fresh green and the hint of something spicy and not unpleasant in the breeze, letting go of everything but the moment. Even the soreness in her body seemed a thing distant from her, until the sun began to set, the air cooled, and the outline of Patch Junction appeared in front of them.

They entered Patch Junction proper as the last sunlight was streaking the clouds overhead with pale orange light. Izzy tried not to feel intimidated as they rode down past storefronts that rose two stories high, brightly whitewashed, with painted shutters and flowers set in window boxes, tidy enough to say that folk with some wealth lived here. She'd known Flood was plain, but she'd never thought it dowdy before.

She firmed her chin and pulled her shoulders back, as though daring anyone to point at her as a poor relation. Flood was the boss's town; it didn't need to prettify for strangers.

The town was half again the size of Flood and three times as crowded, from what she could see, the main street angling off the road away into the plain, two smaller streets crooked off of that, like a preacher cactus. She caught a glimpse of single-story buildings and garden plots down those streets before they rode on, past the saloon where Izzy had thought they'd stop, and the mercantile to their left.

The saloon had a handful of men lingering outside the door, while there was a wagon being loaded in front of the mercantile, two men working while a third talked to the shopkeeper in his apron, both intent on their discussion. An old man in a dark suit leaned against the front of the barber's, while two women walked along the raised sidewalk across the street, heads bent together in gossip, and a gang of small children played in one of the side streets, tagging each other and whooping as they ran. Gabriel kept riding and Izzy followed, all the way down to the far end, to where a small one-story clapboard building was set noticeably apart. Nobody looked twice when they swung down out of the saddle and hitched reins to the post out front.

Gabriel tilted his head back and studied the small building, his eyes squinting under the brim of his hat, looking up at the tree-and-world sigil carved and painted dark red on the door.

"You check in every badgehouse you come to?" she asked, more tartly than she'd intended, wishing that her thighs would stop shaking so badly.

"No," he said. "But you will."

Izzy pressed her hands against her skirt, the back of it buttoned up again, and paused just before the half-open door. The sigil seemed to taunt her, asking her what she was hesitant about, what made her heart stutter. It wasn't fear; there was nothing to be afraid of here. She was the Devil's Left Hand, duly contracted and sworn, and the marshal stationed inside should answer to her, not the other way around.

Except she knew better. The marshals answered to Territory law, not the boss, for all that they gave him due respect. And she might be his Left Hand by contract and Bargain, but she hadn't proven herself, hadn't done anything except ride a day's length from her home, under someone else's protection.

Izzy felt the childish urge to stomp her feet against the doorstep. She didn't even know what she was *supposed* to do, since the boss hadn't seen fit to tell her anything except she had to leave. She didn't want to go in there and deal with a stranger. She was tired and sore; she wanted a bath and a hot meal and a full night in a warm bed, and something familiar to cling to, an unbroken routine. . . .

Izzy flushed with shame, aware that she was behaving like a baby. She had asked for this. She had *demanded* it. That thought alone forced her feet to move, carrying her over the doorstep and into the marshal's domain.

The inside of the badgehouse matched the outside: plain walls and bare wooden floor, handbills and notices tacked to a board behind the long desk. She noted the iron bars of a cell toward the back, the cot inside currently empty.

"Ma'am." The marshal behind the desk was old, not ancient but too creaky and worn to ride the roads any longer. What was left of his hair was white, and his hands were withered and sun-darkened, but the eyes that lifted to hers were a clear, bright hazel, and his teeth were surprisingly white and strong. "How can I help you?"

Izzy took a deep breath, brushing her fingers against her side more gently this time, trying to calm her heart. "Just checking in," she said, aiming for casual and missing it by a mile. "Isobel née Lacoyo Távora of Flood. The Devil's Hand."

It was the first time she had said it out loud, and the words felt awkward on her tongue and lips; she was too aware of the effort it took to shape them. *Silent, unseen,* she heard the boss say. But Gabriel said the marshals were to be told.

She had hoped that those words would be enough, that the marshal would know who she was, what she was supposed to be doing. Instead, he merely pushed back in his chair and looked her up and down once. Judging, but not offensive; more like how Marie looked at someone who swore their silver was good, no need to test it, like you might be telling the truth but shouldn't take her for such a fool to assume it. "Are you, now. And I'm presuming you have the papers to prove it?"

She bit the inside of her mouth and handed him the oilskin packet she had taken from her saddlebag. "I do." What had she thought, that she would walk in and they would somehow know, would see it in her? She wasn't the boss, so full of his own power, it spilled from him. She wasn't even Marie, who'd soaked up enough of his easy ways that she could reflect it right back at you until you couldn't imagine questioning her. She was . . . green to the road, Gabriel had said. Unproven. If this man had taken her at her word, he'd be a fool and unfit to carry the marshal's badge and sigil.

He looked over the papers, careful, not just skimming the ink, then finally, after what seemed forever, held one up to the lamp to check the watermark. "New to the road, are you, then?"

"New to the road, but not the Territory," she said, trying to pitch her voice like Marie's, just sharp enough to deflect the teasing but not sound as though she were taking offense. He shuffled the papers back into the packet and stood. He was taller than she, and while his plain brown tab-collar shirt bore no insignia, she thought she would have known him for a marshal nonetheless.

"Welcome to the Junction, ma'am," he said, handing her back the packet. "Any aid we can offer, please don't you hesitate to request."

He waited, and she nodded once, holding the packet under her arm, and turned and left the office.

The light had changed while she was inside, shifting from afternoon to dusk. Gabriel was nowhere to be seen, but the gelding's sideways sidle, as though he were moving away from something, led her around to find her mentor cleaning the gelding's back hoof with a pick. Gabriel finished, letting the leg down gently and patting the horse's side as though to say it was done for now.

She expected him to say something, ask for a report, but he merely glanced at her, then looked up at the sky and shook his head. "Took longer than I thought to get here. We'll restock tomorrow. Come on."

Their next stop was a stable, where Gabriel handed over the reins and the mule's lead line to a man who grunted instead of speaking, then he led her down one of the branch streets to where he said they'd be spending the night. It didn't look like much from the front, just a one-story structure wider than it was deep, but it was clean, and the beds were separated by tall wooden screens, giving an illusion of privacy that Izzy hadn't known she would need until she dropped her pack on the cot and realized that she was, effectively, alone. With the Junction being the last civilized stop for most folk heading west, there were two others staying there that night, but she couldn't see or hear anyone moving behind their screens. And Gabriel had taken a space a bit away from hers, near enough at need but not right up close. It was foolish—they'd be sleeping in trail sites much after this, and she knew you stayed close in those circumstances, but this first night . . .

She would not turn down some privacy, and a real bed, and—

"They have a tub out back with a pump," Gabriel said, making her jump. She hadn't realized he'd come around her screen. He'd taken off his hat, holding it in front of him in both hands, and his hair was sweat-soaked underneath, pressed against his forehead. "You could probably use a decent soak, ease out your bones. Although I'd suggest waiting until later." He cast a look down the hall, significantly, and Izzy nodded. So, that was where the others had gone to.

"Dinner first?" she asked, and his eyes crinkled in that way that meant he was smiling, even though he wasn't.

"You're learning the second rule of the road: eat when you can, especially if someone else is cooking."

She availed herself of the basin and jug of water by her bed to freshen up, washing her face and hands in the tepid water, then repinning her braid, and then met Gabriel by the door. He had cleaned his face as well, and changed his shirt, too, leaving Izzy all too aware of the faint smell of sweat and horse that were likely embedded in her skirt, now. But he merely indicated that she should precede him out the door, without comment.

They walked into the saloon, swinging doors separating the dining area from the gambling, drinking, and music on the other side. Despite the flash of longing that shook her from shoulders to soles, Izzy held back the urge to pass through that door, lose herself in the familiar chatter, instead following Gabriel to an empty table. It wouldn't *be* familiar on the other side of those doors. It wasn't home.

A serving girl came over quickly, but despite their pleasing smell, the first taste of buttermilk chicken and biscuits turned to dust in her mouth. Izzy took a sip of tea to wash it all down and ease the sudden lump in her throat. Distraction. She needed a distraction. Her gaze flicked to Gabriel seated across the table, tucking into his meal like he hadn't eaten in days.

She didn't want to speak of the men they'd met in the road, not sure if such a thing was considered polite table conversation, but she didn't want to talk about home either, not with the push of regret and fear still in her throat. And she had no stories to tell, nor any idea what stories to ask him for. . . .

"You done this often? Mentored, I mean." She'd wondered but been afraid that might be prying. Now the words fell out of her mouth without preparation, and she wished, after the fact, she could take 'em back. Like a devil's Bargain, you never asked another man what he'd done unless he offered first. Not even your mentor. Wasn't polite, and it wasn't safe.

Although she didn't think he'd hurt her for asking. Not the once, anyhow.

He was still busy tucking into his own plate, and she thought at first he wasn't going to answer. Then he pushed back a little, wiped his hands on his napkin, and pursed his lips. His hair had dried sticking up in places, his face rough with stubble, making him look like a man she wouldn't want to cross, but his eyes were soft and thoughtful, and he didn't seem to have taken offense.

"A time or three," he said. "Depends on how you're counting."

She frowned at him. Surely he knew how many times he'd done a thing. Was he teasing? No, she thought maybe he was testing her. Not the way he did on the road but the way the boss did, checking to see if she'd thought something through, looked at all the angles.

"Counting by times . . . or people? You mentored two at the same time." It wasn't a question; she was certain she had the answer right.

"Near enough. Chimera."

Izzy did not choke on her tea. It took some doing, though, and she could feel the near miss of heat floating too near her lungs. "You mentored a chimera?"

"Not intentionally, I assure you." His faint, mocking drawl was back, and she'd swear he was pulling her leg, except that wasn't the sort of thing one joked about. Chimera were *dangerous*. Not so much as demon but harder to find, at least until they revealed themselves. Ghost-ridden, some folk called 'em. But the boss said they weren't so much ridden as dancing, twining themselves around, half living and half dead, until you couldn't much tell the difference between.

The problem was, sometimes the half-dead part wasn't all there anymore and pretty much always drove the half-living part crazy, too.

She tried to think of something to say. "I guess I seemed like a lot less trouble after that."

Gabriel gave her a look, one she couldn't quite read. "Not sure I'd say that."

She felt her forehead scrunch in confusion. "You thought I'd be trouble? Then why offer?"

He shook his head, laughing a little, although she didn't know what she'd said that was so amusing. "You don't offer to mentor someone because it'll be easy, Isobel."

"Then why did you?" Whatever agreement he'd made with the boss—and he had made an agreement, she knew it: a low thrumming in her veins when she thought about it, the knowledge where once she wondered—it had come after he'd made his offer to her. She'd been no one to him then, just a girl taking away his drink, a saloon girl he didn't even think was pretty.

"I was born here," he said. Izzy had no idea what that had to do with anything, but she'd learned to listen in the saloon and not interrupt, to let people get to their point in their own time. "Grew up in a little town just south of Fort Victoria."

Fort Victoria was outside the Territory, only just, where the local tribe allied with the French and skirmished against the British and Americans alike. She tried to remember the last time the fighting had crossed over into the Territory: four years, maybe closer to five. There had been riders coming into Flood on a regular basis with reports, and finally the boss had saddled up and ridden out, then come home weeks later, tired and mean, but the trouble stopped.

She hadn't paid much attention at the time, finishing up her schooling and more interested in the looks she was getting from the oldest Turville boy. Now she wondered what had happened, what she might have learned if she'd been paying attention.

"And you took to the road when you were old enough?" Some folk stayed where they were put until it was time for them to be planted six feet down. Some didn't. Obviously, he hadn't.

"Not right away. My ma sent me off to school." He paused, then went on. "Back East, down in Virginia, then Philadelphia. And before you ask, it's just . . . It's a place. Noisy and crowded and strange, but no stranger than anywhere else. I spent two years there, studied at the bar, and then came home." His tone said that was all he was going to say on the topic and she'd best respect that if she had sense. "I suppose I could have used what I learned there, but setting out my shingle didn't call me. And I'm not cut out to be a judge nor a marshal; too many rules." There was a dark glimmer in his eyes, like he'd said something that wasn't quite funny. "So, I took to the road on my own. Been on it ever since."

Despite the warning tone, Izzy had to ask. "Ever think about going back there? East, I mean." She thought about what Ree had said, how many people were out there, and still couldn't imagine it.

"No. I belong here." He flicked his gaze up over her. "You do, too. And that's why I offered. Because . . . I could see the Road in you."

Izzy had no idea what he meant, but it warmed her nonetheless, in a way she hadn't felt since the boss told her she'd have to leave.

Gabriel lay on the too-flat mattress, the thin, stiff blanket pulled up to his chest, and stared at the ceiling, although it was too dark in the bunkhouse to actually see it. The only noise came from one of the other boarders snoring, a heavy, wet noise occasionally broken by a cough or grumble as the man turned in his sleep. No matter that he'd spent most of his life inside walls and under roofs, it still made him uneasy to be cut off from the sounds of the night. He ached to be outside, under the stars, where he could breathe.

There was no sound from where Isobel slept. She had come back from the baths looking slight and vaguely bedraggled, her long hair damp around her shoulders, despite a thorough toweling. No matter how much time she'd spent in the hot water, she'd be more sore than she could imagine in the morning. But there was no point in coddling her. There was a pressure in him to get her back out on the road. All her fierceness, the bone-deep strength he saw in her, wasn't enough to toughen her for what was to come. She couldn't hesitate, couldn't doubt. All pretense to civility and law went by the wayside the moment she chose her way, even if she didn't know it yet.

I would be in your debt if you did this, the devil had said.

Debt was a two-edged blade. Gabriel wanted no debt-owed from the devil, only payment. And only if he succeeded. Only if he turned this girl-child into a rider. If he taught her to harden against the dust and sun, the bad food and hard beds, to be harder than the folk she'd find. If he showed her how to become whatever it was the devil intended her to be.

Gabriel'd seen potential in her, certain. Had seen the promise, the wildness of the Road, clear in her face. But this . . . This was too much to ask. This was far too much to demand of a child, even if Isobel thought it was what she wanted. But he'd agreed, had of free will taken what was offered, had been caught by the thing he'd determined not to ask for only to have it offered, for the cost of a thing he'd have done for free.

He should have known a devil's Bargain would be a damned uncomfortable thing.

There were no windows where they'd slept, and Izzy opened her eyes to pitch dark, unable to remember at first where she was or how she'd ended there. Slowly, the dark was lightened by the soft glow of lamps set in niches along the walls, mimicking the rising of the sun, and she remembered it all: making her Bargain, leaving Flood, coming to Junction with Gabriel. . . .

She lay in her narrow, unfamiliar bed, listening to the sounds of the others getting up and moving around, so different from the morning sounds she was accustomed to, the cluck of chickens and the subtle sounds of bodies moving belowstairs. These voices were deeper, masculine, boots hard on the floor next to her, laughter boisterous, not hushed. The air brought not the tang of hot metal and baking bread but gingery hair tonics and Castile soap.

She knew that she should get up as well, wash her face and brush her hair, dress for the day. Her body had other ideas.

"Isobel?" Gabriel's voice, just beyond the screen.

"I'm awake." She tried to shift her body again and couldn't hold back a groan this time. Even her skin hurt, all the way down to the bone.

"I've brought some willow bark tea. It'll help with the aches." There was a pause. "Isobel?"

"Please," she said, and he came around the screen even as she was sitting upright, pulling at the collar of her night rail where it had shifted while she slept. He averted his eyes, trying not to look at her, and she laughed. "I hadn't thought you for the delicate type."

It seemed as though her laughter reassured him, his shoulders relaxing even as he handed her the cup. The heavy stoneware was warm, and she cupped both hands around it for a moment, as though the hot water alone was enough to ease her body.

"I suppose I revert back to my upbringing when in civilized surroundings," he said, and this time he met her gaze briefly, the edges of his eyes pulled into his smile.

The deep red tea was bitter, but the warmth felt even better in her throat than it had in her hands, and if she was drinking, she didn't have to think about how uncivilized she must seem. She'd been raised in a saloon; she'd seen drunk, half-naked men reeling through the halls before one of the girls could corral them or Iktan toss them out on their ear; she'd been raised among women who were as comfortable in their skins as a bird was in its feathers. If he thought she needed to be treated like a delicate town flower . . .

She scowled down into the tea. If he thought that was what she was, he was gravely mistaken.

"That should help," Gabriel said, and she startled, then realized he was talking about the tea. She'd finished it, even the bitter dregs, without noticing. He took the mug from her, stepping back a bit. But was looking directly at her now, which was a relief. "Wash up and get dressed. I'll settle the bill and meet you outside for breakfast."

It might have been the tea, or simply that she was more awake now, but getting out of the bed was easier, although she was still stiff and sore, particularly in her shoulders and hips.

It made her slightly dizzy to realize, as she fastened ties and laced her boots, that only a day had passed since they left Flood. That two days before, she had been serving drinks and folding linens, worrying over what her future would bring, impossibly confident that once she turned sixteen, everything would be easier.

Izzy sat down on the edge of the cot to braid her hair, fingers moving in familiar patterns, the motion soothing her thoughts, until the braid was tied off with a leather thong. She started to pin it up, the way a grown woman should, then remembered the feel of sweat on her scalp the day before, how heavy her hair had felt, and left it down instead. It felt strange, but when she turned her head and felt the weight of the braid brush against her back, it made her almost smile.

Gabriel met her in the hallway. He was wearing a different shirt this morning, this one brown and open at the neck. The dust had been cleaned off his boots and long coat, but there were still mud splatters on his trousers from where they'd forded the creek. The memory of him as the casual, flirtatious cardsharp was so at odds with the man standing in front of her, that first man might as well not have existed.

Maybe the girl she'd been, Izzy-as-was, didn't exist anymore, either? It would explain the way she felt, confused and hazy.

"Feeling better?"

She nodded, attempting to hide her aches, but must not have been convincing enough.

"Don't worry. Food will help."

Food did help, even though the bread was nowhere as good as Ree's, and the meat too greasy. The coffee was strong enough to singe her tongue, and the familiar note of chicory washed away the grease and the last lingering taste of the willow bark tea. The dining room was far busier than it had been the night before, the long tables seating men filling their stomachs as though they wouldn't see another meal for days, intent on their own thoughts, or reading a broadsheet boasting the latest news. There were two women at another table, apart from the others. They ate more delicately, their heads together, speaking quietly. Izzy watched them, curious. One wore a brown traveling dress, high-necked and demure, with a small leather case on the ground next to her feet. The other woman was older, with silvering hair tucked into a neat coil, but she was wearing trousers and a collared shirt much like Gabriel's, a leather coat folded across the back of the chair next to her. They, and she, were the only females in the room. Izzy wondered if the woman in trousers was local, or also a traveler, and if so, had she stayed at the roadhouse as well? But asking such questions without an introduction would be rude.

"We'll be leaving after breakfast?" she asked Gabriel instead, hoping to get some detail of where they would be heading once they left town. She was like the mule, trotting along in Gabriel's trail. Her entire life, she'd done exactly that, taking orders without hesitation or doubt; it should not itch at her now. And yet it did.

"Soon enough," Gabriel said. He'd been watching the people, too, and she wondered who had caught his attention and why. She didn't know how to ask, though; the easy comfort of the day before was gone, like morning mist once the sun rose. Her stomach felt tight, and she pushed the remains of her meal away, no longer hungry.

Although anything to put off getting into the saddle again seemed a good idea to her, the insides of her thighs and her shoulders still aching, she couldn't imagine why they would delay longer in Patch Junction.

"What are we doing, then?"

Gabriel grinned at her, and the spark of mischief in his eyes both reassured and alarmed her. "Shopping."

The look of relief on Isobel's face when she realized she wouldn't have to saddle up just yet made her look very young, and Gabriel was annoyed at his reaction—he needed to toughen her up, not coddle her. But the faint pink burn on her nose had rebuked him this morning, a reminder that she needed a hat before she spent another day on the road, and there were items he'd need as well, things that the devil's Right Hand, however efficient, hadn't considered.

Fortunately, he'd been given enough coin to deal with that as well.

Gabriel finished his breakfast, tucking payment under the plate before leading Isobel back out on the street. There were more people about by then, the sun full over the horizon, and the bustle was enough to make her flinch slightly. He supposed it was louder than Flood ever was on a normal day, though nowhere near his memories of Williamsburg, much less the city of Philadelphia, with its constant rattle and creak of commerce.

He raised his face to the morning sky and breathed in deep. He might have resented coming home, but he couldn't regret it. Not when the air smelled of milkweed and tall grass and honest earth underfoot, and the sunlight stretched without interruption, turning dark to pale blue, not a cloud in the sky.

He hated the Territory some days, but leaving it had been worse.

"Come on, then," he said, and led her down the main street to the mercantile. No sign announced its purpose, but the single glass window with its display of dry goods around a too-ornate saddle made no mistake of its purpose.

"That's a very large store," Isobel said, her voice faint.

He scanned the building—a single story, but twice the width of any other storefront—and nodded. "Patch Junction earned its name by growing out of an old crossroads," he told her. "Used to be smack on top of it, in fact."

She blinked at him, unsure if he were joking or not.

"That's what they say, anyway." He shrugged. "The second road's long gone now; not sure it was ever more than a track to begin with, but Junction's still where folk come for supplies."

That was why they had a badgehouse here, too. The crossroads itself might be long gone, but marshals were known to be cautious. Where there was power, there was usually trouble, too.

He could almost see her brain taking that fact in, looking around her with different eyes. He wondered what she saw, if there was some trace of Patch Junction's past lingering in the decades of wood and iron built up over it.

If there was, she gave no sign of seeing it, and he felt an odd pang of disappointment. To cover it, he gestured for her to precede him up the stairs and into the store.

The clerk looked up as they entered, the bell over the door jangling sharply, and gave them a professional once-over. "Morning."

"Morning," he said in return, hearing Isobel echo him, and cast an eye over the dry goods displayed up front. He wasn't the sort to need for much, but the money he'd been given weighed heavily in his wallet, the devil's lucre, and he was eager to have it be gone. Isobel needed a trail hat, and he wanted to try another saddle pad for her, and while they were at it, a new coffeepot would not be amiss. The one he'd been using was right-sized for one man, but the way she'd put the brew down this morning told him she was no delicate tea-sipper. Not unless it was medicinal, anyway.

"Iz." He got her attention away from the soaps and lotions, and pointed toward the display of hats. "Nothing frilly," he warned her, and smiled at the face she made, as though offended that he thought she might opt for a cap of lace or something bedecked with feathers. "Practical, to keep the sun off your face and the rain out of your eyes."

She nodded and moved over to the display, reaching for a severe-looking black gambler that he could tell would be too large for her. But a hat was a personal choice; he wouldn't interfere.

Gabriel did his own shopping and then picked up a broadsheet from the pile on the counter and skimmed the bold print headlines, thinking he should pick up some more shot and powder, too. The broadsheet was two weeks old, but the news was not the sort that would blow over anytime soon: the Spanish protectorate was rumbling again about heretics and salvation, while the Métis and British were snapping at each other over trapping and timber up north, and the States tried to play each side for a better advantage.

Reading between the lines on that last, of course, since the paper'd come straight out of Philadelphia, home of the fine upstanding leaders of said States. Twenty-five years, they'd been trying to see where an advantage lay and never once gotten anything for it save more war. Gabriel pushed down the wave of disgust he felt, the memories he was trying to forget, and dropped the broadsheet back down on the counter.

Isobel appeared at his side with a simple tan hat, wide-brimmed and low-crowned, the only ornamentation a black fur band around the crown. "This one," she said, as though expecting him to disagree. He picked it up out of her hands and tested the work, feeling the weight and the nap of the felt. "That'll do," he said, giving her an approving nod.

He paid for the items they'd collected, seeing the coins go into another man's hands with something like relief. He kept half of the quartered pieces in his pocket and handed the rest to Isobel. "Not that we'll have much use for these the next few weeks, but it's always best to have pocket money in case."

And better it rest in her pockets than his.

Izzy waited nearby while Gabriel paid for their purchases, unable to shake the feeling that people were looking at her, no matter that Gabriel'd said that the town was used to strangers. Had the marshal told someone who she was, and they'd told others? Or was she imagining the side looks, the quick glances away?

Maybe she was. She felt itchy all over again, exposed and oddly vulnerable, and she didn't like it. What had the boss said? That the Left Hand wasn't to be seen until he *wanted* it to be seen? But who'd listen to her unless they knew who she was? How could she be invisible without being ignored?

She took the coins Gabriel handed her without thinking, staring at them a moment before slipping the quartered bits into her jacket pocket. Having the coins made her feel slightly better, more solid somehow, but not enough. She didn't know why she had been sent away, what she was supposed to be learning, and the frustration added to the itchiness and the discomfort until she wanted to stamp her foot, knock things off shelves, scream at the top of her lungs to be noticed; at the same time, she wanted to disappear, to run back to Flood and beg to be allowed to stay, to be Izzy the saloon girl again, where everything was familiar and made sense.

"Here you go." And Gabriel was standing in front of her, the hat in his hands. She took it from him, feeling the smooth felt slide under her fingertips, the leather tie and beaver fur band inviting touch.

It was only a hat, nothing special, but it was hers, something she'd chosen, bought for her to wear, to keep the dust and the sun away. Eventually, the glossy finish would become battered like Gabriel's, her jacket would be covered in dust, her boots scuffed and muddy, and people would look at her with respect, too.

He ushered her out of the store with two fingers gentle on her shoulder, but as they stepped back into the sunlight, he stopped her, turning to look into her face as though he'd seen something that disturbed him. "You all right, girl?"

"Yes. Yes, I'm fine." She wouldn't take offense at him calling her girl, not with coin in her pocket and this new hat in her hands, the felted brim smooth under her fingers and a shiver in her bones that she couldn't explain.

He gestured for her to step down the sidewalk, falling into step beside her. "We've one more errand to take care of, then, and—"

"Izzy?"

A woman's voice calling her name, so unexpected in this place that it was as though someone had touched a piece of ice to the nape of her neck, making her jump, before she saw who was coming toward them, hands outstretched.

"Oh." Izzy clutched the brim of her new hat more tightly. She had forgotten entirely that she knew someone in this town, caught up in the newness of . . . everything. Or not forgotten, exactly, but Izzy had figured the odds of them seeing each other had been so slim. . . . She wasn't prepared.

Only the house can play the odds safely. The boss liked to say that, usually when someone had done something stupid.

"April! I wasn't sure if we'd run into each other while we were here." *If you can avoid lying, you should.* Gabriel's voice-memory this time, not the boss's. She stepped forward into the other girl's embrace, a brush of a kiss on her cheek before they were apart again, taking stock of each other. April was older than Izzy, her once-pale complexion now browned by the sun, her light brown hair artfully curling from under a simple bonnet. She had gone off to marry a farmer, although Izzy could not remember his name.

"I saw you across the street and I thought I was dreaming at first." April's outward appearance might have changed, but her eyes were the same wide brown, and her voice was still the older-sister-scolding that Izzy remembered. "Why didn't you let me know you were coming to visit?"

Izzy licked her lips and forced herself to smile. "It's not a visit exactly. . . ."

Gabriel stepped forward then, and she turned to make the introductions, welcoming the time to gather her thoughts. "April, this is Gabriel Kasun. He's mentoring me on the road. Gabriel, this is April . . ." She couldn't remember April's married name.

"April Cortez," the woman said, offering her hand to Gabriel. He took it with a smile, the easy warmth Izzy had seen the first night in the saloon rising to the surface again, as though he'd no other purpose in his life save be charming. She was not proof against that smile but kept her attention focused on the other girl. "Izzy, you're taking the road? Truly? I would never have thought it of you."

Never mind that Izzy had never thought it of herself either, April's tone rankled something inside. "You thought I would be a saloon girl the rest of my life?" Even as the words came out, she wanted to slap herself. There was no shame in that. Simply because she wanted more . . .

But she did want more. There was no shame in that, either.

"No, but . . . Oh, this is no place for such a discussion," April said, exasperated. "Come, join me for a cup of tea. You have time for that, certainly? We may not be fancy here, but we have a tearoom that would be the envy of ladies even in Fort Cahokia."

There was no room allowed for argument; April shifted her basket to the other arm and slid her right into Izzy's, towing her along. Gabriel, rather than objecting, offered to take April's basket for her and followed at their heels, an obedient, if amused, dog.

The tearoom was in fact a room off the baker's, with a shaded porch and cloth-draped tables. Gabriel held the chair out for April and then sat down himself, arranging his longer legs carefully under the table. Izzy glanced at him under her eyelashes and tried not to smile. He might be able to charm, but any fool could see he was better suited for a saloon than a tearoom.

But then, so was she. Izzy placed her hat on her lap and settled her skirt, imagining how Peggy would act. Calm, reserved, and slightly amused, she decided.

A young woman came over, offering them tea in a fancy china pot, and a platter of biscuits, which she placed on the table when April nodded.

There was a little posy of flowers on the table as well, the blue petals drooping slightly. April touched them with a finger, lifting them from underneath, and when she took her hand away, the posy looked fresh-cut, the petals firmer and the colors more vibrant.

"You've gotten better at that," Izzy noted, glad of something to say. April had a gift for living things; she'd been in charge of the herbs Ree grew for the kitchen, and they'd always survived the cold and heat when she tended them, although nothing like the touch she'd just casually displayed.

"Living on a farm will do that," April agreed. "Skills only grow if you use them. But you already know about me"—and Izzy had a moment of guilt that she hadn't stayed to listen when the girls read April's last few letters out loud—"now tell me about you, Izzy! How on earth did you take the road?"

"Taking the road" could mean different things—marshals took the road. So did peddlers and traveling men like curanderos and law's advocates—Gabriel said that he'd chosen to ride rather than set out a shingle. But she wasn't going to stay a rider forever. She'd go *home*.

"I haven't," she said to April. "Not truly. When I go home, I'll be working with Marie." April had grown up in the saloon, same as Izzy. She should understand what that meant. "But first, the boss wanted me to see the Territory." Izzy lifted her hand, palm down, and moved it from right to left, as though fanning cards out on a table, ending with her thumb pointed in toward her rib cage. It was the boss's gesture when he spoke about the Territory, all the places and people who lived at his sufferance, and Izzy used it intentionally, to drive her point home. April's eyes widened a little, and her mouth made an O shape before she recovered, sipping her tea. Then: "You mean you *work* for him."

Izzy narrowed her eyes at the odd emphasis but nodded. "Yes."

"Oh, Isobel." April put her cup down, the china clinking faintly against the saucer, and sighed. She looked carefully at Gabriel and seemed to consider her words. That was new: April had never been the most careful girl, more prone to spilling her thoughts than hoarding them. "Do you really think that was wise?"

Izzy put down her own cup, still untasted. "What are you talking about?"

"Don't mistake me," April said quickly, glancing again at Gabriel as though she thought he might stop her. "We know who we've to thank for our safety, the way things work here. There's not a soul who knows better how fair he is, nor how he's kept the natives calm, and we respect him greatly."

Izzy could feel the way Gabriel tensed, even across the table.

Something had changed, something important, but she had missed it. Her gaze rested on April, trying to read her. Earnest, worried . . . excited? She held a secret inside, but so deeply, Izzy couldn't see.

"I hear a hesitation in those words," Gabriel said.

April turned to address him, her eyes alight, her hands fluttering like butterflies. "It's only that there's so much else, too. So many opportunities for someone able to—" She turned back to look at Izzy, her voice more plaintive than excited, now. "The Territory hasn't changed for a hundred years, Isobel. But the rest of the world moves on, embraces change! Don't you ever wonder if things might be different?"

Isobel's eyes remained narrowed, and she saw Gabriel tense slightly, as though anticipating what April might say next. "Different how? I have no desire to leave the Territory." She thought of how Ree had described cities, how Gabriel had spoken of his time across the Mudwater, and wondered how April could think that would be better.

"Not to leave, no, of course not, but we could bring change here. To keep what is good and bring in what is better. Mister Kasun, surely you've heard of things occurring beyond our borders, to the East, and in Europe?"

"I have," he said. "Some of them good, some bad. But I take it you're thinking more to the good? Mister Murdoch's gas lighting, I suppose?"

"Oh, things, of course, yes. But more than that, Mister Kasun! With Mister Jefferson as president, the United States are—"

"Are across the river," Gabriel said abruptly. "Where things are very different."

"Yes, but—" April seemed unwilling, once started, to heed Gabriel's warning tone or the distinct chill in the air around their table. Izzy's heart raced, and her palms were clammy with sweat, reacting to some threat she couldn't identify. Surely not Gabriel; Gabriel would never hurt her or April. Would he?

"Isobel." Gabriel rose from his chair, his expression still pleasant, but she could read his intent to be gone without delay. He took out his wallet and placed a few coins beside the teapot. "We'd best be on our way."

Izzy made her apologies to April, who had the most hurt expression on her own face, then followed him out to the street, her heart still hammering too quickly for comfort.

"What was all that?" she demanded, daring to grab at his elbow. "That was incredibly rude!"

He stopped and swung back to face her. "You're green and you don't know better; that's why I'm here, to keep you from trouble. And that woman inside there is trouble, Isobel."

"For admiring the States? The boss himself—"

"The devil may do as he pleases, and he will." Gabriel's voice had lost all of that slow, soft drawl, clipping his words as though they'd been shaped with an ax. "But don't ever start thinking he'd welcome folk looking 'cross the River for their governing. Because there're folks there who would take that interest for an invitation."

Izzy bit back a retort, aware again that they were beginning to attract attention from other people on the street. "It was still rude," she said instead, as prim as she could manage.

"Yes, it was." He sounded utterly unapologetic as he started to walk down the street again, without waiting for her.

Izzy drew in a sharp breath, then dropped her chin and hurried to catch up with him. She had read him as a sharp, yes, but not one easily angered or driven to cruelty, particularly not to a woman who had offered him no direct insult. And the boss had given her over into his guidance. So, if Gabriel thought April was somehow a danger, a risk, she needed to abide by his decision and learn from his lessons, even if they didn't make much sense to her. At least until she knew enough to argue against them.

They'd taken a half dozen more too-long strides before she judged it safe to speak again. "We are going to reclaim the horses?"

He glanced at her and slowed his pace down to match her legs. "One more thing left to do in town first."

‡ ‡ ‡

Isobel thought he was angry, Gabriel knew. It wasn't anger that drove him but fear, irrational and overwhelming. The years since he'd been East fell away, and he could feel it again, the sense of wrongness, of unease and discomfort that had hounded him those years, had driven him back to the Territory simply so he could breathe again.

And this girl, this ignorant *child*, thought it would be better to bring that *here*?

But he said none of that to Isobel.

Confident that she would follow, Gabriel turned left onto the side street, heading for the way station. Like most stations, it was a simple wooden box twice as wide as a man and about as high, its once-bright yellow paint faded but still clearly visible, as was the devil's sigil, the *infinitas* encircled, burnt into the wood: a warning to all that the contents were protected, not to be tampered with.

There was customary law, the rules that kept the Territory orderly, tended to by judges and marshals, and then there was the devil's Agreement, which kept all else secure.

The letter he drew from his pocket seemed to weigh more than two sheets of paper possibly could, and he hesitated before shoving it through the narrow opening as though glad to see it gone.

When the post rider came through next, they would add that letter to the packet they were bringing back East. With luck and good weather, Gabriel's letter would reach its destination within the month. He felt a twinge of shame for being a hypocrite, for snapping at the girl, April, when he himself kept correspondence with his former classmates, now members of the very government he did not trust. But that lack of trust was *why* he maintained contact: not to aid them but to keep himself safe.

The devil had promised him an end to that. If he succeeded.

"Are you mad at me?" Isobel's voice was soft again, not frightened but seeking to placate.

"No. No, I'm not mad." He turned to face the girl. She was wearing her new hat tilted too far back on her head, and he reached out to pull the brim down slightly so it shaded her eyes and nose properly. "You're under a hard weight, being green and needing to be whatever it is he's wanting of you," he said. "Likely your thoughts are all a jumble, and being away from home's only making it worse?"

She nodded, clearly reluctant to admit any such thing.

"That's to be expected," he said. "A few weeks from now, I mightn't have interrupted, but you don't need more confusion in that handsome head of yours. Not just yet." She didn't know what the Territory was yet, not really. She needed that before people started filling her ears with nonsense and trouble. Although, having a bit of doubt planted in that sharp mind might not be such a bad thing. . . .

"When people start telling you how to fix things, Isobel, it's best first to make sure those things need fixing."

He looked down the street the way they'd come, then, his trouble-sense pricking. Maybe April, maybe something else, maybe nothing, but the need to be shed of town and back on the road gnawed at him. "Let's collect the horses. We'll head west, give you a taste of the wide-open lands."

He'd planned to head for Widder Creek, a few days out, then they'd follow the road into the high plains and, eventually, De Plata. That should take a few weeks, allow him to see the folk he needed to see, and give Isobel the chance to get a little dirty without actual harm before they swung back northeast, to civilized towns.

"I know what the plains look like," she said, scowling.

He smiled at her indignation, briefly. "No, you don't. You've spent your entire life in a protected circle, sheltered by the devil's name. But you'll learn, right soon enough." Her scowl didn't ease, but he could tell she was thinking on what he'd said, wondering what was out there. Good.

They collected the horses and mule at the stable. While Isobel double-checked their tack and started reloading the mule's packs with their new acquisitions, the boy who brought the beasts out waved off his pavement.

"The devil pays for his riders," the boy said, giving Steady an affectionate slap on the flank. "And yours weren't no trouble at all."

The mare's tack was marked with the devil's sigil, but his wasn't. But he didn't want to shame the boy by insisting. "For your time, then." And he slid a quarter-coin into the boy's hand, then clapped him on the shoulder. "A good horseman's worth his weight in silver, no mistake."

"True words, those," a voice behind him said. "You heading out of town?"

"We are." Gabriel wasn't caught off guard, had sensed the man moving closer, with no attempt at stealth. He turned, his hip against Steady's saddle, to face the newcomer.

An older man, ordinary enough, with bright hazel eyes under sparse white hair forming a crown over sun-weathered skin, dressed as though he might have cause to throw himself onto horseback at a moment's notice, age or no.

The marshal, no surprise, even without spotting the sigil pinned to the loop of his belt. Never mind that Isobel had checked in the day before—by association he, Gabriel, was worthy of a look-over as well. Perhaps even more so: he might be useful—or dangerous, depending on how the marshal stood. Gabriel kept his ears open when he traveled, and he heard what was spoken in a low voice; like Isobel's girlhood friend, not everyone was pleased with the status quo, and marshals, for all their oaths, were still men, and prone to their own opinions.

He might be overcautious, likely was, but even an indirect threat to the Territory put him on guard, and his trouble-sense was rarely wrong.

"You're riding on the devil's business?" the older man asked now.

"Greening run, is all," Gabriel said.

"Same as makes no nevermind," the marshal said, still casual. Too casual, for a man trained to caution. "To a lot of folk."

"Makes a whole world of nevermind," Gabriel corrected him, checking Steady's girth and tightening it a notch. Turning your back on a marshal wasn't an insult but a sign of trust. "She's just learning her way, no challenge to anyone."

"She's his Hand, boy." The marshal had enough decades on him that Gabriel let that pass without comment. "She may be green, but there's going to be those who won't care—or who will take that green for an easy kill. You know that, right?"

"I know it." And his right hand was on the marshal's shoulder, the dagger pricking his stubbled neck, while his carbine rested easy in his left hand, cocked and aimed at the man's knee. "And I aim to see her trained, not dead."

"Good." The marshal wasn't even sweating, although he was careful not to move suddenly. His face was battered and wrinkled, but the eyes meeting Gabriel's were clear, untainted by age. "That's good. We ride the same road, boy. Now put your toys away before I make it hard for you to hump that saddle."

Gabriel looked down then and saw the marshal's own knife, a good ten inches of straight steel, pointed directly at his crotch.

Isobel chose that moment to finish with the mule and join them. "Gentlemen? Is there a problem?"

"No problem at all, ma'am," the marshal said, stepping back. His blade had disappeared by the time he turned to face Isobel, and Gabriel made his own weapons do the same, the dagger sliding back into its sheath, the gun reholstered on his saddle. Isobel was standing on the wooden walkway, her head tilted at an angle, her expression curious but unshadowed, and for a moment, Gabriel wanted to send her home, tell the devil the deal was off, to send her off to some boarding school where they taught girls how to become gentlewomen, not riders.

The moment passed. He'd made his deal; the time for choice was gone. And Isobel had never been meant for a gentlewoman.

"Time to go," he said brusquely, picking up the reins and swinging into the saddle. When Steady took a few steps back, he reined him into a turn and waited for Isobel, with an apologetic nod to the marshal, to mount up and follow, the mule already at their heels.

Gabriel didn't seem inclined to talk once they were back in the saddle, and so Izzy kept her silence as Patch Junction slowly faded on the horizon behind them, the grassland unrolling ahead of them. The dirt road, cut by hundreds of hooves and wheels, was clearly visible underfoot, but when Izzy looked ahead or behind, it seemed to disappear below the grasses, as though they wandered without direction. She found herself looking down at the road more and more often, the pale brown dirt reassuring against the endless lines of the prairie grasses, and expanse of pale blue sky overhead, barely a cloud to break the color.

Gabriel had been right: she hadn't known the prairie at all, not really. Not this terrifyingly wide expanse of same-same-same without the familiar, comforting silhouette of buildings grouped together. There was nothing to rest her eye on save the two of them and the mule, and the occasional wide-branched tree solitary in the distance, and the entire world seemed to undulate if she looked at it too long. Even the occasional bird circling far overhead only emphasized how insignificant they all were, horses and humans alike.

"Is it all like this?"

Her voice was so small against the vastness, she thought it might not carry past Uvnee's twitching ears. But Gabriel slowed down enough that they could ride alongside each other, in response, and that helped, a little. "Not all, no," he said. "Eastwards, there's more hills, and north and west, there're mountains, breaks it up some. You'll see. But here . . ." He looked around as though seeing it all for the first time. "Pretty much like this. Hunting camps and farmsteads here and there, the occasional town where three or four families decided to make a go of it together and succeeded, but mostly . . . like this.

Junction and Flood are pretty rare. Mostly, the Territory's . . . quiet."

"You like it." She didn't mean to sound accusing, but he just laughed.

"I do. Not forever, not always, but there are times when a man just needs to remember he's not all that important in the greater scheme of things, that whatever we do, this"—he waved a hand around them—"abides."

She swallowed against a sudden, unexpected lump in her throat. "You must have hated it then, back East."

"No." That surprised her, how firm he sounded. "I couldn't stay there, but I loved it the same way I love this. When you have so many people, Isobel, it's almost the same as having no people at all."

That made no sense to her, and she said so.

He only shook his head and handed her a tin flask filled with water. "Think about it. Maybe it will."

He lapsed into silence again, and she did the same, taking a sip of the lukewarm water and letting it ease her throat and the thirst she hadn't even noticed until then. When she offered it back to him, he shook his head, indicating that she should keep it, pointing out the slot in her mare's saddle where the fist-sized flask would fit.

That discovery led her to consider the saddle more carefully, noting the loops and ties that she hadn't noticed before, wondering what they might be used for. She suspected, like the flask, she would find out as they went.

Unfortunately, her thoughts soon circled away from the workmanship of the leather saddle and how the bag she'd packed hung so perfectly to how her back ached if she sat one way, her legs protested if she sat another, and how her arms ached from holding the reins, causing her entire body to feel as though Hiram the blacksmith had used his hammer on her, rather than his anvil.

But there was no point in complaining; it was what it was. She would simply have to accustom herself to it, toughen herself to it. Was that what the boss had wanted her to learn? No; she rejected that thought almost immediately. Nothing so simple, she was certain. Her gaze was drawn again to the far horizon, and she felt a warm shiver move from scalp to spine. *This*, she thought, *maybe this*. How small she was, in such a larger world. Or simply, how large the Territory was.

The sun was midrise now, angled enough that Izzy was glad of her new hat, although it did nothing to keep the dust of the road from her mouth and nose. The mule plodded along at Uvnee's shoulder, the mare periodically turning her head to nip at its ears, making it shake its head and snort at her. Izzy smiled and patted the mare's neck, taking comfort in the warm feel of flesh under her fingers, the rise and fall of the mare's flanks under her legs, even the occasional flatulence from the mule and the inevitable sight of Gabriel's horse lifting its tail to relieve itself as it walked. Small, pungent things to bring her back to herself.

She studied the man riding in front of her as well, trying to let her shoulders soften, her backside relaxing into the sway of the saddle the way Gabriel's did. It was harder than it seemed, but after a while, her hips and legs ached less, at least, although her arms and shoulders still burned.

To distract herself, Izzy thought over the confrontation she'd interrupted back in town that morning. She'd watched players stare each other down over the felt, seen Iktan and Marie calm enough fights before they happened to recognize the signs, like two dogs circling each other over a chunk of meat.

The marshal had seemed respectful enough when she introduced herself. And yet his eye on Gabriel had been strange, almost suspicious. Did he not know he was her mentor? Why hadn't Gabriel told him? Or had he, and the marshal was still suspicious?

Izzy worried her upper lip between her teeth, realizing that she hadn't tried to read the marshal. She hadn't tried to read April, either, come to think of it. She'd been distracted, surprised—had assumed that both would speak truthfully to her, not hide anything.

"Presumption gets a body killed," she said out loud, and Uvnee's ears twitched back, as though the mare thought she'd been speaking to her. "Iktan always says that," she told the mare. "That you can't presume someone wants to cause trouble, but you can't presume they *don't*, neither."

If the boss had only told her what to do, what was expected . . . She felt a surge of indignation rise in her chest, just as quickly tamped down. If the boss didn't tell her something, it was because she was supposed to learn it on her own. She'd pay better attention, read Gabriel, read everything she saw, and figure it out herself. Be like Marie, who didn't go running to the boss every time there was a problem.

Huh. Izzy caught her lower lip between her teeth again, her forehead creased at that thought. Had Marie been sent away, too? Or was the Right Hand kept close and only the Left sent away?

Caught up in those musings, Izzy barely noticed the faint rumble rising underneath the now-familiar sounds of horses and mule until she heard Gabriel call her name. "Isobel. Look up."

Her head lifted and she saw he was pointing north, across the grasses. She squinted but could see nothing save a smudge on the horizon, a smear of black between the grey-green and pale blue.

Then the rumbling noise resolved into a mighty thumping, and the smudge became thicker, and her breath caught in her chest even as the thumping found its way into her bones, making her heart speed as though to catch up. "Oh."

She had heard the stories, of course, about the great herds. She had seen the dark, shaggy pelts, thick enough to dig your fingers into, warm enough to laugh at a winter's storm, but a pelt did not move, did not thunder, did not fill the world until there was nothing else but the immense, incalculable swarm of creatures moving across the land, dust raised for leagues in their wake.

They were too far away to pick out individual details, the long black smudge and golden dust behind spreading seemingly forever, and she thought that maybe the herd would never end, that it would continue forever, even after they had ridden on, pouring from the horizon until the sun set again, thick hooves setting their medicine into the dirt and stone.

"Can you feel it?" Gabriel asked her, and she nodded, unable to speak. Like the river when it was in full flood, or the boss when he was angry, restrained but powerful, pressing against her until she couldn't breathe and didn't need to breathe. The thundering of their hooves *was* her heartbeat, the beat of the stone beneath their feet, the air heated by the snort of their breath, and the warmth of their shaggy hides the pulse of blood under her skin. . . .

And then the herd let go of her, so suddenly that she fell back into the saddle, not even aware that she'd risen in her stirrups, trying to see better.

"Breathe," Gabriel said. "Your first time, it can be overwhelming."

She nodded, her left hand pressed against her chest, watching as the herd shifted and moved away, fading again into a near-silent smudge in the distance. "Oh," she said again, unable to find more words than that.

Gabriel rode close enough for their legs to brush against each other, reaching out to press his fingers around the silver band on her finger. "If you're ever any closer, hold hard to any silver you've got. It should keep you safe."

She wasn't sure there was enough silver between the two of them to keep that much power at bay. "How does anyone manage to hunt them?" she wondered, feeling her heartbeat return to herself again.

"You don't charge in and start shooting, that's for certain, although some fools have tried. There are rituals. You speak of your hunger and your need, and ask the herd to give what is needed. I've never seen it performed myself." He chuckled. "I'm a decent enough shot with the gun but hopeless with the bow, and you don't have time to stop and reload when you're in the middle of a hunt."

Izzy touched the sheath of the knife strapped to her saddle and thought about the fact that she didn't own a gun and had no idea how to shoot a bow, and decided that she would rather observe buffalo from a distance as well.

"Ways to go yet," he said, and moved his gelding back into motion. She pressed her knees into Uvnee's side to get the mare to move, and they continued west, following the sun as it arched overhead and down. The road was well-traveled enough to be packed hard, and wide enough for them to ride alongside each other with room to spare, the mule bringing up the rear. A solitary hawk soared overhead, and the *wuffle* and snort of the horses was matched by the occasional yip of something hunting in the tall grasses around them.

"How far until the next town?" she asked finally.

"A ways."

Izzy rolled her eyes, hard enough he must have felt it.

"I told you, places like Patch and Flood, they're rare enough and mostly alongside rivers. Out here . . . Nothing's permanent. Season changes, hunting camps move, villages shift when the soil gets tired. You're town-bred, used to people about, things staying in one place. It will take a while to accustom yourself. But you will. Or you won't."

"Is that a challenge?" Her chin lifted, even though he couldn't see it.

"A fact," he said, and looked over his shoulder at her, eyes shaded under the brim of his hat, impossible to read. "Which in and of itself is enough of a challenge."

Izzy tugged her own hat farther over her forehead and urged Uvnee to a slightly faster pace, passing Gabriel and Steady just enough to claim the lead. Never mind that she didn't know where they were going; the road stretched ahead of them, and if he wanted her to stop, he could call out and say so.

Behind her, he began to sing softly, in a language she didn't recognize, rolling syllables that weren't quite nonsense, rising and falling more like a chant than a song.

They rode like that for another handful of hours, the sun glaring down from in front of them, and just as she was beginning to think that the road would roll on forever without a single change, they came to a small stand of trees, stunted against the landscape but still taller than anything they'd seen all day. Gabriel took the lead again and turned them south just after, leaving the wide road for a narrow track, barely visible through the grass under the horses' hooves. She could hear the mule behind her, muttering its own opinion about this turn of events. Old Elias at the livery stable used to claim that mules were wiser than horses, and most people, too. It was certainly opinionated enough.

"What's it saying, Uvnee?" she asked the mare. "Does it think we should have stayed on the road?" One pointed ear flicked backward, as though to say, "I never listen to mules." Izzy laughed and then looked around again, trying to understand why her mentor had chosen this route. The flowers she had noticed the day before, the tiny blue ones, were thicker here, competing with the taller grasses, and a low brush grew in almost a hedge to their right. She couldn't identify anything, although she noted some bramble that might have been blackberry, and her mouth watered a little. If it were later in the season, she might have suggested they stop and pick some, bring them back for Ree to use.

That thought gave her pause. It would be a while before she tasted one of Ree's pies again. She knew that, had known that, and yet the sense of loss struck her again, displacing any contentment she had found.

She looked at the brush, and then back at the stand of trees they'd turned at, thinking of the taller, thicker cottonwoods growing by the creek back home, the sagebrush they'd seen outside the town, and frowned, trying to see what made the difference here. Why had Gabriel turned there?

She needed to ask things, she reminded herself, even if it meant exposing her ignorance. "What happened here? Why does it look . . ." She stumbled for a word. "Different?"

"Good eye," Gabriel said, not bothering to look back, and she felt a flush of satisfaction at his approval. "Was a farmstead. Fire raged through here a few years back. Nobody'll live here now, so the grass is taking it back."

Once land'd been cleared and planted, it generally didn't get abandoned, not if there wasn't a strong reason. Izzy looked more carefully. She didn't see the remains of a house anywhere, but there was a shape to their left as they rode by that might have been a well once. That would explain why nobody took the land once the original settlers were gone: easier to build closer to a creek, where there was fresh water, and not have to rely on a well year-round.

Or . . . "Someone died?"

"Entire family, plus an indentured boy."

"Oh." Izzy didn't shiver; she had no fear of haints, and they'd no reason to be angry at her. Still, the grounds were tinged with a melancholy knowing. She touched the silver of her ring and thought of the wardings on Flood's boneyard that kept the dead at rest.

Gabriel didn't tell her anything more, just sang a few more lines of those chant-sounding words under his breath, and then asked, "You see anything useful?"

This was a test, then. Izzy looked around again, trying to see it in a purely practical manner. "Berries are only just starting to ripen. Probably serviceberries growing now, though, if you want to hunt for them. That's elderbow; it's edible if you're real hungry. Coneflower for illness, and the stems make a useable dye. There's . . ." Her gaze was caught on something and she brightened. "There's the remains of an old chimney over there if we needed to make a fire, cook dinner." She was sure there were things she was missing, a hundred and ten things her mentor must see without half trying. It was just experience, she told herself. She could learn to do that, too. Every new rider had to, right?

"And the path we're on?" His voice came over his shoulder; she couldn't see his face but he sounded amused, and her cheeks flamed at the thought that she'd missed something obvious. Izzy looked down past Uvnee's neck at the dirt churned up by the mare's hooves, and then looked behind her.

"It's . . ." It was narrow—she had already noted that—and barely visible through the wild profusion of grasses, but there was something else there too. Something she hadn't seen before. She looked, and listened, and licked her lips before she finished the sentence. "It's maintained."

Once she saw that, it was painfully obvious, same as reading a person. She'd never thought about reading a place before; how could she, when she'd been in the same place near her entire life?

"Maintained?" Gabriel's voice didn't tell her if she was right or wrong, but she knew she was right.

She held the reins in her left hand and gestured with her right. "Everything else is growing back, but the brush and the taller grasses, they don't cross it. This was a road once."

"Still is, only not much in use now that the farm's gone. That's a thing to remember, Isobel. No true road ever disappears entirely. You just have to know how to find them."

Her curiosity flared at the idea of a true road versus what—a false road? A temporary one? "How?" *How did you find them*, she meant, but more *how did you know true from false?*

He was laughing at her now, or perhaps only laughing. "The same way you do anything."

"Experience," she muttered, pulling her hat down more firmly on her head and glaring at the spot between his shoulder blades. He sounded like the boss just then, all hint and nothing solid, and the frustration was a real thing, hot under her breastbone. "I—

Whatever she meant to say was cut off by a harsh scream overhead, and they both looked up into the sky, Gabriel pushing his hat back to see better. Izzy's breath caught in her throat, somewhere between fear and awe at the outline of a massive bird floating overhead, wings coming between them and the sun, all other birds suddenly gone from sight. She couldn't see distinctive markings, but she didn't need to: only one thing could be that size.

"Reaper hawk," Gabriel told her, reining in his horse to take a better look. "They don't usually call unless they're hunting. I wonder what brought them out here." He cast a glance at her, as though to gauge her reaction, then looked back at the sky. "Gorgeous, aren't they?"

That was one word for it, although not the one she might have chosen. Izzy had never seen a Reaper before, but she'd heard about them. People said they were large enough to take a human the way a regular hawk would catch a rabbit. Looking up at the creature soaring overhead, she could believe it. Like the buffalo herd, there was something powerful in the creature, powerful and disturbing.

"Some of the native tribes claim they're strong medicine, that a feather from one in the fletching leads an arrow straight to prey."

She could believe that, too; it seemed impossible to think the creature could ever miss once it stooped.

"Only some tribes?"

He shrugged, that one-shoulder rise that told her to take it or leave it as she saw fit. "And some tribes think they're ill omens. Death-bringers, like owls."

Despite the narrowness of the path, the mule had sidled up closer to Uvnee again, seeking comfort against the predator overhead. "It's not hunting us, is it?" She felt a fool for asking, but anything that worried the mule worried her.

He cast another look overhead. "They generally know better than to go after people, particularly on horseback." Before she could breathe a sigh of relief, he added, "But be careful when you're alone, especially if you're knelt down. You look smaller to them then, and they might take a dive before they realize their mistake."

He might have been joking with her, but she couldn't tell. Another hawk joined the first one. She could see that this one was slightly smaller, circling just below the first. "Its mate?"

"That's the male. Prettier but less fierce."

He was mocking her then, she was certain, but she bit her lip and nodded. "Is there a nest nearby? Are we threatening their chicks?" It was spring; they'd have chicks somewhere. But looking around, she couldn't see anywhere that might have hosted a nest for a scrub jay, much less a creature that size.

"They nest higher up in the hills, come down to hunt. Bit far to see 'em here," he said thoughtfully, looking up at the sky again. "Probably looking for a pronghorn that wandered off, maybe tracking something injured. I've been told they'll sometimes take on a bear, but I'm not sure as I'd believe it."

Izzy had seen the trophy belts some marshals wore, bear claws hanging from them like polished bone daggers, each twice as long as a man's finger. She looked into the sky again, trying to imagine the clash between the two, and shuddered. She had always thought of Flood as being protected from attack from the ground—winter-hungry wolves, or a would-be bandit new to the Territory who didn't know yet who lived there and thought it would be easy pickings. Not death from the sky.

The two birds circled again, then, finding nothing of interest, wheeled again and disappeared into the sun's rays. When they emerged, much farther away, Izzy found she could breathe easily again, like a rabbit when the shadow passed.

Ill omen? The boss didn't believe in any such, said man made their own fate, sometimes good, sometimes ill, but always their own decision. But Iktan always carried a jet carving of a cat, what he said was a jaguar, to ward off ill-wishings, and Molly would rub her rosary when she was worried something would go wrong. . . .

She shook herself, even as Uvnee shuddered under the saddle, and shifted her gaze from the sky back to her surroundings. The tall grasses, scattered with tiny flowers as far as her eye could see, the grit of the dust on her skin and in her mouth, the stink of warm horseflesh and leather, the flat, warm taste of the water she'd been drinking; it reconnected her to herself, shook off the unease the birds had left behind. She reached her right hand to touch the silver band on her left, rubbing the shining metal gently. Like the buffalo, she didn't think it could do much if a creature like that turned its attention to her. Hopefully, she would never find out.

"Seeing them's a good reminder," Gabriel said, urging Steady forward along the path, forcing both Uvnee and the mule to follow or be left behind. "What other than a Reaper do you need to worry about on the road?"

"Bears," she said promptly, relieved to be on more familiar ground. Every child knew about bears: the grizzly could knock you dead with one blow, and the black was smaller but still fierce. "Wolf packs. And cougars." There were none near Flood, the plains too open and low for the big cats' liking, but she'd heard stories from men passing through the saloon, about the solitary hunters called ghosts, who were heard but rarely seen save for glowing eyes in the dark and the blood they left behind.

"And how do you fend them off?"

She knew that, too. "By not being where they're hunting."

That time, Gabriel was laughing *with* her, she was pretty sure.

"Wise, but not always enough. Your boss said you were a fair shot with a blunderbuss, and fair enough's likely all you'll ever need for the big cats or bears. They don't like loud noises and they don't like the smell of powder; most times, they'll scatter in favor of something that won't fight back. When we stop tonight, if there's light, we'll see how you handle the carbine." He looked back at her, his face shadowed once again by the brim of his hat. "And your knife," he said. She touched the blade sheathed against the side of her saddle, then nodded. Ree had taught them all how to use smaller knives, both for cooking and defense, but she'd never thought of it as a weapon, not truly.

It was, Marie would say, time for that to change.

They made camp soon after that, Gabriel simply reining his gelding to a stop and sliding from the saddle without warning. He stood still for a moment, his eyes closed, then nodded once and set off, walking about ten paces before stopping again, his head tilted to the side as though he were listening for something. Izzy, uncertain, waited for direction.

"Not much water, but enough for the night," he said, and she edged closer to see that there was a tiny creek running at his feet where he'd stopped, barely a handspan wide and mostly hidden by the grasses. Her eyes went wide; she'd heard of water-finders before but never knew one. Like April's plant-sense, it wasn't a thing you could learn, only came on some folk, some medicine born in 'em.

She'd never had a use for it, never felt jealous of it, when April coaxed up the herbs. But water-finding . . . She pushed the feeling away. Useless to envy; she wasn't, she couldn't.

She was the boss's Left Hand. She'd find her own use soon enough.

"Get your mare settled," Gabriel told her, "then find a flattish place without too many rocks, and settle it down for sleeping. Check for holes, too. Nothing quite like waking up and discovering you've got a gopher in your bedroll."

It was easier dismounting this time: her legs didn't shake or tremble when she tried to move, and lifting her pack didn't make her spine cry in agony.

Uvnee seemed delighted to have the saddle off, leaning into Izzy while she brushed away the worst of the sweat from her hide, then meandering away to dip her muzzle into the creek alongside the mule.

Suddenly craving cooler water, too, Izzy moved slightly upstream of them and refilled her own canteen and the tin flask Gabriel had given her earlier.

Gabriel came around after they'd all finished with the creek, and wrapped a series of ropes around Uvnee's left legs, leaving just enough slack between that it didn't tangle. "Hobbles," he said, before she could even ask. "She can walk just fine, see?" And he patted Uvnee on the haunch; the mare ignored him, placidly pulling at the grass. "Just means she can't run off if they get spooked. I trust Steady, he's well-named, that one, and the mule knows better than to wander off, but your girl's still got to prove herself. And having to track down your horse in the morning might be one way to gain experience, but it's not one I recommend."

Izzy studied the way Uvnee moved, making sure that the mare wasn't bothered by the hobbles, then nodded reluctant agreement. Lacking a stall or corral, it seemed reasonable and still gave the mare room to defend herself against snakes or predators if need be.

"There's enough grass here, but we won't always have good forage. Once they're rested, give 'em some grain, too," he said. "I'll show you how much."

The grain was in one of the packs slung over the mule's backside. It looked at her curiously as she unloaded it but, other than an eye-twitch, didn't seem overly worried about when it would be fed. The pack was heavy but no larger than her saddlebag, and she frowned at it, wondering how it could contain enough grain for the entire trip. Maybe they would refill it when they reached the next town? But Gabriel had said . . .

She reached a hand in and felt the soft, scratchy pellets against her skin. The bag seemed deeper inside than it did out, and she pulled her hand out again and frowned at it, as though something might have changed while it was out of her sight.

If Gabriel wasn't worried about running out of grain, she decided, then neither would she.

Once she'd chosen a reasonably flat patch of ground and laid her bedroll down, Izzy gave the animals a handful of the feed each, then wandered over to see what Gabriel was doing. He had cleared a small space of grasses, baring the soil underneath, and was knelt down next to it, laying fist-sized rocks in a small circle. "Has to be a small fire tonight," he said. "These grasses won't burn quick, but they'll smoke so badly, we wouldn't get any sleep after that." He placed a small brown object the size of his fist at the center of the circle.

"Is that . . ." Izzy reached out to touch it, then drew her hand back, hesitating.

"It's all right; you can touch it now."

The coalstone was rough to the touch and slightly chilled. She rubbed her fingertips together, then looked at him. "How do you light it?"

He reached his own hand out, placing his palm on the coalstone, and pressed. "Like that."

When he drew his hand away, the coalstone was a pale grey, and within seconds, tiny yellow and red flames licked over its surface.

"Useful for when there's no fuel to burn," Gabriel said. "Trail tricks, not the sort of thing you needed in Flood, I suspect."

"No." She cocked her head to the side, still watching the flames but thinking back. "Our blacksmith got coal in, every month; boss made sure of that. Ree said wood made the best bread, but mostly we just used cow chips." She grimaced at the memory, having spent too many hours when younger collecting the dung for drying, and Gabriel laughed.

"Coalstone won't burn particularly hot, but it's handy. Chips are better for cookfires; we can stop to gather some, if you prefer. . . ."

"No, no, that's quite all right," she said hastily, embarrassed when he grinned at her.

"And while dinner boils," he said, arranging a triangular stand and hanging a pot over the flame, "we'll see how well you do know how to handle a weapon."

The answer, Izzy quickly learned, was "not well." Gabriel's gun was lighter and longer in the barrel than the blunderbuss she'd learned to shoot, and only added to the aching of her arms and back until holding it steady proved impossible from the shaking of her muscles. He finally took pity on her, taking the carbine away and telling her to draw the longer blade sheathed at her saddle instead.

A few passes with that, Gabriel's arm wrapped in his long coat for protection, had him nodding thoughtfully. "We'll work on it. For now, time to eat."

The fire might not burn as hot, but it warmed the beans and pork hock well enough. Izzy lay down on her bedroll that night with her body aching but her belly full.

The flickering glow of the fire lingered to her left, her mentor a lightly snoring lump a few yards away, the horses quiet shadows a little beyond that. Overhead, the sky was a glittering scatter of stars, the moon full and round. An owl hooted, and insects chattered close to her ear, and suddenly it became too much, the vastness and strangeness and new experiences overwhelming her. She pulled the blanket over her head and the world went away, until suddenly Gabriel was shaking her shoulder and it was morning.

Izzy's first campfire breakfast was johncakes and lard, served up on thin, worn tin plates, and washed down with bitter coffee that left her teeth fuzzy and her tongue dry but her mind clear.

"It's horrible stuff," Gabriel admitted, "but riders can't be choosers. And after a while, you get used to it."

She doubted that but didn't say so.

They scraped the plates and dumped the coffee, and repacked, then she watched while Gabriel poured a double handful of dried beans into one of the refilled canteens and hooked it to the mule's pack, snug against the animal's side. That was how they'd had beans ready to cook the night before, she realized: soaking in water all day as they rode, then he'd poured both beans and water into the pot and added the dried hock.

"Pork, beans, and hardtack," Gabriel said, seeing her watching. "It's not exciting, but it's better than thinking you'll be able to hunt along the way, and then starving."

Izzy had never hunted for anything other than prairie hen eggs, but nodded anyway. A rabbit or two added to the beans would be even better, and she was reasonable sure she'd be able to catch a coney, even if Gabriel didn't think she could hit the broad side of a buffalo standing right next to her.

They saddled up after that, still heading southwest by the sun. The ground was uneven here, the dirt road no longer smooth but studded with rocks, the grasses on either side still shading from winter brown to the pale green of new growth. The occasional narrow creek cut wedges in the turf, deep and narrow, but never seemed to cross the road. Or the road never crossed them; Izzy couldn't be sure which was true.

Occasionally, something would rustle the grass, and once Gabriel pointed out a small grouping of wild horses in the distance, black-and-white patchwork hide and flying tails. Her eye tracked them, something leaping in her chest—different from the way the Reapers or buffalo made her feel: softer, more like comfort than fear. Buzzards circled occasionally, and blue-winged swallows swung in dizzying swoops through the air around them, their faint calls the only sound other than the wind and the steady *clop* of hooves, and those things too brought comfort. Although she couldn't quite say why.

The landscape itself remained unchanging, endless sway of grass and occasional rock crops, but Izzy remembered her vow to pay attention, to read everything she could, and practiced on what she had. By the afternoon of the third day after leaving Flood, Izzy felt she had an understanding of her mare, the way Uvnee would spook at the too-close swoop of a swallow but not even blink when a colony of sod dogs scolded them for riding too near their burrow, and of the mule, who didn't care about anything except solid footing and his next meal, and was happiest when jowl to shoulder with one of the horses.

Gabriel was a harder read, though even the boss would admit that it was difficult to learn a man by the set of his shoulders and a hat pulled down low over his brow. She'd already known he had a pleasing charm, and a gentle kindness inside. But she knew more now. When he dropped one shoulder, he was about to show her something, or test her. When he shifted to his left, he'd go quiet for a while and didn't want to be disturbed. And as he went to the evening chores with quiet competence, and showed her how to load and unload his carbine with quiet, calm instruction, she got the feeling that he was a deep man, the charmer she'd met in the saloon only the surface paint.

He was born to the Territory—she knew that from what he'd

said—and had left for a while to study in the United States and then come back. He'd been on the road a while, didn't seem to have a sweetheart or any place he called home particularly, and he was patient as a rock when it came to teaching.

And sometimes she'd wake midway through the night, and he'd be sitting there, his back against his pack, not doing anything but staring out into the darkness. She never spoke, even though she knew he knew she was awake. Whatever coiled in him, violence or sorrow, he didn't care to share it, and she'd respect that.

The morning of the sixth day since they'd left Flood, the first he'd allowed Izzy to set the coalstone and make johncakes she didn't burn too badly, the landscape changed again. Izzy noticed less green and more brown, the grasses growing shorter, low brush hugging the flat, featureless ground in sparse patches over bare rock. She couldn't imagine anything growing here, anyone living here, and said so.

"No?" Gabriel said, clearly amused. She frowned at him, shifting her weight in the saddle from one buttock to the other almost automatically, then let her gaze rest on the horizon, the way he'd taught her, and slowly dragged her eyes back, not looking for anything in particular until a movement or odd shape caught her attention. There was the occasional jagged spar of stone rising out of the grass, higher than a man was tall and strangely ominous in their solitude. The grass swayed in places despite the lack of breeze to move them: invisible birds or small animals creeping along, hiding from predators, she supposed. So, there was that much life here, and the flash of something moving further distant, a jack or grouse maybe, but nothing that would make him say—oh.

"Someone was there," she said, pointing at something in the distance. The barely visible framework was old, a rounded skeleton bleached and broken down by the wind, but obviously manmade. "A hunting camp?"

"Maybe a month ago," Gabriel said. "Niukonska, probably. There's not enough water to support a long-term camp here; they were just passing through, maybe hunting or observing some ceremony."

But people did live here. She took the rebuke silently, her jaw clenching slightly. She'd known better, she had. The native tribes, los nativos do país, Ree called them; they farmed, some of them, and hunted, and didn't settle in towns the way whites did but went where they would and didn't pay much attention to Law or the devil unless they chose to.

Suddenly, the empty land around them seemed less empty, and Izzy wasn't sure if that were a good thing or not.

They rode closer, past the bleached, bent sticks that had once stretched a hide between their ribs, and she saw two small charred circles where fires had been built, but nothing else left behind.

Gabriel broke the silence again. "Your boss teach you anything about the tribal alliances?"

"A little." She considered how very little that had been. "He had me study a map once. Listed all the tribes, as far as we knew 'em, and who they traded with, who they were warring with. Boss said it had to be updated all the time because they'd move, change who they were friendly with, who they weren't. It's not like Spain, where they have one border and keep to it."

"Nations are different creatures," Gabriel said. "They think about land different. They think about war different, too. That's a thing your boss has been able to keep from the Territory so far."

He was sad . . . no, he was angry when he said that, and she knew suddenly that he'd been in a war maybe, or been close to one, close enough for it to hurt. But he was too young to be part of the Americans' rebellion, wasn't he? Some folk aged differently, but he didn't *seem* that old.

And it was none of her need-knowing. *Stop poking*, she told herself, hearing Marie's tone in her thoughts. *You read what you need to know and you leave the rest alone. That's only polite.*

Izzy shifted in her saddle, taking a sip of water from her canteen and letting it slide down her throat. The road had widened enough there that they could ride abreast, the mule still plodding along behind as though it didn't matter where or what, so long as it didn't have to lift its head. Izzy felt sympathy; the sore tenderness of those first few days had faded into an ache every bone in her body felt, from heels to elbows, and sweat had run and dried and run again under her clothing. She would have taken off her hat to let the breeze touch her scalp, except there was no breeze to be found. How was it so warm, so early in the season?

"Doesn't it rain here?" The sky was such a pale blue, it was nearly white, the only clouds high and loose-formed, like a breath would make them disappear, and even the air smelled dry and dusty.

"Not so much as where you're from, or up in the mountains proper, but it does." He looked around, and she saw that expression on his face, a quiet sort of concentration, like he was listening to something she couldn't hear. "Rains are late this year; when it comes, everything will bloom all at once. It's . . . impressive."

Izzy tried to imagine the ground around her suddenly turning green, maybe with flowers, the occasional cottonwood's bare twisted branches hidden under green leaves. And then she thought about the mountains, the long ridge called Mother's Knife, where the Territory ended. Across those distant peaks was Nueva España, where her parents had maybe come from, and maybe where they'd gone back to. She tried to imagine it, tried to imagine mountains, and on the other side, towns and cities filled with people who'd come from somewhere even farther away, and failed utterly.

Her distraction was broken by an itch at the back of her neck, as though something crawled across the fine hairs under her braid, but when she reached back to brush it away, there was nothing there. Maybe a spider'd hidden in her collar, she thought, and shuddered, brushing the back of her neck again for good measure.

"Will we go up into the Knife?" she asked.

"No." He hesitated. "We'll get closer, though. Despite your boss picking the route, there are some folk I need to see. There are a few settlements over the ridge, good places to touch ground and talk to people."

The sudden urge to talk to people, utter strangers, caught Izzy by surprise. She wasn't normally much for talking, but she supposed a week with only one person—and three beasts—for company could make even the most sullen man a chatterbox.

And meeting people, learning who was out in the Territory, learning their needs, was what she'd been sent here to learn, to do, like Marie did for the folk who came to Flood. At least . . . she *thought* it was.

She shifted in her saddle again, rising in the stirrups to stretch her legs slightly, then extending her arms one at a time to work the ache from her back. Uvnee twitched one ear but otherwise ignored her rider's behavior, having decided it did not indicate a threat about to eat them both.

She let Uvnee fall behind slightly as they wound their way past a series of those tall, jagged rocks, slowing to look more closely at the way the rock was layered and cracked like sugar candy. She could have reached out and touched one as they passed, but instead kept her fingers wrapped around the leather of the reins, her free hand resting on the fabric of her skirt. She looked away from the ridge of rock, focusing instead on the now-familiar set of Gabriel's shoulders in front of her, his dun coat nearly matching the dust Steady's hooves were kicking up. Her boots were coated in the same dust, her hat no longer brightly new, if not as battered as Gabriel's own, her dark braid stiff with sweat no matter how many times she brushed it each night.

She remembered that last night in Flood and wondered, if she looked in a mirror now, who would she see?

The back of her neck itched again, but she ignored it. There was no insect, no cloth fluttering there; it was only nerves, and she would not let nerves control her. She would go where she was sent, and speak to the people she met, and learn their names, their problems.

Be the boss's eyes and ears and his voice, just the way he'd told her to be. She could do that. She'd been frightened the day she first served drinks, too, and that had turned out to be easy . . .

"Ho-wa, riders."

The voice came from out of thin air, halting them in their tracks. Ahead of her, Steady was true to his name, planting all four hooves firm on the ground, not startling at all. Uvnee shifted uneasily, even as Izzy pulled the reins in and looked around, tightening her legs in case the mare bolted.

Izzy would have panicked as well, save Gabriel seemed completely calm, as though he heard voices from nowhere every day. She forced her breathing to ease, her body to mimic his, as she'd done so often in the saloon, taking her cues from the older, more experienced women.

"Who are you?" the voice asked.

"I am Gabriel Kasun, also known to the Hochunk as Two Voices." Gabriel wasn't as calm as he seemed; she knew him well enough to pick up the faint tremor in his voice, even though his body was perfectly still. Too still, maybe. Gabriel normally sat loosely in the saddle, the same as he had in the chair in the saloon, his limbs relaxed but ready, not this close-held tension.

"And the girl-child?"

Izzy wanted to bristle at being called a child, but uncertainty and training kept her well-spoken when Gabriel nodded at her to respond. "Isobel née Lacoyo Távora of Flood."

A dry cough was the only response to that. She found herself trying to see where the voice came from without obviously searching. Gabriel was looking off to the left side of the road, but she couldn't see anything there, save a single jut of stone rising hip-high and some scrub. Anything hiding behind it would have to be on their belly, coiled like a snake.

"Have we crossed a barrier unknowing?" Her mentor shifted in his saddle and pushed his hat back, as if to give someone a better look at his face.

The voice came from a different angle, as though the speaker had moved, though Izzy had seen nothing. "Riders always do."

Gabriel chuckled, low and amused, not alarmed. "I suppose we do. Have we given offense?"

Izzy gasped as a man appeared at Uvnee's side, a bone-handled knife held crosswise at her leg. She did not doubt that it could cut through cloth and flesh down to the bone if the wielder chose. She swallowed a squeak of protest, even as Gabriel turned his gelding slowly so he could keep both her and the road ahead in clear view.

"If you had given offense, you would be dead, not speaking," the stranger said, not the same voice that had stopped them. He was looking at Gabriel, not her, as though she were of no more importance than the horses or mule.

Insulted, she brought her gaze up from the blade, refusing to let her fear rule her. The man holding the knife was clad in a sleeveless tunic made of tanned leather, what looked like black horsehair hanging in a fringe across his chest from shoulder to shoulder, a body no broader than her own, and smelling of something faintly acrid and sweet. The skin of his arm was lighter than she'd half expected, lighter than Ree's skin, coppery-red rather than red-black, contrasting with the bone handle of the knife in his hand and the pale brown of the leather. His hair was long and clotted with stone-dust, but black as a crow underneath, darker even than hers, and when he lifted his face to look at her, his eyes were dark as well, deep-set in a wide-boned face. Older than her, she thought, but not by so very much. Once past the blade still held to her calf, he did not seem threatening at all—but then, he did not have to be, holding that knife.

Natives find their own trouble, the boss's voice echoed in her memory. *They need nothing from me and want less.*

She remembered the story of her parents, and their dilemma was suddenly real to her for the very first time. If these warriors decided they did not belong here . . .

"Two Voices, and the Old Man's Hand," came the second voice again. The boy eased the pressure off the blade but did not lift it from her leg. "Why does the Old Man walk our lands?"

If he could have sworn without making matters worse, Gabriel would have. But there was nothing he could say: the question had not been asked of him but Isobel.

He nodded at her again, telling her to respond.

"The devil walks where he will," and wasn't she cool as midwinter rain, for all that she had to be terrified? "He does not challenge you, but he holds the Territory nonetheless. The first people ceded him that right."

He bit the inside of his cheek, waiting to see the reaction to that. No one knew how the devil had come to the Territory, or why he claimed it; nobody knew what accommodation he'd come to with the native tribes back then, or if it had been a negotiation or bloody battle. Even children and old drunks didn't speculate, although if you'd asked anyone, they'd probably have suggested the devil'd won it in a card game. And you of certainty didn't sass to a native about that, not if you valued your skin or your scalp.

Except she wasn't sassing, he realized. She was just saying what she'd always been told. And odds were, it was going to get them both killed, nothing he could do to stop it.

"The Old Man protects the bones," the invisible speaker said. "All know this. But can he protect from what he does not see?" It could have been a threat but wasn't. "Bones may be cracked," the voice went on, "and even one such as he should be wary."

Gabriel saw the glint of a blade off to the side and breath caught in his throat, but the visible warrior merely tapped Isobel's leg with the flat of the knife before he stepped away, moving so smoothly they didn't hear him disappear any more than they'd heard him come.

"What—" Isobel started to ask, but Gabriel lifted all five fingers away from his palm, and she fell silent, her hand dropping to her leg where the knife had rested. The boy had counted coup on Isobel, letting them know he could have killed her had he wished to, but chose not to. Why? Why accost them at all?

He breathed out and in three times, waiting. Niukonska, he thought, trying to place exactly where they were on the map he carried in his memory. The style of clothing, the hair: almost certainly Niukonska, or close cousins. And hard-learned senses told Gabriel that they hadn't come alone. A hunting party, the same as had made the camp they saw earlier? The game here was sparse, but it was possible.

The other explanations were either a scouting party, in which case they needed to rethink their path to avoid whatever might be brewing, or a religious ceremony, in which case both groups, having made suitable noises of respectful noninterest, could ignore each other hereafter. That would explain why they were stopped with a warning rather than an arrow. But their interrogator had worn no ceremonial paint, had not worn robes nor a headdress. So, perhaps it was merely a hunting party, making sure they had no competition for whatever animals roamed here.

But making assumptions was not only dangerous, it was often deadly. So, he waited, stretching his legs down into his heels, his spine up into his scalp, the gelding's easy breathing matching his own.

"Where do you go, riders?"

The first voice again, now coming from ahead of them on the trail.

"Riding," he said. "This is a mentorship ride. J'enseigne cet enfant comment monter," and then again in Hochunk. *My companion is a child; I am her guardian*, he'd said, more or less. The devil alone knew if it translated into whatever language the Niukonska spoke. He was Two Voices, not All Voices, and the only local tongue he spoke with any fluency was Hochunk. But a mentorship ride should be protected, just as he would steer clear of an initiation rite. That was customary law and tribal law.

"You teach the Old Man to ride?" There was scorn and mockery in the boy's voice now, and he felt an itch to reach for the gun slotted against the saddle leathers, even though he knew damn well the moment he went for it, he'd be holding arrows the ugly side in.

"I am the Devil's Hand." Her voice was like church bells back east, high and fine, and rang out in the air just the same. "And every hand must learn to hold a knife, to wield a pen—or draw a bow. Is this not so, elder cousin? Have you not taught your own hands the same?"

Silence, and Gabriel wasn't sure who was more taken aback by her brass, their unseen interrogator, himself, or Isobel herself.

"This is not he who teaches you." That was the second voice again, now coming from the left side. He was shifting to show he could, while remaining invisible to white eyes? Were there only two of them? No, at least one more, although Gabriel couldn't locate them yet. Sweat dampened his back and arms, the flutter of blood in his veins still too fast for calm thinking, but he needed calm. Needed to find a way out of this before the girl got them both killed.

But they'd called her the Hand first. They'd known she belonged to the Old Man. Would they really injure one close to the devil himself, or her guide, for a passing offense?

When in doubt, be cautious. When cornered, be bold. When dealing with natives, be aware that likely whatever you do will be wrong.

"I've taken the Old Man's silver," he said. "Taken oath to protect her." He wet his lips with his tongue and went on. "We intend no offense and will not hunt if these are your grounds, but we are riding through."

It was a risk, adding insolence to her sass, but while they might allow a coward to live, they would not respect him, and he needed to ride these roads even after the girl was gone.

There was silence, almost deep enough to hear the brush growing and the rocks cracking, before the sensation of being watched abruptly disappeared. Under his legs, Steady let out a groan, his sides expanding as though he'd been holding his breath too.

"Are they gone?" Isobel's voice shook, now.

"I don't know," he said. "But we should be." He kicked Steady into movement, trusting her to follow.

They rode the rest of the day without stopping, save to let the horses graze for a bit. When her stomach grumbled, Izzy ate a piece of charqui from her saddlebag, having stolen most of it from the mule's pack days before. The dry-cured meat tasted like Ree's kitchen smelled, slightly spicy and warm. It tasted like home. Today, though, that brought no comfort, and she put the strip back half-eaten.

Occasionally, Gabriel would drop back a little, look at her like he was about to speak, and then reclaim the lead without saying anything. Izzy was thankful for that. She had questions—she had a hundred questions—but she didn't know which ones to ask yet, or if she should even ask any of them. And she didn't have answers to anything he might have asked.

She'd never encountered a native before, not up close. Once or twice, a party had come to Flood, but they'd stood outside the town's boundaries until the boss went out to treat with them. They never came inside, and she'd never been allowed to serve the meals he took with them, either; Marie and Rosa had done that.

Why had they been stopped? How had they moved so quietly? And what had they meant about the devil being wary? What had they meant about bones cracking? Was this something she need warn the boss of? And if so . . . how? She had no carrier pigeons, no way to send a letter until they reached the next town with a carrier-box.

Every shred of confidence she'd gathered since Patch Junction seemed scattered again, leaving her shivering with doubt. By the time the sun began to sink into the horizon, casting long red fingers across the sky, Izzy had convinced herself that she'd done something terrible, committed some awful mistake, and to speak of it to Gabriel, to ask any questions, would simply prove her failure further.

"We'll camp up ahead." His voice was rough from a day's disuse, and he coughed, then tried again. "There's a spot that I've used before, assuming nothing has disturbed it."

Animals were known to get into caches, Izzy knew, or a winter storm. . . . Izzy could only imagine what might have happened during one of the storms that swept through the prairie during the winter months. But when they came to it, they found a cleared area just off the road, with a thin line of scrub trees behind, a charred circle where previous fires had been lit, and a small stone-built cache of dried chips for fuel. There was no source of fresh water, but it otherwise seemed near perfect.

"Unpack the mule, pull what you need for the night, stash the rest of the packs there," Gabriel said, pulling the saddle off Steady and placing it carefully on the ground, as though she hadn't already learned to do just that. Before she could bristle at the reminder, he bent to retrieve something and then walked off without another word into the scrub.

"Huh." Izzy stared after him, then untacked Uvnee and placed her gear near Steady's, then turned to deal with the mule, who was waiting patiently for its turn.

"At least you don't take moods," she said, petting the smooth hide above its nose-whiskers. "Good boy. And do you even have a name? We just call you 'boy' or 'mule' all the time. That's hardly polite."

The mule flipped one long ear and lipped her other hand, clearly wondering why she was asking about silly matters when there was a hungry mule to be unpacked and fed.

Once the animals were cared for and the packs stacked where Gabriel had indicated, Izzy looked around, trying to find a good place for her kit. Not too far from the fire, for warmth, but not so close she risked sparks catching. . . . She frowned, trying to determine a proper distance, then set about clearing the area of as many rocks as she could find, pitching them away from where the horses were grazing with perhaps a bit more force than was necessary.

Why had Gabriel just gone off like that? Was he was angry with her?

She should have followed his lead, not sassed? But looking back, she thought that the knife the boy had been holding was for show. If the natives wanted her—them—dead, they would have been left on the trail for buzzards and crows, the horses and mule and all their belongings taken or abandoned. That had been . . . a warning? A test?

A test she'd failed?

"If someone would only tell me what I'm sup—" She broke off the complaint midway through, ashamed of herself. If the boss'd wanted her to know things, he would have told her. He'd had the training of her entire life, hadn't he? She knew how he worked. And Gabriel seemed to go the same way. So, either she would learn what she needed or she already knew and just hadn't figured it yet.

"So, come on, Izzy," she said to herself. "What do you know?"

Gabriel wasn't back yet. She found a flattish rock nearby large enough to sit on, drawing her knees up and wrapping her arms around them. The stone was cold through her skirt, but it warmed up, and the sun was warm on her arms and face, the faint scent of something spicy carrying over the dust and grass.

They'd spoken English, at least a little, and Gabriel had spoken to them in what she thought'd been French. But he'd then said something else, the same language she'd heard him singing in before. Two Voices, he'd called himself, had mentioned a tribe who'd called him that.

Natives who wanted to trade learned at least a little English, Spanish—or French if they were up north, she supposed. But what if she encountered natives who hadn't learned? How could she make herself understood?

"No. It's not the words; it's what he said. How he said it." Gabriel had known how to speak to them, how to behave. Like playing faro or poker, there were good cards to hold and cards you folded on. That was what she needed to know.

Izzy tried to recall the map the boss had set her to study, all brown lines and black lettering, sketching out the mountains and rivers, the borders where Spain pushed in and where the Americans and British lurked, and the names of the native tribes who lived within the Territory. Like she'd told Gabriel, the boss knew them all, the tribes and who they allied with, the treaties and bargains they came to among themselves. Who hunted where and who traded with whom.

He'd shown them to her, and she'd not paid enough attention. She should have studied that map more closely, memorized more. She would, she promised herself, when she returned to Flood.

Assuming she returned. Izzy felt the ghost of the knife against her leg again and reached for the small blade that now hung at her belt, for reassurance. Gabriel had said he would teach her how to better use it, and the larger one strapped to her saddle, how to shoot the carbine, not just load and hold it. She needed to learn all that, and never mind how tired she was when they made camp. If the natives had taken exception to her, had decided they'd . . . What had the other voice said? Given offense? If they had, they'd be dead now.

And if she'd had a gun? If she'd had a knife to hand? She'd probably still be dead. The only thing that protected her was who she was. What she was, whatever that was.

The palm of her hand itched, and she rubbed it against the rough fabric of her skirt, frowning at the sensation. She could feel the sweat forming under the brim of her hat, the weight of it suddenly unfamiliar again. She removed it, wiping an arm across her forehead, and placed the hat carefully by her side. She must look a sight, nearly a week on the road since Patch Junction, but there was no mirror to check her hair, no extra water for even a sponge bath. She would go to bed coated in dust. This was her life, now.

I am the Devil's Hand. What had she expected to happen, that they would jump away, that a thunderclap would sound, or the boss himself would appear to scold them? Foolishness. He had sent her away to stand on her own, not to rest on his boots. The thought came for the first time, creeping on the heels of her doubts, that she was not worthy of his expectation.

That she would fail.

"Ho, the camp!"

Izzy felt her heart near leap from her chest and found her hand resting on the blade she'd just been contemplating. She pulled it from its sheath slowly, tucking it against her forearm, the blade out of sight, and stood to greet the newcomer.

"Easy, girl. If I'd meant harm, I wouldn't have hailed, and I'd not still be standing outside your fire." The woman gestured to the charred line in the grass around their campsite. Izzy had noted it when they rode in but not thought anything of it. Of course, and now Izzy felt even more a fool. The line was a fire-ring, to establish the boundaries of the campsite. And the woman stood outside it, not intruding—and not presuming on the hospitality required within that border. Either of them could pull weapons, break promises, without censure.

Except, of course, the only weapon Isobel had was the small knife. Hardly effective at a distance, and the carbine was so far out of reach, it might as well be back in Flood.

The woman was wearing an oilcloth coat that came to her knees, her boots rising almost that high, mud-splashed even though there hadn't been enough rain to wet the dust in days. She didn't bother with a skirt for modesty, her legs long and unashamed in trousers, and Izzy felt a curl of envy in her stomach that overrode her fear. The woman's face was round and sun-browned, her hair long, pale brown and braided over one shoulder like Izzy's own, and as Izzy watched, the woman lifted her hands away from her body, palms forward and fingers up in the sign for peaceful intent.

"My name's Devorah," the woman said. "I left my beasts tethered over there"—she jerked her head to the left, where a yellow horse and a brown-and-black jenny with ridiculously long ears were contentedly munching on the grass. "There's a patch of sweetgrass there; your mule might like it too. Helps their digestion." She grimaced. "Mules need all the help they can get."

Something itched against Isobel's neck again, but this time, she didn't try to brush it away. Her palm tingled, and her fingers twitched. *Caution*, they seemed to whisper. *Caution*. Where was Gabriel?

"Cautious girl. But there comes a time, caution turns to pure inhospitality." Devorah took a step forward and turned slightly, as though to show she carried nothing behind her back, either. "I only thought a girl traveling alone might welcome some company on the road."

"She's not alone."

Devorah turned, and her face went from stillness to surprise and then delight. "Kasun? I will be washed by the Jordan, who knew you were still alive?"

"Devorah." He was standing a few yards off, and while Izzy noted he knew the woman, he didn't seem anywhere near as pleased to see her. "I've been here and there. Still alive, yes." He sighed and took off his hat, flapping it at her in vague welcome. "Enter and be welcome at our fire, although we haven't quite gotten it going yet."

"The offer is as good as the action," she responded, stepping over the charred line. "And who's your companion?"

"That's Isobel. First year on the road."

"You're mentoring?" That seemed to amuse Devorah, and Izzy felt her hackles rise. Gabriel met the woman's laugh with a stone-still face until her amusement faded, and that made Izzy feel slightly better. "Well. Welcome to the road, Isobel." She made a gesture to the mule. "I've a fresh-caught rabbit to add to your pot, if you're in need of meat."

Izzy's mouth started to water, and she hoped Gabriel said yes. She was awfully tired of beans, dried pork, and charqui.

"We wouldn't say no," Gabriel said. "Isobel, if you've the need, there's a patch thataway. . . ." And he jerked his head toward the trees where he'd disappeared to.

She nodded her understanding and headed away from the campsite, curiosity about the newcomer losing to the need to empty her bladder in private, and the awareness that he wanted her away for a reason. After relieving herself, Izzy took her hair down from its braid and finger-combed it out, scraping her nails along her scalp, and then rebraided it, wishing again for a mirror and a comb. "And while you're at it, a warm bath and fresh-milled soap?" she mocked herself.

She would settle for rabbit.

Judging enough time had passed, she went back to the camp. If they'd exchanged words, it wasn't clear, or it had been settled peaceably. A small campfire was crackling, deep red flames licking at the cow chips, the coalstone a sullen black glow in its center. Devorah was cross-legged in front of it, preparing the rabbit for cooking, a pile of bones on a piece of leather at her side. The knife in her hand was small, with a wicked curve that slid through flesh easily, and her movements reminded Izzy of Ree's, that same casual comfort dismembering things.

She was a rider, Izzy thought. Like Gabriel. Only a woman. Like the woman she'd seen back in Patch Junction, the one with the leathers, and the silvery hair?

Gabriel was knelt down, unloading items from his pack. He frowned at the leather packets and replaced two of them, keeping one out. She studied the newcomer, then walked—practicing her steps to see if she could move as silently as the native—to stand next to him.

"Devorah. You are friends?" She spoke quietly, pitched only for his ears.

"Not so much friends as two people who have known each other for a very long time," he said dryly. "There's a difference." He stood, brushing dirt from his knees. "I trust her at our fire. And I'm not about to turn away fresh meat I didn't have to hunt."

Izzy hesitated, then plunged on. "What did she mean about you still being alive?"

"Nothing. An old scar she feels the need to pick at, to see if I will flinch."

It wasn't nothing. Izzy had learned to read men in the smoke-filled interior of the saloon, to judge their words and actions. Something bothered Gabriel about those words. But she had risked pushing, and he had refused. She dared not push again.

‡ ‡ ‡

Whatever else Devorah might be, Izzy admitted that she was good company. Hearing a third voice with new stories—and the willingness to share them—had been a pleasure added to the fresh rabbit.

The last of the bones had been salted and cast into the fire, the grease wiped off hands and mouths, and they were down to the last dregs of the bitter black coffee. Things called out in the darkness, and there was the occasional rustling in the grasses, but whatever was moving in the night saw their fire sparking and avoided it. Devorah pulled out a flask when the coffee was done, and Gabriel had taken a long pull, but Izzy shook her head; she'd had whiskey before and not liked it.

"Been down south the past year, myself. Led settlers in, dropped them off at their site, then wandered for a bit." Devorah's voice was casual, almost too casual, and Izzy lowered her mug and listened intently.

They'd been exchanging stories about the road—or rather, Gabriel and Devorah had, with Izzy silently listening. For the most part, it had been minor things, of new boardinghouses like the one they'd stayed in earlier, or a road washed out by rains. But this was different.

"De Marquina still trying to poke holes in the border?"

"Not so's they'll admit, no more than usual." Devorah sounded disgusted. "But the folk along the border are skittish, keeping watch on everything that moves and no little that doesn't."

De Marquina, Izzy knew, was the viceroy of Nueva España. He ruled the territory to the south and along the western flank, holding it in the name of the faraway king of Spain, whose name she could not remember. Spain, who thought the Territory evil.

"But what of the Agreement?" she asked. "Does Spain wish to cause trouble?" The boss had stopped them years before; he would have to ride out and remind them if they pushed, same as he'd done to the north.

"Spain wants nothing that will cost money," Devorah said. "But I doubt her king pays overmuch attention to the push and shove of borders, so long as nothing official occurs. And if a farmstead or three is consumed along the way? Eventually, it'll be like the land was always theirs, no cost to them. Everyone wins."

"Except the people along the border," Izzy said.

"Most people don't care overmuch whose rules they live under," Devorah said. "At least, not until it inconveniences them."

"Still, a few border incursions shouldn't be making them skittish," Gabriel said, frowning at her. "They know how this game is played, a push here and a push back, and a formal apology when the devil turns his eye on them."

"You wouldn't think so, would you? The fact is, they don't know *why* they're upset, only that they are, and that's what makes me nervous. You know me, Kasun; I see no reason to staying where things are unpleasant. I'm heading northeast, far north as I can get before I have to deal with the damn Métis and the British. At least they know enough to keep out of our way."

"They were a bit distracted by the colonists in recent years," Gabriel said dryly.

"You would know, wouldn't you?" Devorah looked sly in the firelight. "So, what do you think; are these United States going to survive?"

"The boss thinks so," Izzy said, finally having something to add to the conversation.

"Does he, now." Devorah didn't sound disbelieving so much as wanting to be convinced, and Izzy felt her fingers clench into a fist, a sudden spurt of irritation flooding her thoughts. She didn't like it, and forced her fingers to ease, straighten. As she did so, the irritation also faded, and she could hear the insects chirping and trilling again beyond the fire. Had they halted, or had she merely been unable to hear them in that heartbeat?

Devorah was still waiting for an answer, Gabriel staring into the fire, his legs stretched out in front of him, but from the tilt of his head, she knew he was listening too. "Yes." She thought of the conversations she'd overheard, the scattering of rumors and fact brought by travelers and the boss's messengers. Nearly twenty-five years since the colonial rebellion, longer than Izzy had been alive, and the original lands had expanded to press against the River, press and stop—for now. Because the boss had said *thus far and no farther.*

"And does he think that they, too, will test our boundaries and steal lands?" Devorah asked.

Izzy allowed a faint smile to curl her lip, not of amusement but superiority that she knew this and the older woman did not. "Why do you think they haven't already tried?"

Both Devorah and Gabriel grunted at her comment but asked no further questions, which was as well, because that was all she knew. She hadn't paid the messengers all that much attention then, and she cursed herself for that now. But the fact that she knew more than they did, she admitted to herself, made her feel a little better.

Soon after that, they turned in for the night, wrapping themselves in their bedrolls, far enough apart for privacy but close enough for comfort. The coalstone still glimmered in the ashes of the fire, but the rest of the night was pitch, the stars muffled behind clouds, the moon a faint, hazy sliver. Izzy could still taste the bitterness of the coffee in her mouth, clinging to her teeth. Her tongue felt fuzzy, her eyelids gritty, and there was a rock under her bedroll despite her having cleared the ground before she laid it out. To her left, Gabriel snored lightly, barely a dark breath against the darker rustle of air. Devorah, on the other side of the ashes, slept silently.

Izzy sighed and shifted, trying to get comfortable enough to sleep, when something moved, just at eye level.

Her entire body tensed, although she managed to keep her breathing steady, pretending she were still unaware, half-asleep. It could be anything—a badger or skunk looking for its evening meal, or . . .

"Sisssssssster."

Or a snake.

Izzy exhaled, no longer pretending to sleep, and opened her eyes as wide as she could to find the shape in the shadows. An arm's length from her face it uncoiled, the body rising up from the ground to nose height. Whatever colors its scales might be were turned to muted shadows, but the vertical-slitted eyes seemed to glow from within, and the shape of the tail, pointed toward the sky behind it, was clear.

Thankfully, the rattle remained silent. Whatever the snake wanted, it did not see her as a threat.

There was movement behind her, the reassuring pressure of Gabriel's hand on her shoulder, and then his calming words—but he was not speaking to her.

"Good evening." His whisper somehow managed to sound polite as well. "Are we in your way, elder cousin?"

Always be polite to a rattlesnake was the first lesson every child learned. Elsewhere, they might be vermin; within the Territory, the wise knew better. While they might make people jump for their own amusement, rattlers, like owls, also carried wisdom.

The snake's tongue touched the air, then it spoke again. "Curios-sssssssss. Ssssssstopping by to sssssseee the devilsssss toy."

Izzy started, only the hand on her shoulder keeping her from doing something drastic and startling the snake into an unfortunate reaction. Its tongue flickered out a second time, testing the still night air. In the distance an owl hooted, and something rustled in the trees, but the snake didn't seem to notice.

"I am no toy," Izzy said hotly, her shock knocked aside by irritation, milder than what she'd felt before, but sharp and hurtful inside to be dismissed so.

"Who sayssssss I sssssspeak of you?" The snake's wedge-shaped head turned to her, the tongue flickering out again, and she could hear the amusement in its tone. "Little sssssssisssssster. You do not yet play a role in thisssss sssscene."

"And now you have seen us," Gabriel said, his voice still a whisper, still polite, but backed with more authority than before, as though he felt himself on firmer ground despite the snake's mocking.

"Be wary and beware," the snake said, its eyes still on Izzy. "Your enemiessssss are not who you think." It hissed what might have been a laugh, and flicked its gaze to Gabriel. "But then, neither are your friendssssss. The land twistsssssss."

Izzy wanted to ask what it meant by that, but its dismissal of her still stung, and her pride kept her mouth shut. The snake hissed again, in amusement or maybe approval or something else entirely, Izzy didn't know. Animals that gave warnings . . . that was a medicine for natives and magicians, not . . .

Well, she stopped that thought dead. Why *not* her? If Gabriel could speak to it, get answers, why couldn't she?

But by the time she thought of what she'd ask, the snake was gone, the space in front of her empty save for some crushed grasses and the cool, now-silent air. Gabriel's hand lifted from her shoulder, but his presence remained behind her.

"It called me sister," she said quietly, grasping that one thing. "Not little cousin. Why?"

"I don't know," Gabriel said, his hand still warm on her shoulder. "Likely it smelled the devil's touch on you. Puts you one ahead of the rest of us mere mortals."

He was joshing her. Or mayhap not. "You think it meant . . ." She didn't finish the sentence, didn't look over her shoulder to where Devorah still slept, but he took her meaning nonetheless.

"I don't know," Gabriel said again. "But when you hear warnings, even if they don't make much sense at the time, you tuck 'em away until they do. And you play it cautious until then."

"I—I wanted to ask it—" and she was horrified to feel hot tears forcing their way past her eyelids, the feeling of having worked up her courage only to be denied making her want to yell, to make exactly the kind of fuss Marie would have frowned at. Biting her lower lip until the tears stopped, Izzy shook her head as though to say it didn't matter.

"It's gone. Go to sleep, Isobel," Gabriel said, rising to move away. He didn't understand. Izzy sank back down into her bedroll, ignoring the rock still digging into her, and closed her eyes.

The tears flowed then, silently, until she fell asleep.

Izzy felt the sunrise under her lids even before she opened them to see the stretch of morning light reaching into the sky. Her head ached, and her lashes were sticky with sleep, but her body, for the first time, didn't immediately remind her of every ache and bruise. She stretched cautiously, and there was a faint burn in her arms and calves, but that was the kind that would ease as the day went on, not get worse.

Before she could celebrate, she turned her head to where the snake had been the night before. The ground was bare, no sign that anything had occurred, but the memory of it—of being dismissed by the snake—still rankled. But . . . had the snake done something to make her feel better? Could it do such a thing?

No, she decided. It was coincidence.

Then she heard the rustling noises that meant someone was already awake, and she pushed away the doubts of the night before. The snake had called her *sister*. Any warning it had to deliver had been aimed at Gabriel, not her. Nothing was going to go wrong.

When she pushed her blanket aside and sat up, she almost believed it herself.

"There's water for washing," Devorah said, seeing she was awake.

Izzy rubbed at her eyes, pulling the sleep from her lashes, and gave the other woman a polite smile in thanks, a smile that turned into something brighter when she tested the water in the pan, and realized that it had been warmed just enough to counteract the morning chill, something Gabriel never bothered to do. She washed her face, then used the face cloth to scrub her arms, legs, and feet until she felt clean again.

Izzy was still uncomfortable being half-dressed outside, and she quickly buttoned her skirt and blouse over her chemise, and pulled on woolen stockings before checking her boots for anything that might have crawled into them overnight, and lacing them up. She felt a moment's regret for clean linens, but the scent of dried lavender they used in the drawers was a near-lost memory now, under every day's horseflesh, smoke, and sweat.

"Coffee'll be ready in a span," Devorah said. "Himself's already awake and grumbling like a bear."

Gabriel woke early, but he didn't wake easy. She wondered if Devorah had tried to speak with him, or if she knew better. She wondered how well they knew each other, and for how long, and what wound had scabbed over that the other woman tried to pick at. Izzy wondered those things, but she didn't ask. It was enough that they were here, sharing the road and the predawn silence.

The fire Devorah had started was small but offered a comforting warmth, and the coffeepot sat on its tripod over the flames, the smell making Izzy's nostrils flare and her mouth water. In all that was still strange and new, the bitter smell was familiar, a connection home, and as the sky brightened to a clear blue, the light filling the air, it was hard to remember the darkness and shadows of the night before, hard to remember the feeling she'd had when the snake slipped up to her face, the words it uttered, and she was half thinking the exhaustion and uncertainty and rabbit for dinner had combined to give her a too-real dream.

Except she was too much a child of Flood to discount any dream that real.

Izzy sat on the flat stone nearest the fire, curled her legs underneath her, and accepted the battered tin mug Devorah handed her. The warmth was nearly enough to burn her fingers, and she put it down on the ground next to her, to let it cool before she drank it. While she waited, she unbraided her hair, letting the strands fall down her back. Her scalp felt dry and itchy, but when she ran her fingers through her hair, the strands felt unpleasantly oily.

"Men don't talk about it," Devorah said, watching her, "but after a few weeks on the dust roads, you'll be daydreaming of a bath, and after a month or two, you'd trade your companion to the nearest demon for a safe pool to wash in. That's my advice for you: never turn down the chance to wash your hair."

Then she reached into her pack and handed Izzy a small brown paper packet. "Soda ash. Rub a little into your scalp, only a little! That will help. Keep it dry or it becomes useless."

"Thank you." Izzy took the packet. It fit into her hand, lightweight, with something soft and granular moving inside the paper. She'd never been given a gift before, not from someone she didn't know, and she wondered if she should give something back in return.

"I don't know why you've taken to the road so young," Devorah went on, "and I'm not going to ask. But there are damn few of us riding, and every trick needs to be shared." The older woman gave her a sideways grin and flicked her own braid over her shoulder. "No need to tell the boys."

"Tell the boys what?" Gabriel's suspenders hung down at his waist, his hair sleep-tousled, and he needed a shave, the rough bristles covering his cheeks and chin with shadow.

"Girl things," Devorah said, not cheekily, not saucy the way Molly might, but matter-of-factly, as though that were the end of the discussion.

Gabriel snorted and reached for the coffeepot. "Then I thank you for not sharing."

He wasn't sure what sort of conversation he'd stumbled back into, but he caught the long-suffering glance Devorah gave Isobel, woman-to-woman, and hid a grin behind his coffee. The girl'd spent her entire life in the relatively sheltered environs of the saloon; devil or no, all this—him—had been an abrupt change from what she'd been used to. Not that Dev was what you'd call the mothering sort, but she was female, and he supposed that mattered.

Good influences were for preachermen and stay-at-homes. Isobel was going to be the Devil's Left Hand, whatever that ended up meaning. She needed a different kind of influence.

"Weather looks to hold another day or two." He took a seat by the fire, Isobel to his left, Devorah across the low flames. "You were heading north, you said? The trails should all be cleared by now, but be careful. It was a cold winter; the momma bears are going to be taking anything that looks like food up there."

Devorah made a rude gesture with three fingers. "I'm always careful. You know that."

"I've never seen a bear," Isobel said.

"Try not to," Devorah said. "They're large, smelly, and mean."

"Only in the spring," Gabriel said.

"They smell all the time," Devorah said, wrinkling her nose. "Worse than you."

"Feel free to make your own campsite next time," he said without offense, steadfastly ignoring the look the two women gave each other. He was a fine friend to soap when he had it, but when you were on the road, you smelled like the road; that's all there was to it.

The conversation lapsed after that, a comfortable, lazy silence taking over, until Devorah turned her mug upside down, spilling the dregs of her coffee into the dirt. "Well, it was good to run into friendly faces," she said, tucking the tin mug into her pack and standing up, "and I appreciate the shared fire."

"Good to see you still breathing," he said, raising his own mug in salute. He'd been true to Isobel: the two of them weren't friends, but they had known each other a long time. It was good to see her well and kicking.

"You take care, Isobel," Devorah said to her. "Don't let this one sell you for a wife."

"Not a soul here who could afford me," Isobel shot back, and Devorah laughed.

"Yeah, you might just do, Isobel, you might just do."

Dev picked up her pack and hauled it to where her mule waited, ear to ear with their own mule like a pair of gossips. She saddled the horse and loaded the pack onto the mule, tightening straps and checking the fit, then led the beasts onto the trail, disappearing around a bend, the way they'd come the night before.

Gabriel turned back to the fire and looked at Isobel. "You look like something bit your nose. What?"

The girl's hair was loose around her shoulders, and it made her look too young. "She didn't say good-bye."

"No more than you did when you left Flood," he pointed out. "And you knew those folk a sight better than she knows you—or me, for that matter." She still looked upset, and he shook his head. He'd forgotten she was green, for just a moment. "You don't say good-bye," he told her. "Not unless it's the last farewell. The road curves on itself, and you'll turn around and there she'll be again, maybe tomorrow, maybe ten years from now."

That wasn't entirely true. Once you took to the road, you didn't expect to see anyone twice again, but why assume the worst? Leave it open, leave the farewells unsaid. That was how he'd sorted it, anyway. He didn't know how other folk felt.

"Is that why the snake just left?" She said it quietly, as though it weren't a question, and she didn't mean for him to hear.

"Snakes are just bastards," he said anyway. "Wise, but bastards."

If possible, her eyes got wider. "So . . . it really happened?"

That made him laugh, the sound rough in his throat. "If it didn't, we both had the same dream, and on the road, that's the same thing as it really happening." Towns pulled in tight, people setting up protections as they were able. Outside, especially on the road, you were more vulnerable; things could get in. She should know this already. They'd sent a child out with him, for all that the law said otherwise. What had the devil been thinking?

He made a face at that thought. The devil kept his thoughts to himself, and an honest man was thankful for that.

"Why did it speak to us? Was it truly a snake, or . . . ?"

At least they'd taught her that much caution, to not even indirectly call the dancers' attention. Territory had enough trouble in it; no need to give the land itself ideas.

"It's hard to tell with rattlers." Rattlesnakes were prone to sticking their noses in, and they'd been unprotected, off the road. And stories claimed rattlers had an affinity with the devil and his kin, making sense it'd called her little sister.

But he'd been drawn to Isobel's side when he should have been sound asleep, and they'd managed not to wake Devorah, who normally would be alert at the first movement. And it hadn't made a lick of sense, what the snake had said. All that called for it being a dream. It hadn't felt like one, though, not the least because he'd been unable to fall asleep again after, staring at the sky overhead until first light chased the last stars away.

He wasn't sure which would be worse news, if a dream-dancer chose to poke into their dreams, or a snake had something to say to them. But Isobel was waiting on his answer.

"I'm pretty sure it was actually a rattlesnake. I'm too tired for it to have been a dream."

His reassurance didn't seem to have reassured her a bit. Fair enough: he'd managed to unreassure himself. If a rattler were paying attention to them, that meant other things might be too. So, there was her next lesson.

"There are things out here, Isobel. Things we understand, and a hell of a lot more we don't. Not even your boss does entire, I'm thinking. Maybe the tribes, but they've each got different stories to tell it, and they don't share 'em all with us. What I do know is that our visitor chose to stop by for its own reasons, spoke to us for its own reasons, and it may not be in our best interests to poke too deep into those reasons or worry too much about what it said until we've got some idea what it was talking about."

She looked away, but some of the tension left her face. "Do you think it lied?"

"Snakes don't lie." Not in the flesh, anyway. Wasn't a soul alive could tell what a dream-dancer might do. "They don't tell the truth, neither, not the way we see it. Didn't they teach you any of this, Izzy?"

"Not enough," she said, a sour twist to her mouth. "Obviously."

"Right. Once we're on our way, we'll remedy that. Start with snakes and work our way through." Odds were, a rider wouldn't ever encounter one spirit animal, much less more, in their entire life—and at that, they had more chance than most. But as Isobel was the Devil's Hand, he wasn't going to assume anything.

It wasn't until she'd nodded and gone off to pack up her own kit that he realized he'd called her Izzy, the way that girl had, back in Patch Junction, instead of Isobel. He dumped his own coffee and stretched, arms reaching to the sky until he felt something in his back crack. He'd need to watch that. "Izzy" might be fine for a saloon girl, but not the Devil's Hand. And he could not afford to take liberties or see her as anything other than the woman she'd need to become.

Everyone might be equal in the territory, but only a fool didn't acknowledge power, be it a gun, a knife, or medicine. And the Devil's Hand would carry all three.

They broke camp in a silence that was somewhere between comfortable and awkward, and if Gabriel saw her glancing off to the side several times, checking for anything that might slither, he didn't mention it. Her silence continued once they saddled up, and they rode northwest along the curve of a shallow-cut creek, both of them wrapped in their own thoughts.

By the time they paused to stretch their legs midday, he'd had enough. The creek had widened into something that could honestly claim the name, and he distracted Isobel from her thoughts by showing her how to spot sakli and trout in the shallows, to stand so that the sun didn't cast a shadow and scare them away. He was already a few days off schedule thanks to taking it slower on Isobel's behalf; another few hours wouldn't make a difference to where they were going, and fresh fish was always a welcome change.

And watching her face when she took that first bite of fish, the skin crackled and crisped with a dab of molasses, the flesh practically falling off the knife, was worth it.

"Ree never made fish like this," she said. He guessed Ree had been the saloon's cook.

"Soup or fried," he guessed. "Makes sense. Fish feeds a lot more that way. But there's nothing like pan-cooked trout, in my experience. Makes fishing worth the bother."

The delay meant it wasn't until nearly dusk that the road brought them to a small copse of black cherry, the circle-and-square burned into one of the older trees telling him they'd reached the first of his scheduled stops. A narrow path led off the road, through the trees to a bridge spanning the river, the planks rough-hewn and weathered, and when Isobel turned to look at him, her expression dubious, he nodded.

"Home sweet home for the night," he said.

"That bridge looks . . . old."

He snorted. "Older than you and twice as strong. Go on, Isobel."

Isobel gave the bridge another dubious look but sent Uvnee over it without hesitation, Gabriel following once she was on the other side, the mule, as ever, trailing faithfully behind. He had confidence the bridge was still strong, but there was no point testing it with two horses at once.

On the other bank, the land had been cleared of grasses and replaced by a small garden patch, beyond which were three cabins draped in darkness.

He was about to call out to the house, announce their arrival, when Isobel reined the mare in suddenly, her spine and shoulders rising up on alert. Gabriel had his hand resting on the carbine's butt even as he caught up with her, glancing at her pale face before following her gaze to the structures a few hundred yards down the path.

"What happened?" Her voice was a scarce whisper, as though she were afraid of startling something, and her gaze darted nervously, as though expecting something to attack.

"I don't know. Stay here."

Gabriel swung out of the saddle, feeling his feet hit the ground with a jolt. They'd been sleeping rough since leaving Patch Junction, and he'd been anticipating a real bed all day. But he'd been on edge too since the snake's visitation, although he hadn't let himself acknowledge it. The rattler's words had been for him as much—maybe more—than her, and he didn't like so much of the medicine world paying attention to him all at once.

But the nights since then had passed unmolested, other than a badger who'd taken offense at their campsite, and nothing of the uncanny had crossed their steps.

Until now.

Widder Creek barely qualified as a dot on his map: three one-story cabins set in a curve of the river that gave it its name, just enough farmland cleared to support a family and not much more. The couple that'd settled there had come with two sons, who'd both married Hutanga girls. There should have been small children playing in the courtyard, movement in the field, someone doing laundry or chores in the shared barn.

Instead, there was stillness and silence.

Next to him, Steady shifted, restless, and Isobel exhaled, a tiny breath that should not have sounded so loud. "Should I . . ."

"Stay here," he repeated. He unlatched the carbine from his saddle and took a moment to load it. But even as he did so, he knew that it wouldn't be needed. Not to put down a threat, anyway.

He hadn't even reached the door of the first cabin before he smelled it: the horrible, too-familiar sweetness of decay and shit. He didn't want to go any farther but forced his body to keep moving, one sleeve over his mouth in a faint hope of keeping the worst from his lungs.

There were two bodies sprawled on the floor, just past the doorway. Adults, a man and a woman, fully dressed, the visible skin blackened and bursting. His gorge rose, and he gagged it back down again, not wanting to befoul the scene more. A quick glance into the house showed no sign of violence or bloodshed, and no sound coming from deeper inside the house.

He backed out, closing the door behind him, and then bent down to rub his hands in the dirt before dusting them off on his trouser leg. He would not vomit. He would not.

"Gabriel?"

"Stay where you are," he said, but could hear her walking toward him already. He shook his head and turned to glare at her.

"They're dead." She wasn't asking.

"Yah. Looks like sickness. Something fast." Not influenza, not the way the bodies had fallen. There hadn't been plague in the Territory for years that he'd heard of, but he didn't hear everything. "Stay out here; I need to check the other houses."

"No."

"What?" He stopped, staring at her. She lifted her chin defiantly, the brim of her hat not hiding the determination in her eyes or the stubborn set of her chin.

"I don't know if these people made a Bargain with the boss, but they were part of the Territory, and if a sickness did kill them all, then I need to know. Don't I?"

He couldn't fault her logic, only the application of it. "You can know as well waiting here as going inside."

"You think I haven't seen the dead before?" Isobel's expression, if anything, got harder. "I've seen death."

His gut instinct was to tell her, again, to wait here. She was only—

"You're not supposed to be coddling me," she said, so matter-of-fact that he had no comeback. "I need to see."

He sighed, rubbing the back of his neck, then nodded and lifted his other hand, indicating that she should take the house to the left while he went to the right.

They burned the houses and the barn as night fell, not bothering to pull the bodies out first. Flames purified same as deep earth, and faster. Izzy braced herself to watch the roofs fall, the walls collapse in on themselves, the homestead slowly disappear in black smoke and sparks. Gabriel paced back and forth, checking on the horses and coming back, then walking away again, but she stood still, watching. There was an ache inside her that wasn't sadness—she hadn't known these people, to sorrow at their passing—but something deeper, the same blood-red heat as the sparks she was watching, the same charred remains left in their wake.

She had not lied to Gabriel; Izzy had seen the dead before. Age, injury, even influenza struck Flood, same as any other place. She'd helped wash bodies before burial, and stood vigil a time or three, once she was old enough. She knew not to linger overlong on what the body became once the spark was gone. But they had been here once. They deserved to be remembered by more than charred earth and smoke.

She turned away from the fire, went to Uvnee, and pulled the notebook she'd found on her dresser the morning she left Flood out of her pack, then turned to Gabriel, who had followed her. "What were their names?"

"What?"

"Their names."

"I . . ." Her mentor stopped to think, running a hand through shaggy hair, leaving that hand resting on the back of his neck and looking up at the night sky, as though the answer were there. "Karl was the old man. Karl and Sophia. Oldest son was . . . Simeon; younger was also Karl. I don't remember their wives or any of the kids."

She nodded and wrote their names down. *Karl and Sophia of Widder Creek. Their sons Simeon and Karl younger. Wives and children, names unknown. Dead of unknown causes,* and then the date, near as she could recall. Izzy squinted at the paper, barely able to see it in the firelight. It was likely still May—they hadn't been gone that long—but the dates slipped away without chores or deliveries to mark the days.

Gabriel didn't ask what she was doing or why. If he had, she wasn't sure she could have told him.

As soon as the ashes burned out, they saddled up and left, not wanting to linger overnight in proximity to the dead. The wooden planks of the bridge sounded fragile under their hooves, and Izzy felt a shiver coat her arms as they rode over, but neither of them paused until they reached the point where the turnoff folded back into the main road. Only then, with cleaner air in her nose and the memory of what lay behind them hidden by trees, did Izzy let herself feel sick.

Gabriel reined in beside her, a darker, more familiar shadow in the night, and pulled out the coalstone, clenching it once to create a faint glow in his hand.

Izzy wasn't sure if the pale red light made things better or worse. She turned her face away so he couldn't read her expression and asked, "What do you think killed them?"

"Could be anything. Like I said, sickness can come fast, especially them all living on top of each other like that."

She looked back at him then. "Even the animals?" There had been three horses in the barn, dead in their stalls, and a litter of pigs and chickens in the coop, a mess of feathers predators had not touched.

He shrugged. "It happens sometimes."

Not often. Not like that. Not so swiftly that they didn't have time to bury the first victims. She felt chilled, worse than cold rain on a winter's night. "The snake's warning. Now this . . ."

He picked up what she wasn't saying. "Things happen, Isobel.

Sometimes they're connected, but more often it's just . . . chance. Random."

"You think the snake was random?"

It was the first they'd spoken directly of it since that morning, and she couldn't imagine a time she wanted less to talk about it than now. Saying the words felt like she'd been punched in the stomach.

Gabriel looped Steady's reins around the pommel horn, then took off his hat and ran his fingers through his hair with his free hand. "Creatures like that are . . . like your boss. They're a law unto themselves, even in the Territory, and if you try to figure out the why or wherefore, you'll never get out of that hole. I told you already: if there was a deeper meaning to it, we're not going to know until it bites us on the nose, so there's no point worrying about it."

He was harsher-spoken than he'd been before, and Izzy felt a pang of guilt: he'd known these people, known their names, most of them, had maybe shared hospitality before. Whatever she was feeling, it had to be worse for him.

Folk had died there. Folk who should have been protected.

Make this right, she heard inside her head, a voice like water, like wind, crackling like fire. *Make it safe.*

She dismounted, her body moving without conscious direction, and pulled a square package, wrapped in an unbleached cloth, out of her saddlepack. Inside, there was a cylinder of hard-packed salt about the length of her hand and three fingers thick. She had packed it the way she'd packed everything else she'd been given, without question, assuming it would make sense in time.

Now, she went back to where the two paths diverged, knelt carefully, and dragged the cylinder across the dirt where the two trails met, leaving a clear line of salt glittering white against brown, clearly visible even in the darkness away from the coalstone's glow.

She could hear the horses shifting behind her, leather tack creaking, and the gentle sound of Gabriel exhaling, the way he drew his thoughts together before he spoke. "You think there's enough left in the ashes for a haint to linger, you need to lock it down?"

"S'not for them," she said. "It's to protect anyone else." He thought she knew nothing, and maybe she didn't, not the way he meant, but she knew this. Salt and blood to protect the living. She bit her lip, staring down at the line, then took the knife from her boot and nicked the pad of her left thumb, letting a drop of blood fall down. Just a story she'd heard, maybe a thing the boss mentioned in passing, even if she didn't remember where or when.

The blood hit the salt and *spread*, one single drop staining the entire line a deep red that glowed like an ember before fading to dark.

When she looked up again, the track they'd followed to the bridge had disappeared, the trees closing together as though no path between had ever been there, and she—even knowing the tiny settlement existed—felt a push to move away, go elsewhere. This was one road that would not be found again any time soon.

"Even folk who knew it was there, they'll forget," she said. "And nobody else will think to venture in, or wonder why the trees are there. Give the land time to reclaim the ashes, clean the land." She knew that the same way she'd known how to do it, the kenning in her like she'd lace her shoes or make a bed. Maybe the boss, or Peggy's brother the marshal, had spoken of it, told a story of doing the same, and she'd forgotten until it was needed.

Maybe. And maybe it was something else. Izzy let that thought settle in her bones, heavy and cold, as she wrapped the salt stick back in its cloth and replaced it in the pack, then swung back into Uvnee's saddle. Her hands were still lightly dusted with salt, and her mouth tasted of ashes and smoke.

"That was well done," Gabriel said quietly, his face showing the same exhaustion, and she nodded, although she didn't agree. It was what she was supposed to be doing, nothing more.

Make this right. Make it safe.

"We should keep going."

She knew that he had intended for them to stop a while at Widder

Creek, overnight there. But his suggestion that they put some distance between themselves and the ashes was one she agreed with wholeheartedly. Even the division she'd placed on the ground didn't banish the uneasy feeling she'd felt on first seeing those too-quiet houses.

Gabriel thought it was illness had killed those people, and she couldn't say it hadn't been. Illness came fast and hit hard, and could burn itself out like a match once it had nothing more to live on. And yet. And yet.

Make it right. Make it safe.

She felt the unease tremble on her skin, curl uncomfortably in her stomach, and she pushed Uvnee to go a little faster, put that much more distance behind them before night fell. The mare seemed to agree, matching Steady's longer stride without further urging.

Gabriel wasn't a fan of riding after full dark—too easy for a horse to misstep and break a leg, he said—but they didn't reach a place both of them felt comfortable stopping at until well after the waning moon had risen. He'd kept the coalstone in one hand, urging more light out of it despite the discomfort, but there was a limit what it could do without causing actual flame.

"Not perfect, but it'll do," Gabriel said finally, looking at the starlit horizon rather than the patch of grass he'd indicated. "Saddle down."

Since leaving Flood, Izzy has learned to ride all day without ache, identify a small animal in the underbrush as they rode, hit a target six times out of ten with Gabriel's carbine, and sleep through the night no matter what rocks found their way underneath her bedroll. In short, despite being shaken by what they'd found at Widder Creek, she felt capable and competent. So, when she slid out of the saddle and felt her knees buckle when she hit the ground, forcing her to grab the stirrup to stay upright, Izzy let out a swear word she wasn't supposed to know, humiliated at the way her body had failed her.

"Iz?"

Gabriel was there suddenly, holding her elbow.

"I'm all right. I just . . ."

The faint stomachache from earlier resettled low in her gut now that she was standing, a too-familiar sensation, and she let out a sudden, irritated huff of air. "I'm fine." She removed her arm from his grip, pushed away from Uvnee, and went to pull her kit from the saddle. "I'm fine."

She wanted to ask him to finish untacking Uvnee, but then he would ask what was wrong, and nothing was wrong. So, she finished the chore, making sure that the mare was settled and comfortable in her hobble, before settling her bedroll a few feet away from Gabriel's, then picking up her pack and walking a safe distance away from the camp.

She'd gotten accustomed to doing her personal business by walking far enough away, maybe behind a rock or taller grasses for some privacy, but there was nothing here save grass and more grass, and a small hill too far away to be safe. She was uneasy going too far away from the camp, as though the illness might have followed them in the darkness, lurking like a wolf for stragglers. But she trusted he'd keep his attention on the camp, and anyone else who might be watching . . . well, there wasn't a thing she could do about that.

"Idiot," she told herself. "Losing track like that." Back home—but back home, the days hadn't melted into one another the same way. She remembered Devorah and how comfortable she had seemed in her trousers, and the woman in the restaurant back in Patch Junction, so dignified in her leathers, remembered thinking she might try the same some day. For now, however, she was just as pleased for the modesty of a skirt, as she removed a set of clean rags from her pack and folded them the way she'd been taught, placing them inside her drawers.

It wasn't perfect, but it would do.

Next to the rags in her pack was a fist-sized paper wrapper. She opened it and took a pinch of the crumbled yellow buds, keeping it in her palm as she replaced everything, and returned to the campfire.

Gabriel had started a small fire already, despite the lateness of the house. He watched her but did not ask what she was doing as she pulled out a battered tin pot and set water to boil for a tisane.

Gabriel watched out of the corner of his eye as Isobel crumbled leaves into the pot of water, murmuring something under her breath. He'd been worried at first, thinking her collapse was a reaction to everything that had happened that day, and short of offering her a slug of whiskey, which she didn't like, there wasn't anything he could do to ease *that*. People died, sometimes badly, often unfairly, and that was just that. The tea suggested women's medicine, though, which he could stay out of with clear conscience. She likely wouldn't welcome any comment, no matter how kindly meant.

Nonetheless, he visualized the road in his head, trying to determine how far they could push tomorrow, and if he could call a halt earlier than usual without making it appear as though he were coddling her. By the time she'd poured the concoction into her mug and taken it back to her bedroll, where she'd curled up in a clear sign that she didn't want to talk, he had a rough plan in mind. Originally, he'd thought to stay overnight at Widder Creek, then push through until they got to Clear Rock, a few days' ride west. But now he thought they would swing north and stop at the Caron place instead. They weren't always the friendliest of folk, but if Isobel were one of those women who became snappish during her time, she'd have a suitable foil with the missus, and if she needed coddling, well, they'd have a warm bed and another woman's comfort to offer, without him being obviously complicit.

And it would be good for both of them to see living folk.

Satisfied, he pushed against the ground, meaning to get up and start preparing the evening meal, when something made him pause. A faint whisper from the stream deep belowground, the taste of rotted meat and fouled water in the back of his throat, all gone as quickly as he'd noticed them, leaving the lingering weight of something behind him. He knew the clearing was bare, the lack of cover proof that no one was watching.

And yet he knew they were being followed. They were being watched.

He tried to convince himself that it could be anything—a big cat, curious about the smell of humans and horses, or even a bear, fool-hungry after a winter's hibernation. Risks, but known ones, things you could deter and avoid, and run off with gunshot if needed. But none of that would have touched the water that way.

He looked over his shoulder at where the horses had been staked for the night. Steady had his head down, cropping at the grass, Uvnee already dozing, her weight on three legs. Only the mule was alert, looking up, but not even remotely spooked, the way he would be if an animal predator was around.

He hadn't lied to Isobel. There wasn't any point in worrying about what the snake had said; whatever was coming would come, and they could only hope being alert would be enough. But first the snake, then Widder Creek, and now this?

He thought that being alert might not be enough.

Those thoughts made him glance over to where she lay curled on her bedroll, the empty mug still clutched in one hand as though for comfort. He should tell her, warn her.

He reached down to touch the silver clasp on his boot, a habit he'd picked up when he was still green on the road himself. No, best not to alarm her, not when they were already spooked enough.

He wouldn't coddle her, but he would measure out how much she had to carry and when.

"There's still a potato or two left," he said instead, raising his voice enough that she'd hear. "Common cheese and roasted potatoes sound good to you?" It wasn't really a question; that was all they had left. He'd been counting on trading for fresh supplies in Widder

Creek, maybe convincing the old man to slaughter a lamb for them. Obviously, that hadn't worked out so well.

Isobel lifted her head as though it was an effort, her legs curled up into her stomach, arms around her knees. "I'm not hungry."

"That wasn't what I asked."

"Potatoes and cheese sounds good." She made a face, scrunching her mouth up and her nose down. "Mostly I just need the tea and to sleep."

"Real bed tomorrow," he told her. "And a bath."

She smiled briefly at that. For a moment, the events of the morning were not forgotten but shifted somewhere out of sight.

"Eat something, then sleep," he said, turning back to the fire to give her at least the illusion of privacy. "We're back on the road at sunrise."

Odds were, whatever he'd sensed had moved on by then. And if he was wrong, if whatever was watching them followed? Well, he'd deal with that then.

Justice Caron was exactly as mean-tempered as Gabriel had warned as they approached the homesteading. The man stared at them from the front of his house, a sod-and-timber shanty that looked as though the next strong wind would finish knocking it over, and lifted his bearded chin stubbornly.

"Why shouldn't I fill the both of you full of lead?" His beard quivered with indignation, but the hands on his ancient blunderbuss were steady.

"Because you're too cheap to waste shot on us," Gabriel said, clearly exasperated. "Old man, we're not here to rob you blind, just to ask for shelter for one night, and perhaps a few drops of human kindness, if you've any left in your bones."

"Hrmph. You think there's room for you here?"

Gabriel glared back. "I know for a fact that you've a shelter out back that's fit for your young 'uns as well as the occasional traveler. Seeing as how I've slept in it a time or three before."

Izzy bit the inside of her cheek to keep from giggling at the expression on the old man's face as he realized he was turning away someone he knew or at least had hosted before.

The old man squinted harder, as though that would improve his eyesight. "Gabriel Kasun, is it? You weren't traveling with no flippit back then."

"She's hardly a flippit," Gabriel said before Izzy could ask if she was supposed to be insulted by that or not. Apparently, yes. "This is Isobel née Lacoyo Távora, late of Flood." His voice went dry as a summer creekbed. "You have, I presume, heard of Flood before?"

"'Z'at a place or a person I'm supposed to know about?"

Before all this, before she'd taken the road, Izzy would have assumed the old man was lying or mad. Anyone who survived more than year in the Territory knew about Flood and who lived there. But this man, his broad shoulders stooped, brown skin grizzled, blocking their way like an old bison facing off against wolves, nearly convinced her of his ignorance. Then she looked past the surface, and something in the old man's face, or the minute way he shifted, was like a shout. He knew and was trying to get a rise out of her for some reason.

Izzy had been raised in a gaming house, and two could play that hand easily as one.

"It's all right," she said to Gabriel, making sure that her voice carried the distance between them and the shanty. "I would take no hospitality from the unwilling. If Master Justice wishes to shut his doors against travelers who have given no offense, that surely is his right. It takes a strong man to stand *entirely* alone against the Territory."

Her words weren't a threat and weren't a promise, exactly—she didn't have authority to do either thing, far as she was aware—but Izzy was pleased with the curl of curtness she put into the words, leaving the old man to wonder if there had been a threat or a promise made after all.

He sneered at her. "You Scratch's kin? Scrawnly little chicken like you?"

"Don't," Gabriel said quietly, and she wasn't sure if he was warning her or Caron. He needn't have worried about her. A girl didn't get to be a woman without running into his sort. A female wasn't supposed to have an opinion, much less authority.

"I was raised in the devil's house," she said, "and I carry his sigil." The papers in her kit had been enough for the marshal, although she strongly suspected Caron would be unable to read them. Still, the sigil would be enough. It wasn't the sort of thing a person took on without they had reason. Sigils had power of their own, like crossroads.

"Hrmph." The old man glared at her. Instinct told her to stare back; training warned her to let him have his bluster. She softened her gaze, not retreating but refusing to fight, as much a compromise as she could make.

"Old man, are you pretending that you have any say about anything that happens in this house?" The question came from Izzy's right, and she turned to see a woman standing there, her fists on her hips, glaring at the old man. She had grey hair piled in a knot on top of her head, a gingham dress that had seen better years, with a dark blue apron tied around her waist and a glare that could set a tornado back on its heels. "Because if so, you've clearly lost what few wits you were given at birth."

At her side, Gabriel coughed into his fist, and she suspected he was hiding a grin. "Miz Margaret. It's a pleasure to see you again."

"Shush, boy. It's no pleasure to see me; not even the angels could say that. But you'll get your shelter for the night and a meal besides, because we do not turn away travelers who've offered us no harm, despite what that idiot old man likes to pretend."

Gabriel doffed his hat in a half bow and slid out of the saddle, giving Izzy a tap on the leg as he did so. She dropped down off Uvnee's back, feeling the soles of her feet touch ground at the same moment her hips and knees began to ache from the change in position.

"And you, girl," the older woman said as Izzy came to Uvnee's shoulder, reaching up to ease the mare's reins. "You got a name?"

"Isobel, ma'—Miz Margaret."

"Hrmph." She sounded so much like her husband, and yet not, Izzy felt a smile slip free. "You let your man take those beasts into the corral and shuck their gear. You look like you need a hot meal and a warm compress, and to get off your tail for a bit; am I right?"

She didn't wait for a response but plowed up the stairs, past her dumbstruck husband, clearly expecting Izzy to follow.

So she did.

The inside of the shanty was one large room, with a brightly patterned blanket slung on a rope across the back end, hiding what Izzy assumed was the sleeping area. A long, narrow table took up half of the room, roughhewn stools pushed underneath. A stone fireplace was built into one wall, a cast-iron cooking stove set into it, and a pile of split wood beside. The fire was burning, but the air was surprisingly clear of smoke. Izzy must have looked puzzled, because the old woman—Margaret—tapped her on the shoulder and pointed to the roof, where an open chimney let fresh air in—or, Izzy realized, excess smoke out.

"There's a hatch for bad weather, but mostly, we leave it open. Learned that from the old man's people."

Izzy looked around again, this time noticing the dirt floor, hardpacked enough that no dust rose when they walked, and the sturdy, simple furniture that was draped not with the usual worn linens or wool blankets but deep brown and russet furs.

"You're trappers?"

"We were, back north. Less to hunt here, but we still keep a hand in when a bear doesn't know what's good for him or too many badger start hanging around." Margaret went to a chest against the far wall, lifting the lid and reaching inside. "You sit now, child. Something that won't move under you, for a change, and let me fix up a warmer and some tea."

Suddenly, nothing sounded better to Izzy than exactly that.

"Your time, is it?"

"Yes, ma'—Miz Margaret." Izzy didn't bother to ask how the other woman knew; the women at the saloon had always known, too. It must be a skill you learned as you got older, or maybe when you were young, it carried on your face as well as your gut.

"Men don't never understand," Margaret said under her breath. "Old man's lived with me near forty years, and every month he was still surprised, like it'd never happened before. Don't envy you being up on that beast. Good that your man thought to stop here 'stead of going on all day. Nonsense, that; nowhere you need to be so bad, it can't wait."

Izzy quickly determined that her hostess did not require responses, was just as happy to have someone not her husband to ramble on to about the tea they had to brew, the lambs they'd had born that spring, her useless children, half of whom'd run off and gotten married and never visited with their own children. . . . "And here you are; eat that up," she said, handing Izzy a bowl filled with soup from the pot on the stove, placing the mug of tea on the table in front of her. Izzy couldn't have said what was in the bowl if her life depended on it, but it smelled rich and meaty, and her mouth watered before she'd even lifted the spoon.

As though drawn by the smell, the men came in as well, trailed by another figure, who turned out to be the youngest of their sons, going by the name Esaias.

"Only one of my brood still home, though the next-youngest boy's out with the flock," Margaret said, ladling out more soup and placing the bowls on the table. "Sit, all of you; don't gawp around like you were sheep yourselves. Sit!"

After they'd finished supper, Margaret shooed her son off to sleep in the shed, offering them his quarters for the night. Gabriel thanked

her politely, as did Izzy, although he would have been just as pleased
to spend the night with the livestock rather than in that boy's mess,
given his druthers. Sheep would be cleaner, he suspected.

Also, there would be more room to sleep. He looked at the tiny
space and made a face. They'd had more privacy on the road than they
did here.

"I promise to leave your virtue alone," Isobel said tartly, coming up
in the doorway behind him, stripped down to her chemise and a dark
blue shawl. Her hair was down and she was clutching what looked like
a small . . . sheep?

Seeing where his gaze rested, she held it out for him to see better.
"A hot water bottle wrapped in wool. It's for . . ." She blushed slightly,
ducking her head and cuddling the bundle back to her stomach. "I
have stomach pain," she said, and he nodded once, then turned back
to the bed. Women's issues were for women; he wanted no part of it,
even in discussion.

He eyed the bed again as though it had teeth and an uncertain
temper. "They assumed . . ."

"I know what they assumed," she said, her tartness lost under her
blush. "You're not old enough to be my father, so you're either my
brother, my husband, or my pander. Either way, there is only the
one bed and I'll not be sleeping on the floor."

A gentleman would take the floor without hesitation. But this was
not the East, where society would raise an eyebrow and gossip, nor
Spanish-held lands, where the Church judged women harshly. This was
the Territory, where practicality ruled, and they would have a long
ride ahead of them the next day.

He pulled off his boots, dropped his suspenders, unbuttoned his
vest and overshirt, and lay down on the bed next to her. The mattress
was thin but softer than the ground they had been sleeping on, and
while he preferred the open sky above him, there was much to be said
for walls and warmth.

"We used to bundle when we were younger," she said quietly.

"During the winter. The young 'uns all shared a room, and it would get cold, so we'd pull the mattresses to the middle of the room and pile the blankets on, and bundle. The boys stopped before the girls did, though. Got so's they'd rather be cold than too close."

He didn't think that she was looking for him to say anything in response, so he didn't. Eventually, her breathing evened out, and he fell asleep listening to her faint snores.

He dreamed, knowing that it was a dream. That happened sometimes, usually when he had too much on his mind, so it wasn't a surprise, even as he stood in the middle of a river and watched the blue-winged hawks turn and swoop. The sky was deep blue, but overhead hung the moon, not the sun.

None of this was real. And yet everything was.

Old Woman Who Never Dies delighted in dreams like that. But there was no dream-figure, no fellow traveler here, no message writ on the chalk cliffs along the river or the clear water around his ankles, fish swimming past him deeper below. Just the moment, cold clear air in his lungs and his heartbeat in his ears.

The world was never that silent.

Standing out in the open like that made his back itch, like there was a shotgun or bow lining up on him, but his feet wouldn't move. The water rushed past, the hawks hunted, the clouds slid past, and the moon shifted phase, but he stayed locked in place.

"Mother, pity us," he whispered, but no message came. He did not know what the blue-winged hawks meant, did not know what the fish at his ankles meant, did not know what the silence meant. He had no medicine more than his water-sense, and he could not interpret signs.

"All right," he said. "All right." He acknowledged Old Woman, acknowledged himself, acknowledged his helplessness and his willingness to learn, and he woke to the smell of grease and the sound of someone yelling at the chickens outside. Isobel was already awake and gone, the mattress next to him cool to the touch.

A rattlesnake, and now Old Woman.

"All right," he said to the empty alcove, letting every pound of his unhappiness weigh down the words, then he got up to join the others.

It was Isobel he had heard, out in the packed-dirt yard between the house and the shed where they'd slept, trying to coax the chickens out of their coop. From the noise and fluster coming from within the sturdily built structure, they didn't seem in the mood to cooperate.

He stood and watched her for a while until she stopped, her hands on her hips, and glared at the birds like they were the cause of every sorrow in the world. A single black-and-white banded feather was caught in the crown of her braid, while others floated gently around her.

"Something scared them last night," he said finally.

"I know that," she snapped. "But they need to get out so I can collect the eggs. Miz Margaret said they're tetchy if you try to get under them."

He watched as she tried again, bending nearly in two so she could reach inside the coop, then shifted his attention to the landscape around them. Chicken were easily frightened, but for them to still be flustered after the sun rose and the threat slunk away was a curious thing. He stepped out of the hard-packed dirt of the yard, beyond the low fence, and studied the ground there. In the near distance, the horses snorted and jostled each other, reaching for the fresh feed and water that had been laid out for them. They'd been in the stable all night with the sheep and the boy. Nothing had disturbed them. So, it had been after the chickens only. A fox, then, or ferret.

He turned again but saw no pawprints, no marks or disturbances where a creature might have slunk along the fence. A snake, maybe?

He felt a touch of unease, despite the fact that snakes were surely a common enough predator here, along with everything else that would find a penned hen or fresh egg tasty. He had no reason to assume malice where natural hunger could explain. And yet.

A rattler and Old Woman had come to warn him to be wary, to watch and be ready.

He looked up as though expecting to see the blue-winged hawks circling above, again. But the sky was bare even of clouds, the sun bright where the moon had been cool. Still, he felt caution creep over him like a second skin, and he moved closer to where his charge was coaxing the flustered, squawking hens out into the yard.

The Carons were doing well enough, but their homestead had nothing to appeal to a dream-dancer or demon . . . save themselves, him, and Isobel.

"Iz."

She looked up at him, the chickens not so much abandoned as suddenly secondary. They'd progressed that far that she could read his tone: good.

"Are any of the chickens missing?"

She shook her head. "One per nest, and no stray feathers or blood. They're merely upset."

He wiped a hand over suddenly dry lips. "Stay alert. Something passed this way last night. And if it wasn't here for fowl, it was here for something else."

It might be nothing. It might be whatever had been watching them before. But there were limited protections to be made this far off a road, away from any town. And the dream had been too full of nothing not to disturb him.

Izzy wasn't altogether surprised when, immediately after breakfast, Gabriel told her to pack up and be ready to go. He had been odd since he woke up: quieter, more cautious. And it hadn't been the chickens that had him so; that had deepened his mood, not caused it. Every time he turned around, his forehead creased, his eyes distant and look-ing inside, she could feel herself worrying up, too.

Miz Margaret didn't seem overly surprised, either, when they made their farewells, only tucked the hot water bottle, now emptied, into her hands and told her to keep it. The boy had barely said a word to anyone over breakfast, disappearing immediately afterward, while the old man *hrmph*ed and grumped and muttered about strangers where they weren't wanted. But she noticed that he, too, kept looking past the table, out the window, as though half expecting something to come up to the house.

Izzy knew that the old man and Gabriel were both uneasy, their bodies braced as though for a blow. But she couldn't tell *why*. More, she could tell that they didn't know why, exactly, and that made her feel worse, as though it were her responsibility to know, to suss out what they couldn't.

It *was* her responsibility. That was what being a Hand meant: it was the strength of the Territory, the boss had said. The cold eye and the final word, he'd said, the one who could do what others couldn't.

She had known how to close the sickness off from the rest of the Territory before. The whisper had told her. But it was silent now, and her sense of *knowing* slithered away, leaving her fretful and restless.

Izzy waited until they'd left the sod house and the farmstead behind, the sound of hooves on the packed dirt of the road echoing below them, and the mule's occasional grumbles a familiar lullaby, thinking he'd be more open to speak when they were alone.

"Something happened back there. Something that worries you."

Gabriel settled into his saddle, glanced sideways at her. "It's likely nothing."

"But possibly is?"

They were riding alongside each other, the road there wide enough for a wagon to pass without risking the grass, and she tilted her head to look back at him. "Possibly is?" she repeated, as though he might not have heard her, or misunderstood her.

"Possibly," he agreed, and his eyes were shadowed. There was something he was hiding, something he wasn't telling her. "You open your ears and your eyes, and tell me."

Izzy opened her mouth to ask what, exactly, she was meant to be looking and listening for, then clamped her mouth shut so hard, her teeth hurt. Something worried him, even more than what they'd found at Widder Creek. This wasn't another test. This was real.

PART THREE
DUST AND BONES

GABRIEL TURNED THEM WEST AGAIN after leaving the Carons' farm-stead, taking a rougher trail through dry plains, where the sky seemed impossibly far away and small brown birds hopped through the scrub brush, away from the sound of their hooves. Despite the uncertainty of that first morning, Izzy found herself near falling asleep in the saddle several times over the next few days, waking abruptly once when she thought she heard the hot rattle of a snake, but when nothing appeared, she wrote it off reluctantly to nerves. There were far fewer trees there, even the wide-spreading cottonwoods looking parched and broken, and the creeks they passed by were all dry and dusty. They made cold campsites and used their water sparingly and mainly for the horses.

After three days, the dust seemed embedded in their sweat, crusting on their skin during the colder nights. Devorah's words about how badly she'd desire a bath came back to Izzy, and her dreams each night were filled with water deep enough to sink into. The soda ash had been keeping her scalp clean at least, but she was running out, and the sliver of soap Miz Margaret had given them was near-useless in a handful of water, leaving more behind than it cleaned off.

They saw no one else as they rode, the land around them empty of everything save brush and the occasional rabbit or deer gazing at them thoughtfully. Rabbit could be trouble, Izzy knew, but neither it nor the fox she spotted early one dawn gave any indication they were anything but what they appeared.

The third day, Izzy looked up to see a smudge of grey in the near distance, swirling like a child's top, but although she noted that Gabriel's shoulders tensed up again each time and he reached for his knife like it gave him comfort, the dancer never came close enough to be of concern.

Izzy watched them more out of boredom than real interest. Everyone knew dust-dancers were harmless, mostly. They might confuse a traveler or obscure a trail, but that was it.

Yet something about them spooked Gabriel, and that preyed on Izzy's thoughts, churning with what had happened back at the farmstead, and what had happened with the rattler, and the growing prickle at the back of her neck.

But he didn't speak of it, any of it, and she didn't ask. They both only waited and rode on.

A day later, with the landscape changing only in the type of birds they saw and the prickling growing more intense, impossible to ignore, Izzy finally spoke up.

"Someone's watching us?"

"I think so." No praise for figuring it out, which irked Izzy, but he hadn't scolded her for not realizing sooner, either. "Someone or something. For a while now. Since just after Widder Creek, I think."

Well, that wasn't disturbing at all. She huddled deeper into her bedroll and looked up at the sky, the half-moon bright enough to blot out some of the stars, casting odd shadows on the land. But there was nowhere anything could hide, not unless it was knee-high to a grasshopper. They hadn't even heard a fox or coyote hunting in the past few nights. In fact, the only thing they'd seen was . . . ah. But dust-dancers weren't anything to be feared of, certainly not someone as road-savvy as her mentor, and he'd been worried days before they saw the first one.

Since Widder Creek.

She swallowed her uncertainty and spoke into the chilled darkness.

"You think whatever it was, it was what spooked the hens, too? Back at—"

"Maybe." She couldn't read him in the darkness with that single terse word.

"Might not be a threat."

"Might not."

He didn't think so, though. She could see it now, in the way he moved during the day, the way he looked over the area even as the horses picked their way along the trail, the way he'd drawn the mule in closer instead of letting it amble at its own pace, keeping it within reach. As though he thought something might attack, going for the unridden animal first.

She considered the terrain again, trying to see it the way Gabriel might. A ghost cat might blend into the brush, and they'd never see it coming, but the horses would smell it before it got close, surely. What could be silent, near-invisible, scentless, or . . . oh.

Izzy swallowed hard and touched the silver ring on her finger, rubbing it until the smooth metal warmed under her touch. She wished she had something larger, more than the handful of coin Gabriel had given her, tucked into the pocket of her jacket folded just out of reach with her dress and stockings. Like natives, demon acknowledged the boss's power but didn't fear or need it. She'd never thought that she might need to fear *them*.

What had the rattlesnake said, again? The memory had turned to haze, but it had been something about enemies and friends and not being who they thought. Demon weren't friends. And the snake had been speaking to Gabriel, not her, hadn't it?

Her palm itched, and she scratched it absently, then inspected the skin for sign of bite or rash. But there was nothing there other than an ordinary bruise on the heel of her hand and a line of dirt under her nails.

Just nerves.

Izzy went to sleep that night trying to remember the familiar, comforting feel of her old coverlet under her hands, the sounds of the saloon at night, the smell of brimstone and smoke in the morning air, but her dreams were filled again with the sound of running water and the dry, whistling sound of the something crackling underfoot.

The next day, they both woke tense and watchful, the small fire put out as soon as Gabriel had poured the last coffee grinds into the dirt. Izzy reloaded the mule's packs and saddled Uvnee with only half her attention, the rest torn between the sense, still, that something was following them.

They saw no more dust-swirls in the distance, and eventually, the feeling of being watched faded. She caught Gabriel's eye at one point, and he nodded slightly: he'd felt their watcher leave too.

Izzy let the reins drop to her lap, trusting Uvnee, and stretched her arms to the sky. Her menses were gone for another moon, her muscles felt loose and limber, the sky overhead was blue, and the air, while still too dry, now smelled of fresh growing things, and the watcher was gone.

"Things come and go out here," Gabriel said. "Best never to assume anything. And pick up the reins. Uvnee's a good horse but even good horses can spook."

Chastened, she picked up the reins again and paid attention to her surroundings.

The change in mood seemed to make her mentor more talkative, and he picked up her lessons again. "What was that?" he asked, lifting his chin to the left of the trail, at the form disappearing into the grass.

"Grouse," she said. "Young one?"

"Do you know, or are you guessing?"

"Guessing," she admitted, bracing herself for the lesson on how to identify a bird by the flick of its tail feathers.

Midmorning on the fourth day since leaving the farmstead, they came to a split in the dirt track. Gabriel led them onto the left fork, slightly wider but otherwise unremarkable from the trail they had been on, and Izzy reined the mare in a few paces after that, feeling an odd shock run through her body. It was like what she'd felt when she crossed that first stream but different, somehow. She turned in her saddle and looked back, the mule looking at her quizzically, as though to ask what she thought she was doing.

The trail behind them looked the same as it had before: dry, packed dirt surrounded by brush and rock.

She looked ahead. The trail they were on looked almost the same. But almost wasn't the same. If she were trying to read it the way she'd read a person . . .

It was half again wider. The ground underneath was smoother. And it . . . felt different.

"This is a road," she said out loud. "That wasn't; this is." The difference between a road and not-road, that she'd asked Gabriel about when they passed the burned-out homestead weeks ago: this was it. Not a thing to be seen but to be *felt*.

The realization, the knowledge that she could tell the difference, made her dizzy, enough to catch at the pommel so that she didn't fall. She looked back again, letting her gaze linger on the ground, then rise up into the sky, the pale colors around her whiting out around the edges, her eyes watering until she blinked, pressing the heels of her hands against her eyelids.

When she opened her eyes again, the world had gone back to normal, the sensation of difference gone. But she had felt it. She *knew*.

The knowledge—the ability to *see*—tucked into her hands like a precious thing, she urged Uvnee on to catch up with Gabriel, who had not paused while she figured it out.

Her lessons continued as they rode. Snakes, despite their reputation, had been simple: be respectful when you crossed paths, listen when they speak, and if you have an extra egg to leave out for them, do so, but don't feel obligated; they disliked being obligated in turn. Mostly, though, they left people alone. Rabbits were tricky, buffalo were power-ful, so were ghost cats, and best left alone unless you had a powerful need. Bears could be approached but never twice, and Gabriel told her stories from several different tribes of what happened to foolish hunters who failed to heed that.

And that brought them to the creatures of air.

"If an owl calls three times, what does it mean?"

"That there's medicine being worked," she responded. "If it calls a seventh time, someone will die."

"And five or six times?"

"It's a noisy bird?" She grinned at him, almost impish.

Gabriel kept his expression stern. "Why three and why seven, but not four, five, or six?"

"Because . . . I don't know." She pushed the question back to him. "Why?"

He shrugged one-shouldered. "Nobody knows. It just is."

She flicked the underbrim of her hat with one finger, clearly liking the sharp thunking sound that made. "I bet the boss knows."

"I bet he does." Unspoken in his response: but the boss wouldn't tell her, even if she asked. Although Gabriel had no idea what the Hand would be privy to once she returned to Flood.

The thought was also a reminder that this, her company, was not a thing he should be becoming accustomed to. When he felt she was blooded enough, that she understood the road enough to travel it herself, the mentorship would be over.

And, having completed his half of the bargain, the devil would pay in full.

All he had to do was keep her safe until then.

They both fell silent. Gabriel drank water from his canteen, then passed it over to her, a silent reminder to stay hydrated, while he scouted the road ahead. Just because their shadow had disappeared for a while, there was no reason to assume all was peaceable up ahead.

Five days since they'd left the Caron farmstead, and the ground was changing, hillocks and valleys making the riding more difficult. The pale, blue-shadowed shape of the Mother's Knife was barely visible in the distance, if you knew how to look, and that meant nothing could be taken for granted.

"Do I get to ask questions now?" she asked.

He made a sweeping gesture with one arm, indicating that she had his full attention. He was curious to see what she felt important enough to ask, half a month into her first ride.

"How are we able to feel the road underneath us, or the buffalo herd, but it's not dangerous the way crossroads are?"

"Ah." He fell silent, thinking about how to answer her. "That's a thing, Isobel."

"A thing?"

"A thing I can't tell you until you already understand."

She kneed Uvnee sideways, then took off her hat and swatted his shoulder with it. "That's not fair."

"It's not," he agreed. "But it's the truth. Never assume that the two will ride side by side."

"All right." She had clearly heard some variation of that before, from the twist of her mouth, and he could only imagine the look in her eyes. "But why do you refer to every road we've been on, every true road, I guess, as just the road? As though it's only one, even though they're not? And is a road always a road? Or it's a trail sometimes, like the one by the burned-out farm?"

"Ah." He sorted through her words, determining that she was actually only asking the one question: what makes a road a road? It was a reasonable question and one that he could explain with what she already understood. "Remember what I told you before about saying good-bye?"

She frowned. "That you didn't."

"Why?"

"Because . . . the road curves around again." She squinted, staring at the grass around them in a way that suggested she was seeing something else entire, and he could practically smell the thinking going on inside that handsome head. "But that don't make sense. The boss's map showed dozens of roads, all through the Territory. Most of 'em run straight unless they have to go around something they can't get through or over. That's how we get crossroads."

Uvnee stumbled slightly in the road, and she steadied the mare with knee and rein without thinking, adjusting her weight as she did so. Another few weeks, and he thought she'd be able to sleep in the saddle without falling.

"You're still thinking like a townsie stuck in one place," he said, that observation triggering his response. "Think like a rider." He'd actually expected this question earlier, but to be fair to the girl, other things had happened to distract her. And, likely, she was using this now to distract her from *that*.

"Roads go from one place to another," she said slowly. "Sometimes, like the path from town to the river, it's people walking, making a trail. Like an animal trail, 'cept it goes somewhere we want to go, so more and more people use it and it widens. Paths that don't get used disappear. Paths that are used, they turn into roads?"

He could see her turning that idea over and over, handling it to find the flaws or see where a new piece went.

"And like . . . like the Law, once it becomes a road, because everyone *agrees* it's a road. It's . . . Once it's a road, it's like every other road . . . like water goes from the mountains down creeks, into lakes, but it's all water?"

He raised an eyebrow, impressed. "Very like," he agreed.

She was quiet for a while, then: "It doesn't work that way outside the Territory, does it?"

"Not so much, no." He thought of the roads in Philadelphia, cobbled over and dead under his boots. "Maybe they are elsewhere; I didn't travel much. But not in the cities."

"But why? And what makes a road safe and crossroads not?" She glared between Uvnee's ears, as though that particular spot were to blame for her failure to understand.

"Don't think so hard about it, Isobel. Let it come. It will." He could see that she didn't believe him at all. He took another glance at the road ahead of them, letting his awareness open to anything that might be moving. There was nothing but silence until he pointed to where the road led into the hills. "Clear Rock's up ahead. Last one to the marker-post buys dinner tonight!"

It was a useless bet—Izzy didn't have enough coin on her to pay for a meal, even if there'd been a saloon in town to offer one. But the road was clear, and the horses could use a leg stretch after a slow but steady walk all day. He dug his heels in and let Steady go, aware that the mare and her rider were hot on his heels.

Clear Rock was less a town than it was a stronghold. It sat in a cut on the side of a long hill, looking out over the rolling plains to the east, and was the last decent place to stop before you headed into the foothills proper and the western borders of the Territory. To reach it, riders had to pass by a massive trunk, wider than a man could reach around, hewn from somewhere else, stripped of its bark, and set into the ground just as the road curved around and up the hill.

Steady, with his longer legs, reached the post first, but Isobel managed to stay on his heels the entire way. Reining the mare in, she wheeled around the post, her hat falling off her head until she caught it, jamming it back down over her braid. "Why is this in the middle of the road?"

"Border towns use 'em, especially when there's only one way in and out of town. Slows people down if they're looking to enter town in a hurry in a group. You ride through here in a group of four or more, you have to slow down and split up." He frowned at the post, reading the marks carved there by recent travelers. None of the marks looked to be less than a month old. Not that Clear Rock got much traffic, but he'd have thought, with spring coming on, there might have been riders coming down from the mountains, or a marshal on their rounds. "Up here, supplies can get scarce, and folk aren't always known for asking permission if they need something."

Marshals didn't keep a set route—they weren't that predictable— but the last sigil carved into the post looked to be months old, maybe even a year past.

She reached out past where he was looking and touched the marshal's motto burned into the wood just at eye level. "Act with ill intent and you will be found."

"The marshal's solemn vow," he said.

"But sometimes, they don't find them," she said.

He looked at the year-old mark again. "Sometimes. And sometimes they're just too late. The Territory's wide, and horses can ride only so far, so fast. Even if we had a hundred more marshals, it still wouldn't be enough."

"That's why the boss has me." Her voice wavered a little, as though she was only now starting to realize what she'd let herself in for.

"I doubt he expects you to be able to track down raiders or outlaw posses all by your lonesome," he said, although for all he knew, that was exactly what the devil expected. The old man might look human, but anyone with a drop of Territory water in them knew he wasn't, and what he thought and expected couldn't be counted on to match what normal folk thought.

"Maybe" was all Isobel said. "But he . . ." She shut her mouth as the mule caught up with them, its ears more annoyed than usual. Whatever she was going to say, she didn't share, and they started down the slight slope into the town proper.

Clear Rock hadn't been built to be pretty. The first buildings were low structures: storehouses and pigpens. Then there was a corral, blocks of hay shoved in one corner, a horse-sized shed in the other. The houses, built of stone, not wood, were huddled in the center, eleven of them, their doors painted bright colors as though to make up for the ochre dullness of their walls. It was an odd way to build a town, until you remembered how isolated they were, prey to any posse that rode through.

"Where is everyone?" Isobel asked when no one came out to greet them.

"I don't know." The last time he'd been there, he'd been challenged just after the marker-post, by a young lookout sitting high up on a rock. The rock had been bare when they'd ridden past it.

There was a dog sitting in the corral, a lean, dun-colored beast, regarding the newcomers with calm curiosity. But that was it. There were no other animals in the pens, no people on the street or in doorways.

Gabriel removed his hat, letting it rest on the pommel of his saddle, and ruffled his sweat-streaked hair. "Hey, the town!"

There was no answer, no movement.

Unlike Widder Creek, there was no stench of illness or decay, and the silence was less ominous than simply . . . empty.

Isobel looked around, her gaze skimming from left to right, alert for any movement despite—or because of—the silence. She was a far cry from the girl who'd ridden out of Flood two weeks before, and he felt a touch of pride despite the situation. "They . . . all went somewhere?"

"Maybe. Stay on your horse and be ready."

Isobel gave him a long look, then settled her backside more firmly in the saddle and touched the long knife sheathed next to her leg. She still wasn't as handy with it as she was her shorter blade, but the only guns they had were on Gabriel's saddle, and he wasn't inclined to pass her one. She was still as likely to shoot him as anything that attacked them.

He rested his handgun across his lap, half-hidden by the brim of his hat, and kept the reins in one hand. The mule shoved its way between the two horses as though it wanted to hide from something. Isobel reached out a hand and touched its neck lightly. "Easy, boy," she said. "Whatever's wrong, we'll protect you."

It snorted, judging her words and finding them wanting, and despite the tension, she laughed. That gentle sound seemed to fill the street, far louder than had come from her throat, bouncing off the stone walls and echoing as though more than one person were laughing, even after she had stopped, a hand clamped over her mouth.

"Oh, that's not upsetting at all," Gabriel said, listening to the lingering echoes. "Isobel, take the mule. Head out of town, back past the post."

She didn't argue.

There wasn't a taint in this town as far as he could tell. It was just . . . empty.

Sometimes, he knew, towns went empty like that. Harvest failed one time too many, or illness left 'em too dispirited to go on, or they got into a foolish scuffle with the local tribe and lost. But Clear Rock had a purpose in being there, a *reason* for people to stay. And if they left . . . what had come through while they were gone?

Gabriel holstered the pistol and dismounted from Steady's back, tying the horse's reins loosely to the fence of the corral so that if anything happened, the gelding could break free on his own. The dog had disappeared, and Gabriel felt faint relief: a dog that'd gone feral or sick was a problem he didn't need. He felt no worry leaving the horse behind; if it returned, Steady—unencumbered by a rider—would dispatch it with his hooves if it were a threat.

Every inch of his body alert, he loaded the carbine and carried it easy in his arms. If anything were to attack, he'd have the one shot, but after that, the gun would be as much use as a club, and he'd have to drop it to use his knife, anyhow.

But nothing jumped out at him. Nothing moved inside the buildings, not on two legs or four. There weren't even any vermin that he could see, and usually, they'd be the first to move in when a place was abandoned, right after the birds.

That made the dog's presence even more unnerving.

He looked up into the sky, half expecting to see carrion birds wheeling overhead. Or raptors, the way they'd been in his dream . . .

He stilled, the memory of that dream coming back to him. The stillness as the water rushed past his legs, the fish swimming below and the hawks above, but nothing living save himself on the ground . . .

Mostly, Old Woman Who Never Dies left him be now that he'd come home. But he'd hitched himself to more powerful things, so it was pointless to complain now when they dragged him along behind. She and the devil could argue over him when this was done, but he wasn't fool enough to ignore warnings, even if he didn't know yet what they meant.

"All right," he said out loud. "All right."

He'd fought against this all his life, run from it, crossed the Mudwater, buried in the laws and rules of another country, and come home because he had no choice. But that didn't mean he'd given in. He'd listen to warnings, but he'd do this his own way.

He had to be certain, though. Gun cocked, he opened the door of the nearest building and went inside. No bodies. A chair was overturned and beds were unmade, but there were no other signs of violence. Whatever had happened there had happened quickly. But there was no smell of illness, no bodies too long unbreathing and untended.

A quick pass through the kitchen made him pause and back up.

The cookstove was cold, the fireplace ashes swept up, and the narrow pantry's shelves were empty. It was spring, yes, and they might have run down their supplies something fierce, but there still should have been some staples, the last dregs of even a hard winter, the last of the potatoes, or . . . something.

Not empty shelves, not even an onion left in the bin. They had taken everything edible with them.

Or something had eaten it.

He went through every house, quickly but carefully, then back-tracked to the corral, untying Steady and putting their back to the town, as quickly as he could.

The town of Clear Rock, some five days' journey west from the farmstead of the family Caron, in the foothills of . . . Izzy stopped, frustrated. She didn't know what these low hills were called, where they would appear on the boss's map. She closed her eyes, trying to visualize the map unrolled across his desk, place herself on it, move herself along the road that would take her there. They had gone north briefly but then turned south, even as they went west. . . . If she could feel the road under her feet, surely she could feel where she *was* on them?

The nape of her neck itched, and something pricked the palm of her left hand, sharply enough that her fingers flexed, making her drop her pencil, breaking her concentration. She looked around even as her right hand went to the knife at her side, a new and still-uneasy reflex.

Nothing was visible on the road save Uvnee and the mule, both of whom were looking at her curiously. The feeling intensified, thrumming through her, and then . . . disappeared.

"I felt something," she said, glaring back at the mule as though daring it to say something. "I know I did." Not the way she'd felt the road under her feet; more like how she'd come to know something was watching them, a sense of unease that had no obvious source.

Was their unseen companion back? If it had been a dust-dancer . . .

how had it come off the plains into the hills? What did it want? She didn't know, didn't know enough without Gabriel here to explain things, and she felt her frustration build. Where was he? Had something happened to him? If something had happened to him, what would she do?

The mule flopped one long ear at her and went back to contemplating the air in front of its nose as though her panic was of no consequence to it. Whatever had made her tense didn't bother it or the mare at all. She wished that made her feel better.

Izzy frowned, realizing that she'd once again forgotten to ask Gabriel the mule's name. Somehow, that failure calmed her: something so ordinary and stupid, a balm against her panic.

The sound of hooves made her turn back toward the town even as she reached down to pick up the pencil from the dirt, tucking it back into her journal and replacing them both in her saddlebag. Gabriel was leading Steady by the reins and looking like he'd just eaten something that disagreed with him. She waited, calmer now, but still feeling the sweat on her skin and the slight pinch of her boots, the smell of horse and leather and her own skin, and the sensation, still lingering, that something had been *watching*.

"We've got trouble," he said.

She bit her lower lip, feeling how dry the skin there was. Did she tell him about the feeling? No, wait, let him say what he had to say first. "They're all gone?"

"Gone, fast and hard. And their supplies are gone, too. Everything edible, down to the last dried apple." His mouth was a thin line, his eyes unhappy, and her worry deepened. People didn't just up and abandon their homes, pack up all their supplies, not unless something drove them out.

"But not illness." Again, she meant.

"No bodies, no stink, no new graves less'n a few months old. I'd say no."

Some of her fear eased then. Two instances of a fast-moving and deadly illness, this far apart, would have been terribly bad news. Not that this puzzle wasn't worrisome too.

Gabriel took off his hat, running his hands through his hair until it stuck up in tufts. He'd shaved before they left the farmstead, but his chin was covered in thick dark stubble again, and there were shadows under his eyes that hadn't been there when she met him. She didn't know if that was normal for being on the road, or if all this was more trouble than he'd been expecting. If she were placing a bet, she'd say the latter.

She also suspected she didn't look much better. Not having a mirror might have been a blessing after all.

"I'd been counting on resupplying here," he said. "Their well was clean, so I refilled my canteens, but I'm not going back in there with the rest, and we're too low on supplies to continue on into the mountains. We need to get back into the plains, let me do some hunting, maybe find the nearest tribal encampment and see if they're open to trading. I don't suppose you have any extra shiny we could use?"

"You told me not to bring fripperies," she said tartly.

"That'll teach you to listen to me." He smiled, but it clearly took an effort, the surface charm of the man she'd first met scraped dry to the bone.

Her hand ached again, as though someone'd jabbed her deep in the palm, and she rubbed it, frowning at the skin as though it were to blame for everything. Her thoughts chased each other until she forced them into order, looking back up at him. "We can't go yet. We need to know what happened." It was just common sense: This town was too close to the southern border, a waypost, Gabriel had said. If something were causing trouble here, the Spanish viceroy, de Marquina, would hear of it, use it to his advantage.

She might be called the Devil's Hand, but she was his eye and ear, too. Same as any who worked for him. And she was the only one *there*.

"What happened is that nearly a half hundred souls are gone,"

Gabriel said, his voice harsh, "and we don't know why or how, or if whatever spooked 'em is going to come back around again while we're waiting here."

"If I'm to be the Hand . . ."

"You need to know what's happening. Yah, I get that." Gabriel threw his hat to the ground, then stared at it, bent, and retrieved it, slapping the dust off against his leg. He wanted to saddle up and ride away; she could see that in him. Every bone in his body yearned to be away from there as fast as Steady could carry him. But he wouldn't. Not if she said no. The sense of power she'd expected to feel didn't come; she just felt tired. Sad. Scared.

"I've been thinking," he said. "That maybe this is related to what Devorah said? About things getting worse near the border?'

"I don't know." Izzy realized she was still rubbing at the palm of her hand, and forced herself to stop, willing the ache away. "But the boss would say that's a suspicious hand."

He sighed and stared at the ground, like it would tell him something useful. "Yah," he said finally. "Yah. You're right. All right. So, what now?"

He was asking her? Izzy shook her head. She'd called rank as the Devil's Hand; what else would he do?

"I need to know what happened," she said, not so much to Gabriel, or even herself, but that *sense* inside her. The one that had told her what to do outside Widder Creek. "I need to know . . ."

She had to be careful. If that knowing was from the boss, odds were it worked the same as anything the boss gave away: you had to know what you wanted and what you were willing to give, and you mostly only ever got one shot to make it right. And if it wasn't, if it was some other medicine . . . well, all the more reason to be careful with what she asked for.

The salt-stick was where she'd replaced it in the pack, and she took it out, holding it uncertainly and yet certain that this was what she'd need. The silver band on her finger seemed to weigh more all of a sudden, curling her little finger in toward her palm. Silver and salt—they were protection, not weapons.

"But knowing is protection, isn't it? And I need to know why they left the way they did." She crumbled a little of the salt off the stick, letting the grains rest in her left hand, and curled the finger with the ring inward. "*Maleh mishpat*," she told it, the words forming in her mouth without conscious thought. She didn't know what they meant, but the *sense* told her they were important. "I am the strength of the Territory, the cold eye and the final word. And I *must know what happened.*"

Gabriel was speaking behind her, but she was aware of the sounds rather than hearing them. The mule was directly in front of her, dark brown hide shuddering as it flicked a fly off its hindquarters, but it seemed far away, not within arm's reach. The world spun around her, and she was spun within it, her arms too heavy to hold up, her head too large to stay on her shoulders, her knees too wobbly to support her.

"Isobel? Izzy!"

The words were distant, impossible, incomprehensible, nothing to do with her. She was stone and bone, dust and wind, the steady roar of water deep underground, the cold bitter bite and stifling heat. . . .

Darkness came, sweeping low over the western horizon. Storm clouds spread too far, piled too deep, hiding something within. Does not belong, *something told her.* Does not belong. *And the darkness slid through the jagged mountain peaks, sliced into thick ribbons, still rushing forward, dispersing into the sky, soaring up and dipping down, down, and one of the ribbons fell onto Clear Rock and ate it whole. . . .*

"Izzy!"

She was being shaken roughly, hands gripping her arms hard enough to bring her back to her flesh, eyes focusing, letting go, and remembering who she was . . .

"Izzy?"

"Yes," she said, answering the unasked question. "Yes."

"What did you see?"

"Something came . . . out of the sky. Something fearsome and dark, and . . . "

And consumed every living thing in the town.

"What now?"

Izzy blinked at him, her jaw dropping slightly. "You're asking me?"

He made a sound of exasperation and ran his hands through his hair again before flinging them wide. "I'm out of my depths here, Isobel. Natives? Rockfalls? Sickness? I can handle all those and more. Mysterious storms that leave behind empty towns? I've got nothing. So, I'm asking you, Devil's Hand: what do we do?"

The panic that had quieted when Gabriel returned roused again at his words, pressing against her ribs and her throat. Her heart beat too quickly, her blood raced as though she'd been running too hard, and she realized suddenly she'd clenched both hands so tightly, there were red marks from her nails on the flesh of her palms. She wasn't the Hand, not properly, never mind that she'd been able to *see* what happened, all the confidence she'd had when they rode out sucked away by weeks in the saddle, weeks of people not being impressed by her at all, by not being able to do something as simple as collect eggs from chickens or save people from being ill.

She looked up at Gabriel, intending to throw the question back to him—he was her mentor; he was supposed to *know* things. But what she saw there stopped her cold.

His face was calm now, only the slightest pinch between his brows. His jaw was unclenched, his head tilted just slightly to the right, and his eyes . . . his eyes were half-lidded but alert, curious. Waiting.

He trusted her to know what to do. He had confidence that she would be able to think of what to do.

She shook her head, panic replaced by lingering confusion and helplessness. "I don't know."

That seemed to turn a key in him. "All right. What do you *think* we should do?"

She swallowed, still feeling the panic pressure, still queasy from being spun around by the vision. But his certainty didn't allow her to question herself, didn't give her room to back out.

Another test, she thought to herself. Just pretend it's another test.

"I want to turn tail and ride home," she admitted. Go home to Flood and lay this all out at the boss's feet. Have him ride out, handle it. "But . . ." The words she'd spoken earlier, the words the boss had said, came back to her. "I am the strength of the Territory. I need to know what's happening." She was the cold eye and the quick knife, and the final word. Her, not the boss. No matter how woefully unready she felt.

"I don't understand what's happening." Here, or to her. "But I think I know what to do."

His confidence in her had limits.

"I don't want you going back in there." Gabriel had his arms crossed in front of his chest, staring down at her, and Izzy spared the thought that he wasn't as good at that look as Marie or William. "Listen to me, Isobel. When a situation's gone that bad, you don't plant yourself in the middle of it while you poke."

She crossed her own arms and glared back. "Then how'm I supposed to poke it?"

Izzy was certain that whatever had happened to the people of Clear Rock, the only way she'd be able to find out—assuming she could find anything at all—was to be there when she looked. Gabriel, though, he was dead certain that she could do it just fine from out there, same way she'd seen whatever it was that came down in the first place. And he had all the logic on his side, like the boss would say, but it didn't feel right.

And all she had to go on just then, much as she hated it, was how things *felt*.

It was the first time she'd ever truly challenged him, terse-voiced and tight-gestured, and he was answering back the same. "Isobel. Listen to me. My job is to keep you safe. And I know you need to do this; I'm not arguing with you, am I? But whatever you saw come down—"

"It's gone now!"

He let out an almost-not-quite-growl and lifted his hands in exasperation, like he wanted to punch something but couldn't. "Is it? Are you certain? Could you raise your hand in oath and swear whatever did this is gone?"

The words caught in her gullet. No. No, she couldn't. In fact, she knew—the way she knew all the things she could not possibly know—that it lingered.

She set her jaw, not willing to admit that he had a point. "I have to know what it was."

"You can poke at it from here. Outside."

Beyond the post-marker. Beyond the town's boundaries. "Whatever words they had, it didn't save them from this. It won't keep it contained, either." The road-post would not slow down the storm she had seen.

"Isobel." His mouth was a flat line again, eyes narrowed, the charm replaced by a low-burning anger. "This isn't up for debate."

She tried to hold on to that feeling, that certainty that she needed to get closer, but it slipped away under his insistence and her own fear. "All right."

Battle won, Gabriel stepped back, his arms hanging by his side as though unsure what to do. Izzy almost laughed despite the fear, because it wasn't as though she had any idea either.

"If this is you, boss," she whispered under her breath, into the air, "you might've warned me." Some folk might be fine being thrown into the creek; she preferred to know how swift the current was first. And now, this was a river, not a creek, and the water was well over her head.

Gabriel wouldn't let her drown. Not if he could stop it, anyway.

Following her first instinct, she made herself comfortable in the middle of the road, the post-marker directly in front of her. The ground was sun-warmed but hard, and the dust clung to her skirt. She rested her hands on the ground, the grains of salt still clinging to her palms pressing into the dirt, then she lifted her left hand and made the devil's gesture again, circling out and in toward her rib cage.

"Show me," she whispered. *"Maleh mishpat."* She felt the words echo inside her ears, drumming like rain on the roof, washing through her body, and though she still didn't recognize the language, she understood what the words meant. *Fulfill justice. Be* filled *with justice.*

That time, she was half-prepared for the sensation of being spun, the ground under her backside cradling her even as it swallowed her, *standing in the middle of the night, thick black clogging hunger need need hunger seeking taking swallowing consuming searching eyes eyes turning looking at her looking* seeing *her how hungry coming at her coming too fast too—*

The ground spat her back up, and something hit her hard, swooping her up and tossing her into the air, into a saddle. The reins were shoved into her hands, her fingers closing around them instinctively even as she struggled to open her eyes, and then she was moving, her body leaning forward, legs closing around Uvnee's ribs, elbows tucking against her own body as the mare surged forward.

Behind her, she could feel it, despite her pounding head and skitter-stop heart, the overwhelming sense of *hungersearchingtaking* reaching for them even as the horses galloped back down the road, instinct sending them fleeing from whatever had been woken in Clear Rock.

The horses ran until they ran themselves out, gallop slowing to a trot, and then falling into a slow walk. Izzy could feel Uvnee's chest blowing, her ribs rising and falling with a bitter rasp, and leaned her cheek against the mare's neck, tears wetting the sweat-damped hide. "I'm sorry," she whispered, her voice cracking, not sure what she was apologizing to or why. She had only a hazy memory of what had happened: the last thing she clearly remembered was Gabriel stalking away while she made herself ready to . . . to what?

Her fingers were numb from clutching the reins and Uvnee's mane, but she forced herself to ease upright, unclenching and stretching her fingers, and only then did she realize that Steady was stopped a few paces ahead of them, his proud head dropped, his rider leaning against his side, stroking his neck and making sure that all the straps and packs remained secured on his saddle.

"You okay?" His voice was raspy too, and he didn't turn to look at her.

"I think so." She risked looking behind them, although she knew that Gabriel would not have stopped if it wasn't safe. The road behind them was clear, only puffs of dirt still swirling in the air. How far had they run? "It didn't follow us."

"I'm pretty sure we didn't outpace it," Gabriel said, still petting Steady's neck. "I don't think it wanted to leave the town."

She thought of what she'd felt when she called up the storm, and shuddered. She should have tried to contain it, not call it out. Now it was there, awake, alert, and coiled inside the town, and she still had no idea what it was, or where it had come from—or why.

As they watched, a small brown smudge came into view down the road, a familiar, irritated set to its ears. Despite herself, Izzy smiled, surprised at the relief she felt that had little to do with the return of most of their supplies.

"We need to name the mule."

"What?"

It seemed impossibly important now. "We almost left it behind, and it kept up. It deserves a name."

Gabriel turned his head just enough to look at the mule trotting toward them, then at Izzy, as though certain he'd told her this before. "His name's Flatfoot."

"Flatfoot?" She shook her head, finding some refuge in teasing him, as though they hadn't just barely outrun something terrible. "From the man who named his horse Steady, I should have guessed."

From the shaky grin he gave her as Flatfoot finally reached them, Izzy thought maybe Gabriel was taking the same comfort in their exchange.

"Do you think . . . it's okay to just leave it there like that?" She was surprised at how ordinary the question felt, as though they were discussing if they should make camp there or ride farther on.

"First rule of the road, Isobel." And just like that, his voice was serious again. "Don't pick up more than you can carry. You tried, and you failed."

She winced, but he went on, relentless.

"You almost got us killed. Or . . . whatever it did to everyone else in that town. And going back there to cut it off from the road, whatever you did back at Widder Creek, isn't an option. It's still there, it's gotten a taste of you, and we are not getting within reach of it again. Understood?"

"Yes, sir." The mule had reached them now and rested its head against Izzy's leg, pushing gently. She reached down to scratch its ear. "Sorry, boy," she said to it. "I'm glad you didn't get eaten."

"It's just us out here, Isobel; we need to think of ourselves first. Supplies, some rest, get to our next destination. You can send a message back to Flood from there if it will ease your mind. And maybe they'll know more there. Maybe word's gotten out about what happened."

Izzy gave the mule's ears one last scritch, then settled herself back into the saddle and gathered the reins again, letting Uvnee know it was time to walk forward. "I suppose." The mule let out a groan but stayed at Uvnee's heels.

Gabriel was right. And yet the memory of that storm driving through the mountains itched at her, not letting her thoughts rest. Why had it come to Clear Rock? And how long would it be content to stay there? What *was* it?

"How did I know how to do that?" was what came out of her mouth instead. "I mean, I, that was—"

"You took the devil's Bargain; you expect nothing to change?" His voice, though gentle, carried a hint of both scorn and amusement. "You see things when you take the road. Things you can't explain, things you don't understand. Things nobody understands. Just the way the Territory is."

"It's not like that outside?" Beyond the devil's hold, she meant. Across the River in the States; over the Knife in the Spanish lands.

Gabriel snorted, unamused. "If so, I never saw it. You cross the river, and things are . . . different. The Territory has its own way of doing things. The dime store novels have that much right, at least. Though they paint your boss a little different."

"Oh?" Anything, anything to keep her mind off what they'd left behind.

"They dress him up like a greenhorn dandy, all lace and flash."

Izzy tried to imagine the boss fancified like that and shook her head.

Gabriel kept talking. "We call him the devil because they did first. The tempter, the deceiver. The bargain-maker. They don't understand. Not him, not the Territory. Folk who come here, they're mostly desperate. But when you're born here . . ." He stumbled over his words, something he wasn't saying, or didn't want to say, she thought. "It's hard to be anywhere else. Even the air feels wrong."

She had thought about leaving, hadn't been able to fathom it. April—even unhappy, she'd seemed shocked at the idea of leaving. But her parents had left. Had they been born here? She'd never wondered before. "Why?"

He shrugged, a casual motion that she could tell wasn't casual at all. "You'd be best off asking your boss that, not me."

"But you—" She was about to ask about his time back East when Gabriel's head went up, his gaze on something on the road ahead of them. Izzy tensed until she saw what had caught his attention. A man walking along the side of the road.

They'd gone days without seeing anyone down in the grasslands. Finding someone here in the hills? She understood why Gabriel tensed, but all she could wonder was if this man had come from Clear Rock, and if he could tell them what had happened there.

"Stay behind me," he said.

"One man alone isn't a threat."

"Bandits put out lures sometimes," he said sharply, and she subsided, letting Uvnee drop back a pace. She remembered the four men they'd met the first day out, and how easily they could have been trouble if there hadn't been a haint-bounty they'd wanted more.

They kept walking, the horses moving faster than a man on foot, until they were near abreast with the stranger. He was tall and lean, dressed in drab-colored trousers and a long coat of the same hue, his head bare, sandy hair tousled and long. All in all, she thought, he was as unremarkable as the rocks on either side of them, and colored much the same. Then he turned to face them, and Izzy took back all her previous thoughts. His skin was rough like a man who'd spent his life in the wind and sun, his nose a sharp beak, his forehead a high dome, and the eyes that studied them were as dark and deep as the earth itself.

The smile that he flashed them, though, was that of a predator, a coyote upright on two legs. "Well met, well met indeed, on this dusty and not quite so deserted as I'd thought road! Well met, my friends."

"I've no claim to call you friend," Gabriel said, his chin lifting, "and you none to so name me."

The stranger blinked, but the smile didn't waver, and something prickled all over on Izzy's skin, some sense of things not right. Nobody should be that friendly out there, particularly not when Gabriel had been rude in return, not unless they were up to no good. Even green to the road, she knew that.

The stranger cocked his head, gaze still intent. "You are riders on the dust road, not marshals nor brigands but honest souls. Why should we not be friends?"

The burn on Izzy's left hand flared as he spoke, almost as though someone'd touched her palm with a hot brand, and her hand clenched into a fist, then released, dropping limply against her thigh. She knew, even the moment Gabriel named the stranger.

"Honest souls have no truck with magicians."

"If you ever see a magician, run. Do not pause, do not speak, by all that you value, do not catch their attention, just run."

Izzy stiffened her spine against the shock and watched the magician warily. She was the Left Hand of the Devil and she would not run. But she was no fool, either, to think the creature in front of them harmless—or even benign. She knew what the common folk whispered about magicians, that they'd sold their soul entire to the devil for the power they held, that the things they could do were a twisting of power for evil.

The boss had set them straight on that late one night. Two magicians had been causing a ruckus northward in the Territory, so much decent folk got tired of it and sent a rider for the boss to put things right. Only, the boss said he didn't have any hold on magicians, any more than he did on demon. "They are what they are," he'd said, leaning back in his chair, toying with the cigar he'd cut and lit but never drew into his lungs, watching it burn down bit by bit. "Like wind and drought, you live through 'em, you don't control 'em. Trying's pure foolishness. Just be polite if they look your way, and eventually they'll get bored and move on."

The magician was looking clear at them, and Gabriel had already been rude. Izzy's thoughts were razor-sharp, rain-clear, aware that she couldn't trust anything she read, aware that everything hinged on this moment. Polite, perhaps, but she'd learned that polite and the road didn't always ride together, and the magician hadn't seemed to take offense at Gabriel's words. . . .

"What do you want of us?" she asked.

Sandy eyebrows raised, mock surprise. "Why do you assume I want anything?"

The mule snorted, a rude, wet sound, conveying Izzy's own disbelief perfectly.

"Perhaps," the magician went on, "I merely seek companionship on the road. Seeing as how darker things have begun traveling it."

Her eyes narrowed, the razor of her thoughts cutting clean through his words. "And would you know anything of that darkness?"

"No more than you, devil's daughter," the magician said. "Oh, yes, I know you, or know the mark you wear, at least. You have the smell of your boss about you." He lifted his nose and sniffed once, a showy affair, and then tilted his head and smiled at her, though his eyes remained dark and still. Dangerous eyes, she thought again. Not a coyote—a wolf.

As though hearing her thoughts, that smile this time showed too many teeth. "I bear no grudge against the Master of the Territory, little Hand. I am not your foe."

She could feel Gabriel's tension, and the way he waited for her to respond. "I believe you," she said, finally. "But I don't trust you."

"You'd be a fool if you did, and I would lose all respect for you. But there are weaker links that have bound allies before."

"Allies in what?" Gabriel asked, suspicion in his voice. She might halfway believe the magician when he said he meant no harm, but her mentor didn't.

"In discovering the source of the darkness," the magician said, as though that ought to have been obvious to a child. Dark eyes narrowed, staring at her. "You know of it. You have seen it?"

There was something hungry in the magician's voice, and Izzy forced herself not to give way before it. If he was a wolf, then she would be a horse, or better yet a buffalo, and he would beware her hooves.

"What do you know of it?" she asked in return.

"That it chills the wind and trembles the earth, disturbs the bones. But I do not know the what of it nor the why. I would know these things."

There was a hunger in his voice, naked and unashamed, and some sense of him was clear to her then.

"I am Isobel," she said abruptly. Gabriel might object, but the magician offered them no obvious threat and spoke of things that she had seen in her vision, that had scratched and worried at her thoughts. For that alone, she wanted to keep him near. "My companion is Gabriel."

"Farron Easterly." And he made a sweeping bow, long limbs surprisingly graceful, his hair falling over his shoulder before he flicked it back. "A fortuitous meeting, indeed."

Magicians took their surnames from the winds, the boss said. Eight winds, each with their own strengths—and weaknesses. But he'd never said what those weaknesses might be, and she had never thought she'd need to know.

"You'll need to walk if you travel with us," Gabriel said, accepting her decision but clearly not pleased with it. "The mule already bears a load."

The magician—Farron—took no visible offense. "I shall endeavor to maintain the pace, to avail myself of your companionship."

And then he smiled again, a too-wide, too-pleased grin, and Izzy thought she might have made a mistake.

Letting the magician tag along had been a terrible idea.

Gabriel paused while unsaddling his horse, took off his hat, and rested his forehead against Steady's neck, gathering strength from the solid muscle and calm breathing. He'd called an early halt to the day the moment they'd come to an acceptable place to set up camp, although "acceptable" meant only that they'd gotten far enough away from Clear Rock that he no longer felt overly twitchy.

But at least one cause of his unease had come with them, striding alongside the mule with a pace no human could maintain, cool and talkative as a crow.

Magicians were dangerous. Unpredictable. You avoided them; you didn't travel with them. And if one of them asked to travel with you, you took off in the other direction; you didn't say yes! What had Isobel been thinking?

"Damned if I'll ever understand women," he said under his breath, aimed only for Steady's ears. "And girl-women least of all."

The magician chuckled softly behind him, and Gabriel jumped, his hand already on the grip of his knife before he gained control of himself again.

"Your mistake is in thinking of her as a woman."

He turned, leaving his hand on the weapon, and stared at the magician. "Beg pardon?"

"She is female, assuredly. Subject to all the ills and frailties of that flesh. But she is also the Hand, rider. You have no understanding of what that means." The magician looked up at the sky, not bothering to shield his face from the setting sun. "And neither does she."

The magician's tone, half-mocking, half-thoughtful, didn't help Gabriel's mood. "And I don't suppose you're going to tell us."

The magician tilted his head and smiled brightly at him. "Now, where would the entertainment be in that?"

Gabriel sighed. This had been a *terrible* idea.

Isobel no longer required guidance when they set up camp, and he left her to it, moving away from the campsite only long enough to find a patch of nopales nearby, gathering enough of the flat, spiky paddles to griddle for dinner. It wouldn't be particularly satisfying, but he'd survived on less, and worse, before.

He knelt next to the area he had cleared for a fire, placing the coalstone in the center and asking it to burn. It stuttered slightly, then warmed under his touch, warning him to move away before flames emerged. Not that they needed much of a fire: the night promised to be comfortable after the day's warmth, and they didn't need a large fire to cook on, only enough to keep the night at bay.

"The coalstone's dying, isn't it?" Isobel said, coming up next to him.

"Coalstone don't last forever," he said. "I'd meant to trade for a new one when I could. But we seem to be having bad luck with that."

There was a weighted silence, then she asked, "Do you think that's all it is? Bad luck?"

He sat back on his heels and looked up at her, thought of how he'd first seen her in the devil's saloon, hair pinned in a fancy knot, a pretty dress and a sweet, sly look on her face. The figure watching him now was sun-baked despite her hat, the tip of her nose and the stretch of her cheekbones darker than the rest, her eyes shadowed and tired, her hair a long, messy braid flipped over one shoulder, her hands ragged-nailed, holding not a tray or fine glassware but her knife and a whetstone.

She was still weak after whatever it was she'd done back at Clear Rock, and he'd told her to sit and rest while he set up the fire. The magician, of course, was useless, wandering off to stare into the distance, hands clasped behind his back, the moment they made camp, rather than offering to help. He had no gear—he could conjure up a cabin for himself or sleep suspended in air, for all Gabriel knew. Or it was entirely possible that magicians didn't sleep. Rumor said they'd started human but weren't any more, giving themselves over to the spirits in exchange for their powers. Rumor said they weren't to be trusted.

Gabriel was pretty sure rumor was right on all those matters.

"If you were anyone else, I'd say yes," he told her honestly. "With you?" He shrugged, letting his gaze drop down to where the tiny flames were now curving around the coalstone. "I don't know. What was that you said about suspicious hands earlier?"

"The boss calls it that," she said. "When things go one way too consistently. The world is random, he says, like the deal of cards. A good player can manipulate what they get, but they can't control the deal, not without cheating. So, if you call the high card every time, it might be luck and it might not."

"You're calling all this a high card?" He couldn't help but be amused.

She let out an exasperated sigh, as though she couldn't believe she had to explain this to him. "It's too much. Too consistent. Bad luck, yes. But all this, the illness in Widder Creek, the . . . *thing* in Clear Rock, and a magician who happens to meet us in the road and offers us his aid? And something following us, maybe for days?" Isobel had been checking each item off on a finger, then folded them all against her palm. "The boss taught me how to conjure the odds. Can you say that this doesn't feel"—she expanded her fingers, like a bird taking flight—"suspicious?"

"Sometimes a run of bad luck's just a run of bad luck, Isobel." But once she'd presented the evidence, he couldn't not see it. Not all of it, but some; if he were gathering evidence, it might be enough to sway a judge and jury.

"Pfffft. Bad luck or manipulation, what does it matter?" The magician stepped out of the dusk, not even pretending not to have been eavesdropping. He had shed his long coat and rolled his sleeves up, looking like any other rider at the end of a long day, if you didn't look too closely at his face.

Gabriel looked at his face. The eyes were golden brown in the faint flickers of firelight, the sharp planes of his face giving him a feral, worrisome look.

"You think there's no connection?" Isobel had too little caution of the magician, but Gabriel carried enough for them both. He hoped.

"I say you worry too much of what is and what isn't, little rider. The winds blow, and the world turns, and things change. You have no control over any of this."

The magician—Farron—cocked an eye at the coalstone, then shook his head in mock sorrow and bent down, holding out his hands. It looked as though he were trying to warm his fingers, but a faint breeze rippled around then, and the flames grew twice their size, crackling as they fed on invisible fuel.

Gabriel shifted uneasily but didn't say anything. Knowing that power swirled throughout the Territory, that was one thing. Seeing it used so casually . . . He glanced at Isobel, who seemed unflustered by it all. Then, she would be, wouldn't she? Growing up in the devil's own house. He might seem just a man, but the few natives Gabriel had spoken to on the subject said the devil's medicine was bone-deep, powerful enough to level mountains, much less one magician.

But the devil wasn't here, and no matter what Iz was proving herself capable of, she was still just a girl and his responsibility.

"It is my obligation to do something," she was saying now. "I may not be able to control the wind, but if a storm is coming, I can at least get people out of its way."

The magician tipped his head to her, the sardonic edge of his smile softening slightly when he looked at her. "You may try, little rider. You may try."

The creature's informality raised hackles and an immediate need to remove his attention from Isobel. "So, how did you know of this . . . darkness, you called it?"

The magician didn't even bother to look at Gabriel. "I know everything the wind knows."

"That's not an answer."

This time, his smile was a closed-mouth smirk. "It is the only one I have."

"Farron." Isobel sat down, the knife and whetstone now placed by her knee, and leaned forward, staring intently at the magician. "You offered your assistance, said you wanted to know what happened back in that town too. We allowed you to come with us, have offered you hospitality by our fire. You will not repay us by mockery or evasion."

It was her voice, but those weren't her words, not entirely. Gabriel had recited enough speeches, mouthed the words of others for effect time enough to recognize the difference. The cadence was another's entirely. The only thing he didn't know was if she were merely imitating her boss, or if his hand lay on his Hand, even at this distance.

The air crackled, the fire snapping in the night air, sparks arcing to the ground. In the distance, an owl hooted twice, then fell silent.

"As you will," the magician said with an overly dramatic sigh. "I know because the wind told me. Every turn and twist it takes, every new thing it carries, I feel and I hear. When something new digs into the ground and strikes stone, I know. And this . . . this *darkness* is all the wind and the stones will speak of, for days now."

"You hear the wind? How?" Isobel leaned forward even more, her braid coming perilously close to the flames. Gabriel, unnoticed, tucked it back over her shoulder.

The magician leaned back, as though drawing away from her intensity. "How? How, indeed. For every gift, there is a cost. For every cost, there is a gift." He lifted his arms in a shrug, and it felt, to Gabriel, the first honest thing he'd done since appearing. "You might as easily ask how I wish or dream. The wind warns of something coming. Something with power. Power and ill intent. We can taste it."

"We?" The last thing Gabriel wanted, after a magician in their party, was more than one magician anywhere nearby. "No, never mind. You said you could help. How?"

"I felt you push at the bones," the magician said to Isobel. "You are . . . half-trained and weak, and could only rouse the beast, not question it. My skills are greater, but I lack the strength to face this storm on my own." His admission had nothing of humility in it, only simple fact. He tilted his head again, the pale strands of his hair tinged red in the firelight, his eyes glittering. "I admit, our meeting on the road was not entirely coincidental. I felt you on the winds and waited for you to find me."

Gabriel watched Isobel, watched how she leaned into the magician's words. They were appealing, even he could feel it, but there was something sticky in them, too, unpleasant like a spider's web.

"Your strength and my skills, we could ride this storm, make it our own."

"Magicians do not share." Gabriel made his voice harsh, attempting to break those honeyed webs, his heart pounding at the risk he took. "Nor do they merely *borrow* power from another. You lie, magician."

The magician's chin lifted, and he stared at Gabriel, Isobel forgotten for the moment. "Have a care, rider."

The power in his voice was a stranglehold, but Gabriel forced the words out of his too-tight throat. "Threatening allies? How quickly you revert to type, *magician*. I say again: you lie. You do not want a partnership; you want *her*. You need Isobel's skills and her power, too, no matter how weak you claim they are, because you're afraid and can't do this yourself."

This was dangerous, Gabriel knew, like waving a fish in front of a grizzly. But the magician lied, was attempting to manipulate Isobel, and Gabriel'd learned over years that the surest way to find truth was to make someone mad enough to spit it out.

"You're a coward and a liar."

The magician stood in one smooth movement, uncoiling until he towered over them, his hair pale against the dark sky, the fire cracking with renewed vigor until he seemed limned with flame. "I ride the east wind. Do you have any idea what that means, mortal?"

Gabriel stood as well, showing his teeth in a grin as cocky as he could muster. "Show me."

Izzy could barely breathe, feeling the air around the small fire thicken as Gabriel goaded the magician, pushing with his words, saying things he had no place to be saying.

So, why was he saying them? The boss's voice asked the question in her head, forcing her to stop reacting, start *thinking*. Why was he doing this? Gabriel Kasun was a solid man, a thinking man who counted the cards and considered his bets. He had offered to mentor her on a whim, but even then, he'd had his reasons. So, what was his reason here?

Her thoughts were too slow, and she shook herself, irritated and impatient, her palms warm with sweat as the two men squared off, words threatening to explode into blows.

"You want to know what a magician may do? How powerful I am?" The magician was beyond sense now, the snarl of a dog in his throat. "I will show you."

But he didn't do anything. He merely stood before them, staring out at something she couldn't see. Izzy clenched her fingers, knuckle rubbing against the silver of her ring. The sun was below the horizon now, shadows filling the crevasses around them where the flames could not reach. Too late, too late; power was best worked at dawn and dusk and when the sun was direct overhead. Every fool knew that; surely a magician would not—

A breeze stirred the flames even higher and lifted the edges of Izzy's jacket, making her shiver, though the breeze was not cold. The magician raised his hands to shoulder height, fingers splayed, palms facing out, and the ground underneath them rumbled.

Unnerved, Izzy wanted to look for Gabriel, move closer to him for reassurance, but could not take her gaze off the magician. She could *see* the wind wrapping around him, feathering his long hair, sliding under his skin and then back out again, and her breath caught at how simple it was, how clean and simple, not complicated at all, as though all she had to do was reach out and touch it, and it would be part of her as well.

Such power, she thought. Not a quiet rumble at all but a roar, the scream of a ghost cat in the night, the howl of the coyote, the rush of buckshot as it left the muzzle, knocking her back and making her hands tremble.

"Don't," she said, unsure if she spoke to the magician, or Gabriel, or the gathering power itself.

None of them listened.

The magician's hands stretched forward, as though he were attempting to take hold of something, and the air opened around his hands, a reddish-black splotch that grew and deepened, tendrils reaching out of like—like ribbons, she thought, even as they spread, shadows in the darkness, tiny flickerings that she could *hear* as well as see.

"Blessed angels and all the gods protect us," Gabriel swore, even as the ribbons snapped outward, raptor wings on a downward strike, and wrapped around the magician's torso, fighting the wind for his body, rocking it back and forth.

She thought, for just an instant, she saw the magician's expression change, eyes widening, teeth bared in a fierce grimace. This hadn't been what he'd expected, what he'd thought would happen.

And then a shape thrust itself through the opening, leering out of the blotch, a head elongated like a horse but with teeth like no horse ever had, long curved eyeteeth jutting over a jaw that opened impossibly wide. They snarled at each other, beast and magician, then the beast struck, its head jolting forward, jaws digging into the magician's chest with a hot, meaty *thunk-crunch.*

There was a long, silent second, Isobel struggling to find air to scream, and the head pulled back, drawing half of the magician's chest with it, ropes of gore and bone exposed in a steaming, salty mess.

Her voice was still lost, but a scream rose out of the wind itself, piercing Izzy's ears with its agony and outrage. The storm-snake pulled back in through the splotch, teeth grimed with blood and gore, shaking like a dog to splatter blood into the fire, until the splotch squeezed smaller, smaller still, and disappeared.

The magician's body teetered, rocking back and forth on the balls of its feet even as the wind whistled into his skin and out again, wrapping around the bloodied, torn flesh and carrying it away, fading bit by bit, until there was nothing left but the smell of blood and shit, and the cold, sickly sweat Izzy could feel laying thick on her skin.

The faint noise of grasshoppers came back first, then the call of a distant owl, three ghostly hoots.

"What . . ." Her voice was clogged in her throat, choking her. "What happened? Gabriel?"

And then Gabriel was behind her, holding her shoulders, turning her away from the fire, away from the gore splattered at their feet, letting her face rest against the rough cloth of his jacket, his arms warm around her.

"New rule," he said, his voice soft, steady against the shell of her ear. "Don't stand too close to magicians. Ever."

"Poor bastard." Gabriel's words hadn't been meant for her, and she tucked her forehead against his shoulder, pretending she didn't hear, pretending that none of it had happened, that they'd never encountered the magician in the road, had never seen the empty street of Clear Rock, had never ridden up into the hills, had never ridden out of Patch Junction. Had never seen, never felt, never smelt . . .

Her nose was pressed against Gabriel's jacket, and he smelled of dirt and dust, of well-tanned leather and horseflesh, of chicory and coffee, and the faint sharp smell that was somehow Gabriel alone, that she hadn't even known until she recognized it.

She touched the ring on her finger and *felt* the tarnish dulling its surface.

In the distance, a coyote called to the moon, a long echoing noise, and Izzy shivered, although the sound had never bothered her before.

"Get your gear," Gabriel said, pulling away. Izzy shivered again, the night air colder after his warmth, but lifted her chin, determined to do whatever he told her. "I want to be on the road as soon as you're ready."

Away from here. Away from—she didn't look at the ground, still splattered, but nodded once and turned to gather her kit together.

While she was doing that, he put out the fire, and the night closed in around them, the stars too dim and the moon too low to bring relief. When he nudged at her shoulder, she jumped, half turning to see him offering her several strips of the paddle-shaped plant he'd brought back for dinner. "You can eat 'em raw," he said.

The thought of eating anything made her stomach roll, but she watched as he took one and began chewing at it while he rolled up his own kit. "You'll do better with something in your stomach," he said without looking back at her. "Just small bites."

She nibbled cautiously at one of the strips. The taste was slightly bland but wet, like a pear that wasn't quite ripe yet, and she ate the entire thing before wiping her hands on her skirt and going back to work.

The smell of blood and feces followed her, the horses shifting and shying away when she approached. Even Flatfoot gave her an evil eye when she tightened a strap, his ears flickering back and forth as though he expected something to jump out of nowhere again, this time with a taste for mule-flesh.

Izzy couldn't bring herself to fault him. She still felt wobbly, and she couldn't blame the darkness for how her vision was disturbingly unclear. But closing her eyes to get rid of the tears was worse: she could see the fanged mouth darting forward, heard the meaty thunk as it connected with the magician's flesh, and she was aware of the fact that it was aware of *them*, that they were ignored, not unobserved.

Her hands slipped on the leather, jabbing herself with the buckle hook, and she swore, forcing herself to concentrate. The horses would calm themselves only if she were calm.

She felt Gabriel behind her, likely carrying their packs. Her hands stilled, and she tilted her head to look up, looking not at the brightness of the waning moon rising on the horizon but the deeper black overhead. She wished for the warmth of the oil lamps of the saloon, the sulphurous reassurances of the blacksmith's forge, even the steady flicker of a tallow candle.

"What was that? What did he do?"

"I don't know." Gabriel's voice was terse, his words bitten off. "I don't . . . I told you, this is beyond me, Iz. He wanted to show how strong his medicine was, so he probably called on a dust-dancer, or maybe it was what was made lunch out of Clear Rock. I don't know. He was a magician; who knows what they do or why. Whatever it was, whatever came when he called, it was more than he could handle."

It had torn his chest out and eaten it.

"That . . . that thing wasn't what I saw before. In Clear Rock." Her voice wasn't as even as she would have liked, but Izzy was proud of the fact that she got the words out at all.

"Wonderful, so there are two things out there eating people?" Gabriel moved to double-check Steady's gear. Izzy didn't take it as an insult; he needed to do something too, same as her. She finished checking Uvnee's girth, pushing the mare's stomach a little to force her to exhale before tightening it a notch again, then scratched Uvnee once on the poll just between her ears in reassurance, and went to mount. By the time she was settled, Gabriel was already moving Steady back onto the road, the mule's lead rope tied to his saddle for the first time since they'd left Patch Junction.

Izzy had seen death before, she'd watched people die before, but never like that. The sheer swift violence of it, the lack of warning—had the magician thought he could control it? Had he even known what he was calling up?

"You pushed him into it," she said, returning to the last thing that had made sense. "You goaded him. Why? He could have been useful! He *wanted* to be useful." She felt anger flare, a satisfying burn. If she was angry, she had no room to be afraid.

"Iz . . ." It was difficult to see his expression; he was a silhouette beside her, from the brim of his hat to the cut of his long coat over Steady's flanks, and his voice was nearly as blank. "What are magicians?"

She sighed, but somehow the fallback into question-and-answer settled the last of her nerves, as did moving away from the stink of the campsite.

"They're white men who style themselves on medicine men, on dream-talkers. They've given themselves to the wind in the crossroads, eaten the power there until it fills them entire." She knew that, everyone knew that, the same way they knew that magicians weren't the same after that. Not bad, not evil, just . . . different. Unreliable.

Just run.

She'd been fooled by the magician's appearance. Had seen the surface and discounted what was below, even though she knew better, had grabbed at the idea that someone could help her, carry her responsibilities for her. She'd failed, and Gabriel had been right. And the magician had died for it.

A small, disloyal voice in her thoughts said, *Because Gabriel had goaded him.*

"In civilized places"—listening to his voice in the darkness, she thought that Gabriel sounded tired, like he knew he'd goaded the magician into it, as well—"magicians—conjurors, witches, wind-talkers, whatever name you settle on, those who claim the same skills—they're driven out, same as the rest of what roams wild in the Territory. White or native makes no difference. There's no place for that in civilized places. But the Territory isn't civilized, not yet. Maybe not ever, if your boss has his say."

Tired and regretful, like he wished it were different. But Izzy couldn't tell *what* he wished were different.

"You meant to drive him out?" After she'd invited him to come with them—Izzy felt insulted, then betrayed, then felt a sudden rush of relief that her mentor had been able to overrule her if the magician had been that dangerous, if she'd made such a terrible misstep. And then she remembered how the magician had died, and felt guilt at her relief.

"No. But I knew he was dangerous. Prideful, arrogant." Gabriel *tsk*ed with his tongue, a sharp, wet noise. "Maybe they've a right to be, magicians. They can do things most of us can't, and if they pay a high price for it, well, that's their business. We all make our bargains for what matters to us. But my obligation is to protect you, Isobel. And if *he* was looking to us for something, adding to all we've already seen in recent days? That made me wary.

"Challenging him the way I did, I knew he was bound to show off, to prove to us—to himself—that he *wasn't* afraid. I was testing him, under as controlled a situation as I could manage. Testing his control. And I won't apologize for that or for what happened."

For a bit, the only sound was the clop of hooves on the road and insects singing in the grass, broken once by a distant howl echoed by several more. Too far away to be a worry, Izzy judged, and moving away from them, not toward.

"What was it?" she asked, finally. "The thing that took him." It hadn't been the thing she saw at Clear Rock; she was near certain of that. It had *felt* different.

"I don't know," he said again. "The tribes have stories . . . All I know's there're things out here that nobody's ever seen, at least not to talk about it. Maybe your boss knows. I'm just hoping that eating what summoned it was enough and it doesn't feel the need to come back and find *us*."

Wasn't much to say to that, so she didn't.

Despite all that had happened, the familiar motion of Uvnee's walk eased Izzy back into a sort of sleepy calm, her hands easy on the reins, her body soft and comfortable in the saddle. Part of her knew she was half-asleep; the other was alert to everything around her, the sounds and smells of the night air. She tipped her head back and studied the glittering sweep of stars, the moon now a bright silver glow casting down a hazy light. Izzy had never ridden at night before. Despite the conditions, she thought she might like it. But they were moving in the wrong direction.

Izzy frowned, then pulled Uvnee to a halt. Gabriel rode on a few paces more, then stopped, sensing she was no longer following.

Why had she thought that? She pulled at the feeling, kneading and stretching it under her hands until it firmed. The words came to her, certain and firm. "I need to do something. About what happened in Clear Rock."

Even in the moonlight, she could see the stubborn clench of his cheek. "You're not going back there."

"No, I know." She didn't want to go back there either. Just the thought of it made her chest hurt. "But what the magician said . . . He was telling the truth. He really was worried that something's come into the Territory that's scaring . . . that's that scary. And it's not enough just to leave it be and hope it doesn't get hungry again."

She didn't want to go anywhere near that thing, didn't want to even think about it, but saying the words eased some of the discomfort she'd felt all day, maybe for days now. "That's . . . that's why I'm here, isn't it? Not to run away, not even to run back home with warnings, but to *do* something about it."

He shifted, the saddle's creak too loud in the thin night air, interrupting the insect chorus around them. "Do what?" He wasn't challenging her; he wasn't dismissive. He was asking.

And she knew. As simple as kneading bread or folding linens, she knew. The way the cards flipped onto the felt, the pattern of the deal, the shuffle and fold of the pasteboards between the boss's fingers, one at a time but each one part of the whole, she felt something rise inside her. Not the twisting, tossing sensation of before, but a grounding, her backside firmly in Uvnee's saddle, her awareness stretching through the mare's legs and hooves into the ground, even as the breeze touched every inch of her skin and the coyotes' distant howl was clear and close in her ears.

"I need to clean the town."

Gabriel might have said something; she couldn't hear. Her left palm rested against the fabric of her skirt, but it was touching the ground, too. Connected. Listening. More than listening, some sensation she couldn't name, couldn't grasp, fire under her skin, stone grinding against her bones, and it *hurt* but she couldn't stop, couldn't break away.

The moment when she had seen the storm-thing descend remained with her, remained within the stones and bones of Clear Rock. She reached for it, stretching the connection tight between them, flipping a single card from the boss's deck into it. Low card: dealer wins.

Flickerthwack. The card landed, a line of flame circling it, racing inward. When it reached the center, a silent explosion filled her awareness, trying to rock her out of the saddle. Some part of her held firm, touching the stones below, wrapping the wind around her, and her inner vision cleared.

In the town of Clear Rock, every external wall now bore the boss's sigil, pulsing with power.

I did that, she thought with awe, then the need to do more pushed through her. She gathered the sigils together, imagined the medicine in them like a coil of hair braided into something stronger, wrapping around the town, and then she set it on fire.

The sigils flared like the blacksmith's forge, so bright she half thought it would be visible from where they stood, racing from the external walls inward, until the conflagration met at the center and went out with a brutal snap, only cold ash left behind.

The town shuddered and was still. Cold, empty. Safe.

Izzy was allowed a flicker of satisfaction, then her own body resurfaced, screaming in agony. She swayed and fell forward onto Uvnee's neck, bumping her nose hard enough to send shock back down her spine. When she steadied herself, her left palm spasmed, all the pain centering there. She looked down, and her eyes widened. In the center of her hand, where the burning sensation had been, where it had prickled before, pale red lines picked out a sigil. The same sigil she had left on the town of Clear Rock.

The devil's mark.

"Oh." Her voice was faint, weak, stunned, her fingers curling over the mark, skin stretched tight and hot.

"Isobel? What did you do?"

She could only shake her head, unable to answer. The power that had flowed through her, the knowing—it wasn't hers, nothing she'd done. She had no power. It was all his. She had given herself entirely to the boss, had signed a Bargain that could never be broken.

She was the devil's tool, nothing more. Would never be anything more. The bitterness of it rose in her throat, gagging her.

"Iz?" Steady was pushing against Uvnee's side, his square head at Izzy's elbow, while Gabriel leaned in, trying to take her face in his hands. She shook him off, tipping her head down to let the brim of her hat hide her face, refusing to show weakness. Not there, not then.

He took the hint, pulling Steady back a pace but still watching her. "It's done?"

"Yes."

"Good." And he turned Steady back and started down the road again.

The set of his back, his shoulders, reminded her: regret was pointless. She was what she had chosen to be. Had done what needed doing.

Izzy lifted her chin and pushed Uvnee forward to follow.

Something was screaming. Lightning strikes rained down into rock, and flesh burned. A coyote howled and a shadow swept overhead, and deep within the earth, something shifted and groaned . . .

Izzy woke within the echo of her dream, her heart pounding and her face bathed in sweat. Four mornings now, the same not-a-dream, and annoyance was starting to win over the fear. Gabriel wasn't sleeping well either, the shadows under his eyes deepening, the tension in his shoulders increasing. They didn't mention it to each other. They spoke of very little beyond what was necessary, making and breaking camp with practiced efficiency, riding toward some point Izzy assumed Gabriel knew, south and westerly by the sun's track.

They were riding to see a friend of his, he'd said. Someone who might be able to cast light on the things they weren't speaking of.

Despite all that, despite what lurked unmentioned behind them, Izzy felt strangely comfortable. The saloon, the press of people around her, the everyday noise of life in Flood, seemed impossibly far away and unthinkable now. Where the quiet had been oppressive at first, now it allowed her to hear the yet-quieter noises, the creak and groan, squeak and scream of the smaller life around them.

She avoided thinking about her Bargain the way you avoided a pit in the ground: skirt around it, don't fall in, and it might as well not be there. She knew it was foolishness, but she couldn't do anything else, not just then.

They were riding through grasslands again, the shadow of the hills a constant companion to their right. Gabriel pointed out signs that buffalo had passed by, trampled and grazed-down grasses and drying chips, but the herd had clearly moved on. She watched a small herd of elk move slowly in the distance, saw fox kits tumbling about their mother at dusk and hawks glinting golden in the morning sun, waited while a sleepy-eyed brown bear lumbered past, nodded in cautious greeting when three native boys ghosted by, their bare skins painted, leading a horse equally daubed with color.

"What are they doing?" she asked, when they were alone again.

Gabriel merely shrugged, watching where they'd gone. "Doesn't concern us."

Although there was no defined trail under their hooves, if Izzy concentrated, she could feel the hum of the road underneath, barely enough to reassure. Every so often, Gabriel would rein Steady to a stop and tilt his head, listening, and then start on again.

The fourth or fifth time, Izzy asked, "Can you hear it all the time?"

"It's like listening to a creek or the rain," he said. "You hear it, and then you don't hear it, but when it stops, you hear the not-hearing it."

She thought about that as they rode on, turning more westerly, back toward the shadow of the hills. Overhead, a flock of smaller birds swooped and dipped in a black shadow, scattering when a larger predator dove into the ranks. They'd seen no hint of Reaper hawks since that first, nor any other predator, although they heard coyote song in the early evening, and the coughing call of a ghost cat had kept them company the last night. She had woken several times to see Gabriel sitting upright, the silhouette of his carbine clearly visible in the moonlight.

There had been no hint of whatever had killed the magician, and her ring, freshly polished, stayed bright, as did the buckles on Gabriel's boot and the inlay in the stock of his rifle.

They both stayed alert.

They broke camp before dawn each day, and when the sun reached its apex, they paused to let the horses rest while they stretched their legs and had a quick meal, then saddled up again. They were both sore sick of bean-bread and molasses, but she had to admit that it filled her stomach and cleared her head. Gabriel took to setting four quarters of a coin and a sprinkling of salt at the edges of their lunch-time camp: noon was a powerful time, and no matter that nothing ominous seemed to haunt them, the slight bit of protection made the meal go down more easily.

There was still a while to go yet before they would break that day. Izzy rubbed the palm of her right hand against her skirt, feeling the texture of the cloth scratch her skin, and frowned. She'd been able to rinse out her chemises and stockings two days ago, when they camped near a stream, but after nearly a month on the road, she felt the intense desire to dump her skirts and shirtwaists into a tub of warm, soapy water and give them a proper scrubbing.

She thought about Devorah and her words of advice, and wondered if the woman had made it safely north, and what she would say about all this. Likely "ride away as fast as you can." Instead, they were riding into toward the mountains. Into the storm. Something twisted in her stomach as she raised her eyes to stare at the still-distant blur on the horizon.

Darkness came, sweeping low over the western horizon. Storm clouds spread too far, piled too deep, hiding something within. And the darkness slid through the jagged mountain peaks, sliced into thick ribbons, still rushing forward, dispersing into the sky, soaring up and dipping down, down . . .

She dug her thumb into the palm of her left hand, pressing into the flesh without looking at the mark there, until the memory went away. Gabriel said he had a friend in the mountains, but he hadn't told her more, and she hadn't asked.

They were both waiting, silenced, still holding their breath against another blow.

Movement to the north caught her attention, and Izzy let her eyes rest quietly on the distance, thinking that maybe she'd seen a rabbit or a small deer, something they could catch for dinner, although the thought of butchering a carcass without water nearby was enough to make her lose any appetite. But she quickly realized that the source of the motion had been much farther away than she'd thought. "Is that a rider?"

It was, riding a splotched pony, white hindquarters clearly visible, heading east, away from them. Although the rider wore plain buckskin, the colors of the States were clearly visible fluttering from his saddle, red and white stripes and a field of blue.

"American?"

"Government rider," Gabriel said. He was sitting straight and easy, his hand at the brim of his hat, shading his eyes to see better. There was something weirdly yearning about him, as though he wanted nothing more than to hail the rider, speak to him. But he did nothing.

Anyone could ride into the Territory, if they'd a mind to. Bearing colors gave a rider protection of a sort: nobody thought the Americans would start trouble, but nobody could say for sure they wouldn't, not even the boss.

Easier to let them come and go, he'd said more than once. They'll see what they see and say what they'll say, and telling them they can't is worse than saying they may.

And those that see, stay, Maria had said once, and laughed. But the boss hadn't.

SILVER ON THE ROAD

Izzy watched the rider lope away from them and thought of April back in Patch Junction, how she'd sounded, speaking of the American States as though they had some secret she needed to know, and Gabriel's worries about what she'd said. And then she thought of the boss sitting at his table, flipping pasteboard cards in front of him, listening to the flow of conversation and gossip, and for the first time, she had the sense of him playing not cards but people, places, flipping them over and reading them, sorting them, sending them where they needed to be . . .

She clenched her fingers around the ache in her left hand, and wondered what card represented her.

They camped that night next to the bank of a tiny river snaking its way through the grasses. The horses and mule drank their fill, then wandered off, grazing contentedly. Izzy had meant to groom Uvnee, aware that the mare's coat and forelocks were caked with dirt, but she stopped, midturn, and felt her jaw drop open.

"That's . . ." She gained control of her voice again and said, louder, not looking away, "That's the Knife?"

Gabriel looked over where she was staring, shading his eyes against the setting sun. "Yep." He gave her a curious look. "Ah. Never seen 'em before this close, have you?"

"No. I . . . No." Her chest felt tight, and she swallowed. "How . . . how far away are they?"

"'Nother two days' ride, probably," Gabriel said.

"Oh." Her voice had gone faint again. The jagged smudge rising above the hills, lit from behind with the scarlet of the setting sun, was that far away? She tried to gauge how tall they must rise and failed utterly.

"We'll be there soon enough," he said. "Try not to worry about it until then, and come help me set traps for dinner, or we'll be eating bean-bread again—and we're near out of molasses."

The thought of fresh meat made Izzy's mouth water. Fortunately, they were lucky enough to catch a plump rabbit while making camp, mainly by dint of Gabriel stumbling over it, startling it into Izzy's hands.

"Catches with Open Fists," he teased her. "That's what the Hochunk would call you."

He kept mentioning that name. "Who are the Hochunk? How do you know them?"

He gutted the rabbit and dumped the remains into a hole she'd dug by the creeklet, and she put soil back on top to keep predators from it while they camped there. "I stayed with some of them when I came back," he said. "They're good people. They hunt up near the Great Lakes, near the border, do a lot of trade back and forth across the river. Smaller tribe, not like the Niukonska or Lakota."

"You stayed with them a long time?"

"A year, more or less." He tossed her the gutted, skinned rabbit and got up to wash his hands, ending the conversation.

The coalstone had spluttered and died several nights before, but they'd collected dried dung—*bois de vache,* Gabriel called it—and shoved it into one of the now-empty bags strapped to the mule's back. He used a handful now to build a small, intense fire, and she set the meat to cook.

"Most folk don't interact much with natives," she said, picking up the conversation again as they ate.

"Most folk aren't riders, Iz. You had the one poor experience, but you can't judge from that. Mostly, we ignore each other unless we've cause; there's room enough to do that."

"Your old friend we're going to see. He's native?"

"He's . . . something." He cracked a bone and tossed it into the remains of the fire. "Not sure what tribe, though. Never asked. A man living alone like that—"

"You don't ask where he came from or why," she finished. "I know."

"Just checking, greenie."

She took the teasing as a warning to stop poking and pulled her blanket more closely over her shoulders, resting her head against the pack. "Good night, Gabriel."

The sky was clouded that night, the stars hidden, and the faint flicker of their fire made the night seem even darker and more vast. For the first time in five days, with the mountains lurking in front of them, Izzy fell asleep wondering about the tribe Gabriel had spent a year with, rather than the magician, and Clear Rock's fate.

Her dreams, if she had any, were washed away when the sky opened just before dawn, waking them with a sudden downpour, and they were quickly soaked and covered in mud, the grass beneath them now slick and slippery. There was a mad scramble in the dark to get their belongings under cover of the oiled tarp that protected the tack from dew, the animals setting themselves side by side and bearing with the deluge as best they could.

Once that was done, Izzy looked down at herself and started to laugh, swinging around wildly as the rain fell down, feeling her bare feet squelch in the mud, her hair sticking to her back, her chemise clinging to her limbs. Izzy had almost forgotten what rain felt like. She turned once again and had her hand caught up in Gabriel's, his other hand settling at her waist, and they performed a slippery, messy reel of sorts, ending when one of them slipped and fell, dragging the other down to the ground with them. They lay there, the horses watching them, until the rain ended, and pale light began to creep into the eastern sky.

"We're a right mess," Gabriel said, slicking his hair back from his face, and looking at himself in dismay. "Into the creek with both of us, and hope there's a towel still dry afterward."

Izzy paused a moment, digging into her pack for a sliver of soap, then grabbed a reasonably dry cloth and joined her mentor by the water's edge. She stopped and watched as he tried to dunk himself in the water, which even after the rain was barely deep enough for fish, much less a full-grown man, and laughed again before sitting down at the edge and leaning back slowly, so that the water rushed over her, rinsing the mud from her hair and skin without effort.

"Smart girl," she heard him say, and then he sat down in the water alongside her and did the same.

She reached out her hand and shared the soap, then rinsed her hair out and, leaving him there, picked her way carefully back to the tarp covering their packs. She found dry clothing to wear and stripped off the utterly soaked chemise, abandoning it on the grass. Her skin prickled from the damp cold, but any shyness she might have had once at being nearly bare like this had faded a long time since. She dressed, then shoved her stockinged feet into damp leather. Thankfully, the shelter had kept the tack safe, and the horses had dried out quickly once she'd brushed the worst of the mud off them, too.

"Too wet to even consider a fire this morning," Gabriel said. "Think you can manage without coffee?"

"Can you?"

"Two more days' hard push, and we'll be there. Coffee and someone else's cooking."

That promise got her back into the saddle, although the slightly crazed relief of the rain slowly faded into a twitch of unease in the back of her head that only got worse as the day went on, and what had been a faint blue-grey smudge in the distance slowly rose up as they rode, until it seemed to block the sky.

She tried not to let her apprehension show, but eventually, Gabriel noticed. "You all right, Iz?"

"It won't fall on us, will it?"

The bastard laughed at her, and she bridled, perfectly willing to burn off the feeling with anger.

"You're plains-born," he said. "I forgot that." He reached over and touched her arm lightly. "They're not going to fall on you, Isobel. The bones dig deep, and these mountains don't move. And we're only going into the foothills, really. No need for worry."

She took a deep breath and then let it and the anger flow away.

Gabriel didn't lie to her. If he said it was safe, it was safe enough. Then his words came clear, and she twisted in the saddle. "Wait, there are mountains that *do* move?"

His laughter was her only answer.

Gabriel lost the road for a while soon after they broke camp the next morning, and while he'd waved off her concern, telling her that "aim toward the Knife" was a perfectly valid direction, the sense of relief she felt when the horses' hooves touched the road again was mirrored in his own expression.

And it *was* a proper road, the first she'd seen since . . . since they'd ridden away from their camp at night, fleeing the creature they still weren't speaking about. Too narrow even for a cart, the edges were still clear and the reddish-brown dirt puffed around their hooves as they rode, distinct from the grasses around it. Izzy looked down at the swirls of dust and the hard-pounded dirt below, and wondered at its existence so far from anything at all.

"Riders ride," Gabriel said, as though he knew what she was thinking. "And this is the only way into the Hills."

"You ride this way often?"

"Once a year," he said. "Sometimes more, depending."

"To see your friend."

"To see my friend," he agreed. "And to carry messages to De Plata occasionally. The mail doesn't come all the way out here, and the ore trains aren't always agreeable to carrying anything other than their own profit."

"There're silver mines here?" She tried to remember the boss's map spread out across the table: there had been red triangles along the western border, but they had seemed impossibly far away then.

She was impossibly far away now.

"Three, last I heard, although one was about played out. Your boss takes his cut, and the rest goes to Red Springs, down south, to be smelted."

LAURA ANNE GILMAN

Silver for coins, silver for safety. She touched the ring around her finger and wondered if it had begun its life here, in the hills ahead of them. Coins, or the inlay of a knife, or the buckle on Gabriel's boot, the links on the boss's cuffs. She knew mines were safe, they had to be, but . . .

"Ease down, Isobel," he said, matching Steady's pace to Uvnee's so they could ride side by side. "Living silver's rarer than a white buffalo."

And far more unlucky. Silver ore was malleable, usable. Living silver resisted, often with terrible results.

"When was the last time?"

"Eleven years ago, when Kinchester Mine blew."

"Oh. I remember that." She shuddered. "The boss had been mid-deal at the table, when all of a sudden everything stopped. *Everything.* Not even the lamp lights flickered. It felt like I couldn't move, couldn't even breathe. Nobody could. And then the boss stood from the table and walked out into the night, and everything had started again, but he didn't come back home for three days." She leaned forward and patted Uvnee's neck, as though the mare needed reassurance. "We only learned later what had happened."

"Usually, it's so deep down, doesn't get bothered. Deep veins, miners know to avoid."

"But nobody knows for certain before they reach it?" Before it killed them.

Gabriel rubbed fingers across his mouth, then made an "I don't know" gesture. "Magicians, maybe. Your boss, probably. But they're not the ones down in the mine."

She had never thought about the miners before. The idea that someone went into the earth to pull the ore from the ground . . . She had seen the rough silver come to town every year, of course, ready for shaping on the forge, but she had never thought about where it came *from.* That was almost enough to distract her as the road slowly went higher, taking them into the rougher, steeper terrain, the rocks rising up around her, casting thick shadows. Almost.

Gabriel reined his gelding in, and as though they'd discussed it beforehand, they dismounted to stretch their legs, walking side by side. The horses trailed behind them, Flatfoot slightly ahead, his ears alert and interested, as though he was glad to be out of the endless flat expanse of the plains, even if there was less to graze on.

"Gabe . . ." She reached her hand out without thinking, relieved when a warm, calloused hand took it up, fingers twining with her own. Her breath came more easily after that, despite the impossible-to-ignore feeling that despite his assurances, the mountain *would* fall on them.

But the moment that fear eased, Izzy realized that the prickling on the back of her neck had returned, and this time, it came with the ache in her palm, dead center of her left hand.

Izzy hesitated, testing that prickling sensation, then said, "It's back, isn't it? Whatever was watching us before?"

"We're definitely being followed. Can't say it's same as before, though." He turned to look at her and tipped his hat back enough that she could see his face clearly. His stubble had grown thick over his chin and lip, and there was a bruise over one cheekbone that he'd likely picked up during their scramble during the rainstorm, but his gaze was clear and surprisingly unworried. "What do you sense?"

She licked her lips, thought about how to explain it. "My skin's too tight," she said, finally. "It makes me nervous."

"Could be anything," he said. "Native hunter wondering what we're up to, or someone come up over the border, poking their nose in. Or a cat or maybe that coyote gotten too curious, wondering if we're good to eat. Maybe a spirit-dancer, drawn by all the devil's medicine you've been using."

"None of that's making me feel any better," she told him.

"Or it could be a demon."

She liked that idea even less.

"Unlikely, though," he went on. "Demon aren't travelers; they tend to pick an area and stay in it. And generally, if they're going to cause trouble, they do it; they don't lurk."

213

"But they do eat people?" Her voice did *not* squeak.

"Sometimes. Not often."

That failed to be reassuring.

"I don't know," he said again. "I don't know what it is or why it's so interested in us, or if it's the same as was following us down in the plains. But I aim to fix that." He adjusted the brim of his hat, letting his hand linger over his mouth. "You keep going on; take Steady with you. I'm going to circle around and see what I can see." He handed the gelding's lead to her. "Just keep going."

"Gabriel." He paused but didn't turn back. "Be careful."

She felt foolish after saying it; of course he would be careful. He was the cautious one, the experienced one. But something prickled under her skin, all over her body, and the tug she gave Steady's reins might have been harder than was strictly necessary. She looked ahead, then unlatched her canteen and took a long drink, trying to look unconcerned for the benefit of anything that might be watching, then started walking again.

The road they were on was wide enough now for both horses to walk abreast without crowding, Flatfoot wandering ahead, occasionally looking back to make sure the rest of his herd was within sight. She kept moving, feeling the strain in the backs of her legs; although she'd become used to riding all day, she was unaccustomed to this kind of climb for any length of time. But walking had an advantage. She could feel it now if she concentrated: not a sound or a touch, exactly, but an awareness of the road under her feet. If she pressed down on the forward step, hard but gentle, she could feel it deepen, humming not in one place, but many. She thought, although she hadn't said as much to Gabriel, that if she pressed a little more, she might be able to trace every road, a lattice stretching throughout the Territory. But each time she thought that, the connection broke, and she could feel nothing at all.

Gabriel had said she would learn to sense it, that every rider could, eventually. Unlike before, when the boss's power had flooded through her, this was her, all her. She clung to the connection for that and kept walking.

‡   ‡   ‡

Gabriel stepped off the road and dropped to his knees on the ground. Scooping up a handful of rock dust, he coated his clothing and face as best he could. Not that his clothing was brightly colored—even if it had been once, years on the road had worn most everything he owned to shades of brown and grey. But like called to like, and the more he could blend with rock and dirt, the better.

He spared a thought for Isobel. She'd been on edge since Clear Rock, more so than he'd expected. He'd assumed that, growing up as she did, she would be aware of the nature of the bargain she had made with her boss, what might be expected of her. He might have been wrong in that assessment. Damn the devil for a cold bastard; no doubt he had his reasons for sending her half-trained and half-blind, but they weren't ones Gabriel could fathom.

But there was nothing he could do about that now, if at all.

There was no visible trail save the one they had come along, and damn little cover to hide in. He backtracked along the road, moving slowly, alert for any flicker or twitch that might be another living thing. But save for a rock-mouse that paused to stare at him before deciding he was no threat, there was nothing else on the trail.

Except he *knew* there was.

He hunkered down to think. This was Hinonoeino territory, but if they had been following, they would have left some sign, if only to taunt him with his failure to catch them at it. He knew this tribe: so long as he offered no offense, he would be allowed passage. And Isobel was the devil's. Here, so close to the border, that could be both a plus and a danger, depending on the Hinonoeino's relations across the mountains—he wasn't fool enough to believe they didn't have regular contact with the Spanish, if only through the endless parade of hopeful padres looking to save heathen souls in exchange for Mexicana silver.

But if it was not them, and it was assuredly not another rider, and he truly didn't think it was anything on four paws, the remaining obvious conclusion wasn't one he wanted to make. He'd rather deal with another chimera than a demon, but he suspected he was not going to get much choice in the matter. He exhaled, rubbed at his face, and muttered, "You knew when you signed your name, this was not going to be a milk run."

"Sssssssssso you did. And yet you chosssssssssse anyway, ssssssssssson of bonessssssss."

Gabriel sighed, tipping his hat back and sliding—carefully, looking where he dropped his backside—to the ground. "What now?"

"Sssssssssso gracsssssioussssssss," the snake scolded him, belly to the dirt, head lifted just enough to that he could see the bright black eyes and the forked tongue darting out into the air. Another rattler, this one yellowish-green, with darker black markings toward its tail. It was smaller than the one that had visited them weeks earlier, but Gabriel didn't pretend that it was any less dangerous.

"Forgive me, cousin," he said now. "May I ask why you honor me so with your presence?" *Was it you following us?* he meant. A conspiracy of rattlesnakes made him more nervous even than the thought of demon.

"Sssssssssss." It was laughing at him. "You inssssssert yoursssssself into the doingssss of the world. We did not expect that of you."

"The world is larger than the Territory."

"No, it issssssss not."

He'd had these arguments before, with those who went about on legs, and never won them, either.

"Are you here to warn us about our enemies and our allies again? Or has something new occurred?"

The snake waited, watching him, the tip of its rattle shaking so slowly, it barely sounded.

"Ahead, there issssss danger. Be wary. Know your enemiessssssss, and know your friendssssssss."

The same warning the other snake had given them. And still useless.

"Thank you," he said, polite through gritted teeth. "I—"

He yelped and leapt back just as the hawk swooped down and grabbed the snake in its talons. Golden-brown wings beat the air, driving dust into his face, and then the bird—and snake—were gone.

He let out a shocked huff. "Should have paid more attention to your own destiny and less to mine."

Twice now, snakes had come to warn him. Gabriel was neither ignorant nor a fool. He knew what that meant: he'd stumbled into exactly the sort of mess he'd spent his entire life avoiding. But the warning was near useless without telling him *who* his enemies were. Or, for that matter, who his *friends* were.

Isobel?

No. He refused to place her under scrutiny. She might lead him into danger, but it would not be a willful betrayal.

Warning aside, that still left the question: had it been the snake they both sensed or something else? But by now, anything that had been shadowing them would have moved on or hidden itself. And he needed to get moving as well, or he'd still be walking come nightfall to catch up with Isobel and the horses.

They made camp reluctantly, as the evening shadows made the trail's footing more uncertain. Given his druthers, Gabriel would have kept walking all night rather than making camp where they might be vulnerable, but Isobel hadn't quite mastered the art of sleeping in the saddle yet, and she needed to rest.

While she slept curled up under her blanket, he groomed the horses by moonlight, taking comfort in their soft breathing, aware that if anything were to approach, they would know before he did, but not so much comfort that he could bring himself to sleep as well. That finished, he sorted through their packs, redistributing the weight, and gauging how long their supplies could last. The result wasn't encouraging.

The moment the sky began to lighten, he woke Isobel. Her eyes opened immediately when he touched her shoulder, and she sat up without complaint, alert but aware that he'd not woken her to an emergency—a far cry from the sleepy-eyed girl who'd breakfasted with him in Patch Junction.

"No fire this morning," he said, handing her a narrow strip of pemmican and a canteen, and laughing when she made a face. The fact that it didn't taste as good as the salt-dried charqui was why it was still left when they were down to the very last of their supplies. "Drink all the water you want, though. We'll be in De Plata by noon, and a hot meal for dinner."

"De Plata." She rinsed out her mouth with water, spitting out into the dirt, then repeated the name, imitating his accent. "That's a Spanish name."

"It was a Spanish outpost originally."

He could feel his stomach rumbling, refusing to be distracted by his own strip of pemmican. While Flatfoot might feel better with lighter packs, even Steady, who could feed himself on two tufts of grass and stubbornness, kept trying to mouth at Isobel's hair every time she passed within reach, as though the braid might somehow have become straw. She smacked his muzzle with a gentle reprimand and swung herself up into Uvnee's saddle.

"Well, I don't care if the town was originally settled by an entire pack of magicians and a dust storm, so long as they can provide a hot meal, a real bed, and enough water to wash myself and all my clothing."

"All the comforts of home," he promised. "A priest named Escalante built a church there and brought a few desperate families in, thinking that if he managed to establish a foothold, perhaps convert a few heathens, Spain would have a base from which to claim the rest of the mountains and work their way down into the plains."

"What happened?"

"Natives put up with him for a few years, then tired of his foolery."

Izzy rolled her eyes, unsurprised. "Gospel sharp used to ride through town every year, heading for the native hunting camps. Boss said they got pleasure out of being told no. Never heard that they rode out with more followers than they rode in with."

"A man has religion, takes something major to make him change it. There weren't any plagues or disasters near De Plata, the crops didn't fail, so the padre had nothing to work with. Anyway, once the priest was gone, the villagers he'd brought with him stayed because they'd discovered silver in the streams, and—"

"We're going to a silver town?" Izzy reined Uvnee in hard enough to make Uvnee buck slightly in protest. "Sorry girl," she said, patting the mare's neck in apology. "Truly?"

He shook his head, amused at how her fear was so obviously competing with excitement.

"What do you think De Plata means? But don't get too excited. No matter what stories they tell over campfires and in rag novels, silver mines are boring. Dark holes, grimy miners, and inert silver you wouldn't even recognize in its rough form. But they have something better in De Plata."

"Better than silver?" She was dubious.

"Much," he said, but wouldn't tell her more.

The road they were on soon became a steep slope, with even the normally sure-footed mule having difficulty. The trees grew taller and more thickly on either side, birch and alder supplanting cottonwood, and the ground underneath was a harsh red studded with rocks. The sense of being watched lingered, although Gabriel wasn't sure if the feeling was true or simply the fear of it lingering.

"You're sure they won't fall?"

It took him a moment, lost in his own concerns, to remember what she was asking about. The mountains. "They haven't so far as my father's father knew; there's no reason to think they will now."

"Your grandfather was here to know?" She looked surprised and a little impressed.

"So he claimed." He mounted up again before she could ask more. His family wasn't something he wanted to talk about. Fortunately, from the frowning glances she kept shooting up at the peaks in front of them, Isobel had other things more important to worry about.

The hills didn't fall, and they rode into De Plata midafternoon, the sun casting an oddly overcast light through the trees. The town wasn't much: a shallow bowl between two peaks, consisting of a mercantile, a run-down-looking guesthouse that had seen better years, the long-house where the miners ate their meals, and a ramshackle shack with a chirurgeon's sigil overhead. At the other end of the single street, there was a small cluster of stone shacks, windowless and slumped, where the men slept. Farther past, visible more because he knew than being able to see it, were the entrance to the mine and the furnace where the silver ore was melted into usable form.

There was no stable; the horses and mule were left in a corral on the other side of the shacks, sharing space with a small herd of long-haired goats and a pair of particularly bedraggled donkeys who seemed disinclined to greet the newcomers.

"Where is everyone?" Isobel asked, and he couldn't fault her nervousness, considering the lack of greeting they'd found at Clear Rock.

"Most of the locals will be in the mine," he said. "It's the only reason this town exists. Mine the silver, purify it, send it down into the Territory. That's all they do here."

"Everyone?"

"Most everyone. You don't raise a family if you're a miner, Iz. It's a hard life."

"Not everyone's a miner." Where a minute before they'd been alone, now an older man was leaning against the corral gate, watching them. "Some of us trade, some of us hunt. Some of us deal with the likes of you."

"The likes of—" Isobel started to bristle, all the calm he'd managed to put back into her cracking and falling away with one ill-timed barb.

"Gabriel Kasun," he said, offering his hand to the stranger, his other resting on her arm, a silent warning. The old man didn't take it, and Gabriel let it drop, refusing to take offense. He was white, blue-eyed, and younger than Gabriel'd thought at first, just hard-worn. "This is Isobel née Lacoyo Távora." It seemed like months since he'd first heard that name, not a matter of weeks. He thought about mentioning where she hailed from, then thought about their shadow and decided against it. She either agreed or felt the glitter had worn off since Patch Junction, because she said nothing either.

"Marshal Itchins," the stranger said, turning the inside of his lapel to show the silver sigil pinned there. "Your business in De Plata?"

"Supply run." The fact that this man was a marshal changed things. Isobel *should* check in. But the paranoia that had been growing in him since the Caron farmstead kept him from saying anything. "Then on to see Graciendo."

Itchins's expression didn't change. "You a friend of the old bear's?"

"Not exactly. But he's expecting me." The marshal still looked dubious, so he added, "I'm carrying letters for him."

"Didn't know the old bear knew anyone outside, to be getting letters." The marshal didn't smile. "He expecting you, not her?"

"I'm mentoring her. Is there a problem?" He couldn't remember ever getting this sort of questioning—then again, he'd never encountered a marshal in De Plata before. Had the unrest Devorah mentioned made its way west? Or was something else going on? Isobel had said the storm she'd seen came over the mountains. . . .

"Just cautious," Itchins said. "We only get three, maybe four people here in a year. Seeing two show up at once . . ."

"It's good to see that you are alert, marshal. Especially since there is no badgehouse affiliated with this town, despite the presence of a mine and its proximity to the border." Isobel had stepped forward as she spoke, and Gabriel felt himself move back a pace instinctively. His hand itched to rest on his knife, but he kept it still, away from anything that might be considered a threat.

"I work the circuit through here, from Red Springs on down," the marshal said. "De Plata's a regular stop along the way." His eyes narrowed, studying her. "And you've an interest in my road . . . why?"

Her chin lifted, and Gabriel would swear he saw her grow a handspan taller, her eyes lit with a vigor he hadn't seen in weeks. Being challenged seemed to bring out the fierce in her.

"My name is Isobel née Lacoyo Távora," she repeated. "Of Flood."

His gaze flicked over her, hat to boots, and his jaw tightened slightly. "Long way from home, aren't you?"

"We travel the road we're sent?" She smiled tightly, and it never reached her eyes.

"Hrmph." He turned away, clearly dismissing her, and addressed Gabriel. "You'll want to talk to Angpetu, get a bed for the night. Assume you'll be heading out in the morning."

Neither of them responded to his assumption, merely took their saddles and packs, and headed for the bunkhouse.

They could sense, without looking back, that the marshal watched them walk away.

"He's an ass," Gabriel said out of the corner of his mouth.

"What?"

"The marshal. He's an ass. Don't think that a sigil makes men somehow better. Sometimes it just means they're an ass with a badge."

Izzy scowled and scuffed her toe against the soft dirt of the road, watching puffs of dust form around her boot. It wasn't only that the man had been rude. She could have gone into her pack and shown Itchins the papers she carried, the way she had at Patch Junction, but she could read him easily, could tell that the papers wouldn't mean anything to him this far away from Flood, this far removed. Marshal Itchins didn't care about papers she carried, assuming he could even read them.

She curled the fingers of her left hand into her palm, letting the nails dig into the flesh there, making a fist as though she were about to hit something.

222 ∞

"They're still holding a badge," she said. "And it wouldn't make any difference, would it? If he respected me, it would only be because the papers told him to. I'm not anything more than . . ." She took a deep breath, feeling her eyes itching and her throat clog. She would not cry. She was Isobel of Flood, the devil's Left Hand and a rider— and as such, more than any marshal's equal, even if he could not see it. Even if she did not quite believe it; she knew the importance of a strong bluff. "Tell me about this person we're going to see."

"Graciendo? I could tell you legends and stories and things I've seen and heard myself, and you'd call me a liar. Graciendo is best met personally."

She scoffed under her breath, then thought about all the people who came to see the boss, to look at him, to play against him at his own table, and decided that maybe she'd wait before she judged. The marshal, ass or not, had seemed impressed by the man, and Gabriel rode weeks to bring him letters. . . .

The guesthouse barely earned the name: it was a quarter the size of the building in Patch Junction, and her first look inside confirmed her suspicious. The front room was dusty and dimly lit, with two doors in the back. The only furniture was two straight-back chairs next to a rickety wooden table, and only the small, cast-iron box stove dimly glowing with coals within indicated that anyone had been there in the past few days. Gabriel cleared his throat and dropped his bags on the floor, which creaked again under the weight. There was noise from somewhere, and the left-hand door opened and a woman came out, wiping her hands on a small towel. She was slight-built, wearing a man's shirt and trousers, with the black hair and darker skin of a native, but her hair was cut short to her ears and slicked back against her scalp like a man's. Even in the dim light, Izzy could tell she wasn't much older than herself, eyes bright and skin unlined.

"One square per night for the two of you covers a bed each but not the bath. Meals are another square." She had a voice that carried, husky but clear.

"How much for the baths?"

The owner started to say something, then stopped, reaching for Izzy's hand. Surprised, she let the woman turn her hand over, her thumb brushing over Izzy's palm, then pulling the fingers back gently, as though to expose her hand to someone.

She heard Gabriel make a noise and tried to curl her fingers around it again, but the other woman had a surprisingly strong hold. Held up like that, the mark was clear, the lines darker than before, the looping circles centered within a larger circle familiar to every soul in the Territory.

The woman closed Izzy's fingers around the mark gently, then took a step away, dropping contact as though it burned her. "Room's through there," she said, and pointed to the right-hand door. "Towels are in the bath, no charge."

She took the coin Gabriel handed her and disappeared back through the left-hand door, closing it firmly behind her.

"Iz . . ."

A thousand words in that one syllable, and a question hung between them. She braced herself, but Gabriel didn't say anything more, just picked up his bags and went in through the right-hand door. After a moment, she did the same.

She hadn't been hiding the mark, not exactly, but it felt, now, as though she had.

The sleeping quarters were as barren as the front room, four beds with no barriers between them for modesty, but there were pillows and blankets, and no obvious draft, and it wasn't sleeping on the ground. Izzy dropped her pack on the nearest bed, and touched the striped blanket. Wool, harsh to the touch but likely warm as anything she'd slept under back in Flood, maybe even more so. "She said there were meals included? How does a town this small support a restaurant?"

"It doesn't, exactly," Gabriel told her. "The miners don't bother with cooking their own meals. There's a mess hall, serves up two meals a day. It's not fancy, but it will be warm. And it won't be trail rations."

"I'd eat rocks rather than more pemmican."

"I can't promise they'll have elk, but I remember their mutton as being excellent."

Dinner had been everything Gabriel had promised, the square-chested cook who might have been the guesthouse keeper's older brother serving up warm stew with beans and bacon, and a corn pudding that left her warm and full. But it was the bathhouse—the "something better" Gabriel had promised—that won Izzy's heart. It had been nothing more than a stone hut over a natural spring, smelling of sulphur and filled with steam, but the warm water had eased the last soreness out of her muscles until she was convinced that she would fall asleep the moment her head hit the pillow.

The mattress was thin and lumpy, and the blanket scratched as expected, but there weren't any rocks underneath, and the pillow was surprisingly full. And yet, sleep evaded her. At the other end of the room, Gabriel snored lightly, clearly not having the same problem.

She lay on her back and stared up at the ceiling, finally letting herself think about what had happened since leaving Flood. A month they'd been on the road. Only a month since she'd sat in front of the devil and said what she wanted . . . and she was more confused now than she'd been then. She'd thought becoming his Hand would mean something, would *make* her something, but . . .

She looked at her hand, the sigil on her palm invisible in the darkness, but she could feel it etched into her skin. His hand, moving hers. Nothing she did was on her own; nothing she accomplished was hers. There was no reason for anyone to respect *her*.

Izzy pressed her palm against her chest, feeling her heart beat slowly, a thump and a pause, a thump and a pause. Too slow, too loud. Her palm itched, and her heart pulsed, the air in the sleeping chamber suddenly too close to breathe.

As though still asleep, she rose from the bed, reaching for the dress she had worn the day before, slipping it over her chemise, then sitting down and sliding her stockings back on. She could feel the buttons in the back of her skirt press against her legs as she bent over to pick up her boots, carrying them with her as she reached for her jacket, and slipped out to the front room. It was empty; they had not seen the woman who ran the place since she took their coin. She sat down on the chair to button her boots and put her jacket on.

Outside, the surprisingly cold air slipped underneath her clothing instantly, making her shiver. She buttoned her jacket and rubbed her fingers, wishing for the pair of knitted mittens that were in her pack. But if she went back inside for them, she might wake Gabriel, and the thought of trying to explain why she was awake and dressed before sunrise made her willing to bear the cold.

She looked to her right, down the street to where the mine workers lived, but then turned and walked the other direction, away and out of town.

Behind her, the wind picked up and thin white snowflakes began to fall.

Gabriel didn't think much of it when Isobel's bed was empty when he woke. He figured she'd gone to use the bath again, or merely wanted some fresh air. The room they'd slept in was tidily built, but without windows or chimney, the air became stale overnight. He stretched, feeling his back crack in ways it never did when he slept on the ground, and pulled his clothing on over his johns, gathering his shaving kit. He didn't mind a bit of scruff, preferring that to a cold-water shave, but the steam from the bath would soften the bristles nicely for a close shave. Then he could check on the horses and find Isobel and some breakfast, in that order, if she hadn't already come back.

The outside room was empty and surprisingly chilled, even with the stove still warm from the coals glowing within. When he opened the main door to step outside, he discovered why: the ground and rooftops were draped with soft white snow. Unusual this late in spring, but not unheard-of in the mountains. There were footprints show-ing where people had walked, but there were none leading from the doorstep he stood on. If Isobel had come out this way—and she must have—she had done so before the snow began falling.

He frowned at the snow, then looked up at the sky. The thick cover of clouds, still sending down a light shower of snowflakes, gave him no hint as to how long the sun had been up. Still. He chewed at his lower lip, thinking. If it had been falling more thickly earlier, her steps could easily have been filled in by the time she made it to the bathhouse. Or she might have changed her mind and gone to check in with the marshal. There was no cause to worry: Isobel was a sharp girl, and she knew to be alert. He wouldn't worry. Yet.

The mercantile, as he'd remembered, was much smaller than the one in Patch Junction, with fewer goods and higher prices. But there were the basics they needed and enough more to get them back to more civilized places, and he still had enough coin to cover it all.

"I'm telling you, there's something out there."

Gabriel let his hand rest on the sack of dried beans he'd been about to pick up and listened without turning around. That had the sound of an interesting conversation, one possibly relevant to their situation.

"You're letting nerves play tricks on you." A younger voice, also male, and dismissive.

"Mind your manners, Adam," the first speaker said sharply. "I was working these mines when your mother was changing your napkin, and I know when something's wrong. There's bad air down there and above as well, and it's only getting worse."

Gabriel turned slowly, making it seem as though he were looking at another sack of beans identical to the first, and studied the newcomers.

The three men were clearly miners: broad-shouldered and stooped.

Two of them were older, their grey hair showing scalp beneath, while the other seemed to have barely started growing facial hair. Gabriel ran his hand over his own freshly shaved chin and admitted that the man might have shaved that morning as well, but he doubted it. The younger man had brash words and a brave face, but he held himself like a man about to bolt; he was the one feeling nerves.

"It's not the air," the first speaker said. He was facing Gabriel, his face narrow and long, the skin pale as any Gabriel'd ever seen. The other two men had the square faces and darker coloring of griffe, father and son maybe, but they all had the same wan complexion of men who didn't see the sun often. The mines were no place to spend your life, in Gabriel's opinion, no matter how well it paid.

"Don't start with that again, Will," the other older man said.

"I'll say as I well please, and you'd be wise to listen," Will replied, his words full of heat. "It's not the air; it's the very bones beneath. Some demon's work or worse. It's watching us, lurking where we sleep. The devil's work, I say."

"The devil pays us no mind, so long as we provide," the younger man, Adam, scoffed. "Haul silver down and hold the stone."

"Mayhap it's time the devil does pay us some mind," Will said, but this time his words were tired, as though he'd said it times before and never been heard. "There's three gone, up and into nowhere when they should have been working, and left nothing behind. If it were a cat, we'd've heard it screaming; if it were a demon, it would have taken more; if it were a bear, it would have mayhap killed the one but no more, not once the berries started to bloom. And you think a bear won't leave sign? Nothing. But something's out there, and it's stalking us. Pretending otherwise never makes it go away."

Missing men and no explanation why? Gabriel was done listening. Indicating to the merchant waiting behind the counter that he would be back for the items already gathered, he left the mercantile, intent on one thing: finding Isobel.

The snow had stopped, and the chill of that morning was gone, but the sky was still overcast. Isobel hadn't returned to the guesthouse, nor was she with the horses or in the dining hall, now empty save for two boys scrubbing down the tables. Gabriel made himself stop and think, refusing to allow his worry to turn to panic. Isobel was no flip-pit to wander off. She was a practical girl who'd proven herself already, and he needed to trust her sense. Perhaps she had gone to speak with the marshal?

"No sir, haven't seen the girl." Itchins was found in a small office behind the mercantile, going over a leather-bound journal. He studied Gabriel with a lazy look that hid nothing of the mind behind. He might play the fool, but no marshal ever was. "You've lost one of the devil's get, have you? That won't end well for you."

"She's his Hand," Gabriel said tightly. "I'd suggest you speak of her with more respect."

The marshal tried to raise his eyebrows but succeeded only in making himself look like a bemused, overfed owl. "Then you'd best go fetch her, hadn't you? I've more serious things to concern myself with."

"You mean the missing men? Yes, I know about that." No need to tell the marshal he'd learned it by overhearing gossip; let him wonder. "You'd best be on that, then. Terrible if the Hand were to carry back news that a silver town was being preyed upon and the marshal riding that circuit failed to prevent it."

The marshal scowled at him. "You think I haven't tried? You don't know that's why I'm here, instead of riding on, this past week? But there's nothing. Just a bunch of overly nervous miners and three missing men, who could just as easily have run off on their own soon's the weather cleared."

Gabriel wasn't a marshal, had no obligation to the Law here in the Territory save to obey it, same as everyone else, but he was an old dog with only a few tricks, and one of them was examining a witness. "Nervous how? Because the men are gone, or—?"

The marshal frowned again, but this time it seemed directed inward.

"No. Or, yes, they're worried about that, o' course, but they're skittish. These are folk who go into the bones of the earth on a daily basis, blast and wash the ground under their feet, feed that hot beast of a furnace, and yet something that isn't there has them shivering in their beds."

Gabriel had heard that scorn before but typically not from those born and raised in the Territory. And you didn't generally come to be a marshal if you hadn't been raised there. "You think there's nothing that can't been seen, felt, touched that's dangerous?"

Itchins had the grace to blush, although he kept his bluster. "I'm thinking there's no proof that anything happened to those men 'cept themselves."

"And you haven't felt anything? No sense of wrongness, of being watched, threatened?"

The marshal's hand went to the inside of his jacket, almost as though he didn't realize he was doing it. That was where he kept his sigil; clearly, the touch of the badge a reassurance. "We're surrounded by silver," he said, his protest confirmation of what Gabriel suspected. "We should be safe as babes."

It wasn't enough to turn a judge, but this wasn't a matter for judges. "Should be isn't always. And you're assuming whatever it is minds silver in the slightest." Demon were cautious of it, and magicians steered clear when they could, but Gabriel could attest that the devil himself wore silver, and there wasn't a native alive who didn't know the use of it same or better as any other man.

He hesitated, not sure if telling the man what he knew would help or simply panic him more. "There's something loose in the Territory," he said finally. "We've encountered it down in the plains. Can't say that that's what's taken your men, but I can't say it isn't, either." Isobel had seen it coming over the mountains, hadn't she, in her vision? The sense of urgency grew in him: this was her business, he needed to find her.

Itchins finally focused on him, the intelligence behind those eyes no longer hidden. "Something what? Animal? Magical? Some bastard breeding of both?"

"I don't know," he said honestly, turning for the door. "I'm sorry. Just be careful." He needed to find Isobel.

Izzy hadn't meant to walk as far as she had. The restlessness that kept her from sleeping had driven her steps. She'd thought of wearing herself out, then crawling back into the bed and staying there, letting Gabriel go visit his friend without her. They'd been on the go for so long, so much to learn and understand, and everything she'd seen and heard circled inward: April's words and Gabriel's reaction tangled in the snake's warning, the illness in Widder Creek and the thing she'd seen in Clear Rock, and how she'd known what to do both times, and then the magician's fate, wrapping around the unpleasantly tickling sensation that something was following her. . . . It all settled like a bad pudding in her gut, a scrape of fear down her back that made her move more quickly, as though she could leave it behind if she only walked far enough.

Too late, she realized that she had left the town behind entirely, the snow filling in her footsteps behind her, the tree-covered slope unfamiliar. She was lost. And the sense of being watched was back.

And it was cold, colder than it should have been for even early spring. She cupped her right hand over her left knuckles and breathed over them, trying to bring some feeling back to her fingers, and warmth flared from her palm out, spreading along her arms, down her back and legs, until the air's chill no longer bothered her.

The sigil. She opened her hands and stared at the marking, but it seemed no different, the lines dark and smooth, the flesh taut and warm.

The sensation of being watched increased, along with a quiet kind of curiosity, clear as a touch. But unlike before, the sensation had no discomfort, no disquiet. She turned slowly. There was nothing behind her, only slender, white-barked trees and jumbled rocks. In the distance, she thought she saw something move—an animal, she thought,

231

spooked by her presence. But the feeling of being watched remained. "Hello?"

"You are far from where you should be, nééhebéhe'."

Izzy turned and felt her breath catch, staring at the man standing in what had been empty space before. *How do they do that?* she thought, irrationally annoyed at how natives kept sneaking up on her.

There was a crunch of branches, loud enough she knew it was deliberate, and another figure joined the first. They were both male, older men with narrow faces, dressed in plainshirts under bone-and-cord breastplates, their hair tucked behind their ears and braided in two plaits that came down over their shoulders, feathers woven into the braids. Behind them, another figure—younger, without any adornment and long hair loose—came into view from behind the trees.

"I . . . was just walking. Stretching my legs," she said, trying to remember Gabriel's words to the natives they'd met earlier. "Did I cross a border unaware?" She couldn't read them at all, the cues and hints she'd learned in the saloon useless here, their bodies held differently, their expressions full of meaning but unreadable. Her position, her origin would mean nothing to them; the first natives they had met had made that clear, and Gabriel was not with her this time to intercede.

The fear scrambled at her spine, and she lifted her chin in response. She would not presume, but she wouldn't be cowed, either. "I have intended no offense. My name is Isobel née Lacoyo Távora, and I travel as the devil's Hand."

The first man said something, words she didn't understand, and studied her so frankly, his dark eyes intent, that she felt no hesitation in staring back at him. Neither of them blinked or backed down, even when her eyes began to water from the strain.

The man standing next to him, who had been more politely looking off to the side, coughed and slapped the other man on the back of the head, saying something to him in that same language, only harsher, like he was scolding him. "Your companion will be looking for you," he said to Izzy in English. "Come."

Not knowing what else to do, Izzy followed them.

The walk back to town seemed shorter: Izzy felt a dizzying sensation at one point, like crossing the protective border into Flood, and whispered a thank-you to whatever had allowed her to pass. The older men did not speak again, and Izzy's one attempt to communicate with the younger one had gotten her a blank face in return.

The snow had stopped, and the air seemed to be warming as they walked, as though the storm had existed earlier solely to confuse her steps. Izzy darted a glance at the young man walking beside her and bit her lip. The devil said that no man could work the weather, that it was a creature of its own whim and will, yet magicians could call the winds . . . but natives had their own medicine men, and Gabriel said they spoke with spirits often. But if so, to what effort had they summoned the storm? Surely not malice toward her?

No. More likely this was merely a freakishly late storm and they had been caught in it the same as she. And without them, she might have wandered higher into the mountains and been truly lost, perhaps attacked by a ghost cat, or . . . She had been foolish to wander off, she berated herself. Her distraction had been no excuse.

They came up on the back side of town, past the entrance to the mines cut into the face of a cliff. The lattice of heavy timber that surrounded it piqued her curiosity, but her companions kept walking, and while she was no longer afraid of being lost, she found herself unwilling to linger alone too near that dark opening.

Just past the miners' shacks, she saw Gabriel standing with two other men in dark coats and heavy boots, intent on their conversation. As Izzy and her companions came closer, one of the men saw them, reaching out to slap his companion in the chest, then indicating their approach.

"Isobel!" She was surprised at the note of relief in Gabriel's voice: surely she hadn't been gone that long? The way he wrapped his arms around her, hugging her fiercely enough to force an exhale from her lungs, made her rethink that. Maybe she had?

"You've been gone all day, Iz, you idiot girl; don't you know better than to wander off?"

All day? She blinked at him, feeling foolish all over again. "I . . ."

He shook her once, gently, then released her, turning to face her rescuers. "I am Gabriel Kasun, also known as Two Voices. Thank you for bringing my . . . my notó'u back to me." He stumbled slightly over the odd word, but the one who had spoken to her nodded, as though he knew Gabriel's name already.

"You are the rider Graciendo waits for."

"I am." He waited for them to introduce themselves, but they stared at him, and Isobel saw the way his gaze flickered to the men he'd been speaking with, then back again. Something had upset him, more than merely her going missing. "My thanks for aiding her back to town," he said again. "She is plains-born and not accustomed to the mountains."

The first warrior flicked a hand, as though dismissing Gabriel's explanation. "We would speak with you of things." His gaze flicked to her. "Both of you."

So, they *had* been waiting for her! Izzy wasn't sure if that made her feel better or worse. Why couldn't they just come into town, instead of waiting for her to get lost like an orphaned calf?

Gabriel's expression showed a flicker of curiosity, but if she'd been sitting across the felt from him, she wouldn't have known if he held a good hand or bad. "There's coffee in the mess, if you'd care to come inside and sit down," he said, gesturing toward the nearest building, a low-slung, windowless wooden structure.

"You're gonna let—" one of the miners started to say, then stopped abruptly, like he'd bitten his own tongue.

"They ain't allowed in town," the other miner said. "Sorry, but that's how it is."

Izzy glanced at the miners, then back at Gabriel. That wasn't right. The boss didn't allow for that. . . .

And the boss was nearly a month's travel from here. These miners made it clear they weren't pleased about Gabriel's invitation, and the marshal couldn't be counted on to support anything they did; he'd made quite clear of that. She had no backing, no support save Gabriel. What could she do—and why should she?

Because you are the Hand, her own voice told her. *Because this is the devil's Territory, no matter how far away he may seem, and you are here to remind them of that fact.*

"That may be how it was, but that is not how it is," she said, and her voice wasn't crisp, the way Marie's would have been, but quiet, soft. These men would not appreciate being scolded or hounded. She borrowed instead some of the boss's quiet certainty, thought of the beat of the buffalo thundering underfoot, the deep silence of the open sky and starry night, and looked at both miners square. "This town may bear a Spanish name, but you are within the Territory. If these men have offered you no insult or injury, you may not bar them from going where they will. Have they done you or yours injury?"

It was possible: the tribes warred on each other and occasionally overstepped to raid a farmstead that had offered them no insult. Or perhaps the miners had offered insult, had crossed a border or offended? But the woman who had given them shelter, Angpetu, had been native, hadn't she? Was she of the same tribe? Izzy had been so tired the night before, she couldn't bring the woman's features to mind to compare.

The miners looked at each other while the natives waited behind her, and Gabriel just looked patient.

"No, ma'am," one of the miners said finally. "Or . . . well, it's just that there's been some strangeness around lately, and—"

"And you've decided they're to blame?"

"We don't know rightly who's to blame, ma'am. We'd blame you, 'cept the marshal said you was all right," the younger miner, his face ruddy with embarrassment, said. "But there's men gone missing, and things gone wrong down in the mine, and . . ."

She had heard enough and was beginning to understand Gabriel's unease. Her palm itched faintly, and the thin air burned in her lungs. "My companion has invited these men to speak with us. Are you standing in our way?"

The older miner exhaled and stepped back a pace, pulling the other man with him. "No, ma'am."

She nodded and stepped forward, shoulders straight and every patch of her body alert, as though one of them might suddenly change their mind and try to stop them. She heard the faint huff of a laugh from Gabriel, not quite as hidden as it should have been, and then he and the three natives followed, their footsteps soft in the melting snow.

"That was well done," Gabriel said quietly to her as they gathered in the foreroom of the guesthouse, that being the only place that was private and warm, rather than risk another confrontation with the miners. She lifted one shoulder in a shrug, but his praise warmed her more than the stove could. There weren't enough chairs, so Gabriel and the younger native sat cross-legged on the floor, while Izzy perched herself on the desk, leaving the two seats for the older natives.

"You already know our names," she said, and waited. Away from the miners, would they be more forthcoming?

"I am Rains at Night, also called Aleksander," the older native said, and allowed himself a brief smile at her surprise. "My mother's sister married a French trapper," he said. "I hunted with him for many years. This is my brother, Bear Who Runs." He did not introduce their younger companion, who had yet to speak or even make eye contact.

"The morning's snow was a lucky thing," Aleksander went on. "Another day, our dream-speaker might not have known when you arrived, and we might have taken a different trail and bypassed each other's steps."

Izzy bit the inside of her lip. Why did they take so long to say anything? They were almost as bad as the boss. "You said there were things we needed to speak of?"

Her bluntness made Gabriel lift his head, as though he were about to scold her, then he tightened his mouth and waited. The older native's eyes widened, but she was certain she saw the tip of the other man's mouth curl up. She still couldn't read them, not entirely, but if he'd been scolded for staring at her, she was reasonably sure he wasn't offended by her being rude right back.

"Something cracks the bones," Bear Who Runs said. "Something rides the night wind and bears us no goodwill."

His English wasn't as good as his brother's, choosing his words with hesitation, but those words felt familiar to Izzy, that she'd heard them before somewhere.

Izzy tried to keep her own face from showing expression while her thoughts scattered everywhere, like a mis-shuffled deck. Where had she heard it? In Flood? No. Had Gabriel . . . No. The natives back on the plains had used it too. Had warned her, warned the boss . . . Something shifted in her memory, some time she'd heard the phrase before even then, but it was gone before she could catch at it.

"Something . . . what?" Gabriel asked. "Do you know?"

"You have seen it," Aleksander said to her, and it wasn't a question. He knew without her having said anything. "You have seen the wrongness. The eater."

"Yes." The memory of the storm racing through the sky, sliding across the mountain range, shivered through her spine, all the way to the backs of her knees, and left her needing to sit down. "Have you?" She would not wish that memory on anyone else, but the desire to rest part of the burden on another was immense.

"Calls Thunder has dreamed of it, three times running." She didn't know who Calls Thunder was, but the way Bear Who Runs didn't look at their other companion, she thought it might be them. Why didn't they let him speak? "Calls Thunder says the rocks shiver in the ground when it passes, the trees turn away their budding leaves, and the waters of the streams are filled with birds." Aleksander shook his head. "None of that is good."

"No." She didn't know what any of it meant, but she could agree that it didn't sound good. "It cracks the bones. . . ."

The sensation of wrongness she'd felt at Clear Rock. The tremble and shudder from simply knowing it was nearby. That might not have been what they meant, but she thought she understood now, and berated herself for not seeing it before, for not understanding, when she'd been told, been *warned*.

"You have seen it." Bear Who Runs wasn't repeating what Aleksander had said but asking a different question.

"Maybe? I have seen a thing elsewhere that may be the thing we discuss." She didn't know why she was so hesitant to name it, but they nodded as though they understood. "Something is wrong, not only here." She looked at Gabriel again, but he showed no sign of wanting to pick up the story. This was on her.

"A few days past . . . No. It began before then." She wasn't certain, not the way she'd known other things, but it felt right to start there. "We rode into a farmstead and found all there dead. An illness that struck so swiftly, they had no time to seek help, no time to gather themselves for death." She paused, waiting to see if the others had anything to add. There was silence, the kind that said they were waiting for her to continue. So, she did.

"A few days ride north and east of here, in the red hills, we rode into a town called Clear Rock." It was harder to tell this story, the experience still cold in her bones. "There was no illness there that we could see. There was . . . nothing. No people. No livestock. Nothing left alive."

"They left their town to avoid illness and will return when it has burnt itself out?" Bear Who Runs suggested.

"We thought maybe. Or they had been overrun by bandits, or . . . any number of things we could not determine. So, I . . ." She took a breath and admitted it out loud. "I used my boss's medicine to look."

The memory of the *thing* she had seen roared back, and suddenly the room was too warm, making it hard to breathe.

"Iz?" Gabriel was there, one hand on her shoulder, the other cupping her chin, but she could barely feel it, the memory too much, too strong, pulling at her flesh, the black ribbons trying to sink into her thoughts. Then another hand lay on her arm, and she looked up into Calls Thunder's eyes. The skin was so smooth, so tightly drawn over bones, that she couldn't help but reach up and touch it, her fingers cool as stone against that warm flesh. They lifted their own hand and covered hers with gentle fingers.

They understood what she felt. What she worried about. They worried about it too.

"Something came on the winds. From the west, over the mountains, over the Mother's Knife. It is a living thing, full of ill intent. I saw this. I saw this through the wind and through the stone. It came hungry, and it came angry." She blinked and shuddered, sliding away from Calls Thunder's touch. The eater, they'd called it. "It ate them. It ate the entire town. It would have eaten us, too, when it found us, but we ran."

She flicked her gaze up then to see how the others took that admission. She could not read their faces, still, but the softening around Bear Who Runs's eyes and mouth told her that he, at least, did not judge her less for the admission of fear.

"And then . . ." Somehow, this part was harder to tell, her mouth drying up around the words. "It may not be connected, but we encountered a magician in the road."

No reaction; she might as well have told them she found a dog or a snake.

Oh. She hadn't mentioned the snake. She thought about it, then decided the message had been private, and meant for Gabriel, anyway, not her.

"He was . . . well, what one might expect of a magician, I suppose." He had been arrogant and dangerous, and yet, there had been a humor to him that she might have enjoyed in a travel companion, had it not come bundled with all the rest. "He thought to see more clearly what we had encountered."

"And it ate him as well?" Bear Who Runs asked.

Izzy lifted one shoulder in a helpless shrug. "When challenged to show his power, he summoned . . . something. I . . . cannot say it was the same thing." It wasn't, but she had no proof of that certainty. "But a thing powerful enough to take a magician by surprise so easily? Foolish to ignore it."

Aleksander nodded, grave. "Here, also, a thing has come. Calls Thunder dreamed it, and the white men have gone missing."

"Have any of your people disappeared?" Gabriel asked, speaking for the first time since Izzy had started.

"No."

"Of course not," Gabriel said, barely under his breath. Then, more clearly: "Could this be the workings of another tribe, striking out at those who did not abide by the devil's terms?"

The terms of settlement, he meant. How the devil brokered peace between natives and settlers. Take only what you need, use only what you must, do not tread on another's shadow, do not give offense. Unlike her parents, who had been fools and paid her as the price.

Aleksander and Bear Who Runs looked at each other, then they both looked at Calls Thunder, who said something, finally, but to Izzy's ear it was gibberish. She looked at Gabriel, who shook his head. He didn't recognize the language either.

"There are many who speak with the spirits and may ask them for favors. But none would work such a thing, not so far from their lands, or without cause on those unknown to them." Bear Who Runs's words had a quiet confidence to them, so Izzy merely nodded. The boss might not have accepted their assurance, might have questioned them further, but the boss wasn't here. She was.

"We have spoken what we know. We will protect our lands, but if the eater stalks the larger land, then this is your burden, not ours."

"Wait, what?" Izzy's jaw dropped, and she scrambled to her feet, even as Calls Thunder stepped away from her, turning away toward the door. "But you can't—"

She wanted to demand that they stay to help her figure out what was going on. But they had come out of courtesy; she had no claim on them, no power to demand they stop, help. "It won't stop with us," she said softly. "Calls Thunder dreamed of it. You must know that."

Aleksander paused, turning to look at her. His face had returned to being unreadable, carved from the stone of the mountains around them. "The peoples ceded the Old Man the things he asked for," he said. "Stone and bone are his to protect."

"But . . ." Izzy felt lightheaded, dizzy, and her hand twitched, the palm burning as though she'd grabbed a handful of thistle, warning her to stop. She had given warning and been given warning in return. The agreement was upheld.

Calls Thunder rose with the others but hesitated when they walked out the door, looking back, their gaze looking past Izzy, over her shoulder. A hand reached out, and Izzy extended her own hand instinctively, taking what she was given.

Two feathers, barely the length of her thumb: one banded black and white, the other a pale greyish blue. Her eyes widened, and she drew a quick breath, feeling like she'd failed another test. The exchange of gifts was important, and she didn't—

She smiled then and tucked the feather into her palm, then reached up to her hair with her other hand, pulling the pin from the braid. It had been a fourteenth birthday present, carved from sun-whitened buffalo bone and polished until smooth as milk.

Calls Thunder took it gravely, then followed the others out the door.

Gabriel and she stood in the street and watched the three figures depart. A few miners were also on the street, watching them go but not interfering, clearly glad to see the backs of them.

Izzy sighed, the air rising from somewhere around her hips, forcing its way through her lungs and out in a long exhale. She'd never had a problem so neatly tipped into her lap before.

"Well," Gabriel said. Then, unexpectedly: "Supper?"

Izzy's stomach growled, and the sigh turned into a surprised laugh, reminded that the entire day had somehow passed while she was in the snowy woods. She tucked the feathers carefully into her pocket and made note to pull a leather thong from her tack to tie her braid again. "Yes. Yes, all right."

Whatever they were going to have to do, there was no point doing it on an empty stomach.

PART FOUR
CROSSROADS

THEY RODE OUT OF DE PLATA just after dawn the next day, the supplies Gabriel had bought packed and lashed to the mule's back, plus a new shirt for him and underthings for her. Gabriel was sure that a clean shirt didn't make any of their problems go away, but Isobel had insisted, and it seemed to give her comfort, so he relented.

And he had to admit, if only to himself, that the feel of stiff new cloth was not unpleasing.

The snow had stopped, the air was sharply bright and clear, and the animals, well-rested after two days in a pen, seemed eager to leave. There was no one to say farewell to, the marshal having busied himself elsewhere, and nobody else having an interest in them save that they were leaving coin behind.

"We should have told the marshal what they told us." Isobel refused to let the argument die, even as they left the town behind. "If he's looking into it."

"He won't, not anymore." Gabriel was repeating himself, but she had a determined jut to her chin that told him she wouldn't listen any other way. "I know his type, and you do, too. He'll feel having told you what little he knows lifts the obligation from him." Isobel opened her mouth to argue again, and he held up a hand to stop her. "I'm not saying he's a bad man. He cares about what happened to those men, and I've no reason to think he's a poor marshal. But his purview is fellow-murders, wild animal attacks, and fools lost off the trail. More than that, he knows there's not much he can do. So, he's dumped it on your saddle and called it fair, the same way those Hinonoeino did."

"I . . ." She shut her jaw with a snap and stared straight ahead. He could practically feel the protest rising in her throat, and part of him wished he could let her let it out, pause long enough for her to have the tantrum she was surely entitled to with so much weight put on her shoulders. They both knew he couldn't: green rider or no, something wrong was happening, and her obligation was to track it down and deal with it.

His job was to try and keep her alive long enough *to* deal with it.

Although the snow had melted overnight, the ground was still slick underfoot, and the road that led higher into the mountains toward Graciendo's place was more rock than dirt. The horses picked their way carefully, the mule clumping along behind them, grumbling periodically under its breath; it alone seemed unhappy to be leaving the mining town, where there were regular meals and no heavy burdens to carry. Gabriel had rolled his coat and tied it to the back of his saddle. The morning air still had a slight chill, but he knew from experience that he would begin to sweat the higher into the mountain they went. Isobel had watched him do it but opted to keep her own jacket on, although it was unbuttoned. When he looked at her from the corner of his eye, he saw the dun hat and dun-colored jacket, the dark brown skirts carelessly hiked over the saddle, and if he hadn't known better, he would have thought she had taken to the road a year or more ago, not a matter of weeks.

Was she ready inside, though? Nobody could answer that save her, and maybe not even her, not yet.

"Drink water," he said. "You're not used to being this high up."

She didn't argue, uncorking her canteen and taking a long sip.

"And let me know if your head begins to hurt."

"My head hasn't stopped hurting for days."

"Fair enough," he allowed. So long as she didn't complain of dizziness or lose her appetite, she should be fine.

They rode in silence for a while, birds, invisible in the trees, keeping them company with their calls.

"Calls Thunder," he said, suddenly. "They gave you a gift."

"The feathers. Yes."

"You should braid them into your hair." He should have told her that before leaving, but he'd been so focused on getting the supplies loaded, he'd forgot. "They were a seeing man, a dream-talker." Despite himself, despite all he'd seen, Gabriel had been a little awestruck by that. He didn't hold much with medicine, but he respected it, same as any sane man. "You don't often meet them. And by 'often' I mean never. For them to exchange gifts . . . it's a sign of honor or respect. You should display it."

She bit her lip and a flush touched her cheeks. "Is it medicine? You said a Reaper's feather was considered strong medicine, but these weren't . . ." She touched her jacket pocket protectively, telling him where she'd stored the feathers.

"It's an honor," he repeated. "I don't know the exact meaning they hold for it, but someone we meet might." Graciendo might, if he could think how to ask him. "Anyroad, that meant they were taking it—and you—serious. That's something to think on, Isobel."

"Because of the boss." Her voice was subdued, almost bitter, and he resisted the sudden, unexpected urge to hug her.

"Maybe so, but what I've learned of tribal ways, they won't see the difference: you speak for the Old Man; you *are* the Old Man, in all the ways that count."

Isobel leaned forward and stroked Uvnee's neck, hiding her face. "Why do they call him that?"

He let her change the subject without argument. "Well, he is, isn't he? I mean, he's been here how long? Since before any whites came across the River, or the Maya from down south, since before the conquistadors tried to push their way in, and your boss stopped them cold. That's a long time, Isobel, near three hundred years."

She'd clearly never thought about it, never thought what it meant.

"Flood's only been around for fifty, sixty years," she said. "But Marie's been with him near forever. That's what everyone says. That they're hard-pressed to remember the saloon without her." Marie was the woman who ran the saloon; he remembered that. The devil's other Hand. He would have sworn she was barely a decade older than him—forty-five at most.

Isobel seemed to be thinking hard on that, and he let her lapse back into silence, preferring not to push too hard, not when she'd been so close to snapping in two just yesterday.

"Calls Thunder thinks I'm like them. A dream-talker."

"That you've got powerful medicine, anyway. Because you do."

She shook her head. "Not me. Just the boss."

"Told you, they don't see the difference. Not sure I do, either. Pretty sure that magician didn't, either." Maybe not the best example, but there was clearly some maggot in her head, turning in her thoughts. He had to get it out of her before she let doubt dig in too deep. He might not understand the subtle ways—he needed beating over the head, more often than not—but he knew what doubt could do to a rider. And a rider with strong medicine? Magicians might be the least of what would sniff at her heels out here. "Talk to me, Isobel."

"How can it all be connected?" she asked finally. "The illness, the . . . thing at Clear Rock, the creature that came after the magician, the missing men, the things Calls Thunder saw. It's too much, too much distance, too much . . . It would be madness to think they're all connected."

That startled a laugh out of him, and Steady twitched his ears in annoyance. "Iz, there's nothing about any of this that *isn't* madness.

But your instincts are good; trust them. When the devil's sent a Hand out into the Territory for the first time in how long? And you and Calls Thunder both saw something coming out of the West? In the courts, that might not be enough to be considered evidence but would assuredly raise the question."

"No courts here," she said.

"No."

There were marshals to deal with complaints lodged against men—or women—and to ensure that feuds didn't get out of hand, and judges to hand down punishments at the bench. But no courts the way he'd been trained. No jury, only a posse to hunt you down. Only the devil if you made a deal, and the cold hand of life in the Territory if you didn't.

And the devil's Hand. He studied her as they picked their way up the trail—a trail, not a road: Graciendo lived where not many went. Her hat was slung on her back this morning, a thread of red running through the black strands of her braid when the sun hit it just right through the trees. And when she looked up at him now, her fine dark eyes had lost their snap and gained a weariness.

"I saw it come over the mountains. It had to be the Mother's Knife; there's no other range to the west it could be."

She seemed to be waiting for him to agree, so he nodded. He had no argument with that, based on what she said she'd seen.

"It was like a storm, a massive storm, at first. But then it split. And if one ribbon fell upon Clear Rock, and one here, then where else? I felt a *thing* in that storm, Gabriel. Something alive. Hungry. I need to know what it is, how to stop it. As soon as we're done with your delivering, I need to go back to Clear Rock. I know it fell there; maybe there's some . . . something to tell me *what* it is, where it came from."

"And then what?" The last thing he wanted to do was let her go back there. The last thing *he* wanted to do was go back there ever. But nothing she'd said was wrong, even if he didn't like it.

His job was to keep her alive and bring her back to Flood when he thought she'd learned enough to be on her own, he reminded himself. What the devil did with her after was none of his concern.

"I don't know." She sighed. "But you said it yourself: they've laid it on me. The boss needs to know as much as I can learn, and maybe I can see more if I can feel it again." She stared at him, and he could see the determination behind those eyes. "I'm like silver, Gabriel. The boss tosses me in and I see if it's safe. And if it's not . . ."

His job was to keep her safe. Alive. He needed to be the devil's adversary here, not his advocate. "And if it's not, then what? We've got no defense at it, Iz. We almost got killed the first time you tangled with it!"

"Almost isn't is," a deep, raspy voice said. "Almost doesn't count."

Izzy would have sworn at that point that nothing could surprise her, much less shock her, and yet . . . He stood in front of the horses, hands shoved into his pockets, head cocked to the side, sand-colored hair slicked back from his face, lines deep around dark eyes that squinted at them as though he knew the most marvelous secret ever, and Izzy could *feel* the strangeness in him now, where before it had been muted, hidden behind a mask, a pretense.

She said the first thing that came to her mouth. "You're dead."

"Death, my dearests, is boring." As casual as if he'd commented on the bathhouse being warm or the snow cold. The magician smiled at Izzy, a quick flash of teeth, his eyes too merry for the conversation, too merry for the exhaustion in his face. Whatever had happened to him, wherever he'd been, it hadn't been as simple as he tried to make it seem.

"You're dead," she said again, as though he hadn't heard her. "How are you not dead?" And yet there was no surprise in her voice, no shock. Magicians, the boss said, were a law unto themselves, and then he'd laughed like that amused him.

Something that could die and not die would amuse the boss, she thought, even as the idea sent a shudder down her spine. All things died. Didn't they?

"Dead and eaten." Gabriel's voice *was* shocked, but when she glanced at him, his expression seemed more disgusted than surprised, and she could practically hear him thinking that it would figure a magician couldn't even die right.

Steady reached out his neck as though thinking to bite this new arrival, make sure it was real. The magician flicked a glare its way, still smiling, and the horse pulled back, his ears twitching.

"Perhaps indeed I was, and perhaps I wasn't, and what's dead to the wind and bones?" He still spoke lightly, but there was a deepness to it, deep the way Izzy thought loneliness or sorrow might feel, an ache that stretched from mouth to ribs, a twisting line of darkness, hard and hollow. "Boring is what it is. And so, I am back!"

"Back to pester us?" Gabriel's hand was on the hilt of his knife, and she could see him figuring the odds of it even clearing the sheath, much less hitting the magician, before something dire came after him in return. She felt the urge to place a hand on his arm, remind him that it would clearly be pointless, but it did not seem he would welcome her interruption.

The magician sighed, spreading his arms, and she was reminded for a moment of the Reaper hawks, wide wings blocking out the sun. "If we must be truthful, I would rather be elsewhere. Any elsewhere. I've seen things while I was away, oh, such things your eyes would widen for the telling. I've seen things . . ." His fingers curled, talons clenching at missed prey. "But the wind brings me here, and so here I shall be."

"Seen what?" Izzy asked, her entire body canting forward with her desire to hear. "Did you see the storm, Farron? Tell me! You're a magician; you must know what it is."

The mockery left his eyes, and he looked past them into something that was not there. "This time, I was closer, through no wish of my own. This time, it was clearer. The winds are in confusion, sweeping low to the ground and listening, fearing. . . . A storm has arrived, a bitter storm."

The winds. Magicians took their direction from the wind, and that made them a little mad. If the storms were confused, then would a magician be even more mad? Izzy felt her stomach clench at the thought, a lingering voice whispering at her, *Run*.

She couldn't run. The bones cracked, and the winds were in confusion, and Izzy had no idea what any of it meant, except that everyone thought she would fix it.

"There are balances to be kept, little rider." The magician was looking at her again with those, eyes dark-rimmed and too intent for any kind of comfort. His hand was on Uvnee's bridle and the mare's ears were back, but she was not shying away or retreating. "There are balances that've been tipped turvy. It has to be made right."

Gabriel snorted. "By you?"

"By her. I'm just along for the entertainment." The magician smiled again, bone-hard and brightly, and stepped back, his earlier intensity breaking. "It's always a merriment when the wind changes. And it has changed, my dear ones, oh, lucky ones. The wind whistles me up and down, and it tells me of power and the crackling of bones, spilling marrow into the waters for predators to eat."

Izzy sat upright in her saddle, her hands tightening on the reins, and Gabriel's knife was halfway out of the sheath, as though he had heard a threat in those words.

"Ah, ah. None of that," the magician scolded, and the knife slid back into the sheath, Gabriel's hand flying off it as though it had suddenly burned him. "I am not your threat, rider. Not at this moment, anyway. Show me some respect."

"Are you here to help me, Farron Easterly? Or to claim whatever power you sense?" Izzy felt the brush of something against the back of her neck, the rustle of something softly invisible across her arms, but she refused to shiver.

"If you wish my help, I may lead you to where the wind whistles me, but beyond that, it is not for me to say. As for power . . . it is the only true currency, little rider." The magician looked up again and away, head tilted as though listening to something. "And we should be on our way; it is not wise for us to remain overlong here. How those little diggers spend so much time within the teocuitlatl and still remain dross, I cannot understand . . ."

"The what?" Gabriel was still upset; she could see it in him, the rising need to control, direct, understand, despite none of it remaining still long enough to for them to pin it down, think it through.

"Silver, man, silver!" the magician said. "To touch on the veins and unsheathe it from the bones, purify and form, and still they know not what they handle; they cannot feel it . . . But it would feel you, little rider, as much as it feels me. And we do not want that to happen, oh, no. No waking the silver for us."

Waking the silver? Did he mean . . .

Gabriel looked at Izzy, who gave a faint shrug, as much with her face as her shoulder, then she remembered the feeling she'd had when passing the mineshaft opening, the equal pull of curiosity and push of dread, and this time let the shiver take her, with understanding. It hadn't been *her* feeling that; it had been the ore.

Waking the silver. No. Impossible.

But it might explain why the boss never went to the mines but had them send the silver to him, smelted and tamed.

"We need help," she said quietly. "He may not be ideal, but he's the only one who's offered."

Gabriel ran his hand through his hair and put his hat back on, marking the end of discussion. "He's come back more mad than before, and we're just as mad to accept him. But fine. He may be of help. But I'm not taking him with us on my errand."

"Who?" Farron asked, more indignant than curious. "Who is so important—"

"I carry a package for Graciendo," Gabriel said, and the magician stepped back as though the other man had finally surprised him.

"Ah. Ah, and now I see more, I do." Farron's eyes were merry again, his smile full of teeth. "No fear, rider, no fear. To Graciendo we shall all of us go, thee and thee and me, and see what we shall see."

Gabriel narrowed his eyes, clearly about to protest the magician's inclusion of himself, but Izzy could see no other choice, despite renewed unease. They had no idea what they faced, and the magician claimed to—although she did not look forward to the headache of unraveling his half-mad speech. If he insisted on coming with them to see Gabriel's friend, how much harm could it do?

Izzy twisted the silver ring on her finger, feeling it warm comfortably to the touch, and rubbed the mark on her palm against her skirt. She couldn't risk alienating someone who might have answers. And, she admitted to herself, as unpredictable as the magician might be, for now he seemed to be on their side. Or, she checked herself, the winds that drove him were.

For now, as they followed Gabriel up the trail to meet with the mysterious Graciendo, she wondered what had happened to the magician after his not-death, what he had seen, and why, now, she could feel the strangeness in him.

Had he changed, she wondered uneasily . . . or had she?

Graciendo's cabin was only a day's ride from De Plata, but with the magician on foot, it took them longer than expected, and Gabriel thought it better not to approach the cabin once night fell. They made a rough camp on the trail itself, the ground on either side too rocky for sleeping.

No road led to Graciendo; Gabriel was unsure if the old man had chosen his location for that or simply prevented a road from reaching him, but the end result was the same. The woods pressed around him, as they did each time he made this trip, and he found his neck aching from the times he looked up, trying to see the open sky through thick green leaves and failing each time.

Isobel might feel uneasy in the hills; he could never rest properly if he couldn't see the stars.

He was not alone in being uneasy; they kept the animals close and the fire small, as though to attract as little attention as possible, and declined to step off the trail to hunt, relying on the beans he'd set to soak that morning, and a chunk of salted goat meat.

"Does she know?"

"Know what?" Gabriel knew he was defensive, but the magician gave him no less unease now than he had on first encounter. He fought the urge to flinch, to move away, to find running water and put it between them.

The other man settled too comfortably next to him, resting against the log they'd dragged over for a bench. "What you are."

Gabriel looked over his shoulder at where Isobel was fiddling with something in her pack, the horses a darker shadow beyond, then back to the work at hand. There was enough wood here to make a decent fire, and it had caught nicely, but it couldn't ward off the chill he felt.

"I don't know what you're talking about, and neither do you."

"You think I can't smell it?" The magician stretched his long legs out in front of him and grinned up at Gabriel, teeth too white and sharp to be soothing. He might look human, Gabriel reminded himself, might even sound human, but he wasn't, not where it counted. No magician was. "How many generations?"

Gabriel pulled the coffeepot out of the pack and set it aside, then dug deeper to find the fresh packet of coffee and chicory. "Generations of what?" He was hedging, he knew he was hedging, and part of him wondered why he even bothered. All the years of pushing it down, the denial and the running, and it followed him anyway. The devil had stripped it from him in one sentence, laid him bare and needy, and now this . . .

But what he would give freely to the devil he'd give to no other, not even himself.

"Gabriel Kasun."

His name carried the dry dust of the road and the sour tang of the ocean, the taste of honey from his mother's bees, and the feel of documents shuffled under his hands. Gabriel looked at the magician, his gaze brimming with anger. "Do not attempt to compel me again," he warned, feeling his entire body shift against the need to respond. "Or I'll kill you in your sleep and not have a moment of guilt in it."

"That would presume I slept," the magician said, but relented. The sensations faded, but Gabriel didn't relax. He wouldn't relax for as long as this bastard traveled with them, and not even after that now.

"Fine. I will say it for you. You're bound," the magician said. "As bound to the Territory as I am—nay, more so. Leaving didn't work so well for you, did it? Did nobody warn you?"

The bastard actually sounded . . . concerned.

"I'm none of your business," he said, checking the water level in the bag and frowning. This was the second to spring a leak; they would have enough for coffee tonight or tomorrow, not both, and there was no fresh water until they could use Graciendo's well.

"Oh, give me that," the magician said, and took the leather bag from his hands. He held it a moment and then handed it back.

The bag, half-empty before, now bulged with water, without a single drip.

Farron leaned back, watching him with those uncanny eyes. "I'm not your enemy," he said. "I don't have to be a friend; in fact, you're wise to keep in mind that I'm nobody's friend. But I'm not your enemy. Not here, now, in this time and place."

Gabriel grunted, scooping coffee into the pot and adding water, then placing the pot on its tripod over the flames.

"It doesn't have to be a terrible thing, you know. . . ."

"Leave it," Gabriel said.

Much to his surprise, the magician did.

‡ ‡ ‡

Approaching Graciendo's home at night wasn't wise even for someone who was expected, much less strangers. But it wasn't exactly safe even during the daylight. Gabriel had Isobel dismount as they approached the cabin, the mule halter-tied and the horses on leads.

The cabin itself was barely visible until you were within shouting distance, the planks blending into the trees around it, the roof over-grown with plants, and no windows to let light escape, merely a single wooden door.

"You're both gone distressingly quiet," Isobel said. "Who *is* this Graciendo, anyway?"

"Old," Gabriel said. "Very old and crotchety. And not fond of strangers. You'll stay here with the horses."

"But—" Isobel started to protest, then subsided when he gave her a sidelong look.

"You too," Gabriel said to the magician.

"Oh, believe you me, I have no interest in getting in the old bear's face, and he has no interest in seeing mine. I will keep our little rider company here, and we shall while away the moments until you return."

Gabriel snorted, then took off his hat and hung it on the pommel horn of Steady's saddle, and rooted in his bags for a battered envelope, about the size of a lady's reticule and the thickness of two fingers, and checked to make sure that there were no rips or tears.

"What would you do if it had been damaged?" the magician asked, idly curious.

"Left it on the doorstep and run," Gabriel said easily. "Stay here."

He walked forward, trusting that they would do as they'd promised. But before he could even reach the cabin, the wooden door slammed open and Graciendo emerged.

"Oh, hellfire," Gabriel said.

"You're late." Graciendo, in a bad mood, filled the entire doorframe. He had the bronzed skin and broad cheekbones of half a dozen native tribes, but his chin and cheeks were covered by the same glossy brown hair that ran from his scalp down to his shoulders, curling wildly; his

255

jacket and trousers were styled like a northern trapper's, and his style of speech was curt enough to be American.

"I told you I'd be back in the spring. It's spring. I should have come earlier?" Gabriel went on the offensive, hoping to distract Graciendo from the fact that he'd brought companions. When it had been only Isobel, he could have justified it, playing the girl as weaker than she was, helpless and therefore not a threat. But the magician changed that story too much and—

"And you bring *that* to my door?"

"Technically, I am not at your door, nor even within your yard." The magician's voice carried clearly, but Gabriel was relieved to not hear the usual half-mocking sneer in it. "Consider me passing by, with no interest in your pettish and petulant self."

Gabriel was convinced he was the only one on this mountain with a lick of sense or survival. Well, him and the mule, mayhap, since Flatfoot was quietly minding his own business, grazing on a bush.

"I wasn't talking about you, you misbegotten abomination."

Isobel looked up at that, her eyes wide, and then they narrowed again. Gabriel groaned. She was an even-tempered soul most of the time, but he knew that look, now.

"Iz," he said, getting her attention, and then turned back to his host. "Graciendo. Please. It's been a difficult trip and I'd rather not have to clean blood off my boots if we can avoid it." He didn't bother appealing to the magician's better nature; he had none. "I brought your letters." He held the packet out as a peace offering. The hand that reached out and grabbed it moved faster than expected, but not so fast that the thick claws tipping each finger weren't visible.

"Hrmph." Graciendo didn't even look at the letters but shoved the entire packet into a pouch slung at his side. "Wait." And with that, he disappeared back into the cabin, slamming the door shut behind him.

"Well," Isobel started to say, and the magician placed a hand over her mouth.

"Whatever you were thinking, keep it inside your skull," he advised. "Even the wind skirts carefully around that one when he's in a mood."

The door opened again before Gabriel could say anything, and Graciendo emerged again.

"I thought you wiser than to travel with such," he said to Gabriel. "The Old Man plays games the likes of you should stay away from. He's got nothing to offer you."

Gabriel huffed a laugh. Graciendo was old and had mostly taken himself from the world. He'd forgotten what it meant to live in it. "He had something" was all he said. "This is Isobel," he went on. "She's new come to the roads, and I offered to show her the way."

"Hmmph." Graciendo made no move to go toward her, and she made no move to come forward but inclined her head slightly at the introduction. "And you, Long Nose?" Graciendo said, still not looking at the magician. "What's your reason for venturing near my home?"

The magician made an elegant gesture with his arms and fingers, as though to give the answer up to the heavens. "I go as the wind wills me," he said. "And it seems the wind wills me here."

"With them."

"With them."

There was something going on between the two of them, but Gabriel wasn't even going to try and figure it out. Graciendo was old and odd, and the magician purely odd. Nobody was growling, shouting, or smiting, and that was good enough for him.

"I've a passing fondness for this one," Graciendo said, jerking one clawed thumb at Gabriel. "If I hear you've gamed with him, I'll be displeased."

"He's born bound," the magician said. "What could I do to him that's not already been done?"

Graciendo growled, and Gabriel decided they'd already tested their luck far too long.

"We need be on our way, old friend," he said, not waiting for a token protest of hospitality that would not come. Normally, he would ask to refill his water at the well, but the magician had proven that they need not ask for that, and the sooner they were on the road again, the better for his nerves. Graciendo had never offered him any harm, and he did not *think* he would injure any companion Gabriel brought with him, but he seemed to take Isobel badly, although Gabriel was unsure if was her femaleness that offended or where she hailed from.

He didn't even question the fact that Graciendo knew where Isobel had come from: Graciendo knew everything. And told nothing, save it suited him.

"You'll want to avoid the eastern trail down. Go back the way you came or take the broken trail. It's safer."

Safer and would keep them from returning, if the eastern trail were blocked. Gabriel nodded, and the old man grunted at him, then went back inside. This time, when he closed the door behind him, it was quietly but firmly.

Whatever had been following them had abandoned them at some point—Izzy suspected it was when they'd approached Graciendo's cabin—and had left them alone since then. She looked back over her shoulder, but the cabin was out of sight now, hidden behind several twists in the road.

"Graciendo. He's not . . . entirely human, is he?"

"Not even slightly," Gabriel said, then reconsidered. "Well, slightly."

There was more there, but Izzy didn't push it, still slightly off-balance from the encounter. She focused instead on feeling the stretch of her legs, the faint, ever-present ache in her back, the familiar creak and sway of the saddle underneath her as the horses picked their way down the stone-studded trail they'd found soon after leaving the cabin. Unlike the way up, this was a true road: she knew that even without touching it directly, the way she knew the sun had risen simply for the sky being lighter. If she pushed a little deeper, she could feel it, but it was a comfortable hum, easy to ignore for now. She looked at the back of the magician's head where he strode ahead of them, his moccasins more surefooted than the horses' hooves, his strides longer. His hair was nearly as long as hers, clubbed at the back of his neck, the sandy brown strands untouched by hat or brush, and his hands moved constantly as he walked, long arms waving as though he carried on a conversation with himself—or something the rest of them could not hear.

She traveled with a magician. She had just been insulted by what she thought might be an animal spirit in human form. She was on the trail of a malign storm that could and would kill them if given opportunity. Was this the sort of thing she should expect from now on?

Izzy rubbed her thumb into her palm, but the mark there was quiet, offering no help. A tinge of bitterness crept into her thoughts. The boss knew she liked to have the details well in hand, know every step she needed to take. So, he'd sent her off with no warning, no telling, no idea of what was to come—even discounting what *had* happened—and that had to be deliberate.

Even if he hadn't known what was to come, hadn't seen the storm, predicted what she would find, there was still so much she'd been clueless of, ignorant as a child.

And she thought, maybe, she understood, a little. That didn't mean she liked it. "I'm doing what I can," she told the mark. "But you could have *warned* me."

Uvnee's ears twitched, but that was the only response she got, save an odd glance sideways from Gabriel riding next to her. Nothing came to her, no whisper of understanding or sense of what to do next. She was on her own.

Or not. She had Gabriel. And while the magician wrapped his responses in madness, he hadn't ducked their questions entirely. And he had *said* he wished to help.

"Farron!" she called, loud enough that he could not pretend he hadn't heard her. "What did you mean when you said the balance had been tipped turvy?"

The darkness he'd spoken of, the "eater" Calls Thunder had seen, those she knew. But balance? She thought he meant something more than the dizziness she had felt when the boss's medicine worked through her. He must.

The magician's arms paused midgesture, then his shoulders eased and he dropped back enough for the horses to catch up with him, walking to Izzy's right. He was tall enough that Izzy didn't need to look down to speak with him, his head coming to just below her shoulder.

"Flesh is but the youngest brother. The winds move through it all. The winds sift through the bones, drive water, wear down stone. The wind was here before land, was here before water. Far before flesh."

She waited. He seemed to think that he had explained something, but she was unsure what that might have been. He took a sip of water from her canteen and handed it up to her, as though knowing before she did that her throat had become parched. She took a sip, then frowned. The canteen had been latched on Uvnee's saddle—on the other side from where the magician was walking. With a sigh, she rehooked it in its proper place.

"Wind gives us knowledge, power. We see what it sees, know what it knows." The words came slowly, pulled from him almost unwilling. She silently urged him on, afraid to speak and break the thread. "We see . . . things you cannot."

"And it drives them mad," Gabriel muttered from behind them, and she raised a hand over her shoulder, one finger lifted, to tell him to hush.

The magician didn't seem to hear the comment, or if he had, he ignored it. "The world tilts and tips and rests, events shaking and resettling it, over and again, the rise and fall and rise again. Now, something shakes it, turns it sideways, will not let it settle. That is what we see. Something terrible. Something ill."

He exhaled, and Izzy knew he'd said all he would, or in fact all he could. They moved along with only the clop of hooves and the call of birds in the trees, out of sight, keeping them company. In the distance there was a rough bark, a fox startled out of its midday den, and the answering angry caw of crows.

"The thing that swept Clear Rock clean came on the winds," Izzy said. "The ill wind Calls Thunder saw. Farron, are the winds bringing this?"

"We don't know. Everything is turned turvy and we cannot tell. But it fills the bones and cracks them. Cracked bones cannot bear the weight."

His words were madness, and Gabriel would tell her she was a fool for expecting anything else. And yet . . .

Molly had broken her foot once. The curandero had told her to stay off it for weeks, and she'd spent all evening in a chair, ordering them about like a queen. *Cracked bones cannot bear the weight.* Weight of what?

"The miners said that something was stalking them," Gabriel said, his voice carefully even. "Something lurking in the hills, maybe even under the hills. It may've come from the sky, but it's gone to earth like a badger."

When she looked at the magician, he was carefully staring elsewhere, his lips pursed as though to whistle.

"Badgers . . ." An old story stirred in her head, the familiar echo that had been haunting her taking on more solid form. "Badger shaped the bones of the world."

An old story, a clapping game children played. Turtle dove the waters of the world and brought up the bones, and Badger claimed the bones and buried them, and from the buried bones, Spider spread out the land. . . .

Every people had a story of how the world had come about, the boss said, and every one was as valid as the next and just about as true.

If the storm had gone to ground, cracked the bones that made up the world . . . She thought of the dead bodies in Widder Creek, the sudden illness coming from nowhere and killing everything it reached. Iktan told stories of ill-wishings like that, meant to harm, not heal or grow, to teach a lesson or shame someone too proud. . . .

"How am I supposed to stop *that*?" Her voice might have cracked on that last, and she dared anyone to blame her. A thing powerful enough to ill-wish the Territory . . .

"The old man claimed the bones," Farron said with a shrug, looking back at her, his gaze still distant. "Thus, the bones have claim on him. And by proxy, little rider, you as well. If you did not want this, you should not have chosen this."

"I didn't choose this!" she said, exasperated. "I chose . . ." There was silence from her companions, neither of them looking at her now, and her words fell back into her throat.

"I want to work for you. Not the saloon, not . . . I don't want to work the back rooms or the bar. I want to work for you."

"Respect. Power, maybe."

"And what do you have to offer in return?"

"Myself. All I have is myself."

Izzy felt bile rise in her throat and forced it down, the bitterness in her stomach a match to the taste in her thoughts. He was right: she had chosen this, however blindly. However foolishly. She had given herself over of her own free will. The judge had tried to warn her, and she had said . . .

"All right." She tried to calm herself, refusing to acknowledge the way her heart was thumping, her palms sweating, the sigil etched into her skin silent, useless. If the boss wouldn't tell her what to do, she'd figure it out for herself.

She would earn what she'd been given.

"Farron, what can you—" she started to ask, when the magician suddenly jammed his shoulder into Uvnee's chest, jolting the mare sideways into Steady, who snorted and nipped in protest, even as their riders were hauling back on the reins.

"What the blazes are you doing?" Gabriel demanded, but the magician ignored them both, holding up a hand to tell them to stay still, then striding forward a pace. A rockfall had blocked part of the trail at some point up ahead, obscuring the way. He disappeared around the rocks for a breath, then returned almost immediately.

"What?" Izzy asked, seeing something on his face that hadn't been there before, some flicker of expression she couldn't quite place.

"Something waits ahead."

"In the crossroads?" Gabriel wasn't asking, but the magician nodded once.

Gabriel said something in another language, guttural and harsh enough to be a curse. "Any idea what?"

The magician shook his head once.

"But it means us ill," Izzy guessed.

The look Farron gave her was scornful. "Nothing lurks for good intent, little rider. And never in a crossroads."

"Damnation. The only way around is to go back nearly half a day," Gabriel said, rubbing wearily at the bristle on his chin. "And Graciendo said this was the safest trail."

"So, we go through." Izzy swallowed hard, not feeling anywhere near as brave as she'd tried to sound. "We've silver and a magician on our side; what could go wrong?"

"And to think we once worried about raiders and haints," Gabriel said, and his laughter might have been mostly bravado, but it helped.

Still, none of them moved forward. That, strangely, also helped: she would rather they all be nervous. That made her fears seem less foolish, more wise.

Her hands shook nonetheless, and she rested them on her knees to hide it, the tug on the reins making Uvnee flick her ears backward as though to ask what the matter was. The horses didn't seem fussed at all. She took some courage from that and the fact that Flatfoot was already poking its head around the rockfall and then looking back, as though to ask why they were all simply standing there instead of moving.

"You first," Gabriel said, and she kneed Uvnee forward, only to have him grab at her reins. "Not you. Him." He jerked his chin at the magician.

"But—"

"Your mentor does not believe in the goodness of my intentions," Farron said, his strange, hard smile back in place, "and would happily sacrifice me to whatever malevolence may await us in the crossroads ahead."

"That's right," Gabriel said without shame. "So go."

Izzy wanted to protest: she was the one who was meant to discover what was wrong; it was her duty to do this. But by the time she gathered her thoughts enough, Farron had already gone around the bend again, whistling a jaunty, unfamiliar tune. She wrenched the reins free of Gabriel's grasp, giving him a glare, and pushed Uvnee into a trot to follow him down the trail.

Setting aside pride, Gabriel was right, she admitted to herself. There might be things that could kill the magician and keep him dead, but the cards seemed to be stacked in his favor. She didn't like it, though.

And then she was around the rockfall, her gaze searching ahead for whatever it was Farron had seen.

Izzy had always thought of crossroads as being flat, long roads stretched out for miles in four directions, the point of contact clearly laid out. But the trail here meandered downhill, the intersecting road cutting through rock on one side, then continuing the other side downhill, almost immediately disappearing from sight.

If you didn't know, you might not recognize the crossroads until it was too late. Izzy wondered how many had been trapped by that over the years.

She reined in and waited for Gabriel to catch up with her, her right leg twitching in the stirrup as though she were repressing the urge to swing down and follow the magician as he continued toward the spot where the two roads crossed.

"He's not taking out any silver," she said, worried, and then almost laughed at herself. They already *knew* something was there, and likely all the bits and bobs of silver they had wouldn't be enough to cleanse that ill intent.

"Do you see anything?" Gabriel asked. He looked nervous, his gaze darting, his body that same comfortable but too-still posture she had noted in him before. He was looking for threats from without, she realized, checking every rock, every shadow for a potential ambush.

"No," she said. "I don't see anything." She might, if she went to that other place. If she slipped down into the bones. But the thought made her stomach churn. Before, she had thought that place was safe, protected. Now . . . She had spoken big words about facing whatever had ridden the storm into the Territory, about chasing it down and forcing it to show its face, but this—she didn't even know if it was the same thing that had chased her out of Clear Rock—

it was—

—it was in the bones already, Farron said. Cracking the bones. But cracked bones could heal, couldn't they?

No whisper answered her this time, and she worried at her lip, watching another stride toward what should have been her responsibility.

"He's died before," she said, trying to calm her nerves. "Nothing can really hurt him, right?"

"I don't know."

The palm of her hand ached intensely, and she lifted her other hand to rub at it, thumb pressing into the flesh. The markings there were darker now, still fine-lined but clearly visible, and Izzy wasn't sure if that was a comfort or another thing to worry over.

Suddenly, the sense of urgency swarmed like bees in her skin, the single sting she'd gotten as a young girl intensified until her entire body seemed inflamed and fever-hot. "Farron Easterly!" she called, through a throat suddenly swollen and sore. "Stop!"

She was too late, or he simply could not hear her, his stride carrying him that last step into the crossroads even as the ground underneath burst open, something massive rising from the swirling dust.

"Hellfire," Gabriel whispered in awe.

This was not a storm. It was not a hallucination or embodied spirit. It was a solid beast, rough-skinned and filled with teeth and claw, scrambling to attack anything that moved within its sphere.

The magician had not entered the crossroads unprepared. The first swipe of a gnarled, clawed hand the size of a horse's head was deflected, although those long limbs of his did not move and there was no sign of any weapon, merely the magician standing, chin lifted, feet planted, like he had no plans to move again ever. Her breath caught, her body tightening as though braced for a blow herself, and beside her she heard Gabriel swearing, a low, steady stream in three different tongues.

Fear gave way to anger, boiling like soup under her skin. This was wrong. This was her responsibility, not his; his ego would get him killed. Again. And no matter his flippancy, she could not imagine that was pleasant even for one such as he.

Izzy looked at her left hand, saw that the silver of her ring, brightly polished a few days ago, had tarnished to a dullness, even outside the crossroads. If she'd had any doubt that the beast was natural, that dispelled it. This was some bile of magic, taken form.

The boss had no agreements with magicians. But Farron Easterly traveled with them, by her invitation. *Help me,* she thought fiercely. *Tell me what to do!*

She looked up again, afraid that the heartbeat she'd looked away had somehow been fatal. The crossroads was barely large enough for the both of them; the creature reared over the magician's head, snarling and growling but unable to lay a claw on him. Farron stared up at it, protected but unable to do damage. They were at a standoff.

Izzy took the time to study the creature more closely, although looking directly at it was difficult. It was thrice the height of the magician and whipcord thin, multiple limbs weaving as fast as the magician was still, claws glinting black under the sunlight, skin covered in dark blue scales that glistened as though covered in thick spit or snot. It was built to rend, to tear, to destroy; it had no other purpose.

"Boss," she whispered out loud. "How do we stop this?"

The ache in her hand subsided, and Izzy felt herself drop her stirrups, slipping out of the saddle and landing on the ground with a jarring thud she felt all the way to her skull. The fever heat under her skin worsened, and Izzy wiped sweat out of her eyes, cursing her skirts as they dragged on the dirt. If she survived this, she would buy a pair of pants the same as Devorah and that traveling woman back in Patch Junction, and to blazes with anyone who raised an eyebrow at her. You could not fight in full-length skirts.

"Iz?"

She flicked her fingers backward at Gabriel, telling him to stay put, and moved slowly toward the crossroads. She'd let him call her a fool later, assuming they survived.

Her knife remained sheathed on her saddle, but what was useful against a common predator, two-legged or four, would do nothing there. Behind her, she heard the sounds of Gabriel loading his gun, the rip of cloth and slide of metal, but Izzy thought it would be as useless as her knives, that this was not a thing that could be vanquished with weapons.

And Farron's own medicine could do nothing more than force a standoff.

She clenched her left hand, fingers digging into the sigil, and waited for some arcane understanding to appear, filling her with what to do.

Nothing happened.

She dug deeper, panic thrumming under her chest bone. The boss had to help her. Without his gift, she was useless, just a saloon girl. She knew how to fold laundry, shuffle a deck of cards, pour drinks, and listen to those who needed to talk, not how to kill a monster.

In the crossroads, Farron tilted his head, and this close, she could hear his voice, although she could not make out the individual words, a singsong pattern of nonsense. The creature lifted its own head and roared. The sound should have echoed against rock and sky, should have filled her ears and rattled her bones, but somehow was muffled, hushed.

With every step closer, the air around her felt heavier, oppressive, the thick stillness of a summer storm unsure yet if it would break or swelter. The faintest twist of a breeze ran against the back of her neck, a touch both disturbing and reassuring, and was gone.

Izzy sank to her knees, her palms on the ground in front of her, her gaze held on the scene barely a foot away, close enough to feel the heat the creature was giving off, smell the acrid fear-sweat of both man and beast.

The moment her fingers dug into the dirt, she felt herself slip out of her own body, a sickening jolt and drop, her already fever-dizzy head swelling and then cooling abruptly, as though the fever had stayed behind.

The dizziness she felt now was familiar: colder and sharper, as though she'd been spun too often in a game of blindman's bluff. She felt split wide open and pressed small all at once, a thousand things pressing on her, whispering at her, prying open her eyes and crawling into her ears.

"Oh." Understanding filled her, a comprehension so intense that she couldn't remember not having it a heartbeat before. That was why she had tried to stop Farron, why—

The creature didn't care whatever revelation she was having. With another roar that couldn't escape the crossroads, it reared up and swung its long neck down at the same time its clawed hands came together, closing in on either side of Farron's head. He saw it coming the same instant Izzy did, stiffening his stance and calling something back, a string of liquid words that were gibberish but *sounded* right, sounded powerful. But the creature closed in on the magician, wrapping him in its taloned, scaled embrace, the power he'd summoned either too little or too late to save him.

The blast that threw her backward, singeing her skin and hair, took her utterly by surprise.

‡   ‡   ‡

"Isobel. Isobel. Iz!"

Gabriel called her name and then slapped her face lightly. Her eyes moved under closed lids, and she groaned something inaudible, one hand reaching up as though to brush a pest away. He caught that hand in his own, feeling the firm heartbeat under her skin with relief. When he'd seen her flying backward as though an invisible hand had thrown her, he'd wanted to rush to her side, but holding the horses steady had taken all his strength and focus. Even the mule had bolted, although it came creeping back, cautiously, once everything was still again.

The magician lay in the crossroads, facedown, but Gabriel wasn't going anywhere near him, not until he knew that Isobel was safe, and perhaps not even then.

"Iz, come on, come on now, open your eyes, there's a girl." Her hand was too warm, and he uncurled it to look at the palm. The markings were thick black lines now that somehow seemed to fold into the lines of her skin, echoing the swirls of her flesh rather than being imprinted there.

She sniffled a little, and her eyes opened, staring past him up at the sky.

"Am I dead?"

"Not yet. But you're going to be sore bruised in unpleasant places for a while, I suspect." He helped her sit up, carefully, keeping a close watch on her eyes and the color of her skin. There was a bruise under her right eye, and she looked to be favoring her side; there didn't seem to be any obvious further damage, no blood or protruding bones, and her breath was steady, if a little shaky, so she hadn't injured anything inside.

"Stay here," he told her, and when she nodded, got up and moved cautiously toward the crossroads.

Whatever had been there before was gone; even he could feel that.

269

But the air was still enough to leave him leery of disturbing it: when things went quiet, it meant something was about to break.

He reached into his pocket, finding a coin. He turned it between his fingers a few times, feeling the milled edges worn down over years of handling, the square tips now soft nubs, the etched markings nearly illegible. A quick flick of his arm in a practiced manner, and the coin flipped into the air, arcing over and landing in the dust just inside the crossroads. He waited until the dust settled, then studied the coin.

"It's fine," a voice said, scratchy as though it had been screaming for hours. "A little help, if you don't mind?" And the magician rolled over onto his side, trying—and failing—to get up. "Truth, rider, some help needed here. I just fought some fire-spawned evil; the least you might do is offer me a hand."

Put that way, it did seem the least he could do. But there was still a tremor of unease and distrust as he stepped into the crossroads, half expecting something—beast or magician—to attack him without warning.

The magician's skin, unlike Isobel's, was cool and clammy, but he was able to get to his feet, even if he wobbled once there. His clothing was torn and shredded as though someone had taken knives—or clawed hands—to them, but there didn't seem to be any visible blood, and like Isobel, his breathing was clear and his movements easy enough to likely rule out broken ribs.

"What happened?"

"I was hoping that you would be able to tell me that," Gabriel said, walking just to the side of the magician. He would catch the man if he fell but didn't want to get any closer if he didn't have to. "Last I saw, that thing folded in on you like a bear going for salmon."

"Not an inappropriate metaphor," the magician said, reaching to where Isobel and the animals waited. He swayed a little, and then his long legs gave out on him and he folded down onto the ground like a wobbly foal, blinking a little in confusion.

"You're not dead," Isobel said.

"No. I'm not." He sounded slightly uncertain about that, however.

Gabriel took a step back from both of them, then went to check on the animals. Whatever had happened just then, if they weren't sure, he certainly wasn't going to be the one to figure it out.

"You walk away from magicians; you don't ask 'em to join you," he said into Steady's ears, checking again to make sure the animal hadn't suffered any ill effects. The gelding seemed perfectly unfussed: horses would be the first to spook when something started them, but if it didn't seem like to eat them, they settled down the first, too.

Away from the others, the immediate threat gone, Gabriel shuddered. He hadn't been able to see the beast clearly: it had moved too fast, and there had been almost a haze around it, a constant puff of dust, but it had gotten the upper hand early and never let go. The magician and Isobel both should be dead. But they were alive, and it was gone.

He rested his hands on Steady's warm hide and thought about the mark on Isobel's palm. Thought about how that blast should have broken her spine or at least cracked her skull. Thought about the things he'd seen, the stories he'd heard even as a child. And then he thought about his Bargain with the devil and sighed.

Bound. He hadn't understood, hadn't been told, until it was almost too late. Something in him *needed* to remain within the Territory, even as he *wanted* to be elsewhere. Every day he'd spent in the States had come at a cost, one he'd thought he was willing to pay . . . but in the end, he'd crawled back across the border, only feeling alive again once he'd crossed the Muddy's waters and stood in the Devil's West again.

The Territory might own his body, but it could not have his soul. Or so he'd thought until the devil's promise to give him peace if he would only mentor a young girl on her first ride. . . . But better to live with the fate he knew than be tangled up in *this*.

Too late now. And Isobel . . . His jaw tightened. Bargain or no, magicians and monsters be damned, he would not abandon her.

"Come on, you two," he called back. "Soon's you can mount up and walk, do so. It'll be dusk soon enough, and I don't want to make camp anywhere near here."

Her heart had rested in her throat while they strode through the crossroads, some part of her half expecting the beast to return, but nothing happened, and soon enough the hills were at their backs, and a wide-open grassland spread out in front of them.

Izzy paused and took a deep breath, then urged Uvnee into a swift lope simply because they *could*. The mare seemed inclined to agree, and she nearly lost her hat as they raced down the road, tears forming in the corners of her eyes and her braid streaming out behind her.

When she finally turned Uvnee around and trotted sedately back to where the others waited, she half expected to be scolded. Instead, she found that Gabriel had discovered a creek a little ways off and decided they would make camp there for the night, rather than riding on.

It must have rained while they were in the hills; the long grass was green, seed-tips bending in a gentle breeze, and the soil under their bedrolls was soft, less dust kicked up as they moved about, setting up camp. Here, out of the mountains, where she could see the horizon and the open sky above her, Izzy felt herself relax, if only a little.

But when they'd settled by the fire as the sun began to sink behind them, a lap of bridles for cleaning, that ease disappeared with the magician's words.

"It's not gone, you know."

"I know." She let her fingers linger on the metal of Steady's bit, checking it by feel for any sharp edges or worn areas. She could feel the lingering taint the same way, less seen than sensed, but distant.

"Out of the crossroads, it didn't have enough strength to come after us."

Izzy nodded, but she wasn't sure she agreed. That wasn't what this felt like. It wasn't gone, wasn't dead, but for now, it had no interest in them.

Ribbons fell from the sky, striking ground and disappearing.

"I'd thought I needed to go back to Clear Rock, but now I'm not so sure," she said, instead. "Not if it's following us."

"You think that thing was the same as what was in Clear Rock?" Gabriel asked. "But you'd said . . ."

"It didn't feel the same," she agreed. "But it is. Somehow. Maybe . . . more than one thing came in on the storm?"

"That . . . doesn't make me feel better," Gabriel said. "But it makes as much sense as anything. So, what now . . . we wait for it to come back? We set a trap?"

"What would you do?" she asked in return.

"If I were trying to draw something out but didn't want to show my hand? I'd stick to whatever my original plan had been. Wait and gather more evidence. So . . . continue on the route we'd set."

"That's what we'll do, then." Her words sounded disquietingly like a question, not a statement, but neither man commented on it, merely nodded.

Izzy went back to cleaning the bridles, and Gabriel his whetstone, when the magician asked, "So, I wonder, rider: how did you come to be such a boon and trusted companion to one such as Graciendo?"

From anyone else, it would have been impolite, asking about a man's past. But Izzy thought, once again, that the magician seemed beyond all common courtesy or restrictions, instead like a child asking for a bedtime story, utterly unaware of anything beyond his own desires.

"Purest bad luck," Gabriel said, not pausing in the slow, steady strokes of the blade against his whetstone. He'd finished his, a sickle-curved piece, and was working on Izzy's now, the longer knife she'd been given and was still half-afraid to use. "A year or so after coming home, still full of book-learning and thinking it could replace the things I'd known before—and not afraid to say so." He paused, chuckling at something in his memory. "Graciendo seemed to find me amusing instead of irritating, and so I lived."

"You were fortunate."

"Yeah." Gabriel let the word draw out. "I was."

Izzy could tell that there were things happening beneath the surface, that the magician was saying things he was not speaking, and Gabriel could hear them even though she could not. She did not know if it was because they were male, or because they were older, or simply because she had not been on the road long enough. Or perhaps some blend of all three. The boss always said the simplest answer was usually true, but simple didn't mean it wasn't also complicated.

She thought she understood that better now. Her thumb turned inward, pressing against the meat of her palm. She could feel the markings there, even though in daylight they weren't raised at all, laying flat on her skin. The devil's mark, same as on Uvnee's bridle and her pack. She was no more than a possession, something claimed. . . .

She'd thought power would make her powerful. That the respect people showed would be to her. But it didn't, and it wasn't.

The judge's words came back to her—was she certain this was what she wanted?

"Yes," she whispered to herself in response to his echo, to her own doubts. To belong, to be part of something important, something powerful . . . But the yes didn't fill her entirely this time. Didn't quiet her discomfort, the sense that she'd made a bad bargain somehow.

But there was no denying that she could do things, feel things . . . important things. It was more than the awareness of the road, deeper, letting her sense danger, letting her know when things were well. What else could it do?

Izzy placed her palm down on the ground, and the quiet busy hum of the earth filled her: things moving, stretching, dying, breaking down and reforming, slow and steady as a heartbeat, the crackle of bones and the whisper of winds, and throughout it all the gentle awareness of the roads, like the endless *flickerthwack* of cards against felt, the mumble of voices and clink of glass.

"Isobel."

She jerked up, suddenly aware that she'd slumped forward. "Yes?"

"Go to bed before we have to carry you there," Gabriel said.

She made a face at him but nodded. Her pallet was on the other side of the fire, Gabriel between her and the magician.

Gabriel. He had looked at them both oddly when tending their injuries, and she had felt his unease, his uncertainty, but his manner to her tonight had been the same as before. She couldn't blame him, not entire. And yet, while he did not trust the magician—and neither did she, entirely, for his inability to tell them what had happened in the crossroads, why his magic had exploded the way it did—he did not distrust her.

She thought.

Under the remaining scrap of moon and a deep white splay of stars, Izzy forced all thoughts out of her head, letting the earth sing her to sleep, not noting when a long, lean shadow slid up next to her ear, a pointed tongue flickering as it whispered in her ear.

In her dreams, she stood in the middle of a river, although her limbs were not wet, and the water ran bloody and black around her. She let her fingers trail in the red murk, and where they touched, the water ran clear.

Thisssss isss your power, a voice told her. *To sssstrike and to cleansssse. Embrace it, usssse it, or we all will die. . . .*

Her eyes opened, and she was awake before she was aware that she'd been asleep, the sound of shouting bringing her to her feet and only after the fact realizing that her knife was unsheathed and in her hand. The sun had broken over the horizon: she had overslept, and Gabriel had let her. Gabriel was the one shouting. The fire was not yet lit, but the animals were tethered where they had been the night before, seemingly unconcerned with anything save their morning meal. She took all this in with one glance, hardly aware she did so, even as she was moving toward the shouting.

"You don't do that! Not here, not within my circle!"

"It is my circle as well, is it not?"

"It is not!"

The two men were squared off against each other just beyond the horses, the magician relaxed, amused, looking down with a definite smirk on his lips, while Gabriel ran his fingers through his hair, leaving the strands sticking straight up in his agitation.

"No workings within my campsite, not without permission. Not while we're off the road. Nor while we're on it, either! You've already called one beast down upon us, and it killed you, if you care to remember!"

"Don't you trust me?" Farron asked, and she could not tell if his offense was true or mockery.

"I'll assume that's your idea of humor," Gabriel said. His body was tense, shoulders held stiffly, but he met the magician's gaze squarely, without flinching.

She wasn't sure, suddenly, who was the more dangerous. Everyone knew magicians were powerful, and mad as spring hares, but Gabriel was more than a cardsharp or rootless advocate, even one with water-sense. There was something layers-deep in him, something she hadn't seen before, and it was stone to the magician's blade, solid and unyielding.

They glared at each other, or Gabriel glared and Farron stared back, at an impasse. Izzy wondered if she dared speak up, break their confrontation, or if it would be safer, better, to stay where she was, silent, an observer.

Then the morning breeze picked up, swirling around them, bringing the faint smell of water and mud, and the magician laughed softly, tilting his head like a dog and smiling at nothing in particular. Gabriel did not laugh, but she could tell the moment the fight left him.

"You don't have to trust me," Farron said. "But I've told you twice now: I am not your enemy. Not here, not in this place and time."

Izzy watched the two of them study each other, and Gabriel sighed, tilting his head back to stare at the sky.

"No workings within camp unless I've cleared it," he said. "Give me no reason to distrust you, and I'll work on the trust."

"Fair enough," the magician said, still smiling, then he seemed to notice Izzy standing there, her knife still bared and ready. "And good morning to you, young rider! No reason to fret; your mentor and I were merely having a tête-à-tête over who is lead dog in this ramshackle pack."

Gabriel turned to look at her. "Put the knife away, Isobel. I doubt it would have much use on him, anyway."

"Unless she meant to use it on you?" The magician grinned again at Gabriel's look, wrinkles forming around his sleepy-looking eyes, his teeth too white, too sharp-looking for comfort. Izzy slid the knife back into its sheath, feeling oddly reluctant to return it to her pack.

Gabriel might or might not trust Farron, but she was suddenly unsure if she trusted either one of them just then, that they were so easily brought down by the faintest touch of the wind. With the feel of the earth still beating against her bare soles and the memory of what she had seen and felt at Clear Rock lingering, she wondered how one might tell the difference between a good wind and an ill one, how she could trust anything.

She looked down at her palm, traced the sigil with one finger. Gabriel had made a deal with the devil, made an agreement to protect her, in exchange for . . . something. She could trust him same as she'd trust the boss. Couldn't she?

The feeling of uncertainty was unpleasant. She didn't like it at all.

Izzy went back to her bedroll, placing the knife down on top of her blanket. She tried not to think about the sweat that had dried on her skin: the creek Gabriel had found was barely large enough to refill canteens; she had no desire to try and wash her body in it. Shaking her hair out of its braid, she ran her fingers through the length before braiding it back up again, the feathers Calls Thunder had given her woven again into the plait, hanging just under her ear, over her shoulder. She let her fingers linger over the spines of the feathers and remembered Gabriel's words: Calls Thunder had given them to her as a sign of respect. They were meant to give honor.

The Hinonoeino dream-talker had thought her worth respect and honor.

She slipped a dress on over her chemise, lacing it closed, then drew on her stockings and—after checking to make sure nothing had crawled into them overnight—her boots. Then she rolled her kit back up, and brought it over to where the horses were waiting. By then, Gabriel had the fire started, and the first bittersweet smell of coffee had replaced that hint of fresh water in the air.

"So, where are we heading now?" she asked, sitting down to wait for the coffee to be ready. He handed her an apple, slightly mushy but still edible, and she ate it, waiting for his answer.

"I'd thought to head north after seeing Graciendo," he said slowly. "Originally, take you up to the Lakota and their kin. I've friends there, and they've enough sway among other tribes—willing and otherwise— that they would be useful for you to know."

"Not now?"

He glanced sideways at the magician, who was moving through some sort of slow movements, like knife practice without a knife, away from the fire. "Things have changed. Devorah said there was trouble south of us. And the storm you saw coming in, it came over the Mother's Knife, right?"

She nodded, chewing and swallowing before answering. "Yes."

"That's here"—he drew a wavering line in the dirt with his finger. "The Territory extends here"—he drew another line—"and here"— the line bent away from the first line at an angle. "Devorah was here. There hasn't been any noise of unrest we've heard, north of here"— his finger rested on a spot in the dirt.

"We haven't been that far north," Izzy said, squinting at the make-shift map and trying to place the spots in her own mind with actual locations. "I think."

"You tell me, then. Is the storm north of us?"

She looked at him, but he was completely serious. He expected her to be able to tell where the wrongness was, simply by . . . looking?

She touched the feathers in her braid again, just the pad of two fingers against their raspy softness. She was the one who'd told him she had to know. She was the one who'd demanded they deal with this. Either she could do it or she couldn't, but dithering accomplished nothing.

She rested her palm on the dirt, pressing the sigil to the ground, and reached for that humming sensation again. Doubt filled her: the boss had ignored her earlier calls, so why should now be any different? She might be able to sense the road, but that was nothing; Gabriel said anyone could do it. He was the one who knew the Territory, could sense water, was—

"Iz." His fingers rested lightly on her shoulder, his voice barely audible. "Trust yourself. Trust your instincts. You know how to read this."

Where she couldn't quite trust herself, she could trust his belief, maybe?

The connection didn't so much reach out to meet her as it drew her down into it, settling her, spreading her out. Her skin felt rough, her bones soft; her vision darkened but she did not feel blind. She remembered the feel of the storm, the *wrongness*, the hunger of the thing at Clear Rock, the worry in the eyes of Calls Thunder, and searched the humming for something that echoed that, something that called, like to like.

The connection faltered, shied away, and Izzy forced herself to reach for it, holding and stretching to find the faintest glimmers. Part of her resisted that stretch, knotted tight, overwhelmed. She petted the knot, calmed it. A grim determination filled her, refusing the uncertainty, the doubt. If she was to be a tool, if she was to be a pawn, let her be one, but let her do it properly. Let her claim what power was hers to use, and use it.

There. Her skin shuddered, the unease that was never far gone roaring back to life before she sidestepped, ducked, danced out of its way with her heart beating too fast, her skin sheened with sweat from the effort.

"West," she said softly, forcing Gabriel to lean forward to hear her. "Southwest, deep and high." Her eyes opened, and she stared at him, inches away, without seeing him. "That's where it is. It's spreading, cracking. . . . Feeding."

She was missing something, forgetting something, but to remember would be to go closer, lose herself in the strangeness, and she didn't dare, couldn't dare, not with that hunger crackling around her.

"Will you know it when you see it?" Farron had joined them at some point, standing away and to the side but close enough to hear.

"Yes," she said, certain.

Gabriel stood up. "Then let's go."

Gabriel spoke briefly to Farron, their voices a low, unintelligible, background rumble. Izzy rested her chin on her hands, her elbows on her knees, until she felt Gabriel's hands on her shoulder again, helping her rise. Unlike previous times, the nearly overwhelming, dizzying sense of connection lingered, only beginning to fade when she was back in Uvnee's saddle, leather reins in her fingers and solid horse under her legs. She felt it go with relief. If that was what Farron felt, even a hint of it, and he carried it with him all the time? No wonder magicians went mad. She thought of Calls Thunder again, of his eyes, the boss's eyes, and wondered suddenly what her own looked like now.

She thought she probably should be scared, but she was too tired, worn to the bone. Worn *into* the bone.

Uvnee following Steady without any direction from her rider, Farron walking with his easy long-stride pace along the mare's right side. He did not touch her or the mare, and she was thankful. They traveled in silence, even the magician's usual inane remarks muted.

Izzy rubbed the mark in her palm, staring down at it as though it would resolve into something new if she watched it long enough. But it remained the same familiar sigil, thick black lines curved and flourished in the flesh.

Flood seemed so far away now, a life that belonged to someone else. The girl she'd been would never have understood the sick fear Izzy felt, the ashen taste in her mouth when she thought of Widder Creek, the way her bowels tightened when she thought about facing the thing that had destroyed Clear Rock again, knowing that she would have to, that it was her responsibility now. Whatever she had thought, whatever the boss had planned, none of that mattered. The Territory needed her to do things.

There were more pieces here, things Izzy knew she was seeing, but she couldn't recognize yet what they meant, and she was afraid to dig too deeply, afraid to rattle free anything more. One more thought, one more weight, and her bones might crack too.

She wished she'd been able to talk with Calls Thunder; they seemed to understand the boss, recognize him. Maybe they could tell her what she was feeling, what she had become.

She nudged that thought, let it creep closer to her, breathed steadily as it made itself at home, sunk into her shoulders and down her spine, dropping into her knees, her feet, her fingers. She wasn't Izzy anymore, not entirely. Not the girl who'd sewn ribbons into her best dress or folded linens, but still the girl who'd studied strangers while they studied their cards. Still the girl who'd watched the sunrise and shared morning coffee with the devil. And *she* had been the girl who folded linens, so wasn't she still that same girl, too?

Izzy was so caught up in her thoughts, it took her too long to realize something else had changed.

She moved her mare closer to Steady, letting them match pace for a few strides before she spoke. "It's back."

Her mentor didn't look up, his body comfortably sunk into the saddle, brim of his hat low down over his eyes, his hands relaxed on the reins. "I know."

Farron increased his stride to join them. "What's back?"

"Nothing," Gabriel said.

"Something's been following us," Izzy said. Now was no time to be holding back information, not when the magician might be able to give them answers. Although she wondered at the fact that he couldn't sense it too. . . .

Apparently, he couldn't. "Something other than me? I'm most put out."

The look Gabriel shot the magician would have reduced most folk to silence. Farron made a face and held up his hands in surrender. "Tell me more."

"It's not . . . that." Not the thing that had consumed Clear Rock, had chased her from that place. "It feels different," Izzy said. "We thought it was a dust-dancer at first or maybe a demon. Before we went up into the mountains. But neither one of those would follow us all the way here, would it?"

"Dancers? Barely aware, distracted far too easily. A day they might lurk, but no more. And you, little rider? You'd send them running like a thunderstorm."

She thought he was trying to be reassuring. He wasn't.

"And demon . . ." The magician took that more seriously. "They do not roam willingly and rarely go long without causing some mischief. We would have known by now if they had your scent."

"How long did you follow us?" Gabriel asked. "You said you'd been waiting for us. . . ." He tilted his head and stared at the magician.

"For her, rider, only for her. And only once you entered Clear Rock," Farron said. "And after, of course, once I was myself again. But I intended no harm. I misdoubt this new unease you feel is me— that discomfort should be an old friend to you by now." He shook his head in mock sadness. "You must look to another for this determined affection."

Izzy remembered the feeling of being watched she'd felt in the mountains, how it had felt different from before, and nodded once.

Gabriel saw the nod but didn't back down. "You haven't noticed anything dogging us?" Izzy could hear the challenge in Gabriel's voice, the assumption that the magician was not as alert nor as powerful as he claimed, or that he had sensed it and not told them. But it was a fair question, and she stilled her immediate instinctive urge to smooth things between them, waiting on the magician's answer.

"I have only dogged you once." And Farron showed his teeth in that disturbingly toothy grin of his, then went on. "The winds show me everything, rider. Every pulse in the air, every ripple in the stone, each twitch of flesh. But to separate it out into specifics requires focus, and you have given me nothing to focus *for*." He sobered, his eyes unexpectedly sane for a moment. "And now you know more of my medicine than any who have not paid the wind's price, Gabriel Kasun. Do you wish to learn more?"

They both stopped, staring at each other. Gabriel did not blink away from the magician's gaze, but the way he wetted his lips showed his discomfort, and Steady tossed his head, clearly not wanting to be caught between the two of them.

"Stop it," she said, breaking into their standoff. "We have no time for this, either of you."

"Truth, little rider," Farron said. He blinked once, deliberately, less surrender than truce, then turned to her, resuming his walking pace. "So, what shall we do about this unwanted interloper?"

"You mean the *other* unwanted interloper?"

"I say we do nothing," Izzy said, ignoring Gabriel's taunt and hoping Farron would do the same. "Whatever it is, it hasn't harmed us. It's just watching. We shouldn't provoke it. Like riding near a bear," she said over her shoulder to Gabriel. "Just acknowledge and ride on?"

"Allowing a potential enemy to get within range seems counter-wise," the magician said. "And yet, as you say, lingering at a distance shows no immediate malice. . . . Might it be a local hunter, displeased at our overlarge feet and too-loud voices scaring game away?" His tone clearly indicated that it was they who were too loud, not him.

"It's not a native." Gabriel sounded confident of that, bringing Steady up alongside them, bracketing the magician between the horses while the mule brought up the rear. "They'd have let us know by now, even if they didn't want to confront us directly. And while I respect their hunting abilities, I doubt they could hide for any length of time, even in these grasses. Not and stay close enough to spook us."

Izzy lifted her hat and wiped the line of sweat on her forehead, squinting a little as the sun hit her face. They'd seen no rain since that sudden night storm. She wondered if there might be a creek or pond within a day's ride, and if it would be safe to bathe there. "Another magician?"

"No." Farron's response was immediate. "We are not known for being social creatures, and even less with those like ourselves. We do not linger in each other's company. Another magician would challenge me were our paths to cross, not lurk for days, and likely would not consider the risk of the devil's displeasure worth nibbling on your little morsel. Not unless they were more mad than most, anyway."

"Challenge? You mean a duel?" Gabriel asked.

"Most likely. The impulse to drain each other is nigh impossible to resist." He made a grimace and lifted his long arms in a shrug. "I am not proud of how we are, but it is how we are. We cannot resist the lure."

Gabriel looked over Farron's head, speaking directly to Izzy. "He means they're madmen who cannot be trusted. Isobel, he said it himself; he can't resist. This thing we're chasing, whatever it is, it's powerful, which means for him it's like liquor to a drunkard. He could be using you to find it, and once he does, you—"

"Your determination to protect your charge does you credit, rider, but your suspicion grows tedious and distracts from the true danger. Must I repeat myself a third time and make it an oath?" the magician asked, irritated. "Then so be it." He strode forward and wheeled about, forcing them to pause as well or run him over. He took a deep breath and stared at them. "In this place, in this time, in this cause,

I am not your enemy. In this time, in this place, in this cause, I am your ally. And possibly your only one, as the tribes have determined that this is the Old Man's to deal with, as I suspect you have already learned."

He shot a wicked glare in Gabriel's direction. "If my interest in the power this holds offends you, remember it is also why I aid you as well."

Izzy felt the air waver around them, thickening and then thinning again, cooling and then warming. It felt nothing like the touch of the bones, no hint of the boss's power, yet there was a sameness to it that reminded her of Calls Thunder's eyes or the feel of the road below them.

Gabriel looked at her, and she nodded, swallowing hard. "It was a true oath."

"And," Farron added, an odd glint in his eye, "if I were to chase your morsel myself, it would be in fair contest. I would give her that much respect."

Izzy made a deep bow in Farron's direction, a more flamboyant move than she'd used with the judge back in Flood, and hoped that her lack of amusement was clear in the action. From the way he smirked at her, she suspected he knew and didn't care.

If you see a magician, run.

"All right," Gabriel said, and she could tell he wasn't happy, either, but saw no way around going forward. "So, whatever's lurking, it's not human, and it's not magician, and it's not an animal, because nothing stalks prey this long without attacking. And dust-dancers don't leave the plains, even if they could hold a thought long enough."

Both Izzy and Farron nodded in agreement to that.

"You know what that leaves."

"Demon." She hadn't thought any word could sound so sour as that one did in the magician's mouth. "And determined enough to leave their territory."

"Can't you talk to it? You're both—" she started to say, and he hissed at her, the sheer menace in the sound stopping the words in her throat.

"Never compare us," he warned her, lips pulled away from his teeth, those dark eyes lit from within. "They are animals, made of power but unable to understand it. I am *nothing* like that."

"All right," she agreed, much as she would have tried to calm an angry dog, without moving her body, her voice calm, controlled but agreeable. *But a mad dog would still lunge,* a voice reminded her. And she had no weapon to beat it back, no stick or club. Not unless she used her knife, and how much good would a knife do against a magician? She found her fingers pressing against the sheath nonetheless, the cool metal a false reassurance.

"Your oath," she said, her voice faint.

"I am *nothing* like that," he repeated, but his face eased, and she nodded, letting go of the sheath's ties.

"If it is a demon following us," she said, still alert to every twitch and blink, "why? Boss says they don't much like being around people."

"They don't," Gabriel agreed. He had come off Steady's back when the magician had threatened her, and she followed suit now, the three of them standing within the circle of horses and mule. Anyone observing them would not be able to see their faces or hear their words. "They don't like people and they don't like being alone, so if there's one, there's more than one. Or we've been passed off from one group to another. Anyroad, it's not good news. I'd rather face a war party than demon set on mischief. Isobel, I hate to ask it of you again, but can you catch a whiff of it without it knowing you're looking?"

"You think she can do what I could not?" Farron's voice was tight, controlled, as though Gabriel had finally managed to insult him.

Gabriel gave him a long look that managed to be both considering and insulting. "Can't she?"

The magician gave another shrug and looked away. "She might. Or it might catch and eat her . . . and I doubt she would come back as well from that as I did."

Izzy met Gabriel's gaze and nodded once. They needed to know what followed them and why. She would take the risk, although the thought made her blood chill, uncertain if the magician was exaggerating the risk or not.

Gabriel placed one hand on her shoulder, the warmth of his fingers felt even through the fabric of her jacket. "We're here. We'll keep guard. The last time Steady encountered a demon, he kicked it near into tomorrow."

She smiled at that, the way he'd intended her to, but her insides felt watery, like she was coming down with the flux. Demon might not be as dangerous as magician, but they were bad enough. And opening herself to find it . . ..

Other things might find her.

Izzy rubbed her thumb into the mark on her palm, hard enough for it to hurt. There was a difference between luring the storm-beast in and leaving herself *open* to it.

"Don't look at it, look past it," the magician told her, arms crossed over his chest, his expression closed off. She still couldn't read him, the shifting madness in his brain masking what lay below, but she listened to his advice anyway. "Demon are curious; it will want to see what you see, and show itself that way."

She nodded, her brow furrowed. And if it wasn't a demon that was following them, she thought, not looking directly at it might keep her unnoticed in turn. "Step lightly," Iktan always said. "If you step lightly, most everything will let you pass."

Unless they were drunk. Molly had always added that. Some things were just spoiling for a fight.

She bit her lower lip, trying to think how she might look past something when she didn't know what she was looking for or how she was even looking. Each time prior, she had touched the ground, slid into the humming, let it take her over. And each time, she had been drawn directly to the creature, an arrow loosed from a bow, a bullet from a muzzle, moth to a candle.

She traced the sigil thoughtfully. "Walk past it," she said to herself, an idea unfolding. "Walking to the bar to freshen drinks, all the while keeping an eye on the players at a table." She closed her eyes, visualizing the floor of the saloon, the placement of tables, then imagined herself there, the crowd around her, the way she'd glance and turn. . . .

There was no room for doubt. She had been doing this since she was old enough to carry a tray; the bet was higher but the cards were the same. Bring the things she knew together. . . .

Izzy shifted, turning so that she was at the center of the little group of men and horses, and lowered herself to a crouch. Then she opened her left hand, palm facing toward the ground but not touching it, and thought about being in a crowded room, looking without looking. Then she touched the feeling of being watched, the sensation of something tracking them.

Now-familiar dizziness, steadied by the distant feel of an arm through hers, the press of a body nearby, a horse's whuffling breath and the creak of leather, the sound of human voices wrapped around her, holding her. Dizziness and the drawing-down, crackling and grinding, moving so slowly her breath felt too fast, too obvious, and she tried to slow it, keep it from sounding so loud against the *shhhh shhhhh shhh* of the bones and stones below.

This wasn't like before. There was nothing lurking, slavering, pushing at her. The *shhhh shhh shhhh* wound through her skin, cradling her thoughts, smelling of water and dry stone, tasting of thunder and flame and fur, singing the skittering of things she could not name, but nothing surged at her, nothing took note. She followed it down, searching the way a dowser would for water, seeking unease, upset, hunger. Nothing. She let go, looked instead for the sense of watching, of lurking, of curiosity. . . .

Something brushed against her, dry heat and rasp, and was gone. *Snake. Snake still watches but is not what I seek.*

She looked past, further out, waiting.

Hunger. Not the fearsome scrape and claw but a low thrumming hunger, a *need*. But there was no form she could find, no shape to identify, and then it too faded and was gone. Her eyes opened and she lifted her chin, tilting the brim of her hat back and breathing deep, filling her lungs.

"Iz?"

"Nothing behind, nothing above." She scanned the pale blue sky, able to see buzzards far over them, circling something distant to the left, the peaceful dryness of the single tree in the distance, the slow push-presence of whatever followed them, blending into the push-presence of the rocks, the grasses, the dirt below their feet. The bones of the world, crackling as they moved, slow, so slowly, wind and water rushing over and through. She knew its mood the way she'd know the mood of a player at the table, reading the hundred surface marks and movements that answered her questions even though they never spoke. The unease that had rested in her bones for so many weeks melted and subsided. "I can't find anything," she said, and her voice cracked, dry as the stone underfoot. Gabriel fetched a waterskin from Steady's saddle and pressed it on her, making sure her fingers closed around it so she could drink. The warm, stale water felt magnificent against her throat, as though she'd been screaming for hours.

"There's nothing behind us?" The magician frowned. "But I thought—"

"Something's there, dry and deep below, but I can't . . . I can't see it." She frowned at him, feeling an ache begin to form behind her eyes, that brief sense of contentment gone, replaced by the queasy feeling of having been thrown hard from a horse. She was suddenly hungry, but the thought of food made her want to vomit.

"I can't . . ." She struggled to form words, to explain. "There's nothing to *see*, nothing I can catch at."

"Dry like a rock, or dry like a hot wind?" The magician's voice was hard, cold, and she forced herself to focus on it.

"Like . . . both? But more like wind," she told him. "But it slipped away the moment I reached for it."

"Demon," Farron said. "That's what they taste like: dry and full of nothing."

"Why can't I see it?"

"Because they don't want us to. I scorn their intellect, but we're the interlopers here, little rider. Me and thee and even the People, who claim to remember the lands rising from the waters, we're all invaders compared to them. They're the dust of the first bones, ancient stones. The way we use power, it was theirs first." His voice had taken on that singsong lilt of madness again, his smile distracted, his eyes vague on the distance, seeing something she could not.

"If they're that old, that powerful, maybe they know what sent the storm, too. Let me try again." Her brave words were undercut when she swayed on her feet, nearly falling into Gabriel, who caught her up around the waist.

"None of that, Iz. Back up in the saddle you go, and a good hold on the reins."

She wanted to protest, but the dizziness she'd felt came rushing back like a stampede. It would be foolish to resist, so she let him help her back into the saddle, gathering up the reins and leaning forward to rest her face against Uvnee's warm neck, even as the magician took up position on her right. "You watch the road for me, all right, girl?"

The mare snorted, and she heard Gabriel swing back into his own saddle, and they started forward again.

Gabriel was both amused and worried when Isobel fell asleep as they rode, waking only long enough to help untack the horses when they halted to make camp. Her eyes glazed with sleep, her hair loose over her shoulders, a smudge of dirt on her chin, the facade of adulthood was cracked, if not shattered. He gently pushed her aside when she would have tried to follow her usual routine of cleaning and storing the tack, and made her sit down on a flat stone set just outside the fire circle.

"You did most of the hard work today," he told her. "Rest."

She looked as though she wanted to argue, but he scowled at her, and she ducked her head, busying herself finger-combing the tangles in her hair, then rebraiding it.

"I did no hard work?" the magician said, his voice mock-offended but low, meant for his ears, not hers, as they unloaded the packs from the mule and set up camp.

"I'm not sure what you did today," Gabriel said sharply. "Why would a demon be following us?"

The magician looked down at him, his face schooled in a mask of quiet confusion even as he smoothed a place for the bedrolls to lay out. His hand barely touched the grass, rocks and sticks stirring themselves to the side. "You ask me? It follows you." He cocked his head, considering. "Or her. Most likely her."

"Why?" Gabriel set his own bedroll down a distance away and turned back to face the magician. "As you said, they're ancient and care nothing for our doings, have no truck with the devil's workings, any more than your kind do. Nor do they travel under the open sky." Demon lingered in shadows, in caves or riverbanks, not well-marked roads.

"She is new. It may be curious. That is a trait we all share, even demon." His smile did nothing to warm his face, and Gabriel distrusted it.

"What do you mean, new? She's green, you mean?" Between them, working in surprising harmony, the camp had been established, and only the fire remained to be started. But he hesitated, waiting for the magician to respond.

"There has been no Hand on the road in decades. No—" He frowned, this one an oddly open, honest expression. "Longer than that. The devil had his players, his dogs set to track deal-breakers, his jacks to do his bidding. But none with such . . . authority. None who bear his mark so clearly."

"What does it mean? Why now?"

The magician laughed and shook his head, no humor in the sound or the action. "You ask me to interpret the devil? Madness only drives me so far, rider. But the winds are restless, the natives uncertain, and settlers disappearing and dying, all as she rides by? Something trembles the bones below our feet? You think all that coincidence?"

"I think that not all events are connected. She came of age and offered bargain; that is why she was chosen now."

"Spoken like a true advocate, clinging to the facts. But this is the Territory, and you are bound. You know better."

Gabriel grimaced and turned away from both the man and the comment.

"Whatever the devil promised you, he cannot change that," the magician said, and for the first time, there was neither mockery nor threat in his voice. "He cannot change what you are. And he has no wish to."

"I know."

Gabriel left the magician standing in the gloaming and went to the fire circle, where Isobel had gathered a handful of twigs and small branches, waiting for him to set the new coalstone he'd acquired in the mining camp. It was smaller than his old one and twice as expensive, but it did the trick.

"You should have your own," he said, kneeling to light the kindling. "A rider should always have the means to make fire, unless you've learned to snap your fingers and make it spark?"

Her smile was a faint, wan thing. "Looking to be rid of me soon?" Her voice was low, and she was not looking at him, staring instead into the slender, flickering flames.

He sighed, sinking back onto his haunches. "No. And even were we not on the trail of this thing, not for some weeks yet—I've not taught you nearly as much as I should have by now, and letting you out on your own would disgrace my name." The fact that they'd been distracted and beset for much of that time was no excuse, nor were her own surprising—not surprising, but startling—abilities. Not the first time, Gabriel cursed the devil for sending them out unprepared, ignoring the fact that Isobel was, in fact, no less prepared than any other novice. No other novice was asked to do the things she was asked to do.

If the devil had known what waited for her . . .

"I've been thinking." Her voice was low, and she still wasn't looking at him, but her fingers were no longer tightly clenched, and her shoulders were not hunched forward. He took that for progress.

"Yes?"

"The boss didn't tell me anything. He threw me at you, threw me out on the road, and didn't tell me anything. Not about what I should be doing, not about . . ."—she made a vaguely desperate gesture at herself—"any of this. Why?"

He'd just wondered the same thing, so he had no answer for her. Even if the trouble they'd found was unexpected, had the devil not known what would wake in her? That sort of carelessness seemed impossible, and yet the alternative, that he had intentionally not told her—

That felt right, actually. Cold, harsh, possibly cruel, but right. The Territory was no gentle place, and its lessons were equally harsh.

"I think . . ." He wasn't certain, but he had to say something, not leave her sitting there, looking at him like that. "I think that there are things we need to learn on our own, that being taught, or being told . . . it wouldn't stick. Or we'd take the wrong path because we already knew what lay down the other." That scratched uncomfortably close to home, striking the same sore place the magician had already touched tonight. No one had warned him. Would he have listened if they had?

"So, he didn't say anything because . . . you needed to learn on your own, not what he said was best, not what someone else had done, but what *you* would do?"

She drew sharp, shaky breath in, and he thought maybe something he'd said had been right or close to right.

She was sixteen. Never mind the law, she was too young to commit to anything, much less this. Too young to be so ruthlessly broken, her confidence, however foolish, destroyed, only so the devil could remake her. He bit his tongue and waited.

There was a faint rustle of grass, and the magician sat cross-legged on the other side of the fire, his face lit by the fire, yet still in shadows.

She looked up, and Gabriel was struck anew by the fineness of her bones, strong under sun-weathered skin, and thought again that she would become a handsome woman. And a terror with it, he thought with no little pride. If she survived.

"I could have done anything, gone anywhere," Isobel said. "But I chose this. I chose . . . this." Her right hand made a gesture, fingers spread, making a half circle from her stomach, her thumb pointed inward. "Never mind that I chose for the wrong reasons, not understanding . . . not *knowing*. I made my Bargain."

And at that, she'd had more freedom than he. Gabriel tried not to be bitter over the fact.

"And?" The magician leaned back, comfortable as though there were a wall to support him, and rested his hands on his knees. "Why should I care?"

"You . . ."

"I can't help you in this. I can't guide you or mentor you or whatever lies they tell you any more than your companion over there can." His voice had no gentleness in it, the sharp crackle of fire, the cold cut of winter's wind. "Whatever you call it, witchcraft or medicine, it's power you hold, and there is one truth of power, Isobel Devil's Hand. And that is that there is no moderation, no easement, no gate to shut. You set your fingers to the bones, stirred the dust, and breathed it in. Now it will remake you as it sees fit."

"The boss . . ."

"What is your boss, little rider? Understand that, and you will understand yourself."

Gabriel shifted, intentionally making noise, and they both looked at him, the tension breaking enough that he could breathe again. "That sort of thinking is better done rested and on a full stomach.

Farron"—the name felt odd in his mouth, as though speaking it gave the magician more heft than he'd had before—"we'll need fresh water to soak the beans."

He couldn't see the magician's face, but his voice painted a picture of eyebrows rising high in surprise. "You're sending me to errand-boy to find a creek?"

"Or you can conjure some out of the air; I don't have a particular care," he said. "Just do it." He was going over their supplies in his head, counting what they had left from De Plata, feeding three instead of two. "I'm going to go set some traps, see if we can have fresh meat in the morning. Iz, build up the fire and bury—"

"Bury the potatoes and toast the bread. I *know*," she muttered, and for a moment it was just the two of them again, with nothing more required than preparing a meal and getting a good night's sleep.

"And use the last of the molasses," he warned her, "before it turns on us."

She smiled at that, as he meant her to, while he moved away to see what he could do about the morning's meal.

Everything else would wait until they had some sleep tucked under their ears. He hoped.

Isobel woke before sunrise, her body slipping from sleep to wakefulness with ease. She breathed in and opened her eyes, the trails of starlight overhead casting the world in a silvery light.

A faint movement caught her eye: a tall shadow a ways from camp, performing a slow, graceful routine. Her lips shaped his name: Farron Easterly. To her left, across the faint glow of the coalstone, Gabriel slept, a blanket-covered lump, but she knew that the faintest unfamiliar noise would wake him, alert and armed.

"What is your boss, little rider? Understand that, and you will understand yourself."

Farron's words had followed her into sleep, but she had woken with no more clarity. She thought of all the things she had taken for granted, living under his roof. The Old Man. The devil. Powerful enough to claim the entire Territory, to keep truce with native tribes for generations, to give dearest hopes and darkest desires for a price. . . . She had lived her entire life under his roof and never once wondered *what* he was.

She thought now of his ever-shifting face, how his eyes could be gentle one instant and cold the next, how he never need raise his voice to be heard everywhere, over anything. She thought of his hands dealing cards, shuffling decks, curled around his glass, holding the cigar he never smoked, the sweet smoke rising into the air.

The Devil's Hand. His Left Hand. She flexed the fingers of her left hand, watched the silver ring glint as it caught the starlight, thought of the signet ring on the boss's left hand, to match Marie's, and imagined it on her own. A tool. A pawn. Not Izzy any more, not really.

They called him the devil because he offered temptation, Gabriel'd said. Outside the Territory, they said that. Inside, he was the boss. The Old Man. But what *was* that?

Understand that, and you will understand yourself.

Gabriel threw off his blanket and sat up just as the first rays of light stretched into the sky, and the horses stamped their feet, grumbling for food.

First things first. Deal with what the storm had blown in, stop it from harming anyone else, and then she could worry about all the rest.

Assuming there was a rest to worry about then.

"It's not as easy travel, but if we head across here, we'll pick up the road to the high plains," Gabriel was saying. He had a map open against the saddle, smoothing the weathered canvas, but he wasn't looking at it; she knew he'd more maps in his head than could ever fit in a saddle roll, and she wondered how many years he'd had to ride the roads to learn them like that.

He saw her frowning at the map and said, "It's as much knowing as it is remembering, Iz. A rider's trick; nothing special about it. You feel the road, you ken where it is under you?"

She let her thoughts drift a moment, feeling the now-familiar, reassuring hum of the road below them, then nodded.

"Follow it."

Reach down and sense the *sense* of the road itself, he meant. Touch the presence that made a road a road instead of a trail or a path or . . . well, an ordinary road, the way she'd always thought of it before. She hesitated, remembering the exhaustion of the day before, then firmed her courage. A rider's trick, Gabriel called it. He could do it, Devorah could do it, therefore she could do it. This was nothing compared to what she had already done.

She closed her eyes, trusting Uvnee to keep them steady, and let herself slip down, from neck to shoulders, down to hips, knees, into her heels, and then pouring from her soles, toes tipping forward in the stirrups as though to reach for the ground beneath them, aware of the round warmth of Uvnee's belly under her legs, the warm sun overhead, the delicate, crisp breath of the air on her skin, the distant *thumpthumpthump* pulse of the road neither welcoming nor warning but simply being, endless rolling miles coiling in and out, a pattern on the Territory she could only barely begin to see.

This wasn't like tracking the storm or searching for their lurker. The air pressed against her skin, and the stone drew her in, and underneath the pleasure those sensations brought, she vaguely remembered she was meant to do something, see something, understand . . . The high plains. She was supposed to be finding the high plains from where they were, see the map . . .

Oh. There. Suddenly, Izzy understood why Gabriel refused to explain so much: there was no way to describe the sensation. It didn't happen, it had already happened; the knowledge didn't arrive, it had always been in her, waiting for her to understand.

Was this how he found water, too? Was it simply a matter of knowing to find?

The *thumpthumpthump* drew her in, a sensation of slipping, falling forward but not falling at all, being *drawn* neither swiftly nor slowly but as though one heartbeat lasted forever. She was in Uvnee's saddle, her legs pressed against the horse's bulk, the air on her cheeks and sweat on her scalp under the brim of her hat, the low sound of Gabriel's voice saying something, and she was leagues away, running straight and flat, the air thin and brittle, hoofbeats and wings, the low sound of a man chanting and women speaking in languages she did not know, the softness of clay and the brittle taste of snow still on the mountains.

She could follow it further, she knew. Instead, she drew back, cautious of wandering too far, losing her way back. She followed Gabriel's voice, the smell of leather and horse, the feel of the reins sliding through her fingers. She opened her eyes and looked up, *felt* the road continue on under Uvnee's hooves, felt herself drawn forward without conscious design, the *thumpthump* in her veins. Something was on the road ahead of them, something that should not be there, something that *offended*.

And then she was snagged with knifepoint talons, dragging down her arm, yanking her to the side. A snake's hiss in the wind, the shift of rocks and the high amused howl of a coyote under the scream of a Reaper hawk, and under it all the soft *shhhplash* of water over rocks, the low chant of words she didn't understand, the smell of the boss's cigar, and the *flickerthwack* of cards laid down on the felt.

Who is your boss, Isobel?

She almost understood, almost, and the scream of the Reaper became a man's voice, high and pained, and the connection broke as Uvnee started under her and Gabriel swore. They both pushed their horses into a forward trot, Gabriel in the lead this time, Steady guided by his legs while both hands were busy loading his carbine with skill Izzy would have admired some other time. She was too busy now, pulling the longer knife from its saddle sheath, feeling the handle warm in her grip and wishing they'd had more than a handful of lessons in how to fight from saddleback. Strike away, not in. Keep the blade and the battle as far from Uvnee's head as possible. *If threatened, Uvnee will kick,* he'd said; *do not let her kick at you.*

And then they were on the scene, the source of the sense of offense, the *should not be.*

Five men dressed in rough brown homespun. One down on the ground, curled in on himself—the one who had screamed?—and three others in ready position around him, wooden staffs held in a two-handed grip, while the fifth man grappled with their attacker.

It should not have been a contest. The attacker was slender and pale, bare of any clothing save a clout around its nethers, hair the red of sunrise, long and loose like a girl's, near to its waist and braided with white feathers that fluttered as it moved, limbs twisting in ways more like a snake than a man, impossible to contain.

Izzy gasped, pulling Uvnee up too hard. That pale skin *glittered,* like icicles melting. Her knife would do no good here, nor Gabriel's gun. But Gabriel was out of the saddle, flinging himself on the combatants, and she felt herself slip from her saddle as well, not to join the battle but to circle around, going to her knees next to the wounded man. He did not seem to be bleeding but gasped as though someone had knocked him in an unfortunate place. Izzy sat back on her heels, one hand on his shoulder, uncertain how to proceed.

"Vade foedae rei, quaro monstrante spiritu malum!" the fifth man called, his voice low and frightened, shaking, his hand lifted to show something dangling from his fist. "Quo egressus es ex inferno, et vade ad excutiendam!"

"That's not going to work," Farron told him dryly. The magician had caught up with them and now stood there, arms crossed, lips pressed together to stop a wolfish smile. The mule peeked from behind him, brown nose twitching as though it, too, wanted to laugh.

Gabriel finally got his hands around the demon, then slapped the heel of his hand against the creature's forehead, hissing something in its ear. The demon let out a cry, bitterness and outrage wrapped around an ululation, before collapsing in a thick cloud of white dust that left both Gabriel and the brown-garbed stranger coughing, covering their eyes and mouth.

"Silver and threats," Farron said. "Now, *that* works."

The demon gone, Izzy tried to check the injured man, to see if he'd taken any actual damage. But the moment she reached for him again, he scrambled out of the way, scooting on his backside as though she'd come after him with a heated poker.

"You're more terrifying to him than the demon," Farron said, coming to stand next to her. He showed his teeth to the man next to her. "Ella no va a dañar su alma inmaculada," he said. "Crecer un par ya. Oh wait," he said, switching back to English. "You gave up your pair already, didn't you?"

"You're no one to talk," Gabriel said, tying the horses' reins up and turning to look over the five men. "¿Quiénes soy y por qué estáis en el camino?"

Spanish, Izzy recognized belatedly. He was asking them who they were and why they were on the road. But why . . . She looked over the men more carefully. They were staring back, eyes flicking from Farron to Gabriel, their eyes slipping over her oddly. They did not wear trousers but rather coarse brown coats belted at the waist, with hoods that could be pulled forward or—in at least one case—cowled around the neck. To the side, clearly cast there when they were attacked, were shoulder packs as long as a man's back and braced with willow lattice where they hooked over the shoulder. They had no visible weapons save the staffs they still held at the ready, but Izzy could see they were tipped with iron at either end, and kept her hands visible, her body still, in case one of them should suddenly decide she too was a threat. Her gaze slid upward to the leather thongs around their necks, clearly visible against their cloaks. Not the devil's double-loop nor the marshal's tree, but— Her eyes widened. "They're priests?"

The boss was tolerant of folk crossing borders, but not so tolerant that he'd allow *this*.

"Friars," Gabriel said. "Not Jesuits—Spain's not overfond of them these days. Too tolerant of the heresies, too well liked by the natives." He pushed his hat back on his head and studied the men, his eyes narrowed. "Dominicans? Franciscans?"

Izzy had no idea what Gabriel was asking, and a glance at Farron was no help: he'd gone back to folding his arms across his chest and leaning against some invisible support, smirking unbecomingly. "Does it matter?" he asked. "They're no friends of yours nor mine. We should have let the demon eat them."

The friar who had been doing the actual fighting took a step forward at that, raising his staff, and Gabriel stepped between them, arms outstretched. "Pax, pax. Farron, close your mouth." Then he turned to glare at the men in robes. "Not that I've any love for your kind, Spaniard or Church. Tell me why we shouldn't call that demon back and let it finish you."

The men gathered together in a defensive clump as though convinced that Gabriel could, in fact, summon demon, and their leader glared back at Gabriel, although the way he swallowed told Izzy he was not as confident as he wished to appear.

"You have no authority. You may not keep us from going where we will." His English was oddly accented but fluent, his hair silvering but still full over a round face. His hands, where they gripped the staff, were weathered, his wrists thickly muscled.

"No, but we can keep you from getting your necks torn out," Gabriel said. "Do you know how demon feed? They reach into your innards with talons made of stone and carve your stomach, then your heart, and leave your face for an after-meal sweet."

Izzy blinked in shock at that barefaced lie. Demon did no such thing. Oh, they would kill—they did so regularly enough to be wary—but out of temper or mischief and not in such a way. But Gabriel doubtless had a reason for scaring them; she would not interfere. Not yet, at least.

Why had the demon gone after them? She was quite sure demon didn't care about politics or borders any more than they did anything manmade.

Izzy's palm itched, and she curled her fingers around it, thinking. When she had looked behind them, she had seen nothing. Ahead, the road had sung out of something wrong, something unwanted. But which of them was it, demon or Spaniards?

She stood up, gathering the attention of her companions, although the friars still refused to look in her direction. She still had no idea what to do about the storm, no thought as to how she might stop it, but Devorah had said there was unease in the south, and southwest was where the ill wind had blown from. South and west, where Nueva España's borders ran along the Territory. And now Spaniards—Spanish Churchmen—walked the same road?

She had been raised to see what people wanted, what they needed, even if they would not speak it. And these men wanted something they would not admit to. Something that gave offense.

"He has no authority over you," she agreed. She thought of the boss, who never raised his voice, and of Miz Margaret, who ruled her household by sheer force of will, and shaped her tone after them. "But I do. Your safety depends on me."

Their leader looked her up and down then and scoffed, a low-in-his-throat noise. Because she was female or because she was young and—Izzy acknowledged to herself—road-worn, she didn't know. It didn't matter. She knew, and they knew, that she had the better hand.

"You?" one of the friars, a young one, burst out. "Una niña? Ja!"

The mockery burned, but she pretended the boss was standing behind her, his hand on her shoulder, that familiar, comforting scent wrapped around her, and kept her gaze focused on the clear leader of their group. "You are in a place you do not belong, facing dangers you know nothing of and cannot defend yourself against. I may be female and young to your eyes, but I hold the authority to determine your fate."

Her words carried in the thin air, hanging there for all to hear, and she thought maybe Marie would be proud.

"Why are you here?" she asked more quietly. "That is what we wish to know."

"I thank you for your assistance," the friar said, and she could see that he was trying to be polite, even though he couldn't seem to look at her face, instead directing his words into the ground at her feet. "But we owe you nothing save our thanks."

She glanced at Gabriel. He was staring at them with a grim look on his face, his unhappiness loud as a shout. Farron was nowhere to be seen: he had either left or made himself invisible, either equally possible.

"That is your creed, no?" the friar asked, near mockingly. "That no man owes a thing not willingly given?"

"It is," she said. She could force them to stay; she suspected Gabriel and Farron both knew ways to get words from unwilling mouths. But they had given no offense that she could prove, and taken no agreement, that the devil had claim on them.

"Then we will be on our way." He gestured to his men, who scurried for their packs as though suddenly released from chains. The injured man moved more slowly, skirting around Izzy as though she carried the plague, and hid behind their leader as they turned to go.

"It will only attack you again," she warned them.

"And now we know how to send it on its way," the friar replied, as though he could accomplish that better than she, and turned his back on her with clear dismissal.

Gabriel watched the Spaniards walk away, their habits and packs making them look ridiculous, but he had never felt less like laughing. Isobel rested her hands on her hips and glared at him. "What was that about?"

"What was what?" He refused to feel guilty because a slip of a girl was glaring at him.

"I've never seen you so angry." Isobel's voice was soft again, her eyes worried, and the sharply burning rage he'd felt since he first saw the robes and tonsured heads eased slightly.

"He doesn't like Churchers," the magician said, appearing again as silently as he'd gone, his gaze watching the path where the dust left in their trail was beginning to settle again.

"I gathered as much," Isobel said dryly. "I'm asking why."

She had no idea, Gabriel thought. No idea that her entire tenor had changed, that she had stepped into the leadership of the party without hesitation, without doubt, and not let it go when the crisis was passed. He decided not to say anything; it was enough that she had done so, and done so competently.

"Jesuits aren't so bad," he said finally. "They don't like the Territory much but they deal with it, even if they do so by ignoring it or arguing it near to death. They never went far from their borders, like they knew this wasn't their land."

"The devil had already claimed everything from the River to the Mother's Knife," Farron said. "Wasn't like they had much choice, any more than that fool de Soto did back in 1541."

"The Spanish were the first ones to call him that," Gabriel said. "The devil, I mean. They consider him the source of all sin in the world."

"Stopping men intent on glory and fortune will do that," Farron said dryly. "A pity he didn't send them straight to hell at the time."

Isobel didn't seem to be listening to them anymore. "Do you think they have anything to do with all this, Gabriel? All of this, with what Devorah said, what I've seen, what Calls Thunder dreamed?"

She asked the questions he couldn't answer. "I only know that they're here, and that's never meant anything good before. The Church of Rome is no friend to the Territory, no matter what nation they use to ferry them here. They would see it stripped of its protections, and its protectors, if they could."

She blinked, then understanding dawned. "The boss."

He nodded. "Remember your friend back in Patch Junction? What the States do with the promise of 'civilization,' Spain attempts to do with faith. They feed stories elsewhere, urging people to venture here with tales of gold and silver in the hills, plentiful game, wide-open spaces just waiting for a strong man to come and hold . . . and of the danger that rides the land, the terrible witchcraft, the malicious shadow of the devil. . . . If they could have brought the auto-da-fé into the Territory, they would have, and Flood would be the first put to the flames."

Flood would have been first but not the last. For every soul who could flee, there was another like him, like Isobel. Bound.

He had gone East never meaning to come back, desperate to be away from this land that whispered in his veins, laced around his own bones like the water he could sense the way others smelled dinner. But he had not been able to stay away, the distance tearing at him every breath he took. Two Voices, the Hochunk named him, but Two Hearts might be better suited, or Two Spirits, to yearn for a place and hate it so.

The devil had promised him peace from that if he mentored this girl, allowed her the safety to learn what she needed to know. What he would have done first for her sake, he did now for himself, and the shame of that curled inside him. But the Spaniards would call him a witch for his water-sense and burn him alongside the devil and his people, if they knew. Him, and the girl back in Patch Junction, April, with the plant-touch, and how many others beside?

"They're as much a danger as the storm you've seen," he said to Isobel. "Maybe even more."

"We have no proof they've done anything worse than be foolish." Isobel's jaw was stubborn, but her voice was uncertain; he could convince her if he tried.

"Well, that's a sure way to court death, foolishness," Farron said. "No need for us to do anything but let them find it on their own. Let the demon come back for seconds. Hey-la, problem solved."

"And then their monastery comes looking for them?" Isobel wasn't impressed. "The boss would prefer to avoid further trouble with Spain if we could, and if what you say is true, they'd only use the death as an excuse to prod further."

She was learning politics, however unwittingly. "No. No, you're right," Gabriel said. "Letting them die is not the answer." *Yet*, he thought darkly, and the look in Farron's eye suggested he and the magician were in agreement for once. "It's uneasy coincidence that they're here and something foul's come across the border as well. We need answers from them, if only to know whatever they might know.

"But short of chasing them down and putting them to the knife . . . I've been taught to win arguments, but I'm no match for any trained by the Church. They do not allow doubt, and they believe in a straight path, not the endless roads."

"I could put the fear of the winds in them," the magician offered. "Give me the rising night air, and I could have them wetting their bedrolls before moonrise."

The magician's grin was too gleeful, his eyes wicked, and had he been a horse, Gabriel would have turned him loose rather than get on his back ever. But the temptation was there: let the power the friars so feared and hated be the source of their undoing, send them scrambling and screaming for the other side of the border and ready to shrive themselves to the first soul they saw.

Isobel considered them both for a long moment, and he could practically see her reaching for something, deep within herself. Finally, she nodded. "All right. Do it."

PART FIVE

THE RISING WIND

The moment she nodded agreement, Izzy regretted it. But she did not call him back. "What do you think he's going to do?"

Gabriel met her gaze without judgment. "Do you truly want to know?"

Izzy licked her lips and considered the question. She did. But another glance at the magician's back where he stood, head tilted up toward the evening sky, his hair loose around his shoulders and his body absolutely still, made her think that she didn't, too.

Farron had proven himself an ally, if not a friend. But not even the boss could predict what a magician might do, and there was a cold wind inside him that only a fool wouldn't fear.

And she had set that upon the strangers.

She let her fingers trace the map Gabriel had brought out, seeing the names inked in careful letters almost too small to be legible. She thought, maybe, now she understood what she had been meant to learn, sent away from the saloon, away from Flood. Everything that happened here, within the Territory, reflected on the boss. Those who'd taken bargain with him, those who'd settled there because he kept it safe, those who'd been there before and trusted him to keep his word.

"The left hand moves in shadows, unseen, unheard. . . . It is the strength of the Territory, the quick knife in the darkness, the cold eye and the final word."

She was the quick knife, the cold eye, the final word. Unseen and unnoticed . . . She had spent so much time trying to be *seen*, trying to prove herself, and there had been nothing she needed to prove. Only to accept. The boss didn't rule; he served. And so did she.

She felt herself cracked open and hollowed out by the realization. The road and the ride had changed her, until she wasn't Izzy any longer. Not in any way she'd recognize if she looked in a mirror. Izzy couldn't do this.

But Gabriel's Isobel could, she thought. She could be Isobel.

"Here and here." Where Gabriel's finger touched the map, a faintly glimmering dot appeared, marking the spot. "From Widder Creek to De Plata. I don't know how we missed it; there's a definite pattern. Far in, illness. Closer to the mountains . . . physical attacks."

"Not Patch Junction? The way April spoke against the boss . . ."

He chuckled briefly at that, although she didn't see what was amusing about it. "People have pushed against your boss's rules since the day he laid 'em down, Iz. Always someone thinking there's more and better over the River, or under someone else's rules. Or they just plain don't like being told what they can and can't do. And there's always someone willing to stir it up some for their own amusement. I suspect that's what those friars are here to do too."

"They give offense."

Izzy yelped, high-pitched and unashamed, twisting as she jumped, reaching for the knife at her waist before remembering that it was with the rest of her kit, close but not close enough to reach. Gabriel had his blade out already, though, crouched and staring at their unexpected, unwelcome visitor.

Up close, facing them, the demon could not pass for human. Its skin was not flesh but dust, swirling constantly, thickly enough to seem solid, and to look into its eyes was to fall forward forever, the dizziness she'd felt when first touching the bones. Nothing compared to this, to—

The demon looked away first, deliberately turning its head and closing its lids, to break the fall.

"No offense meant done, no offense meant done," it said. "Put away your blade; open your ears."

"I'll open my ears," Gabriel said, but kept his knife unsheathed, resting it flat against his knee, his fingers still curved against the bone handle. Izzy, on impulse, rested her left hand palm-up on her leg, the sigil clearly visible. But she suspected the demon knew full well who she was already.

"I bring a story. Not a story of the time-before-fire nor a story of time-before-man." The demon kept its eyes away from theirs, its gaze shifting over everything save their faces, a courtesy Izzy hadn't expected but welcomed. "This is a story of the shaking of the bones, when the winds were used against themselves, and ants attempted to carry away the mountain."

Its hands were restless, too-long fingers scratching at the dirt, curling in on themselves, then stretching out again. "We do not know how this story ends. This story has no ending, only endless now."

"You do not travel alone," Gabriel said when the demon seemed disinclined to keep speaking. "Where are your others?"

"Watching," it said. "Watching to see how the story is told." It nodded its pointed chin at the map they'd left unrolled on the ground beside them. "All the places it is being told."

"The friars caused this?" Isobel asked.

The demon looked confused—at least, she thought that might be confusion—then shook its head. "Ants. Ants each take a crumb, and many ants take many crumbs."

"And in the end, all that's left is crumbs." Izzy remembered Ree's fury when ants had invaded his kitchen: he had smoked out the entire saloon, getting rid of them, but not even the boss had complained.

LAURA ANNE GILMAN

"Smoke out the ants," the demon said, and Izzy's head lifted, catching its eye, and she was caught again, swaying forward before Gabriel caught her shoulder, pulled her back. Had it read her thoughts, or had she said that out loud? She couldn't tell, too dizzy to tell.

Demon were ancient. They had always been here. Like the boss. Before the boss.

Like the snakes, she thought. They watched and gave meaningless advice, and then slithered away.

"The problem with smoke is it gets everyone, not just the ants."

This time, the startled yelp came from the demon as it spun around to see the magician standing behind it, and they were all coughing dust as it disappeared again.

"Oh. I scared it away?" Farron didn't seem upset by that—or surprised. "Trusting a demon's even less wise than trusting me," he told them.

"It's all unhappy bedfellows," Gabriel said. "Can we afford to ignore it?"

"No more than you should ignore me," Farron said. "But do not trust it behind you. Demon give no oaths, true or otherwise."

Isobel let them bicker without paying attention, the back-and-forth almost soothing, compared to everything else. They were all ants: the friars but also her and Gabriel, and maybe even Farron. How did one smoke out some ants but not all?

"Have you made them piss their bedrolls yet?" Gabriel asked.

"The winds are too quiet this evening," Farron said, his eyes flickering toward the sky, then back to Isobel. "I need to get closer."

Farron hadn't said they should come along, but he hadn't stopped them from following, either. Or he hadn't stopped her, at least; Gabriel had seemed content to stay behind, only at the last minute swearing, hobbling the horses, and following them.

Along the way, a hand caught her own up, the warm press of Gabriel's fingers against her palm an unexpected comfort.

It took them until after dusk to catch up with the friars, who must have forced a fast pace to get so far. They had camped in a grassy hollow that might have seemed comforting, perhaps even safe, but even at a glance from around the boulder she'd pressed herself against, Isobel could see at least one way they could be surprised while they slept, and doubtless there were more. At least they weren't complete fools: one man was awake, pacing the circuit of their campsite just within the circle. She didn't know if they didn't know what the circle meant in terms of hospitality, or simply didn't trust it. Since she wasn't sure demon would respect it, she thought the latter wise.

The moon was a thin sliver rising in the sky, and the night winds lifted an owl's wings overhead, its call and the crackling of the fire the only sound in the night. Farron had taken cover behind another rock, his long length crouching down while he did whatever it was magicians did before . . . whatever it was he planned to do. Next to her, Gabriel's breath warmed the side of her face, his hand on her far shoulder, his arm warm against her back.

"Stay low," he said, the words scarcely a whisper in her ear, and placed his other hand against the rock in front of them.

"I have to see," she said, equally soft. "I set this upon them. I need to see." If this was done on her order, she could not look away.

He didn't approve, she could tell, but he didn't stop her as she slipped under his arm, moving away, chest to the ground, her chin lifted just enough so that she could observe the camp without being seen in turn. *Like a snake,* she thought.

Your enemiesssss are not who you think. But then, neither are your friendsssss.

Farron, she thought. Neither friend nor enemy. Had that been who the snake was warning Gabriel about?

Somehow, Farron had moved without her noticing, leaving the safety of his rock and circling around the camp so that he approached along the road. She wondered if he was pulling strength from it, the way he did a crossroads, or if the nature of the road kept its power to itself, vulnerable only when they crossed. Gabriel would know. If not, it was another thing to ask the boss when she got home. If she got home.

When she got home.

And then Farron stood, somehow broader and taller than even he'd been before, the wind lifting the edges of his hair and the tail of his coat, the pale moonlight limning him brighter than anything else.

Midnight. A passing-time, like noon or dawn or dusk. Isobel felt her body tense, bracing itself. She wasn't sure what she expected; the confrontations she'd seen before were silent, nearly invisible, save for the press of air and the trembling of the ground, but surely against flesh and blood, there would be more? But Farron merely stood there, waiting for the sentry to notice him.

It only took a few heartbeats, then the man's startled cry woke the others, scrambling to their feet, grabbing their staffs, and forming an outward-facing circle, ready to match any attack. It would have been effective, and impressive, had the attack not come from within the circle instead.

The magician did not move save his arms bent at the elbow, his hands turned upward; his gaze fastened on the camp but otherwise still, even as his targets flailed madly at the whirlwind that grew behind them, reaching out to engulf them.

The cries were terrifying, heartbreaking, and Isobel knew as though Farron had told her himself that each man saw not the dust and leaves of a miniature tornado but the greatest evil and heartbreak they had ever known or feared, striking not at their minds but their hearts and bowels.

It was a terrible thing to do, a vicious thing, and one that would leave no marks, no scars, save what they inflicted upon themselves.

And she let it happen. She had set it in motion.

‡ ‡ ‡

When the first Spaniard broke, it was like watching an ice dam collapse on the river, the weight of pent-up water forcing everything out in one rush. They abandoned their packs, some of them abandoned their staffs, half of them dressed only in pants and tunics, barefoot, racing for the road as though they could outrun the invisible torment that dogged them, invading their very souls. In their flight, they brushed past the magician without seeming to notice him, but his hand flashed to the side, a glitter of dark red in the darkness, and felled them as they passed, toppling face-first into the dirt, seemingly out cold or, Isobel had time to think, dead.

Only one of the friars stood fast: a swarthy man, his dark skin making him harder to see, only the flash of metal at the tip of his staff marking him in the night.

"Sispann ou bèt nan dyab la!"

It sounded like gibberish to Isobel's ears, but the man raised his arms, palms out as though to stop the whirlwind by sheer force, and shouted it again. "Sispann ou bèt nan dyab la!"

Farron laughed, a high, mad noise that made Isobel's skin crawl. This was not the odd, occasionally amusing man who had walked alongside them, given them advice. The wind had taken him full, filled his eyes with light and his body with power, and she remembered the very first warning again: *If you ever see a magician, run. Do not pause, do not speak, by all that you value, do not catch their attention, just run.*

Too late, far too late for any of them to take that advice now. She clung to the memory of his oath, that he was no enemy to them in this time and this place, and hoped that neither time nor place had changed since then.

"Farron!" she cried, trying to drag the magician's attention away from his prey. "Farron, no!"

Only a madwoman would do such a thing, but something snapped and fizzed under her skin, driving her forward, the knowledge that they needed at least one of the friars alive.

They gave offense, the demon had said, and the road agreed—the

Territory agreed. But she needed to know if these men were merely more would-be invaders, or if the storm had been their doing.

Farron took another step closer, and the friar turned, whether warned by her call or some sense of a greater predator approaching, she did not know. He bent and snatched up his staff, a graceful move but one that gave him no real defense against the magician.

"Farron Easterly, *no!*"

Names had a certain power. She did not believe he had been foolish enough to give them a true name; she wasn't sure he *had* a true name anymore. But there was enough of him within it that her call reached him, striking home and halting his hand, at least for the moment.

"We need him alive, Farron Easterly." She swallowed, the faint glow around him showing the savage mask of his face, mouth pulled back in an unseemly wide grin, too many teeth showing, his eyes showing too much white.

"You promised to put the fear of the Territory into them," she said, more quietly now, trusting him to hear her despite the wind and the distance. "You have done so, splendidly. Now let the devil do the rest."

His face rippled, that unnervy grin pulling tighter into a sneer that made her knees tremble before it collapsed, the wind dying with it.

"Have at them," he said, and disappeared—not with the dusty glitter and cold stink of the demon but the way a wind disappeared, with a soft sluffing of breath and then nothing.

Isobel swallowed and stepped forward. The whirlwind, no longer held to its shape by the magician's will and word, was only a soft breeze against her skin, and then it was gone. The friar stared at her. This close, she could see his chest heaving for breath, his face shining with sweat.

"I will protect you," she said. "So long as you answer my questions and do not seek to lie or escape."

His gaze went over her shoulder, doubtless to his companions motionless on the ground behind her, and all breath seemed to escape him. He rested his staff on the ground and went down on his knees. "My parole, it is yours."

"Wonderful," she said, and took the staff from him. It was heavier than it seemed, and the end dipped to the ground before she was able to adjust to it.

"They're asleep," Gabriel said, and she turned to find him a safe distance behind her, eyeing the staff—and then the friar—with the eye of a man who isn't sure the battle is over. "Deep enough that I can't wake them. So, unless we leave them here . . ."

It was unlikely any human would come by to rob them, or cut their throats for sheer meanness, but the demon still lurked, and there were animals that were kept back by fire and voice but would consider silent, unmoving bodies a fair feast, given half a chance.

"We will stay here," she said, letting the heaviest tip of the staff rest on the ground, shifting her grip so that she held it like a flagstaff. "Bring the horses and our supplies."

Hopefully, by the time he returned, she would have figured out what she was doing.

Gabriel's hands were shaking as he removed the hobbles and then saddled Steady, and he leaned his face against the horse's neck, breathing in the familiar scent. The gelding turned its head, pressing him into the crook between neck and withers in a horse's hug.

"Yeah, you didn't like us leaving you here either, did you?" The mare had nipped at him when he'd saddled her first, clearly asking where *her* rider was, and didn't they know that there were *wolves* here and other things that ate innocent horses? Only the mule had seemed unperturbed, looking up from its lazy doze and flopping one ear as though to say, "Oh, you've returned, have you?"

"Damn the devil, and damn her, and damn me, too," he said. "But I'm neck-deep in it and no mistake now."

He'd only meant to mentor a young girl with spirit, show her the road, teach her what freedom meant. But neither of them had a lick of freedom, not really. Her for her bargain, and him . . .

He'd tried to get away, had run as far away as he could get, and discovered it wasn't far enough, wasn't far at all. Three years he'd lasted back East before the Territory called him home, and only constant moving had kept him as free as he'd been, never staying still long enough for it to tangle him down.

He should never have gone to Flood, never tempted the devil's luck, never looked into the clear, bright eyes of a girl who needed him. . . .

He huffed a laugh and scratched Steady under the bridle, scraping away a bit of sweat and dirt. "If wishes were wings, we wouldn't have to ride, would we?"

Strange storms, magicians, Spaniards . . . He didn't like this, didn't like any of it, not a whit, but the devil always paid his price. He just had to keep Isobel safe and bring her home intact. Admittedly, that was proving more difficult than he'd thought at the first, but what Gabriel had asked in return was dear too.

Peace was worth whatever you paid.

Their site packed up, the ashes covered with dirt, Gabriel gave one last look around to make sure there was nothing left behind, and frowned. The magician's pack was gone. Admittedly, the man hadn't carried much, but he was certain that it hadn't been over Farron's shoulder when he attacked the Spaniards' camp, and while he might easily have stashed it somewhere before starting, Gabriel couldn't remember seeing it slung over his shoulder as they followed him, either.

"So, you abandoned us, came back, took your pack, and went on your way. Good riddance." He gathered Steady's reins, slid his foot into the stirrup, and swung into the saddle. He could almost imagine leaving his trouble, his worries, here in this abandoned campsite, letting Steady's tail whisk them away as they walked, Uvnee's lead tied to his saddle, the mule obediently falling in behind. He could imagine it . . . but he did not believe it.

Whatever waited ahead would be no easier than what lay behind.

And the fact that the magician had disappeared left him not reassured but more worried. Because after Farron Easterly had come to them—to *Isobel*—intentionally, after death could not hold him, after vowing to be their ally to find and defeat—or harness—the storm's power, what could have made him leave now?

That question kept him uneasy company all the way to the new camp, without answer.

The fire had been rebuilt to a comforting blaze, casting a pale yellow light, and Isobel and the friar had moved the sleeping brothers out of the road and stacked them on their bedrolls, side by side. It looked uncomfortably like a battlefield morgue, and Gabriel glanced away as he picketed the horses off to the side, where they would not startle any friar who awoke without warning.

The magician had not returned. Isobel and the sole waking Spaniard were sitting across the fire from each other, and he guessed from their vaguely adversarial positions that they had not spoken, save the few words needed to move the bodies, since he left.

Despite himself, Gabriel smiled. What Isobel could do, what the magician was, all that was beyond him. But this—charming people into conversation—he could manage.

"Did none of our sleepers rouse?" he asked, coming to sit next to Isobel, careful to keep enough distance between them to raise no eyebrows. The friar would doubtless be all too ready to cast aspersions of sin at Isobel; he would not add wood to that fire by implying they had any sort of carnal relationship. The other friar had not taken well to a woman with authority—would this one be more adaptable? He hoped that that was not why they stared at each other so glumly. . . .

"None," Isobel said. "Was Farron at the—" She shut her mouth with a snap when he shook his head. So, he hadn't given her notice, either. Gone in the wind, and good riddance.

"And our awake companion?"

"This is Fra Manuel." She pronounced it with the weight on the last half of the name, and when she spoke, he looked up from his hands, giving Gabriel a steady once-over. "He doesn't seem to be a man of many words."

"I'm not entirely sure I can blame him," Gabriel said, infusing his words with as much casual sincerity as he'd ever used in court. "After all, the only times he's seen us, things have gone not terribly well for his group."

Isobel looked at him sideways, looking for his direction. Whatever she saw, it seemed to satisfy her.

"Perhaps," she said, looking back at the fire. "But it was not our fault that his leader insisted on disregarding our advice, to his own folly."

He could *hear* the cadences of her boss in those words and wondered briefly who he was speaking to: Isobel or Hand. Not that it mattered overmuch here, only what Fra Manuel heard.

"Perhaps we can put that to right," he said, still directing his words to her while putting on a show of casual concern for their auditor. "Certainly, the fact that we have cared for his brothers must show we mean them no harm, despite Farron's rather . . . excessive showing."

"You dabble in witchcraft; your souls are forfeit."

Ah. So Fra Manuel spoke enough English to follow. That was good. He was a little snappish about souls and power, though. That was less useful. A fanatic would be useless to them. Unless . . . It was a risk on several fronts, but Isobel had said once that the devil respected a man who played his hand well.

"He thinks his hands are unsullied, his soul clean," Gabriel said, forcing a faint chuckle. "Do you think his master did not tell him what they did here?"

Bless Isobel, she picked up his intent. "I suspect he was told nothing that could not be contained within his prayer book, or he would not use such harsh words on us when he himself is more due them." And that was the magician in her words now. She was a regular mockingbird when she chose to be. Still, from the expressions passing over the other man's face, even in the firelight, it was working

Raising her chin in a now-familiar gesture, Isobel studied their prisoner with a look that would have seemed perfectly at home across the devil's nose as well. "Or he is the very worst of his kind, to lie about the purity of his own soul when it is blackened by false witness."

"I bear true witness," Manuel burst out, his words impassioned, nearly pulling his body upright with the force of them. "You lie!"

Poke a man of God in his virtue hard enough, Gabriel had learned in his time back East, and you'll find what he's made of. "Then why are you here, if not to spread your master's filth?"

"To stop it!"

Fray Manuel's cry was one of anguish, of despair, not defiance. Isobel pressed her palms harder against the log she'd dragged over to use as a seat, her nails digging into the soft bark, but it was barely enough to ground her, as shaken as his pain left her. She wished she dared touch the ground but was afraid to move, to do anything that might set the friar off again or cause him to stop speaking.

Use the pain, she thought, studying him. *It wounds him, and only you can offer solace.*

"Tell me," she said. "Convince me." This was easy, harkening back to all the nights spent listening to the players, learning a secret for the boss or her own curiosity, neither commanding nor demanding but inviting his confidences, the words he clearly so desperately needed to share.

"There are factions in Madrid, en España. They are close to Carlos."

"Spain's king," Gabriel said softly.

"Si. They whisper into his ear that the time is right to claim all of this land, before the Americans expand further. That the plata potencia, the silver of protection, is a thing Spain must control, not savages. And he . . . He sent messengers to the viceroy in Las Californias with orders to do a thing.

"Our abbot, he disagreed, for these orders were not things that the Church could approve, and there were arguments that shook the alcázar. But the viceroy, he determined he would do this thing, to keep his position safe and please the king." Fray Manuel seemed somewhat sympathetic to the plight of a man who answered to a mortal king rather than the almighty one.

"What were those orders?" Isobel asked. "What was the thing the king commanded him to do?"

"No se. I do not know." He swallowed and looked at Isobel directly for the first time. She realized with a shock that he was not much older than she was, for all that he was broad-shouldered. She shoved that thought aside and focused on his words. "I heard this only later, what Fray Bernardo told us. He was there, at the Mission Alta San Diego. We joined him later and were blessed before we crossed the Sierra Madres." He crossed himself, as though checking to make sure the blessing still held.

Isobel waited, but when he didn't go on, she prompted, "Why? Why come here, the five of you?"

"There were twelve first. Three fell ill crossing the mountains and turned back. Two stayed in the Santa des Oro, as planned, to relay news. And two died in a storm two months ago, as we crossed the peak." He crossed himself again and looked down at the thought of those lost companions.

"They tried to cross in winter? Idiots," Gabriel said, barely under his breath. Isobel couldn't disagree. It had snowed only a few days before in the lower hills, and the Mother's Blade was much higher and doubtless colder. She kept her silence, however, and after a moment, Manuel went on.

"We had already lost too much time. Fray Bernardo told us the viceroy, de Marquina, he summoned los hechiceros, warlocks. We were told they made a working in the King's name . . . to undermine the devil's hold and weaken this land to Spain's influence."

He was overwrought at that point, the horror of what he was

telling unmanning him in a way that facing the terrors of the Territory had not.

"It's not a bad plan, as idiocy goes," Gabriel said thoughtfully, then shrugged when Isobel and Manuel both glared at him. "From a purely tactical point of view, I mean." He looked at Manuel. "And the Church disapproves of this why? You've been dying to get your claws across the mountains for decades."

"It endangers the soul of all who allowed it," Manuel said, offended. "And the King, in whose name it was done."

Isobel wasn't sure how the actions of one person endangered the souls of others, nor did she care.

"It is God's will that you recant your ways and come to the light. But this . . . this black magic is not the way. One may not bring salvation through darkness." Manuel glanced at where his companions lay, still oblivious to the world, and sighed. "We were meant to stop it. And now we have failed."

"You never thought to *ask* for help?" Isobel found herself incensed at both the news and the resignation in his voice. "Never thought to tell us what was happening, ask our assistance?"

Manuel blinked at her, as though she'd suggested he ask their horses for help, or the birds overhead.

"Iz." Gabriel's voice was quiet but firm, his hand outstretched to bring her away from the fire. She stared at the friar, then shook her head and turned away, following Gabriel to a distance where they could not be overheard.

"The storm you saw. It was a spell. A dark spell, sent to—"

"To burrow itself into the Territory," she finished for him. "The things I saw, the illnesses, the bad dreams and unease, the missing people . . . all from that?" It seemed impossible. Medicine was a thing that healed, or sent dreams, visions, not this. "How?"

"I think . . . they didn't know what they were doing." Gabriel cast his gaze up at the stars slowly crossing the sky above, as though it were easier to speak when he was looking away from her. "Here, it's a thing we rarely think of: the devil *is*, demon and magicians *are*. You know what a medicine bundle is and how to use silver to clear your way, or you learn, or you leave. Out there . . . it's different.

"When I was across the River, I encountered witches. They knew I was from the Territory and were curious." He sighed and looked back down at her. "They were mostly no more than herbalists and true-dreamers, gifted in some small way, but there's not . . . The winds blow differently out there, Isobel. The wind doesn't speak, the bones lay silent. You can't feel a true road; it's inert, silent.

"I couldn't find water there, Isobel." He shuddered and swallowed. "I don't know why. But only here are there demon and dust-dancers. Only here are there magicians. Only here, of any place I've been."

She tried to imagine that, but it was like a city: too much for her to understand. "Then how could someone—someone from outside—do such a thing?"

"I don't know. I would have sworn it wasn't possible." He rubbed his chin, the soft scratch of bristles an oddly comforting noise. "The monk is useless; all he knows is what he's been told, and damn little of that, I'd bet. Farron could likely tell us if he hadn't flitted, but it's doubtful he *would*."

She felt overwhelmed again, too much being forced onto her and no way to sort it into tidy understanding.

"You ask the wrong person, little rider. The rider refuses to let himself understand."

"I thought you'd gone," Gabriel said, his eyes narrowing as he turned to greet the magician.

"I went to deal with the demon," Farron said, flicking a speck of dust off his sleeve. "It bothered me to leave threads untied in that manner."

Isobel sniffed, picking up the faint scent of cold dust and dry mud surrounding Farron. "You killed it?"

"Please." Even in the starlight, she could see the look of disdain on his face. "Killing them would do nothing useful. I claimed their essence so I might make better use of it."

That was worse. She swallowed, not sure why she felt sudden sympathy for the demon. "You drained them all. Like you would a crossroads."

"Effectively, yes. Don't look so shocked, little rider. This is our nature: they would do the same to me if they had won. And I will be of far more use to you than they would."

The doings of magicians were none of her care, and not wise to meddle with. Isobel took the warning and returned to his earlier words. "What did you mean, that Gabriel won't let himself understand? Understand what?"

"This is not the time or place," Gabriel said, lowering his voice again and glaring at the magician, who glared right back.

"And you say you do not trust *me?*" Farron's expression actually looked hurt, but a heartbeat later, it had rearranged itself to the usual mocking grin, and she knew whatever it was, he would not tell her. "We needs deal with the immediate disaster first, little rider, and toss recriminations and revilement later. For now, it shall be enough to say that this little game has greater reach than those fool Spaniards could imagine.

"Seeing them, seeing the shape they make in the wind, I understand better. It was a thing shaped of ill intent, if no great power, but once here . . . The Territory has its own ways with dealing with intruders, little rider, and not all of them are healthy for we who live here.

"You need to find their medicine, find its shape in the wind, and dig it out before it spreads further. You, none other, Devil's Hand."

Isobel felt panic press on her, her heartbeat too fast, her skin prickling with cold sweat. The magician had his own secrets, appearing and disappearing, and everything Gabriel had warned about him was true. He had his own reasons for being here, his own reasons for helping them. Magicians thought only of themselves, their own power. She could not trust what he implied about Gabriel . . . but Gabriel wasn't denying it.

"Easy," Gabriel said, his hand a calming touch on her shoulder.

"Easy, Iz." He was gentling her the way he might a horse, but she couldn't bring herself to protest, not when that voice and touch eased the cold, calmed her pulse. Gabriel was here. He had made a bargain with the boss to guide her. He was keeping secrets, but none that would harm her, none that would prevent her from doing her job.

And this was hers. Her responsibility. Her obligation. Isobel pressed her right thumb into her left hand, pressing the mark there. The words the boss had said came to her again: *maleh mishpat.* The words had been strange to her, were still strange to her, another language she did not know, but the meaning had rested within her from the moment he had said the words, although it had taken her longer to reach it. The depth of it could not be translated, could not be explained, could not be described, only understood.

Isobel was beginning to understand.

"I am the cold eye and the final word," she said, and when she turned back to the fire and the waiting friar, she knew that whatever differences they might have, whatever secrets they kept, the two men were at her back.

When they returned to the fire, Isobel had merely told them to get some sleep, that they would discuss things further in the morning when the sun was up. When she could see their faces, he thought she'd meant.

For now, Gabriel sat by the fire and watched the soft rise and fall of Isobel's side as she slept beside him. Farther away, close to his companions, Manuel had wrapped himself in a blanket and had his eyes closed, although Gabriel was close to certain the friar was not actually asleep. He couldn't blame him, and he didn't particularly care. His only concern was that Isobel be well rested. Or as well rested as they could manage, anyway.

The magician didn't seem to need sleep at all, spending the past few hours walking around the camp, occasionally disappearing but always, regrettably, returning. He did a slow circuit of the friars still on the ground, then came to stand by Gabriel. "They're waking up."

"Good," Gabriel said, not looking up. "Hauling them around would have been difficult, unless you could conjure up a wagon."

"We could have just—" Farron stopped when that drew Gabriel's glare. "You would have objected?" He laughed softly, the sound not carrying, and sat down beside Gabriel, watching the coalstone cool down as the sky slowly lightened. "You think she should not have blood on her hands?"

"I think she'll have enough blood there soon enough. I've no desire she spill it sooner."

"What, you think that they will simply fall in with us? That our pet friar will not revert back the moment his leader awakens and deem us all fire-worthy scum? And don't think you'll escape his wrath, legacy. You're as tainted as the rest of us. Mayhaps even more so."

The magician wasn't wrong. For all that people had looked at him oddly in the States when they learned where he came from, for the most part it had been curiosity and some fascination that ruled, not fear or hatred. The people of the States saw the Territory as land to be taken, not cleansed, and any white man was considered a potential ally, not a threat.

"I don't suppose you can wipe their memories clean, send them on their way home?"

The magician pursed his lips as though considering the thought. "No."

"Good," Gabriel said. He didn't trust the man already, even less so were he able to do that.

"Of course, if I were, would I tell you? Or mayhaps I've already told you and asked you to forget?"

"You're not fool enough to tangle with someone who rides with the devil's Hand."

"No. No, you're quite right about that. I do not fear the devil but I'm not fool enough to tangle with him needlessly. And she's passing fond of you and would be most displeased with me. Assuming she remembered, of course."

Gabriel hadn't survived nearly four decades without knowing when he was being teased, maliciously or otherwise. But he was too tired to play the game just then. "Harm her, and I will shove a silver blade so far into where your heart should be it will come out the other side, and stake you in the middle of a river." It might not kill the magician, but the combination of silver and running water would certainly make it unpleasant until he worked himself free.

"You're vicious when you're tired," Farron said. "And you do not trust my oath."

"No. I don't."

They sat together in silence as the sun rose and the rest of the camp began to wake.

Isobel knew she was dreaming. She walked slowly through a meadow of water, grassheads swaying lazily in the ripples, making the small creatures swimming at her feet flicker and turn. Voices whispered past her, high and low, dry and soft. The sky was pale grey overhead, the cry of Reaper hawks and eagles distant, unseen. On the banks, something stood, moved, was gone.

She was alone, utterly alone. The winds did not speak to her, the sun did not warm her; her flesh felt loose on her bones, and her bones felt soft, crumbling under every step until she was not sure where she ended and the water began. She was not afraid. She was not curious. She was not . . . anything.

"What am I?"

Her voice stilled the water, silenced the birds, hushed the winds.

"Boss, what have I become?"

No familiar voice answered her. She was alone.

Following impulse, she sank to her knees, letting the water rush over her, small forms bumping softly against her knees and elbows, until the water reached her shoulders, only her chin and face exposed. Her hair ran loose, strands floating on the current, weighing the back of her head down until her back arched, feeling the stretch from her calves to her neck, and yet somehow she was as comfortable as she'd ever been sleeping in her own bed, down feathers and worn, familiar quilt.

The water chilled her skin, then warmed it again, the grey sky soothing when she opened her eyes. All sense of self disappeared, and she *was* the water, rushing over herself, taking bits away and replacing them with others.

Knowing this was a dream, she knew she should be afraid. Instead, she let the water fill her. Running water, to interrupt any conjure, disrupt any spell, even as it cast its own on her, washing her away until there was nothing left, no Izzy, no Isobel, no née Lacoyo Távora, no Hand, only water rushing over bone.

She woke to the smell of coffee and the low murmur of men's voices.

Isobel opened her eyes, and the sky was pale blue, sparked by gold where the sun stretched its rays. No clouds this morning; another dry day. She sat up slowly, feeling every muscle in her body protest as though she had ridden hard all night, her bones oddly numb.

She remembered her dream and clenched her fingers against her palm as though to enclose the mark there. She did not know what it meant, did not know what she was to take from it, and she wished fiercely for the boss's soothing voice and unchanging eyes, or Marie's warm touch and stern tones to set her right.

But she had only herself.

"Here." She took the mug that was offered her, only realizing after the fact that it was not Gabriel but Farron who offered it. She took a sip, feeling the hot bitterness pull her back to flesh, and smiled her thanks.

The magician did not smile back. There were shadows under his eyes, his thin mouth flattened. "Our sleepers have awakened," he said. "You'll need to deal with them."

Panic fluttered briefly under her breastbone. "How?"

He smiled then, but it didn't reach the rest of his face, nor did it mock. "I have no idea, little rider. Your man wouldn't let me kill them, so"—he shrugged—"they are your problem now."

He turned away, leaving her with the coffee and the problem of getting dressed with strangers only a few yards away. She raised her chin at the one man who was looking at her, waiting until he ducked his head and turned away, then reached for her clothing, refusing to be hurried or shamed.

She held their fate in her hand. She would not allow them to make her discomforted.

Clothing properly adjusted, her hair finger-combed and rebraided, the feathers smoothed and reknotted into her braid, she knocked a spider from one boot and pulled them on, then joined the men by the fire.

"Good morning," she said, as civil as though they'd met in proper surroundings like proper folk. She tilted her mug in Gabriel's direction, and he refilled it from the pot. The Spaniards had their own brew, she noted, not coffee but a tisane that made her nose twitch with its astringent smell. "You will be traveling with us for a while," she informed the leader, turning to him even as she spoke. His expression was one of surprise and anger, quickly hidden.

"You may not—"

"I may," she said firmly. "Your companion has convinced me that your intent was . . . not intentionally harmful. But I do not trust you on these roads, and I cannot trust you to return home. So, you will come with us, as we seem to have a shared interest in tracking down the root of this malice and digging it out."

"We are—"

Gabriel stood up, drawing the man's attention away from her. His hand rested on his belt, not on his blade, but the threat was clear. "You are intruders here. Strangers. And at risk from things you cannot, will not understand. We would have slit your throats while you slept.

Only her presence has kept you alive. Be gracious if you remember how."

She had never thought he could look so cold, his eyes narrowed, dark curls slicked back with water, weeks of exhaustion honing his face to stone. In the friar's place, she too would have backed down.

"My name is Isobel," she said, once the friars' leader—Bernardo, she remembered—finished spluttering. "Will you give me your parole, or need we chain you?"

His color still high, Bernardo nodded once in acknowledgment, then said in precisely spoken English, "You have my parole, for myself and my brothers."

They would not attempt to escape, nor to harm the three of them. More than that, she would not trust. The preachermen she'd encountered in Flood had all sworn obedience to their god before any other oath, and she didn't think these would be any different.

"You were heading east with purpose—do you have a way to track the spell?"

When Bernardo looked away, shifty-eyed, Isobel's temper broke, her words hard and precise as his own. "You will answer me when I ask a question, Churchman."

His gaze flickered down first. "We were given a way," he said, and reached into his pocket inside his robe, pulling out a brass-and-wood object the length of his hand.

"A Rittenhouse compass?" Gabriel huffed a laugh. "I would not have taken you for a surveyor, Brother."

"It is bespelled," Farron said, eyeing it the way a child might a mouse found unexpectedly on the table, torn between brushing it away or luring it closer.

"It brings us to the strongest point of disturbance," Bernardo said, his grip tightening on the object as though he could feel the magician's interest.

"Disturbance, hey?" Farron leaned back against the air, now looking decidedly unimpressed. "And what were you to do once you found that disturbance? Pray at it?"

"Farron," Isobel said gently, just his name, but it was enough to haul him back.

He crossed his arms and looked unimpressed at her. "They're fools, young rider. You know what happens to fools here."

She ignored him with the ease of growing practice, looking back at Bernardo. "And there is a disturbance ahead?"

"Yes." He looked at the mechanism. "It has been two days. I will need to take new readings."

"Of course." She gestured for him to continue but made no move to give him the privacy he clearly wanted. The man thought her a fool, a child, or worse: a woman, with no right to command him. He would have taken orders more easily from Farron, for all that he was the very sort of creature his Church preached against.

No traveler dared speak of it while at the devil's tables, but after a few drinks, late at night, she had heard the stories. How the Church called the boss evil, claimed he sullied immortal souls, tempted people into wrongdoing, was the root of all sin in the world. Isobel, even as a child, had known that was foolishness. Desire and greed, and all those other things, they were just what people felt. The boss didn't make anyone do that; they did it themselves.

But Gabriel had been right: they'd burn Flood to the ground if they had their way, and call it a cleansing.

And yet, these men had given her their parole. She was obligated to protect them. She thought that perhaps that was what stuck in Bernardo's craw more than any other. That he had been forced to accept the protection of a woman, in this land.

She felt no pity for him.

He stood and made a three-quarter turn, holding the instrument flat. She was curious, but not enough to crowd in to see what he was doing; she had the thought that the less she asked, the more he would eventually let slip.

"I'm going to see what supplies these idiots brought with them," Gabriel said quietly. "I'll wager it's not enough to keep them decently fed. Don't suppose Farron's got a deer or two up his sleeve?"

"I doubt they would touch any food I brought to them," he said. "Devil-spawn, don't you know."

"They'll eat or they'll go hungry," she said. "Churchers are all about the mortification of the flesh, aren't they?"

Farron shrugged, an elegant motion, and turned away, unlike Isobel choosing to move closer to the friar, shadowing him close enough to be obnoxious. Isobel thought about calling Farron off, thought about the probability that he would simply ignore her, and decided to leave them be for now. The friar seemed intent enough on his work; he might not even have noticed the attention.

"Blast it, you've bewitched it!"

Or perhaps he had.

The magician danced back, his long legs practically folding backward to evade the friar, who took a frustrated swing at him with the hand not holding the instrument.

"I haven't touched the thing," Farron said. "Perhaps your own incompetence fouls it, or you've simply forgotten its use and measure?" He leaned forward as though to look more closely at the device. "I hear tell that such instruments read the souls of their users and, if found lacking, will refuse all service to them. . . ."

The friar growled, a noise that should not come from a grown man, and launched himself at the magician, seeming heedless of the instrument still in his grip. Caught off guard—clearly not expecting a physical attack—Farron landed on his back, the friar over him, fist pulled back to deliver a blow to his face, when Gabriel and another monk appeared at his back, hauling him off with no little force.

"Brother!" The second friar sounded scandalized, even as he was taking the compass from Bernardo's hand. "What has come over you? These people—"

"That is not a person; that is a dust-clotted hellspawn creature, and the compass will not work in its presence!"

The second friar looked at the instrument as though expecting it to speak to him. "It might have been damaged . . ."

"It is that creature! See how it works now—"

Gabriel stepped forward, and Bernardo's jaw clamped shut. "And you, away from me!"

Gabriel stopped in his tracks.

"Do not touch me, do not come closer. In daylight, I see your sins writ on your skin. You are demon-touched, hell-spawned, and the blessing will not work in your presence."

"Isobel," Gabriel said dryly, stepping away from the man before he began to froth or attack him as well, "we seem to have a problem."

Isobel walked closer, eyeing the friar carefully, but he seemed disinclined to lash out at her, at least. "Gabriel, take Farron and go find us something to eat for supper," she said.

"But—"

"It's all right." She understood that he didn't want to leave her alone; she did not particularly wish to be left alone. "They have given their parole; they will not harm me."

The friar was muttering at his instrument now, turning in a half circle to the left, then again to the right, seemingly oblivious now that Gabriel and Farron were no longer too close.

"I will go with them," Manuel said, joining the group, "so each party has a hostage."

"You ever hunt before?" Gabriel asked, half challenge, half honest question.

"I was not always a man of God," Manuel said, his eyes showing amusement. "I can be trusted not to scare away game or ruin a shot."

Isobel nodded at them, and the three men moved off, pausing only for Gabriel to claim his carbine and load it. She had no idea what sort of weapons Farron or Manuel might use, but her worries were more for the man still in front of her.

"If you touch my people again," she said quietly, as though they were discussing the weather, "I will cut off your hands and leave you with bleeding stumps."

The look Bernardo gave her was colder than frost, but he merely nodded. So long as they understood one another.

He turned the instrument and adjusted something, then stilled.

"What do you see?"

"It hasn't moved since the last sounding," he said, and the look he turned to her now was wide-eyed, less afraid than exhilarated, as though the very nearness of the thing thrilled him. "It waits for us."

The longer he spent in the friars' company, the more Gabriel's skin itched. Although he couldn't blame them, not entirely. Every step he had taken since Flood seemed to have scraped something from him, some layer of skin flaking without notice, leaving him raw and exposed. But he'd said nothing of this. He was Isobel's mentor; she needed him to be certain, strong. Dependable.

Hunting—moving quietly, working as much on instinct as planning— was oddly soothing, and neither friar nor the magician did anything to ruin Gabriel's calm.

The hunters returned to camp before sunset, bearing a small mule deer over Manuel's shoulders and feeling reasonably pleased with them- selves. Conditions were not ideal to butcher the entire thing, and they'd have to abandon much of it in the morning, but they'd eat well that night.

Although what Isobel had to share with them when they returned nearly made Gabriel lose his appetite.

"Nearby?"

"For a vague use of 'near,'" she said. "The moment I asked ques- tions, he seemed unable to speak English." She made an exasperated face. "How many languages do you speak?"

"Four," he said. "More or less. A smattering of tribal dialects, enough to say hello, please, and good-bye. You'll learn, and now you know why you need to."

She groaned. "No more lessons, please?"

He patted her on the shoulder and, after making sure that Manuel and the younger friar had the deer carcass well in hand, went to make his own preparations. Soon enough, his pistol rested on the ground next to him, primed and ready. He hesitated, then pulled a small leather pouch from his kit and, after loading the shot, shook a small amount of pale white powder from the pouch into the muzzle, then did the same for his carbine.

"Silver dust," the magician said, crouching next to him in that annoyingly silent way he had. "You may not be an utter fool after all, rider."

The desire to punch him in the face was, by now, easily ignored. "Go make yourself useful if you can," Gabriel said instead. "Scout ahead, and see if the friar is telling the truth, or if we're about to rush headlong into a trap."

"What makes you think it cannot be both?"

Gabriel looked sourly at the magician, who laughed and stepped backward two steps before dissolving into a dusty mist and disappearing.

"Del diablo. Devil's work," one of the friars nearby said, crossing himself and turning away, clearly uncertain that their allies were worth the risk to their immortal souls.

"The devil does far finer work than that, boys," Gabriel said to himself, setting aside the long gun and pulling his knife from its sheath. The edge was fine as honing could keep it, the silver inset running along the spine from the tip into the leather-wrapped grip, brightly polished. He'd used the knife against men, and twice against beasts, but never on a thing that he'd call uncanny.

If it came to close quarters, he was already dead. He could only hope his last strike would matter. "This wasn't what I signed up for, Old Man," he said, perfectly confident that the devil could hear him, if he would. "Mentor her, you said. Get her hands dirty, her eyes opened. Keep her safe. Not battle creatures or shepherd folk who'd as soon strap me to the flames as pass me salt."

And of certainty, there'd been nothing in that about taking on a magician. What sort of fool willingly took on madness as a traveling companion?

"This fool, apparently," he told the knife. "Still. He holds it together well enough. So far." But he would not trust the magician if it came to actual fighting. He wouldn't trust anyone save himself. Not with Isobel's safety.

Too much weighed on her to allow anything to chance.

There was a crackle of sound and quiet yelling—Bernardo, then Isobel. He looked up to watch as the two of them faced off. The friar was burly, broad-shouldered, the bulk of his clothing adding to his silhouette. By contrast, Isobel was a slender reed, her shirtwaist showing signs of wear, her skirt hiked up for ease of movement, showing her boots underneath like a child. But there was no mistaking the authority in her stance, and he smiled a little to see the friar back down.

She might be uncomfortable with what she was called to do, but she would not shirk it.

Bernardo threw up his hands as though asking Heaven for help. When none came, he turned and stormed off, his brothers gathering after him like brown-feathered ducklings. Gabriel looked back down at the knife, then resheathed it and picked up the long knife that had been strapped to Isobel's saddle, studying its edge. She should have practiced more; that was his fault far more than hers. Although in truth, like his own blade, if she were forced to us it, they were all doomed anyway.

"He's not happy with me," Isobel said, coming over to him. She reached up to pull at her braid, one finger running absently over the feathers.

"What is he upset about this time?"

"He wants to go in on his own, banish the creature. He thinks I will be a distraction." The way her mouth twisted on the word, he suspected that he'd said far worse than that.

"We could let him," Gabriel suggested. "Their mess, let them wipe it up?" It was no more or less than what Aleksander and Bear Who Runs had said to them. One white man was as good as another for cleaning up the white man's mess.

She shook her head and glanced down at him. "And when they fail?"

"At least then they won't be our problem anymore," he grumbled, and reached over to check his carbine again. Keeping it loaded had risks, but being caught off guard without it was more of a risk just then.

And not only because of the . . . whatever waiting for them.

They split into two fires at the campsite that evening; the friars were clearly uneasy around them, and Isobel obviously—wisely—did not trust Farron not to antagonize them for the sheer joy of it, nor Gabriel not to hit one of them for looking sideways and lifting their crucifixes at him. Only Manuel sat with them at their fire, although another of the brothers, a young slightly built man who kept looking over his shoulder at them, not with fear but curiosity. The rest seemed oddly subdued, eating as though it might be their last meal ever. Or, Gabriel thought, that they'd been existing on dried rations for weeks, which was likely. Manuel had been a decent hunter, as promised, but he seemed the only one.

Or perhaps it was the news Isobel had shared with him, the idea that the . . . thing, for lack of a better term, was nearby that kept them quiet. But this wasn't the stillness before a battle that he felt.

Then again, these men weren't fighters, for all that they carried deadly looking staffs. Perhaps they were praying.

"We'll need to be on the road by daybreak," Isobel said. "Do you think we'll be able to rouse them in time?"

He'd finished his meal already, his knife stuck upright into the dirt by his feet to absorb the grease, his fingers wiped clean, and the lingering taste of venison making his mood lighten. Unlike the friars, the idea that the storm-creature was nearby didn't bother him overmuch; if it were waiting, it would wait until morning. If it were planning to attack during the night, they were forewarned.

"They're religious men," he said dryly. "I've no doubt they'll be up and on their knees before we wake."

The thought made Isobel wince, and Farron let out a quiet snort.

"I'll take first watch," Gabriel said, standing up and feeling his knees crack slightly. He was more accustomed to riding than sitting or walking. "Iz, you take second?"

"I have the dawn watch?" the magician asked.

Gabriel glanced at him quickly. He seemed sober and sensible, not a whiff of odd humor visible, and so Gabriel nodded. "Thank you." He didn't like the magician, didn't trust him not to do something mad simply because he *was* mad . . . but here and now, they were allies. The only allies they had.

He thought of the snake and sighed. Just once, he thought bitterly, just once a plain warning—*the crazy in the road may be useful, keep him*—would have been appreciated.

Mayhaps, a voice that sounded too much like the magician's for comfort said, *mayhaps if you stopped running and stood still for a bit, you'd hear more clearly?*

He shrugged off the voice, frowning until it faded away.

"Thank you," Manuel said to the three of them, also rising. "I know . . . This place, this land, it makes us uneasy." He shifted uncomfortably, glancing at the other fire, where his companions gathered. "It presses at us in our dreams and does not let us rest. Bernardo, you do not see him as he is, a good man, an honest man. . . . He wishes only to stop this so that souls may be saved from eternal damnation."

Gabriel wanted to scorn the man, to pity his uselessness, but there was something in his words that rejected both scorn and pity. But they were still fools. "Do you have any idea how to do that, or did you race in here thinking that the purity of your souls was all that was needed?"

"Bernardo has the original spell that was cast," Isobel said. She hadn't mentioned that earlier. "He thinks if he can get close enough, he can destroy it."

"He was told how to break it, but he must have some element of the spell itself first," Manuel said. "That is why we have been chasing it. But it taunts us, slipping away when we think we are close, sliding into the ground itself to avoid us."

Gabriel tilted his head, studying the man across the low fire. "You're speaking as though it's alive."

"It is," Farron said, then lifted his hands in surrender when the other three looked at him. "At least as much as dust-dancers are, at this point. Maybe more. I've told you that much already."

"So, they need something to call it to them. Bait." Gabriel raised an eyebrow at Isobel, who looked a little green in the firelight. He didn't want her to do it, either; he wanted her as far away from the thing as he could manage. But it didn't look like anyone was getting what they wanted this week.

"I told you we need to work together," Isobel said quietly. "They have the cure; we will take care of gaining its attention. Bernardo agreed."

"And you were going to tell me this . . . when?" Gabriel asked, his voice dropping to be between the two of them.

"You're in a better mood when you've eaten," she said, and there was just a hint of a familiar, managing smirk on her face. He'd missed that expression in the past few days, but it didn't make him feel much better about her omission.

"Devil's Hand," he said, making it into an accusation of sorts. "I'm supposed to keep you alive."

She just patted his hand, not quite condescendingly, and he sighed.

Manuel turned to go, then hesitated. "Bernardo will, I think, be difficult tomorrow. A woman and a curst man, he will not be happy." He was looking out into the darkness as he spoke, his expression hidden. "I will speak to the others; we may calm him."

"You're not afraid of us, not the way you are this thing you chase, not the way the others are," Farron said, his tone mildly curious. "Why is that?"

"I have seen evil," he said, still facing away. "Men whose hearts are ice, their thoughts filled of black and red, their souls so lost to feuds, they see not the world but only themselves." He shook his head. "I do not have the right words in English. But no, I do not fear you. And although I wish to save your souls, I will wait until you come to me for instruction."

"You'll wait a while for that, then," Farron said dryly.

Manuel nodded his head once. "As God wishes it," he said, and left.

"He's madder than I am," Farron said. "But I rather like him, madness and all."

"You would," Gabriel said. The calm from earlier was gone, and he wanted all of them to go away, go to sleep, so he could find it again.

But when Isobel came to relieve him, the only flicker of sound the crunch of her footsteps on the ground, his thoughts had only circled around and around without resolution. He had allowed the coalstone to cool to a faint red ember so that his eyes could adjust to the night, his gaze sweeping constantly over the huddled forms of the monks, alert to any movement there or beyond.

"Go to sleep, Gabriel," she said, touching his shoulder lightly. "They're not going to do anything foolish in the dark; they'll likely trip over themselves and break a leg." They didn't mention the other threat, as though hoping not to rouse it just yet.

He left her the rock he'd been sitting on and stumbled to his own bedroll, shucking his boots but otherwise not bothering to undress. The night air was just cool enough for easy sleeping, but his thoughts refused to let go of wakefulness. He lay on his back and watched the sky, naming the constellations first in English, then in Hochunk.

When the water slid around his knees, he wasn't surprised. The splash of things moving past him, occasionally bumping and biting at his ankles, was soothing, although he could not see what moved below the surface, the water reflecting the stars back at him, a glim-mering, rippling spread. He lifted his hand to touch the stars, feeling the cool fire under his skin. In the near distance, an owl called, and he felt the swoop of soft feathers, the clutch of talons, and the faint scream of prey and hunter twined together.

Something slid inside his heart, sharp-edged as flint.

The water rippled, as distant as the stars and as silent, and he felt the bones turn and grumble, the air pressing his skin like a father's touch.

You will go, and you will return. The old woman of the Hochunk had stared at him, her eyes blacker than pitch, her skin wrinkled in folds around the bones of her face, her hand when she touched him frail as dried leaves, the nails turned yellow and black. *You flee, and yet you do not escape. There will be no rest for you, Two Voices. There will be no peace in your life.*

He was awake before he knew that he had been sleeping, the dream staying with him even as he sat up, reaching for his boots in the faint reddish light before dawn. By the remaining fire he could see the silhouette of the magician, slump-shouldered and yet giving the impression of alertness, that were anything to happen, he would be on his feet and deadly.

Behind him, there was slow murmuring, and he turned to see the friars on their knees, clearly at some sort of prayer. At least they wouldn't have trouble getting them up and on the road.

A lingering flicker of his dream lashed at his thoughts, and he set it aside with practiced ease. Whatever Old Woman Who Never Dies wanted to tell him, he had made his deal, and he would see it through. And he *would* find peace.

Isobel had thought it difficult enough traveling with one man; trying to perform her morning ablutions, as limited as they were, with seven in close proximity—five of them men to whom a half-dressed woman seemed an affront—became a challenge she could have done without. Finally, she used the animals as a wall of sorts, and if the smell there was less than perfumed, at least she was able to dress in peace, with no sideways glances or glares.

By the time she came back, the sun had chased the last stars away, filling the air with pale light, and they had packed up and were ready to leave.

With six walking, it seemed pointless to mount, so Isobel found herself leading Uvnee, walking slightly behind Bernardo, who refused to look at her but focused all his attention on the instrument in his hands, while the mule wandered through their group at will. Friars seemed to have a fondness for mules, and Flatfoot forever had some treat or another between his strong jaws, or someone scratching his ears. The friars occasionally spoke to one another in low voices in their native tongues but otherwise were silent, the sway of their cloaks and the scrape of their shoes in the dirt of the road the only sounds they made. Isobel become overly aware of the insects singing in the grass, the clop of Uvnee's hooves, the solid placement of her own boots as she walked, even the sound of her breathing, as though simply by existing, she was too loud.

"Ah, the joy of fresh air, the pleasure of the open road, the fractious enjoyment of such fine company!"

Clearly, Farron had no such hesitations. The magician trotted along the outside of the group, coming to Isobel's side, although careful to stay on the other side of the road from Bernardo. "Little rider who is not riding, how are you this fine morning?"

"Are you drunk or merely madder than usual?" she asked in return, but his offensive cheer was irresistible against the quiet glumness of their other companions.

"I've never imbibed a drop of alcohol," he told her. "So, I must be mad." He beamed at Bernardo, who pointedly ignored them both.

"Todos están locos." That came from one of the friars who'd not spoken yet, who had inched closer as they walked, until he was close enough to converse. "Toda esta tierra, todos ustedes, locos. You are all mad." His voice was serious and yet without accusation, as though he stated that the day was dry or the road long. His face was square and lined, with a shock of dark brown hair atop it, and eyes of dark grey-blue that put Isobel in mind of the boss when he was in a kind mood.

"And you have willingly come among us, to face a terror you cannot name, to save those you have never met. I think that makes you twice as mad as we."

"Different mad, perhaps." Having spoken to them, he seemed to lose more fear, falling into pace with their steps. Bernardo glared at them over his shoulder, but otherwise did not interfere. "I am Fray Esteban. I would speak to you of my lord and savior, con su permiso?"

"You may speak but it will not reach my ears," Farron said. "I am given already, my body filled with the winds, theirs to command. But you know that already, for I have placed my skills against yours and bested you."

"And gave us our best sleep in weeks," the friar agreed. "But I offer. And you, señorita? Surely—"

He looked so hopeful, she almost laughed. Farron, without any kindness, did. "My lady rider hails from Flood," he told the friar. "Surely you in your distant safety have heard of that pit of despair, that sunken cavern of debauchery, that—"

"Farron!" But Isobel was laughing now for the sheer ridiculousness of it.

"That's what they think of you, Isobel." His face went solemn, and his bright gaze focused on the friar's, unblinking. "They consider your boss to be the greatest of poisons, the serpent in the garden, the evil they must root out with sword and flame. Never let their smooth tongues and kind eyes delude you: they would put Flood entire to the flame and piss on the ashes."

Something flickered in the friar's face, some sliver of ice, and Isobel felt the answering burn in her palm.

"You may yet be saved, señorita. You are young to be given so to evil."

"You should join your fellows," she said coolly. "And remember at whose mercy you yet live."

He inclined his head and rejoined the others. She felt a shiver of apprehension climb up her arms, making her shoulders hunch even as she uncurled her fingers and relaxed her hand.

"There's madness and then there's madness," Farron said. "And madness beyond that. You're learning, rider, but you haven't learned yet. None outside may be your friend, and few who live within, either."

"Are you my friend, Farron?" She had not spent fourteen years listening and watching merely to serve drunks or read customers. She had been taught to judge—and the time spent on the road had honed that skill. She searched his intent, his meaning, and waited for his words.

"No." He grinned at her, and a wind tangled the strands of his hair but did not touch her own. "And you are not mine. And we are once again being watched."

"I know." She had felt it, the trickling drizzle of awareness across her skin, soon after she woke. "You may have eaten those demon, but it's possible others follow us. They do not love our companions."

"It is an unpleasant sensation, being in agreement with a demon. Could you not have kept the one with the instrument and abandoned the others?"

"They've done no wrong," she said, as much of an answer as she could find. They were offensive but, despite what the demon had said, had given no offense.

"Yet," he said, and she wasn't sure if he was responding to the words she had said or the ones she had not spoken.

"Yet" did not matter. The law of the Territory gave them passage so long as they caused no harm, and she had promised them protection in the devil's name.

His eyes narrowed, and he looked up into the sky. "The demon are creatures of dirt and I am bound by air, but we are in agreement, Isobel of Flood, Devil's Hand. If these men and their god cannot control this thing, then you must. All the winds turn, and the storm is rising. The bones are cracking."

Nothing in his voice changed, but the apprehension she'd felt earlier grew into foreboding, even though the mark on her palm remained quiet.

"Will you be able to aid us when we face it?" He had barely been able to hold off the thing in the crossroads before, but he had consumed the demon since then. Surely he was stronger now?

Farron exhaled and reached for her left hand, turning it so the palm faced upward, and her mark was visible. "I do not know. Whatever it was, it is no longer. We think coming over the mountains changed it, made it both more and less. Consuming it may require such work that I would lose myself entire. For all that I have given myself to the wind, that is a thing I do not choose."

His meaning was clear: she could not rely on him.

Isobel cast a look ahead at the faint blue tinge that marked the southwestern border of the Territory. "Will I be able to face it?" The question she'd dared not ask, not in all this time.

"If you don't know that, how may I?" Then Farron's solemn expression fled, and he grinned that too-sharp smile again, the hunger she'd seen before rising in his eyes. He shoved his hair off his high forehead and winked at her, a slow, terrible thing. "But then, what point life if it's all known? Let the wind blow through you, little rider, and take what it brings. If you fail . . . well, you won't be worrying any more, will you?"

He was about as comforting as a sharp stick.

Isobel swung up into the saddle and urged Uvnee away from him and his mocking laughter, keeping herself alert. The sky was a deep blue, clouds lacy in the distance, and far overhead a pair of raptors soared, and her throat closed in fear a moment before realizing that the wingspan was too small for Reapers. Eagles, she thought, although they were far from any river. They dipped and floated high above her, the sun flashing against their golden wings, turning downward and beating upward, and she could feel the pull of their force, the flap and flutter of their wings brushing against her skin, touching the small feathers braided into her hair, raising a tear in her eyes, a tightening in her muscles as though her claws stretched, preparing to swoop and capture. . . .

She shook herself, aware again of the mare beneath her, the now-normal sounds and smells of people too long on the road around her. Suddenly irritated with them all—too many people around her, shredding the peaceful emptiness with their murmured whispers, their very *presence*—she urged Uvnee to catch up with Gabriel on Steady, leaving the others to walk behind.

Gabriel gave her a sideways look but thankfully held his peace, and slowly—the Spaniards taking the hint and staying back—she was able to calm herself again. When Isobel turned in the saddle to check on the others, Farron was seemingly carrying on a conversation with himself, the friars giving him clear berth despite the narrowness of the trail. Despite everything, she felt her lips twitch in a smile. Farron Easterly might in fact have been conversing with his winds—or he could be pretending merely to unnerve their companions.

But even Farron paid attention when two natives on paint ponies rode up to join their group, seemingly out of nowhere. They were young, bare-chested and bare-legged, black hair flowing over their shoulders, and a single stripe of white across their faces and down their arms. They did not speak, did not glance at them, but rode alongside as though they had always been part of their party.

The friars huddled together, but the warriors took no notice of them, their eyes scanning the distance, occasionally flickering to the magician, then to Isobel, then Gabriel, until she realized that it was an honor guard of sort, safe passage through their lands. When they dropped aside after passing some unseen marker, Gabriel called them a farewell, and they raised their hands in acknowledgment.

"You speak their language, too?" she asked him.

"Haven't a clue what tribe they were," he admitted. "But a little Lakota gets me out of almost as much trouble as it gets me into. *Tókša akhé*, when you take leave of a friend or ally. *Hau*, when you meet them. When you go farther north, French might work, but it might also get you an arrow if things aren't going well."

The language lesson continued as they passed into the deep valley between two hills, and the trail curved and began to rise again, up into the mountains, until Bernardo, still holding his instrument in both hands, came to stand in front of them, forcing them to rein in the horses.

"Isobel." Her name in his mouth had an almost-familiar lilt to it, the way her father or mother might have said it. "Ready yourself, bruja. It comes."

Bruja. Witch.

Isobel stared at the friar, taking in the sweat on his brow, the overeager light in his eyes, and mistrusted him. At her side, Gabriel breathed out quietly, like a horse readying for a race, the horses themselves suddenly restless underneath them.

She swung down out of the saddle. "Farron." The magician was at her shoulder, as though she had in fact summoned him. "Bernardo says that what we seek rests there."

"He is not incorrect." The magician's long hair was slicked back wetly, his skin gleaming with dampness that had not been there last she'd glanced at him. "I had to go closer than was wise, but I could smell it there, curled within the stones of a spring. The winds will not go to it but curve around."

"It rests in water?" Isobel's eyelids flickered, as she clearly thought of something. The two men waited. "Running water breaks spells."

"A spring doesn't run; it pools." Gabriel's wording was precise. "Don't count on that to be useful."

"Pointless discussion," Farron said, and now she saw the wildness in his eyes, the whites rimmed with red, his nostrils flared. "This isn't what it was. Not anymore. It's . . . I have no idea what it might be, save that the self-righteous misbirth of a friar was right: it waits for us."

Farron hadn't been able to explain how the storm-beast had changed, saying only that what he touched in the spring was not the same as what had touched down in Clear Rock, that it *felt* and *tasted* different. Isobel was half-tempted to reach into the road to see if she could feel it too, but fear of what she might find—or wake—kept her from doing so. Instead, she allowed Bernardo to take lead, walking the horses to stay behind him and ignoring the way his chest puffed with arrogant pride at finally taking what he clearly considered his rightful place.

But when the instrument told them to leave the road for a smaller, rockier trail, Bernardo, as Manuel had predicted, turned difficult.

"You must stay here. This is my purpose. I hold the spell that will be its undoing; I will go on ahead and bring the fell beast to God's mercy."

And take the glory home to his people, along with whatever else he could claim along the way. Isobel didn't begrudge him that, but she thought—she *knew*—he was a fool.

She refused to stay behind, not her, and not Gabriel or Farron, either. "This is not your land; you have no idea how to call this thing from its lair. It will come to us." She managed not to shudder at the thought. "And if your prayer-spell does not work, we must be there to finish it." Not that she had any idea as to how she might do that; it was her responsibility to *try*.

"Nonsense." His puffed-up chest moved too close to her, and Isobel stared until he took a step back, but he continued to bluster. "The Holy Father has said—"

"Your holy father isn't here. Your holy father has never been here, has not seen what I have seen. Has not faced the beast your greed and ignorance unleashed on us." She bit off each word, feeling her temper rise, the memories of Clear Rock, of Widder Creek crashing through. All this, because of them. "You are asking us to trust you when it is we who are suffering. No."

He drew himself up, hands clenching at his side, expression caught somewhere between indignant and indigestion. "You cannot—"

The sigil flared, and she clenched her own fingers into a fist, then forced them to relax, letting the heat slide into the rest of her, warming her from the bones. "You keep saying that and do not seem to learn that yes, I can."

There was silence after that, as though they were both astonished at the words that had come out of her mouth. Bernardo stared at her, his face set in hard lines, then raised his still-fisted hands as though barely restraining the urge to hit her.

"Oh, do it," she said through gritted teeth. "Cause offense just once." *Please*, she thought, watching his face. If he did intentional harm, if he acted against the interests of the Territory, against someone within the Territory, she suspected she would no longer feel obligated to protect him.

But he seemed aware of that, muttering something in Spanish and turning away, stalking off. His brothers followed him, Manuel casting a glance over his shoulder to make sure that she was all right. She'd managed a smile, then turned to find Gabriel waiting behind her.

She said the first thing that came to her mind. "We can't take the horses up there."

"We can't take anything up there save ourselves," he said with a practiced glance at the narrow trail. "They'll be fine here for now."

Isobel heard what he didn't say: either they would return for them, or after a sufficient time, the local tribe would take them and their belongings.

She thought of the things in her pack, then thought of the pile of things she had left on her bed back in Flood, the shed skin of her previous life. There was nothing in either place that could help her now.

‡ ‡ ‡

The trail led up, and around, and she would have thought Bernardo was leading them into a trap were he not so determined to find the thing. But eventually, midafternoon, they came to the spring Farron had mentioned. It was half-hidden in the rocks, but a clear-trod path that led to the lip showed someone had been using it recently. The waters smelled clean, not of sulphur or rot, but there was a faint steam rising from the surface that could indicate heat. Or, Isobel thought, something living within it.

She remembered how the creature in the crossroads had exploded from the ground, the thing at Clear Rock forming seemingly out of thin air. And now this, hiding in water. There was no part of the Territory that was safe.

They had done this, *Spaniards,* and she felt the warmth within her burn more intensely, making sweat bead on her upper lip. But Marie would not let anger rule her, and neither could she.

She studied the spring, judging the distance from where they had stopped. "How close do you need to be for your prayer-spell to work?"

Manuel shook his head. "As close as possible. It requires the application of holy water, and I am not certain how strong Bernardo's throw might be."

She glanced at him to make sure that he was not joking. He wasn't. She took a deep breath, unclenched her fingers, and tried not to imagine how the boss or Marie would handle this. Neither of them were here; she was.

"You're all going to die," she warned him.

"We were shriven before we left Las Californias." Manuel smiled at her, and there was humor and resignation in it. "Did you not wonder why we carried so little with us?"

"I thought you were fools."

"Holy fools, perhaps. Bernardo may think to survive, perhaps also

Fray Esteban, who is young. But they hide those thoughts where they think God cannot see them. We have surrendered all to preserve God's will."

Isobel simply shook her head, his thinking giving her a headache. Her braid slid against her shoulders, and she thought she might pin it up for the first time in weeks, mindful of Gabriel's warnings about long hair in a fight. "If you think it's your God's will, then why did your God allow your viceroy to do this?"

"To test us, perhaps?" Manuel made a helpless gesture. "Ours is not to question God's will, only to do as we are called."

"That's an excellent way to get yourself killed," Isobel agreed.

"And are you that much different? You are here, facing a beast we cannot hope to match, filled with evil power, because you have been sent to do so by one you cannot hope to understand."

"We question the boss all the time," she said defensively.

"And does he give you answers?"

She bit the inside of her cheek. "Sometimes. Sometimes he makes us figure it out on our own."

Manuel patted her hand gently. "Perhaps, if we live through this, we may continue our discussion. But for now, Bernardo begins to pace, and your guardia is no less tense. It is time."

He moved off to join his brothers, and she raised her chin and tilted her head, calling Gabriel to her side. "He needs to get close enough to douse it with holy water," she said. "And then, I presume, time to perform whatever ritual the unspelling requires."

"That's not going to end well."

She looked at him, and he ran both hands through sweat-sticky hair, then replaced his hat, pulling it down over his eyes even though the sun was behind them now. "All right. I'm assuming the friars will be useless, outside of praying?"

"That seems a safe way to bet."

"So, we need to rouse it from its lair," he said. "You think Farron will be willing to play bait, instead of you?"

"No," the magician said from behind her left ear. "But I would not have her die pointlessly, either. Might I suggest a distraction rather than a lure?"

"We need to put a bell around your neck," Isobel said, irritated that he'd once again managed to come up on her without a sound.

"If we survive, little rider, you may *try*."

"You're thinking to call it out?" Gabriel asked Farron, curious.

"That is how such things are done," Farron said. "Power to power. We might spend our entire lives without acknowledging one another, but when the winds blow us together, only one leaves." His gaze flicked sideways at Isobel, and she pretended not to notice.

"Neither of you won, last time you challenged it."

"And the time before that, it ate me," the magician said. "Clearly, I'm learning."

It had been the same creature, that first night? But even as Isobel was forming a question, he leaned forward, speaking directly into her ear. "Little rider, this must be done, and it must be done here. I can feel it pressing against its constraints, pressing against the winds that brought it here. It has already changed, and it wishes to grow. That must not be allowed. Allow me to be your distraction. It may be enough to hold it, empty it of power."

"The way you did the demon?"

"The way I would anything with power." He smiled then, an older, grimmer smile than she'd seen on him before, the whites of his eyes so bloodshot now, they were more red than not. "Everything you've ever been told about us is true, little rider. Use it."

Before she could comprehend what he meant, he reached for her left hand, pulled her down, and pressed her palm to the ground. "Call it, then stay very still."

It terrified her, or it would have if she allowed it to, how swiftly the earth swallowed her up now, without hesitation or dizziness, sliding under her skin, bones grinding against bones. The cool tang of water brushed against her skin, under her skin, and she thought she heard something mouth her name before she lost all sense of self, spread into the *thumpthumpthump* of the road above and the long exhale of the bones.

It was there. Waiting-not-waiting, curled at the bottom of the spring, the waters rising up around it, slow breaths exhaling and inhaling. She found it, knew it. Not-breath caught in not-body, the shock rattling the bones, cracking them, and she reached out even as it reached out, *panic fear need hunger* touching her, trying to consume her, fill the gaping *need* inside it.

She fought back, her instinctive response not the burn of power in her palm but the smell of the blacksmith's forge in her nostrils, the *flickerthwack* of cards on a felted table, the pulse of hooves against the ground, the low hum of insects, the harsh-sounding languages she didn't understand, the feel of the rain on her skin and the mud between her toes, the smell of smoke rising from a cookstove, the feel of a coalstone in her hand, midday sun and midnight chill, the low murmur of too many voices like a lullaby.

For half a heartbeat, they were evenly matched, a pulse-pulse-pulse of negotiation, and then something else hit it from above, taunting, teasing, calling a challenge, and it let go of her, pushing her away, and it *screamed*.

Isobel was thrown back into herself, opening her eyes to realize that the magician was gone from her side and the beast had risen.

On the other side of the spring, the friars scrambled down the rocks, and their utter clumsiness might have been amusing any other time and place, but here and now Isobel could only clench her fingers into her hands and wait, cursing the robes they insisted on wearing, even less suited to the road than skirts, tangling their limbs and slowing them too much, taking them too long to get into position.

Tension scrabbled at her, pulling her too tight, making her skin thrum and sweat bead across her forehead and the back of her neck.

Something was wrong, it told her. She'd missed something, done something wrong. . . .

No. This was what they'd planned. Farron stood by the edge of the spring, his hair loose and flowing round him, the south wind wrapping around him, lifting his hair and fluttering his sleeves. She could smell it, the warmer, wild scent cutting through the cooler, damp air, and she could hear his words in it, soft but clear.

"Farron of the Eastern Wind calls you out, unnamed beast. Farron of the Eastern Wind challenges you. Take your form and come face me in fair debate."

She felt the wind rise, although it did not touch her nor any of the others, only wrapping itself around Farron, thick enough she could see it now, shimmering-clear and painful to gaze on too long. The winds were not stable, were too changeable, without stone and bone to ground them, and Isobel could taste Farron's madness rising like ice on her tongue.

Then a friar screamed, and Isobel's gaze cut to the spring itself.

The beast that rose to his challenge looked nothing like the multi-armed creature in the crossroads, nor the half-formed thing that chased her from Clear Rock. Sleek from the water, whiskers quivering, it flipped twice sideways in a sinuous roll, then rose erect, twice as tall as a grown man but slender, its pelt a shimmering brown, four visible paws folded neatly across its chest. It turned its head to face Farron, but tiny rounded ears twitched restlessly, clearly aware they were not alone.

"I was not expecting that," she heard Gabriel say softly, almost amused, but could not spare a glance at him, her attention focused on the Spaniards, who had finally reached the water's edge. She shook her head, aware that something was wrong despite everything going to plan. What had she missed when she touched it, deep in the water? What hadn't she understood?

"Give me your name," Farron said, his voice carrying to all of them. "I am stronger than you, and I will have your name."

The creature's mouth opened, and a long tongue escaped, flickering and forked like a snake's, but it did not speak. Nor did its gaze leave Farron, as though it had dismissed the others as no threat. Isobel's palm itched with prickly heat, a thousand sewing needles jabbed into her skin all at once, and she shifted, finding Gabriel at her back, his hands on her shoulders.

"I will have your name," Farron repeated, no louder but more fiercely, and raised his hands, fingers spread wide. "I will have all of you, and you will have none of me."

She could not have said how she knew when the battle in truth began: neither moved, neither spoke, and the wind did not rise nor settle further, wrapped close around the magician's form, but Isobel *knew*, and some part of her trembled under the knowledge, instinct telling her to flee, to run, to grab all that she cared for and make herself be somewhere far away.

She held.

"Vade et relinqo. Vade et relinqo. In nomine Dei et Domini nostri uos sub praeconem nos explicare vobis misimus ad vos ex nihilo per quem venisti."

Bernardo's voice was not as clear as Farron's, not as strong, and yet it echoed across the water, the air shuddering with the sounds of his spell. Isobel felt her skin shudder as though touched by something cold, although her palm still burned hot, and she leaned back against Gabriel instinctively.

In the spring, the creature spat its tongue into the air again, twisting gracefully so that its body now faced the monks, now deemed the greater threat.

Farron flicked his hands, and the clear shimmer darkened, tinged now with red, but otherwise he neither spoke nor moved, even as the creature shuddered under the joint attack, one seeking to dismiss it, the other to consume it.

"Vade et relinqo!" Bernardo said again, and reached into his pocket, pulling something out and casting it overhand at the creature.

The flask broke against the creature's chest, and it ducked its head to look down, then the two paws on its right side slashed out in unison even as the creature leaned forward, claws raking through the air and tossing men aside as though they weighed nothing. The top half of one man fell forward, the lower half falling back, and two others went down intact but did not move again. Another swipe and Bernardo was on his knees, bleeding from the face, while the last standing friar lifted an arm as though pleading for aid.

Before Isobel could react, Gabriel had stepped around her, raised the carbine, and fired, the sound ringing in her ears. The creature screamed, a mixture of pain and anger, and twisted again, searching for the source of that new attack. Something inside Isobel ached, sympathetic to that pain and anger, and she tried to shove it aside, intent on the fight below her.

Hunger. Such hunger that it nearly swamped her, shaken with pain and confusion, it thrummed up through the bones beneath her feet, weakened her knees, made her shudder under the sheer longing and need.

What had she missed? What had she not understood?

Gabriel placed the carbine down and drew the smaller gun, moving as gracefully over the rocks as the friars had been clumsy, dodging and weaving as he went. The creature let out another wavering scream when the silver shot hit it, followed by a loud, sharp bark, before it launched across the spring, water splashing around it, to meet this new attack.

On the other side of the spring, Farron now snarled and clenched his fists together, yanking them backward sharply as though he were hauling on the reins of a runaway cart horse. The creature jerked backward, twisting in midair, and growled over its sloped shoulder at the magician, even as one clawed paw reached out to grab at Gabriel, who danced back just out of reach.

The magician shouted something, but his words were lost in the winds that rose now, dust swirling around him from his ankles, moving until it reached his chest, then circling around his arms, weaving like snakes, lifting like wings, snarling in hunger and madness. Part of

Isobel knew that there was nothing to see, there was no actual dust, no sound, only the magician calling on the power he had bartered everything for, always reaching for more.

This was the madness that lived in his eyes, the hunger that drove his laughter. Isobel felt it brush past her, sensing her but deeming her both too large and too small to be worth the effort, then slide past, engulfing the creature, twining around it, engulfing it, claiming it.

Fear. Need. Hunger. Defend.

"No," Isobel breathed, unsure if she were protesting that need or her inability to soothe it.

The creature screamed again and lunged for Gabriel, wrapping all four webbed paws around him and pulling him backward into the spring, the splash of water rising higher than the creature before coming down again, soaking the friars and magician, even as the creature and Gabriel disappeared below the surface.

"No!"

She didn't remember crying the word, didn't remember standing or moving, but she was at the edge of the spring, her long knife slack in her grip, helpless. Her words rang out into the air, sank into the stones. "Let him go!"

Farron, his face ashen and blood trickling from his nose, raised his arms again, but before he could ready himself, the water roiled, then the surface exploded again, the beast rising to snarl at the magician, flinging something at him before sinking below the surface again, the water around it turning a murky dark red with blood.

Crumpled on the muddy stones, Gabriel groaned.

There was an impossible silence, deep and loud enough for Isobel to feel all the way through her body, as though the quiet filled the entire Territory from Mother's Knife to the Mudwater River, loud enough for the viceroy to hear it in his capital, for all the tribes to lift their heads and listen, for the boss to pause in dealing his cards.

Then: "That went about as well as I expected," Farron said, his voice as wearied and rough as she felt, and the silence shattered, and the world began again. He reached down to touch Gabriel's shoulder, but the man pulled away, struggling to do so, and the magician sat back on his heels, hands raised to show he meant no harm.

Isobel hurried to join them, skirting around the edge of the spring, offering her hand to her mentor so he could pull himself to his feet. Gabriel hesitated, then grimaced and took the aid, his hand warm and callused against her own.

"Not . . . part of the bargain," he said, and coughed up more water. He was sodden and shivering despite the water's warmth, and the drops that ran down his face were tinged with red, paler versions of the stains on his torso and arms. She could see no wounds on him but blood everywhere, and she wondered if it were any of his own.

"Little rider, you need to—" Farron started to say, but she interrupted him.

"We need to move away from here," she said. The surface of the spring was still, but it was not the stillness of something dead and gone, not entirely. An intense sorrow rose in her, but she couldn't indulge it, not now, and guilt clogged her throat, but she couldn't indulge it, not yet. A thing injured but not dead was twice as deadly as it had been unharmed.

She looked at Gabriel. "Can you . . . ?"

"Yeah," he managed, standing mostly upright, his free hand pressed against his side. His face was tight with pain, but he was able to shuffle forward under his own power, so she merely followed close enough to catch him if he stumbled, and said nothing more. Farron, wordless for once, followed them as they staggered away from the edge of the spring, back behind the boulders, where Gabriel faltered and nearly fell. The magician shook his head once when she glanced at him: Gabriel could not move much farther, not without worsening his injuries.

"Go, quickly," she told him. "Bring our supplies here."

"I will help." She looked up to see one of the friars standing over her, the younger one, who had been staring at them the night before, the one who had begged for mercy from the beast. "Zacarías," he prompted. His mouth was bleeding, his clothing muddy, and there was a bruise purple and green over the entire side of his face, but he seemed otherwise unharmed. She refused to look back at where the bodies lay, forcing all thoughts of Manuel's gentle smile or Esteban's stern faith from her mind, and nodded at him, unable to form the words to say thank you just then.

None of them should have died. And yet she wished they all had, that she didn't have to worry about them now. That guilt, too, weighed on her like exhaustion.

The magician looked as though he would argue, then nodded once and gestured for the friar to follow him. Isobel turned her attention back to Gabriel. "We need to clean those wounds," she said, her hand hovering over one of the bloody stains. "That thing's claws, it might have been infected . . ."

He started to laugh, batting her away from his injury even as he winced. "It was an otter, Isobel. Monstrous-sized, but an otter. I refuse to die from injuries caused by an otter. Do you think we could get its pelt? That'd be a story to tell, not that anyone would believe it. Not even with the pelt."

He was delirious. She pressed her fingers to his forehead, then on instinct pressed her palm instead. He sighed, the laughter running out of him the way a clock might run down, but his skin was too ruddy, his eyes too bright. Had infection already set in? She needed their kit; Rosa had taught her how to draw out a fever, and there was a slippery elm powder she could use. . . . She cast a worried glance at the spring, still quiescent. Dare she use water from there?

"Don't," he said. She glanced at him, and he shook his head, a weak back-and-forth movement. "Too dangerous. Even I could feel it; you must . . ."

"Shhhh." His eyes closed and she sighed, brushing the hair away from his sweat-glossed face and wishing Farron would get back already, even though she knew that it would take longer, coaxing the horses up the steep trail.

Her palm itched and she shook her hand once, briskly. "I know," she told it. "I know, but not now." She would worry about the spell-beast once the others were back to take care of Gabriel.

There was a noise, and she felt her body snap to alert, because it was coming from the wrong direction, from the direction of the spring. Gabriel stirred, opening his eyes and trying to get up as well before she pushed him back down, her hand on her knife, wondering what fresh danger was coming.

Rocks slid down the path and a figure appeared at the rise. It was Bernardo, making his way to join them. His robes were torn and his hands and face filthy with mud and blood, but there was a triumphant glow about him, his eyes too bright for comfort.

"We gave it a terrible blow!" he cried, seemingly oblivious to the bodies of his brothers left on the ground behind him. "The foul beast could not withstand the might of—"

"It took three men dying merely to wound it," Isobel said sharply. "And your magic did nothing save enrage it."

"We knew our lives might be the cost," Bernardo said, brushing off her words. "But we have wounded it, and my prayers—"

"It's wounded, not dead," Gabriel said, pushing himself up on his elbows to glare at the friar from under heavy lids. "And your prayers and spells did nothing. Your men have died for nothing." He winced and pressed harder on the bloody, sodden rags of his shirt. "Iz . . ."

She met his gaze, seeing the worry there, the same as her own. Whatever Bernardo had been told, whatever the spell had been, the creature had not been cowed by it.

Farron had been right; they had both felt it. Isobel remembered what she had seen again, the storm passing over the mountains, shredded into many ribbons by the peaks of the Mother's Knife, falling to ground. . . .

Falling to ground, into the ground. Her breath caught, something flickering at the edge of her thoughts, something *important*.

It was waiting for us. The words echoed in Isobel's thoughts, pushing away any others, keeping her from focusing on the plan she'd come up with, making it harder to breathe. It had known they were coming, the way they had known they were being watched, the way . . .

It had changed, Farron had said. It wanted to grow.

The magician had been able to sense it in the crossroads and in the spring. She had been able to feel it through the stone. But it had not attacked them, not until the magician had appeared. Yet it had killed those in Widder Creek, had done something to every creature in Clear Rock. . . . She needed time to think, to figure it out.

Without this madman crowing uselessly over her.

"Fray Bernardo, if you would be useful, fetch me some water from the spring." She did not deny that she would feel a certain satisfaction if the creature were to return and finish its work, but when the man simply stared at her, she snapped at him. "We need to make a poultice. Surely your god will protect you long enough to scoop water from its edge?"

He drew himself up to argue with her, and Isobel stared him down. "Are you afraid?"

A look of such disgust and hatred flashed on his face that even half-unconscious, Gabriel reacted, trying to reach for his knife. Her hand on his arm paused him. She stared at the friar a heartbeat longer, and he dropped his gaze first, turning to do as she had requested.

"Isobel." Gabriel made her name a command and a question, and yet she shook her head, not able to look her mentor in the eyes just yet. This was nothing he could help with.

"Stay still," she told him. "Farron will be back soon, and we'll get you fixed up."

He leaned his head back, wincing at the cold stone, and laughed, a pained, coughing noise. "An otter. That would make a story to tell along the dust roads, how Gabriel Kasun died at the hands—paws—of a giant monstrous otter."

"That wasn't an otter." She had seen otter pelts before. They were sleek and brown and about the size of a small dog, not . . . that. And they assuredly did not have more than four limbs.

She cast a glance back toward the spring, where the friar was carefully approaching. At his pace, it would take all day to scoop water and bring it back.

"It was an otter," Gabriel said. "Make sure you tell 'em how damned large it was, though, all right?"

"You're not going to die." She turned back to him, trying to shove all her worry and anger back inside, to put on a reassuring, comforting face. But she knew she wasn't very good at it. "You can tell them the story yourself, how you were attacked by a beast and survived." He would have scars, no matter what. She could see them through the cloth now, jagged scrapes that were still bleeding, a pale green pus oozing out along the red. Where was the blasted magician? She needed her herbs, she needed—panic, desperation, a sense of utter helplessness filled her, and she pulled away from Gabriel, wrapping her arms around herself, heedless of her blood-covered hands or muddy skirts.

He was going to bleed out in front of her or die of infection, and there was nothing she could do. She was the Left Hand, not the Right. She was the cold eye, the quick knife, the final word, the decider of protection and punishment. Isobel felt the urge to scrape at her palm, claw the sigil out of her flesh. She could not save, she could not heal; all that power, *useless.*

"Pieces," he said, his eyes fluttering closed. "All in pieces."

"No. Stop it. You'll be fine, I swear. . . ." But his eyes had closed and his body slumped, the damp strands of hair clinging to his forehead, his mouth slack with pain, and something rattled in her throat, a keening noise she'd never made before.

There was no warning before she felt Farron's hand on her shoulder, his voice in her ear, pressing her down, placing her hand on the ground. "Listen," he said, a command he'd never used on her before, and she fell into the sound of her own heartbeat, too fast, panicky, until a slower, deeper echo reached her, the *thudthudthudding* of her heart slowing to the *thud thud thud* of the road beneath her, the dry whisking and grinding of the bones deeper still. They held her, pressed against her, connected her. The panic didn't fade but became manageable, a smaller part of something so much larger.

Brother Zacarías moved her out of the way, gently, and stripped Gabriel's shirt from him, *tsk*ing and muttering under his breath as he appraised the damage. "Brother, you have water?" he called over his shoulder, and wonder of wonders, that caused the older monk to hurry, scooping water into the hem of his robes and carrying it back. Zacarías sorted through the herbs, finding what he needed without Isobel's aid, and mixing it with a handful of water to form a paste. "To draw the poison out," he explained, and Isobel nodded her understanding, watching Gabriel's face tighten with pain as the friar pulled the cuts open to apply the poultice, then bandaged them.

"We wounded it, but the creature still rests under the water." Bernardo ignored the others once he passed them the water, pacing up and down the small patch of ground. "I must finish this, must drive the evil back to its creator, else the stain will remain on our most noble viceroy and, through him, our King. Zacarías, leave off and assist me!"

The other friar ignored him, intent on Gabriel's wounds. What had Farron said? That there was madness, and then there was madness?

You had to be desperate to come to the Territory, abandon everything, take the devil on trust.

"We don't care about your king," Isobel said, reaching for Gabriel's hand and closing his cold fingers between her own. The sigil was silent, still, and she cursed it. Why would it point her at the creature but not tell her how to defeat it? The guilt she'd felt before rose again, and she tried to follow it, knowing that was the key. That was what she'd almost understood before Gabriel had been injured.

"We need to—" Bernardo's rising voice was suddenly cut off with a gagging noise, and Isobel looked up to see the man wide-eyed, his mouth open as though intending to speak, but no noise coming out. Next to him, Farron once again leaned seemingly against empty air, arms crossed over his chest, a disapproving look on his face.

"He annoyed me," the magician said, and the cold, unnerving sparkle was back in his eyes. "Do what you were created to do, Hand," he said to Isobel. "There isn't much time."

"But I don't . . ." Her voice trailed off, the boss's voice clear in her ears, the words of her oath, the Bargain, clear before her memory's eyes. What she had been created to be.

"Justice," she whispered. "Be thou justice." That was what she'd been sent here to do. The cold eye and the steady hand, to keep the Territory safe from without—and within. To ensure that all things followed the Law and the Agreement.

But this thing was no part of either, no more than Farron. Like demon, it should be his fair prey . . . yet he now insisted she deal with it. It had shaken off the unspelling, ignored it . . . because it was no longer the spell that had created it.

It had changed, Farron had said. It wanted to grow.

The *thud thud thud* of the road beneath her was echoed in the *thud thud thud* of the creature's breathing.

The storm had blown over the Mother's Knife and been shredded. Each piece had gone to ground. . . .

Had gone to ground. Had gone to pieces. Had taken shape and form; the longer it stayed, the deeper it went. Whatever intent the Spanish king's medicine-workers had shaped it to do, the Territory had taken it, claimed it.

"Do you see now?" the magician asked. "Do you understand why you must destroy it?"

She shook her head. "No." She couldn't. Wouldn't. It was too much to ask of her.

Farron sighed, exasperated, and stalked off.

He couldn't consume it; the wind could batter it but not take it apart, because, because . . .

"Silver."

She opened her eyes, staring at Gabriel. "What?" He was still delirious, his eyes wide, the black center engulfing the blue.

"Silver. Live silver. Throw you into the crossroads." He coughed weakly, wincing as the monk tightened a bandage around his arm. "Could see it from the start, just didn't know what it was. Shines in you now."

"Stop talking," the friar said sternly. "Drink this."

"Silver, Isobel. 'S'important. Promise me you'll remember."

"All right," she said, and he sighed and drank, his eyes fluttering closed, and his breathing slowing to a scant rise and fall of his chest.

"Will he . . ."

Zacarías didn't look at her. "It is up to God and his own will to live now."

"This is the Territory," Isobel said softly, more to Gabriel than the friar. "His own will is what matters."

"And none of it matters if our wee water beastie gets hungry again," Farron said, having stalked back. "Stop being a child, Isobel." His jaw was tight, his eyes narrowed, and she realized that he was angry. At her?

"I'm not . . ."

He strode forward, brushing past Zacarías to grab her left wrist, yanking her to her feet by it, holding it so that her palm was in front of her face. His gaze was cold, the lines around his eyes no longer soft with humor or fondness. "You have two choices, little rider. Become what you are, or fail. And if you fail, I will consume you and everything else with power here and do what must be done." His eyes glittered with red. "You do not want that to happen."

She stared at him, then back down at her palm. Black lines, looped around each other in a figure eight, encircled by a graceful swoop. She had seen it her entire life, had known what it meant, but she had never truly looked at it before.

"Do you understand?" the magician asked again, cold burning in his voice.

She did. Power consumed power. It would duel until only one remained if it was not held in check.

She was the check. She was the silver on the road.

"You may not have it," she told Farron. "It falls to me now."

He held her gaze, the hunger near overwhelming him, and she saw the moment when he tamed the winds within, held onto the façade of humanity, and chose to give way before the devil's hold.

"Well done, little rider," he said, showing too many sharp teeth, and stepped back—but not so far she did not think he would surge forward again if she faltered.

If you see a magician, run. There was good reason for that warning. But her obligations forced her to stand.

"Whatever it was, whatever the intent . . ." She breathed the thought a moment, then stood and faced Bernardo. "Whatever ill intent your medicine man crafted, Fray Bernardo, once it crossed the border, fed on us, it became part of the Territory now. The viceroy has no claim on it. And thus, nor do you. Go home."

"You cannot . . ." He spluttered, taking a step forward.

Isobel was tired. She was sore, she was tired, she had done a terrible wrong, and there were three men to bury, one of whom might have, over time, become a friend. If Bernardo challenged her one more time, her patience would not stand it.

"We have had this discussion already, Fray Bernardo. Your time here is at an end."

"Our obligation is to wipe the stain of its creation from—"

"Your time here is at an end, Fray Bernardo." Isobel stood, and while she was a full head shorter than the man and half his width, she could feel the menace within her that caused the man to fall silent, although unlike the magician, he did not step back. "You will interfere here no longer."

"I don't understand," Zacarías said, his voice placating, questioning. "You said that the spell was damaging your land, harming people. Why will you not allow us to remove it?"

"Because they are creatures of the devil himself, tools to spread his work. They wish to destroy us by tempting our noble King and viceroy into the darkest sin, confusing them—"

"You're annoying me again," Farron said darkly, and Isobel almost laughed at how quickly the friar clamped his mouth shut. He might not fear her enough, but he feared the magician. She would use that.

"Your spell did not work. It will not work, not on the creature in the springs, nor any other part of it. Not any longer."

"Part? There are more?" Zacarías's eyes went wide.

"They are not your concern," Isobel said. They were hers now.

What she did with them remained to be seen.

PART SIX

SILVER ON THE ROAD

ISOBEL WOULD NOT LET THEM LINGER at the spring any longer, despite Gabriel's weakness. She trusted neither friar nor magician to test her words if the creature came to the surface again.

They bundled Gabriel safely as far from the spring as they felt it was safe to carry him, afraid to jostle him and reopen his wounds. Zacarías settled at his side, Bernardo still silenced, the magician's presence behind him enough to keep him still, although had his eyes been daggers, Isobel would have died of blood loss already.

She didn't care. The sigil still burned, a steady heat telling her that she was not yet done.

A story without an ending, only a beginning, the demon had said. A deck of cards could be burnt once they were used, marked. But a thing of power, a medicine of such fierce intent . . . like the magician, it might not be so easily destroyed. But changed? She felt the weight of the sigil in her palm. Yes, everything changed.

All the places it was being told, the demon had said. How many pieces had the spell been split into? Impossible to know. Until they caused illness or disappearances, or who knew what. Impossible to find until then. Impossible to know how they might change, how the Territory might change them.

But this one, this she had. This one she knew.

This one she was responsible for.

"Farron."

He looked away pointedly, then sighed and looked back at her. "Yes, Devil's Hand?"

"Stop that. I have to go back to the spring. Alone," she added, before he could say anything. "Stay here. Help Zacarías if he needs it. Sit on Bernardo if he needs it."

That made the edge of his mouth tip up.

"What are you going to do, little rider?"

"I don't know yet," she said.

"Ah. That's always the most fun way to do it." But his eyes were clear of red, and she could read only exhaustion in him, not madness, so she only shook her head at him and headed back up the trail.

She stepped lightly over the ridge, but nothing lurked there, waiting, nor did it leap at her as she made her way to the lip of the spring. The water's surface shimmered lightly, a faint steam rising from it, and she rested her hand there, her palm—and the sigil—not quite touching water.

She breathed in, then out, waiting. Thinking.

The ill-wishing had been sent to harm, to weaken, to destroy. But there was power here that did not exist beyond its borders, Gabriel said. Medicine that could heal even that which was sent to destroy?

"I'm sorry," she said out loud, feeling her way. "I didn't know; I didn't understand. You didn't either, did you? All so new, so confusing."

It might be dead, deep under the water. But she thought not.

She plunged her hand below the surface and *called*.

It resisted. It was hungry, it needed to feed, replenish itself, but it would not attack her.

I know, she told it. *I know. Come to me.*

Slowly, angrily, it rose, the whiskers breaking the surface, the ears and eyes, the giant head, but no more. It stared at her, and she reached out to touch the side of its massive muzzle.

It had shape, form, feeling. Whatever the other ribbons had done or not done, this had changed . . . been changed or changed itself, Isobel thought it didn't matter. The Territory marked them all one way or another if they chose to stay.

She had to make it understand . . . or she would have to destroy it. In that much, Farron had not been wrong.

She sank shallowly into the bones, reaching herself out to it again. *You're safe,* she told it. *You may hunt and feed. This spring is yours. But there are certain rules . . .*

Not everyone in the Territory made a bargain with the devil, but they all accepted the Agreement he'd forged: share the land and give no offense without cause. Accepted it or paid the price. Like her parents.

Can you do this?

When she returned to the others, her eyes sore and her limbs trembling, her companions asked no questions, and she did not speak, save to say that the spring was now safe.

The world was a blur, first of pain, then noise, and there had been a time, a brief time, when Gabriel had been reasonably sure he was dead. Even now, slowly becoming aware that he was propped up against his saddle, a blanket drawn over his legs, he wasn't entirely sure that he was alive.

He watched through half-slitted, pain-heavy eyes as the two monks and Isobel brought back the bodies of the dead monks and buried them just beyond the camp's borders, then went to wash their hands in the stream. The magician remained nearby, perched on a rock and watching him uncomfortably, akin to a buzzard watching an injured deer. Gabriel wondered if the magician had disdained manual labor, or if the friars had refused his help, tainted as they thought him.

They weren't burying him, he reasoned, so he must in fact be alive. "How long have I been out?"

"Two days," the magician said. "A close thing, rider. And pointless, when all you need do—"

"Enough," he said sharply, and wonder of wonders, Farron stopped talking.

He knew that occasionally someone had inspected a bandage or forced warm water down his throat, but other than that, there had been only the sharp memory of pain, of drowning and bleeding, rivulets of fire chasing their way through his body, and then there had been nothing, and now there was . . .

Nothing. He could see, he could hear, he could move his limbs, albeit slowly, but he felt nothing. He felt a moment of panic and reached for the nearest water, reassured to feel it trickling past him, a handspan underground. Not all his senses were dulled, then.

He did not reach for anything larger, half-afraid of stirring the spring again and waking whatever Isobel had left there. Or, he admitted, feeling the magician's gaze on him, of waking more within himself than he could accept.

The friar who had been tending him came over, obviously intending to check his bandages again. His name was Zacarías, Gabriel remembered. The only surviving friar other than Bernardo, and didn't that burn, to lose Manuel and keep Bernardo.

"What you feel is normal," Zacarías said now, clearly mistaking his brief panic for something else. "I've caused the numbness to ease the pain of the poison as it leaves your body. As you recover, enough feeling will return to remind you not to do that again and give you time to heal. And once the poison is gone, you *will* heal. Your fever is down, and you can move your limbs; those are excellent signs."

Every curando he'd ever known had that same tone, warmly smug, when they thought they'd saved the day. "How . . ."

"Your companion had the proper herbs, and I have the knowledge." Zacarías had a surprisingly cheerful smile, considering that they'd been off digging graves. "The Lord smiled on you."

If Gabriel had felt better, he might have rolled his eyes. "You know I'm not of your faith."

"Not yet," Zacarías said, patting the shoulder without a bandage.

"Leave him be," Isobel said, coming to kneel next to Gabriel as well. "He's not well enough for to be preached at yet." She still had dirt under her fingernails despite washing up, and sadness that lingered in her eyes. He should have been digging the graves instead of her, not been sprawled like an invalid. He thought about sitting up, showing her that he was fine, but his limbs would not respond to the command.

He settled for glaring at her. She might be the devil's Hand, but she was still a sixteen-year-old girl and his charge, and he resented his body's helplessness in front of her.

"And you, stop that," she said softly. "You kept your word to the boss; your silver shot was what made the beast retreat, not anything they did, and you kept me safe. And Fray Zacarías says you'll be well in a day or two."

"Good," he said shortly. He'd spent too many years moving since coming home, that it felt wrong to stay in a place longer than overnight. Even if he had been unconscious for most of it.

And once he was well again, he would get the full story from Isobel, everything that had happened after . . . after he couldn't remember.

"And you," Isobel said, "are you ready to go home, Fray Zacarías?"

"Si," the young man said, accepting his defeat gracefully. "More than. As soon as I feel confident my patient is well enough to leave."

"We go nowhere." Bernardo strode up to them, as seemingly unaffected by the burial as he'd been by their deaths, and Gabriel saw Isobel's expression change from concern to annoyance. Whatever had occurred while he was unconscious, the man had not endeared himself to her. "So long as the spell remains, my obligation remains."

"You are not welcome here any longer, Fray Bernardo," Isobel said, her voice civil, if only just, with a tempering of steel at its core.

"I do not fear you nor this land. God is with me."

A harsh snort from behind them told them what the magician thought of that.

"We are but two, Bernardo," Zacarías said. "Would it not be prudent to return to where our brothers wait for us, and receive further orders? At the very least, if we are to follow God's will, we need be properly outfitted with food and funds. And horses."

"I am—"

"Your brother is wise." Isobel spoke over Bernardo's posturing. She stood, a head shorter than the friar, her face and fingers smudged with dirt and her braid askew, the two feathers fluttering slightly, and her voice was the roll of thunder moving closer. "Heed him. And tell this to those who give you your orders, that the Territory is not theirs for the taking or the breaking."

For a brief instant, Isobel née Lacoyo Távora was the most terrifying, awe-ful thing Gabriel had ever seen. His expression, he was certain, was purely malicious enjoyment of the moment, and one, when he looked, that was mirrored on the magician's face. In this, at least, they were in agreement: seeing Bernardo toe up to the devil would amuse them both.

"You may not—" Bernardo tried to object again, and Isobel tilted her head to the left, eyes narrowing as though she were contemplating how best to smite him into ash.

Gabriel was reasonably sure she wouldn't do it, even if she could, but if he wasn't mortally certain, only a fool would push her.

Then again, they had already established that Bernardo was a fool.

"We thank you for your patience and your hospitality." Zacarías stepped between them, and there was a worn desperation in his eyes and the set of his mouth that Gabriel wished he didn't recognize. One of the Spaniards, at least, had a lick of common sense, and the ability to know when—and where—they weren't wanted. "We will leave as soon as Gabriel is up and walking."

"Zaca—"

"Be silent, brother," Zacarías said sharply. "You led us by acclaim, not divine right. And I do not acclaim you now. Stay if you will, but be it on your own pride, not God's will."

The silence that followed could have split rocks, but Bernardo finally gave a curt nod of his head, then turned on his heel with precision an army man might have admired, and retreated to where the two remaining Spaniards had set their bedrolls, as far away from the others as was safe distance from the fire.

Isobel was exhausted. Not bone-tired, or even flesh-tired, but heart-tired, she thought. Sore of soul, not body. And while this patch of ground was not where she might have chosen to make camp, particularly with the graves of three men so close, however warded with salt and sigil, it had water nearby, and enough to burn for a fire, and that was enough for now.

It took two more days for the poison to leave Gabriel's body to Zacarías's satisfaction. The magician was gone when they woke on the second day, and Isobel knew she was the only one who felt hurt that he had not said farewell.

She also suspected that she had not seen the last of him. The Territory was wide, but there was only one road, after all.

Gabriel had only smiled when she said that, then closed his eyes and went back to sleep. She sat by his side all day, the same as the days before, unable to close her own eyes for fear of what she might see: too many dead, too many who yet might die as the ribbons snaked their way through the Territory. Not all would change; not all would shift from their original intent.

Whatever Zacarías had done, the wounds had finally stopped bleeding, and the smaller ones were already beginning to scab over.

"He should be able to ride in a day or two," the friar said softly. "But you, too, must sleep."

He handed her a tin mug filled with the tisane she had smelled from their camp before, and she drank it down without hesitation.

Despite her fears, she did not dream.

The next day, Gabriel was using the mule as a crutch, resting his arm across its back as they moved slowly back and forth, wobbly but upright. And when she woke on the fourth morning just before dawn, the sky too overcast for late stars or early sun, Zacarías was packing up their camp, readying to leave.

Isobel sat on a rock, Uvnee cropping grass contentedly at her feet, and watched the road where the two Spaniards had gone hours before. Her elbows rested on her knees, her chin was cupped in her hands, and the sigil was quiet.

Gabriel, who had been double-checking the straps on Steady's saddle, gave the gelding an affectionate pat and walked—slowly, carefully, but steadily—over to join her.

"You're brooding, Isobel."

"A little," she admitted. She reached out to touch his side, where a thick plaster covered the worst cut, and studied his face to make sure he didn't wince. "Thinking, mainly."

"Nothing wrong with that in moderation."

"Now you sound like Farron."

"Cruel woman. I retract my accusation." He watched her, making her uncomfortable enough that she turned away, back to the empty road. She didn't know what he would see, wasn't sure what she wanted him to see.

"What would you have done if he'd persisted?"

That hadn't been the question she'd half expected. Isobel pursed her lips, then shrugged, a faint lift of one shoulder. "Zacarías won't let his brother leave the road until they were well back into Spanish-held lands," she said. After that, they weren't her problem any longer.

He huffed in exasperation. "That wasn't my question."

Still the mentor, even now. Isobel had ducked the question intentionally. If Bernardo had persisted, if he had insisted on continuing his path to find every bit of the spell-ribbons, no matter where they landed, or what they'd become . . . eventually, inevitably, his anger and his refusal to acknowledge the customary law of the Territory would have caused him to give offense. And she, as the Left Hand, would have been forced to take action.

Something inside her twisted uncomfortably at that fact.

The final word, the boss had called her. Silver on the road, Gabriel had said. The curb on power, Farron had warned her. Where she had thought first of the power, the respect, then she had seen only the burden, the shame of being the tool of another, she now understood obligation. Calls Thunder had not shaken off responsibility, nor had the marshals. They had other chores. This was hers, what she had taken upon herself, even unknowing.

Anyone might come to the Territory. But to stay meant living under the devil's Agreement. Even things that had no name. Even things that had not asked to become. And everything under the devil's Agreement was hers to protect.

"I don't know," she said finally.

"Yes, you do." He reached up and tugged the brim of her hat down a little, his expression gentle. "We're going to be riding into the sun," he said. "Don't let it blind you."

She nodded and jumped off the rock, then swung into Uvnee's saddle. East and then north again, they'd decided, riding easy while Gabriel healed. To listen for news of other places where the storm still raged, where bones shattered, illness spread, or strange new beasts lurked.

Eventually, the road would bring her home. But not for a while yet.

FURTHER READING

For further information on my research for the book, visit me at www.lauraannegilman.net/devils-west-bibliography.

ACKNOWLEDGMENTS

The road to creating the world of The Devil's West is long and encompasses so many people; it staggers me as to where to begin. So I'll just mention everyone I can remember, and pray they forgive me if I leave them out . . .

First and foremost, acknowledgments are due to whose work came first, the people who shared their stories in oral histories that made their way—battered but intact—down to my generation; the translations into English of legends and the stories of first encounters and the negotiations and conflicts along the trading routes. Your individual names may have been lost, but your words remain—and remain relevant.

The world of The Devil's West is not ours . . . but the core of it remains true. And that core begins with them.

For their considerable aid, information, and introductions (ongoing):

My driving partner, Christine Hobson, who made every stop from Kansas City to Colorado Springs, no matter how odd, and was patient while I took photos from every angle.

Chuck Bonner of Keystone Gallery & Museum (Scott City, KS), for the history—and the cold water!

Vibeke Adkisson owner of Purgatorie Gallery (Trinidad, CO), for giving us excellent advice.

John Edwards of the Flute Player Gallery (Colorado Springs, CO), for letting me rummage through his reference books.

Jane Lindskold and James Moore

Samantha Cornelius

Fabio Fernandes (for reality-kicking my Portuguese)

Natania Barron (for the Québécoise amendments)

Aliette de Bodard (for the Spanish conjugations)

Constantine Kaoukakis (for the Latin backup)

Aaron Carapella of Tribal Nations Maps

Meg Turville-Heitz

Everyone employed by the New York Public Library, especially everyone who ever had anything to do with the map collection.

Phil Nanson and Peter Morwood, for general weapon and tactical knowledge.

All accuracy is laid at their respective feet; all errors I accept as my own.

And last, but nowhere near least:

John Joseph Adams, who first bought "Crossroads" and "The Devil's Jack," telling me that there was interest in the world of The Devil's West.

The First Draft Alphareaders, whom I put through hell. Thank you again.

Everyone in the WordWar Room, for what remains of my sanity.

And most especially, the folk who attended the SFWA Readings in Seattle and Portland, and the folk at SF-in-SF, in the spring of 2011, whose response to the early drafts of this book kept me going and gave me hope. You guys rock.

ABOUT THE AUTHOR

LAURA ANNE GILMAN is the Nebula Award–nominated author of the Vineart War fantasy trilogy. She has also dipped her pen into the mystery field, writing the Gin & Tonic series as L. A. Kornetsky (*Collared*, *Fixed*, *Doghouse*, and *Clawed*). You can find her at lauraannegilman.net and on Twitter at @LAGilman.